THE
CORPS

─BOOK II─
CALL TO ARMS

W.E.B. GRIFFIN

Praise for W.E.B. Griffin's new epic saga THE CORPS

"W.E.B. GRIFFIN HAS DONE IT AGAIN. This is one writer who can spin and weave some of the most fascinating military characters in today's market . . . *Semper Fi* reads like an M-16 fired on full automatic, leaving you breathless on an adrenaline high. Don't miss it!"

—*Rave Reviews*

"GRIFFIN IS A NATURAL STORYTELLER with a special flair for how military men channel strong emotions."

—*Publishers Weekly*

"THIS MAN HAS REALLY DONE HIS HOME-WORK . . . I confess to impatiently awaiting the appearance of succeeding books in the series."

—*Washington Post*

"PACKED WITH ALL THE LOVE, ACTION AND EXCITEMENT Griffin fans have come to expect."

—*Baker & Taylor*

Don't miss W.E.B. Griffin's triumphant *BROTHERHOOD OF WAR* saga

"A major work . . . magnificent . . . power-ful . . . If books about warriors and the women who love them were given medals for authenticity, insight and honesty, BROTHERHOOD OF WAR would be covered with them."

—William Bradford Huie, author of *The Klansman* and *The Execution of Private Slovik*

By W.E.B. Griffin
from Jove

BROTHERHOOD OF WAR

THE CORPS

BADGE OF HONOR

THE CORPS

CORPS

BOOK II
CALL TO ARMS

W.E.B. GRIFFIN

J

JOVE BOOKS, NEW YORK

The Corps was written on a Sperry PC/IT computer, using Perfect Writer Version 2.0 and Sidekick software, and printed on a QMS, Inc., "KISS" laser printer.

CALL TO ARMS

A Jove Book / published by arrangement with
the author

PRINTING HISTORY
Jove edition / September 1987

ISBN: 0-515-09349-1

Jove Books are published by The Berkley Publishing Group,
200 Madison Avenue, New York, New York 10016.
The name "JOVE" and the "J" logo
are trademarks belonging to Jove Publications, Inc.

PRINTED IN THE UNITED STATES OF AMERICA

20 19 18 17

THE CORPS *is respectfully dedicated to the memory of
Second Lieutenant Drew James Barrett III, USMC
Company K, 3d Battalion, 26th Marines.
Born Denver, Colorado, 3 January 1945,
Died Quang Nam Province,
Republic of Vietnam, 27 February 1969
and
Major Alfred Lee Butler III, USMC
Headquarters 22nd Marine Amphibious Unit.
Born Washington, D.C., 4 September 1950,
Died Beirut, Lebanon, 8 February 1984*

"Semper Fi!"

Author's Note

The Marine "Raiders" of World War II were an elite force of a few thousand men formed soon after the war began. Like British Commandos, their role was to operate behind enemy lines, attacking him where he was most vulnerable. They accomplished this job with no little success, most conspicuously on Guadalcanal later on in the war. Success being no guarantee of permanence, however, the Raiders were disbanded during 1944. Nevertheless, for the short period of their existence these brave and daring men wrote yet another magnificent chapter in the proud history of the United States Marine Corps.

This novel deals in part with the birth and early growth of the Marine Raiders and, specifically, with their first combat operation, an attack shortly after the start of the war on a more or less out-of-the-way and insignificant piece of Pacific real estate called Makin Island.

A novel, of course, is fiction, but a novel based on historical events requires some research. Brigadier General E. L. Simmons, USMC, Retired, the distinguished historian who is Director of Marine Corps History and Museums, was most helpful, providing me with a wealth of material about the Raiders generally and the Makin Operation specifically.

And then, truth being stranger than fiction, I learned over a glass of beer in my kitchen that my crony of twenty years, Rudolph G. Rosenquist, had not only been a Raider but serves on the Board of Directors of the Marine Raiders Association. And from Rudy I learned that another crony of twenty years, Glenn Lewis, had been a Raider officer.

I knew, of course, that both of them had been Marines, but neither had ever talked of having been a Raider. Like most men who have seen extensive combat, Raiders are notoriously closemouthed about their exploits and generally unwilling to talk to writers.

In this case, twenty years of friendship made my friends abandon that Standing Operating Procedure.

Soon after my incredible good fortune in turning up in my (population 7,000) hometown two Raiders willing to give me details of Raider life I couldn't hope to get otherwise, I was talking to another Marine friend, this one a retired senior officer, who asked me what I had managed to dig up about "the politics behind the Raiders." When I confessed I had heard nothing about that, he suggested I should look into it; I would probably find it fascinating.

Shortly afterward, I received through the mail from a party or parties unknown, a thick stack of photocopies of once TOP SECRET and SECRET, now declassified, letters, documents, and memoranda prepared at the highest levels of the government, the Navy, and the Marine Corps during the opening days of World War II.

And these were indeed fascinating: the players; what they wrote; and what lies between the lines. The Marine Corps is itself an elite body of fighting men; and the Raiders were conceived as an elite within the elite. A number of very powerful people felt strongly that an elite within an elite was a logical contradiction and that one elite was all that was necessary. These people did what they could to make sure that their view prevailed.

Since it is germane to my story, it seemed to me that some of this factual material belonged in this book.

The first document in the stack, chronologically, was Memorandum No. 94, dated 6 PM, December 22, 1941, addressed to Franklin D. Roosevelt, President of the United States, from Colonel William J. Donovan, Coordinator of Information. It was originally classified TOP SECRET.

Donovan was a most interesting man. In World War I he had won the Medal of Honor as commander of the 169th "Fighting Irish" Infantry Regiment in France. And between the wars, he had been a successful—and highly paid—Wall Street lawyer and a very powerful political figure. Donovan's power was in no small way enhanced because he and Franklin Delano Roosevelt were friends. They had been Columbia Law School classmates together, and they had maintained and developed their relationship afterwards. In December 1941, for one dollar a year, Donovan was operating as "Coordinator of Information" out of offices in the National Institute of Health Building in Washington, D.C. The job was not, as its title might suggest, about either public relations or public information; it was about spying.

Donovan had been appointed to the position by President Roosevelt, and answered only to him. Roosevelt, using "discretionary" funds, had established the COI to serve as a clearinghouse for intelligence gathered by all military and governmental agencies. COI was to evolve later into the Office of Strategic Services (OSS) and ultimately into the Central Intelligence Agency.

Donovan had unlimited private access to the President, and when he dealt with British intelligence authorities, he spoke with the authority of the President. Thus, when Donovan wrote his memorandum of December 22 to the President, he could be sure that the President would pay attention to it. The memorandum was a philosophical discussion of guerrilla warfare, a form of warfare very close to Donovan's heart; he adored anything that was clandestine.

"The principle laid down," he wrote, *"is that the whole art of guerrilla warfare lies in striking the enemy where he least expects it and yet where he is the most vulnerable."*

He made two specific suggestions for implementing this principle. The first dealt with the Azores and North Africa, where he recommended that *"the aid of native chiefs be obtained; the loyalty of the inhabitants be cultivated; Fifth*

*columnists organized and placed, demolition material cached;
and guerrilla bands of bold and daring men organized and
installed."*

The second suggestion dealt with American military forces.
He asked:

*2. That there be organized now, in the United States, a
guerrilla corps independent and separate from the Army and
Navy, and imbued with a maximum of the offensive and
imaginative spirit. This force should, of course, be created
along disciplined military lines, analogous to the British
Commando principle, a statement of which I sent you recently.*

Just over two weeks later, on January 8, 1942, Admiral
Ernest J. King, the senior officer of the Navy, to which service
the Marine Corps is subordinate, sent a SECRET memorandum
to the Major General Commandant[1] of the Marine Corps,
Major General Thomas Holcomb.

The subject was "Use of 'Commandos' in Pacific Fleet
Area":

*1. The Secretary, [the Secretary of the Navy, Frank Knox, a
close and longtime friend of Colonel Donovan] told me that
the President is much interested in the development and use of
the equivalent of British 'commandos'.*
*2. The Secretary told the President that you have such
groups in training.*
*3. The President proposed the use of 'commandos' as
essential parts of raiding expeditions which attack (destroy)
enemy advanced (seaplane) bases in the Pacific Fleet area.*
*4. Please let me have your views—and proposals—as to
such use.*

Five days after this, on 13 January 1942, a reserve captain of
the Marine Corps stationed at Camp Elliott near San Diego,
California, addressed a letter to the Major General Commandant of the Marine Corps. The subject of the letter was
"Development within the Marine Corps of a unit for purposes

---

[1]The traditional title of the senior officer of the Marine Corps, Major
General Commandant, was in its last days. Holcomb shortly became the
first Lieutenant General of the Marine Corps, and assumed the simple title
of Commandant.

similar to the British Commandos and the Chinese Guerrillas."

It was not common then, nor is it now, for lowly captains of the reserve to write letters to the Commandant of the Marine Corps setting out in detail how they think the Commandant should wage war.

This was an unusual captain, however. He had several things going for him: For one thing, until recently, he had been a military aide to Colonel William J. Donovan, the Coordinator of Information.

For another, he was known to be a close friend and disciple of a very interesting Marine, Lieutenant Colonel Evans F. Carlson, USMCR.

Carlson had begun his military career in 1912 by enlisting (under age, at sixteen) in the U.S. Army. He was discharged as a first sergeant in 1916, but almost immediately returned to uniform to join the Mexican Punitive Expeditionary Force under Brigadier General (later General of the Armies) John J. "Black Jack" Pershing.

Carlson later served in France with the American Expeditionary Force, where he was wounded. He was promoted to second lieutenant (May 1917), and to captain (December 1917). Though he resigned from the Army in 1919, in 1922 he applied for reinstatement of his Army commission, but was offered only second lieutenant.

Unwilling to be junior to his former subordinates, Carlson rejected the commission and instead enlisted in the USMC as a private. A year later, he was commissioned as second lieutenant, USMC.

Carlson began, but did not complete, flight training at the Naval Air Station, Pensacola, Florida, in 1925. And from 1927 to 1929, he was stationed in Shanghai, China, with the 4th Marines. In 1930, he was sent to Nicaragua, as a first lieutenant, for duty with the *Guardia Nacional*. For his valor in an engagement between twelve Marines and one hundred Nicaraguan bandits, Carlson was awarded the Navy Cross, second only to the Medal of Honor.

Carlson returned to China in 1933, where he learned to speak Chinese, and in 1935, following his promotion to captain, was assigned as executive officer of the Presidential Marine Detachment at Warm Springs, Georgia.

Roosevelt, who was crippled by polio, often visited this polio treatment facility. In 1945, he died there.

There followed (1937–41) a number of private letters from Carlson to the President, in which Carlson offered his views of the situation in China, his assessment of the possibility of a war between the United States and Japan, and the implications thereof.

In 1936, Carlson was a student at the USMC Schools, Quantico, Virginia, and took courses in international law and politics at George Washington University. In 1937 he returned for a third time to China, ostensibly to perfect his Chinese. As an additional duty, he was assigned as an observer of Chinese Communist guerrilla forces then involved in actions against the Japanese.

For three months, Carlson was for all practical purposes a member of the Chinese Communist Eighth Route Army. During that time, he came to know and admire both Chou En-lai and Mao Tse-tung. His official reports to Headquarters, USMC, reflected not only that admiration but also his professional judgment that the tactics, the morale, and the discipline of the Chinese Communists were vastly superior to those of the forces of Chiang Kai-shek's Nationalist Chinese forces. In his judgment, the Communists would eventually triumph over the Nationalists, and American foreign policy should be changed accordingly.

In April 1939, frustrated by his conviction that he was being ignored by both the Marine Corps and the United States government, Major Carlson once more resigned his commission. He then spent part of the next two years in China as a private citizen, and there and in the United States wrote two books: *The Chinese Army,* which dealt with the Chinese Communists; and *Twin Stars of China,* which generously treated Mao Tse-tung and Chou En-lai.

He also carried on an extensive private correspondence, much of it unanswered, with prominent Americans, including Douglas MacArthur, as first Army Chief of Staff and then Marshal of the Philippine Army.

In early 1941, he reapplied for a Marine Corps commission. He was offered, and accepted in April 1941, a U.S. Marine Corps Reserve commission as major, was called to active duty, and shortly afterward was promoted to lieutenant colonel.

The lowly reserve captain who, in January 1942, dared to write to the Major General Commandant, wrote a document that was itself only two pages long, but it contained several appendices, including a newspaper editorial from the San Diego *Union Leader* of January 6, 1942, which approvingly described British Commando raids in Norway and Malaysia.

The Major General Commandant, after all, was a busy man. Perhaps he hadn't heard what the English were up to with their Commandos.

Appendix A to the captain's letter was four pages long. It was his proposed organization of *"Mobile Columns (Commandos). (To be called 'Rangers' or some other appropriate name.)"*

In the introduction to the proposed table of organization and equipment, the captain's letter called for *"a closer relationship between leaders and fighters than is customary in orthodox military organizations."*

He then went on to explain how this would be accomplished. First of all, the *"mobile columns"* would not be burdened with ordinary Marine Corps ranks. Each column, to be the size of a battalion, would be under the command of a "commander," instead of, say, a major or lieutenant colonel.

Everybody else in the "mobile column" (except, for example, medical officers and radio operators, who would be known by their specialties) would either be a "leader" or a "fighter." In other words, there would be no captains, lieutenants, sergeants, or corporals.

In the *"Qualifications of Personnel"* section, the captain wrote that all personnel should be prepared to *"subordinate self to harmonious team-work"* as well as to be capable of making thirty- to fifty-mile marches in twenty-four hours.

In the next paragraph, the captain touched on the subject of Rank Hath Its Privileges: *"Leaders must be men of recognized ability who lead by virtue of merit and who share without reservation all material conditions to which the group may be subjected, arrogating to themselves no privileges or perquisites."*

And in the next, on discipline: *"Discipline should be based on reason and designed to create and foster individual volition."*

The captain's letter was submitted on January 13, 1942.

The very next day, Major General Clayton B. Vogel, Commanding General of the 2nd Joint Training Force, Camp Elliott, forwarded it by endorsement to the Major General Commandant of the Marine Corps. The endorsement read,

"The thought expressed in the basic letter is concurred in, insofar as the value of such an organization is concerned. It is believed, however, that the Marine Divisions should complete their organization and train units now authorized prior to the formation of any such new organizations."

It is possible, of course, that General Vogel, having nothing better to do with his time, sat right down and read the letter and the appendices straight through, and came to the conclusion that the captain's recommendations (even if they sounded like the organization and philosophy of the Chinese Communist Route Armies) were touched with genius and should be brought immediately to the attention of the Major General Commandant.

It is also possible that the signature on the letter had something to do with General Vogel's astonishingly rapid action in sending the letter on to the Major General Commandant, and his equally astonishing silence on the subject of throwing out the existing rank structure, and the privileges that went with it.

The letter was signed by James Roosevelt; Captain Roosevelt's father was President of the United States and Commander in Chief of its armed forces.

The very same day—January 14, 1942—Major General Commandant Holcomb, back in Washington, wrote two letters, classified CONFIDENTIAL, that were dispatched by officer couriers. The letters were essentially identical. One went to Major General H. M. Smith, USMC, commanding the Marine Barracks at Quantico, Virginia; and the other went to Major General Charles F. B. Price, USMC, in San Diego.

1. Suggestion has been made that Colonel William J. Donovan be appointed to the Marine Corps Reserve and promoted immediately to Brigadier General for the purpose of taking charge of the "Commando Project."

2. It will be recalled that Colonel Donovan served with distinction in the 27th Division during World War I. He has since then observed practically all wars that have taken place and in particular has specialized in Commando Operations (amphibious raids).

3. A frank expression of opinion is requested from you as to the advisability of accepting this suggestion. Replies will be Confidential and will be forwarded as promptly as possible to the Major General Commandant by air mail where appropriate.

General Holcomb did not indicate—then or ever—who had suggested that Wild Bill Donovan be commissioned a general of Marines. To this day, in fact, the identity of the "very high" authority who wanted Donovan commissioned as a Marine (and thus relieved of his COI responsibilities and authority) has never been revealed, but there are a number of credible possibilities.

The suggestion may have come from the President himself, and then been relayed through Frank Knox, Admiral King, or someone else. Roosevelt was known to be firmly behind the "American Commandos" idea, and he knew that the Marine Corps brass was at best lukewarm about the concept. That problem would be solved if Donovan were a Marine general with "commando" responsibility.

Another possibility was General George Catlett Marshall, the Chief of Staff, who was known to be unhappy with the carte blanche Donovan had been given by Roosevelt, and saw in Donovan an unacceptable challenge to his own authority.

Donovan was a thorn, too, in the side of J. Edgar Hoover, Director of the FBI (even though he held his post in large part because Donovan had recommended him for it), who had already lost to Donovan's COI authority to conduct intelligence operations overseas (except in South America). Hoover was known to be privately furious that he no longer had the President's ear exclusively on intelligence and counterintelligence matters.

The British intelligence establishment was also not happy with Donovan, who had already made it clear that he intended to see that the United States had an intelligence capability of its own, a capability that would not be under British authority. Their objections to Donovan reached Roosevelt via Winston S. Churchill.

But Donovan was not without his promoters; he had a legion of politically powerful fans, most prominent among them his good friend Colonel Frank Knox, Secretary of the Navy. It is equally credible to suggest that Knox, who had charged up Kettle Hill in Cuba as a sergeant with Teddy Roosevelt's Rough Riders, and who viewed the Marine Corps with an Army sergeant's somewhat critical eye, really believed he would be doing the Marine Corps a favor by sending them someone who had not only impeccable soldierly credentials, but the President's unlisted phone number as well.

Nothing has ever come out, it seems useful to note, to hint that Colonel Donovan himself was behind the suggestion, or that the nation's first super-spy ever heard about it until long after World War II was over.

On January 16, 1942, two days after it was dispatched (indicating that the officer courier bearing the letter was given an air priority to do so; he otherwise could not have arrived in California until January 17), Major General Price replied to the Major General Commandant's letter.

In this letter, he didn't appear to be especially opposed to Donovan's becoming a Marine general in charge of Marine Commandos. He wrote that Donovan was *"well qualified by natural bent and experience and probably more so than any General officer of the regular Marine Corps at present available for such assignment."*

General Price then turned to the whole idea of commando forces and the Marine Corps:

If the personnel to conduct this new activity can be recruited almost entirely from new resources it would be the judgment of the undersigned that the entire spirit and plan of employment of the Commando groups is directly in line with the aggressive spirit of the Marine Corps, that it will add immeasurably to the fame and prestige of the Corps, and must inevitably attract to our ranks the most adventurous and able spirits of America's manhood.

If, on the other hand, our very limited resources in trained officers must be further disbursed and if the best of the adventurous spirits and "go-getters" among our men must be diverted from the Fleet Marine Force in meeting the requirements of this additional activity (Commando Project), then the undersigned would recommend seriously against assuming this additional commitment.

That was the official reply. The same day, General Price wrote a "Dear Tom" letter to the Major General Commandant of the Marine Corps. In it he wrote,

There is another thing in this connection which I could not put in my other letter and that is the grave danger that this sort

of thing will develop into a tail which will wag the dog eventually. I know in what quarter the idea of foisting this scheme upon the Marines originated, and I opine that if it is developed along the lines of a hobby in the hands of personnel other than regular Marine officers it could very easily get far out of hand and out of control as well.

It appears pretty clear to me that you are in a position of having to comply and that nothing can be done about it so please accept my sympathy.

Major General H. M. Smith's reply to the Major General Commandant's letter, also dated January 16, 1942, was typically concise and to the point:

(a) All Amphibious Force Marines are considered as commandos and may be trained to high degree under their own officers in this form of training.

(b) The appointment of Colonel Donovan to brigadier general could be compared to that of Lord Mountbatten in Great Britain—both are "royal" and have easy access to the highest authority without reference to their own immediate superiors.

(c) The appointment would be considered by many senior officers of the Corps as political, unfair and a publicity stunt.

(d) An appointment as brigadier general, Marines, doubtless would indicate that he is to form commandos from Marine Amphibious Forces. The commandant would lose control of that number of Marines assigned as commandos. We have enough "by-products" now.

(e) No strictures are cast upon Colonel Donovan. He has a reputation for fearlessness but he has never been a Marine and his appointment would be accepted with resentment throughout the Corps. It would be stressed that the Marines had to go outside their own service for leaders.

(f) It is the unanimous opinion of the staff of this headquarters that commando raids by the British have been of little strategical value. We have not reached the stage where our men are so highly trained and restless for action that they must be employed in commando raids.

And then, as if he wasn't sure that the Major General Commandant would take his point, General Smith added,

(g) I recommend against the appointment.

Meanwhile, another brushfire had broken out. The senior U.S. Navy officer in England, Admiral H. R. Stark, had recommended to the Commander in Chief, U.S. Fleet (Admiral King), that seven Marine officers and one hundred enlisted men be sent to England for training by and with British Commandos, and that when they were trained, they participate in a commando raid somewhere in Europe, under British command.

Admiral King killed most of this idea on January 16. He wrote the Chief of Naval Operations, with a carbon copy to the Major General Commandant, authorizing a *"small group of selected officers and non-commissioned officers"* to be sent to England for about one month, *"such personnel to be used as instructors in the Fleet Marine Force on their return,"* and disapproved Marine participation in British Commando operations.

Three days later, Holcomb wrote to Samuel W. Meek, an executive of *Time-Life*, and a personal friend. After discussing an article someone planned to write for *Life* about the Marine Corps, and expressing the hope that "Mr. Luce[2] will be willing to suppress it," he turned to the subject of Donovan:

The Donovan affair is still uppermost in my mind. I am terrified that I may be forced to take this man. I feel that it will be the worst slap in the face that the Marine Corps was ever given because it involves bringing into the Marine Corps as a leader in our own specialty that is, amphibious operations. Because commander [sic] work is simply one form of amphibious operation. It will be bitterly resented by our personnel, both commissioned and enlisted, and I am afraid that it may serve to materially reduce my usefulness in this office, if any, because I am expected, and properly so, to protect the Marine Corps from intrusions of this kind.

Five days after this, the Commander in Chief, United States Fleet (Admiral King), sent a priority, SECRET radio message to the Commander in Chief, Pacific Fleet, Admiral Chester W. Nimitz:

[2]Henry Luce, founder of *Time* and *Life*, was then functioning as the supreme editor of the *Time-Life* empire.

DEVELOP ORGANIZATION AND TRAINING OF MARINE AND NAVAL UNITS OF "COMMANDO" TYPE FOR USE IN CONNECTION WITH EXPEDITIONS OF RAID CHARACTER FOR DEMOLITION AND OTHER DESTRUCTION OF SHORE INSTALLATIONS IN ENEMY HELD ISLANDS AND BASES X

Admiral Nimitz promptly ordered the Commanding General, Second Joint Training Force, San Diego, to form four company-sized commando units. He wrote that he had requested the transfer of destroyer-transports from the Atlantic Fleet to the Pacific Fleet, for use with the commando units. He also "authorized and directed" General Vogel to "request the services of any personnel who may be familiar with training, organization, and methods of foreign commando units."

Lieutenant Colonel Evans F. Carlson was shortly thereafter named commanding officer of the 2nd Separate Battalion, Camp Elliott, San Diego, California (which was to be shortly renamed the 2nd Raider Battalion), and Captain James Roosevelt was named as his deputy.

And on February 16, 1942, Major General Holcomb finally heard from Colonel William J. Donovan. It had nothing to do with Commandos, Raiders, or his becoming a Marine general. Navy personnel officers, desperate for officers, were scraping the bottom of the barrel and had informed Donovan that they intended to reassign some of the Navy and Marine officers assigned to COI.

Donovan made a reasoned, concise plea not to have the officers he was about to lose replaced by *"a random selection of reserve or retired officers who would I am sure fall far short of our needs."*

If Major General Holcomb replied to Donovan, that letter is still buried in a dusty file someplace. But for the rest of the war, the Marine Corps was far more cooperative than any other service when it came to furnishing personnel to Colonel (later Major General) Wild Bill Donovan's Office of Strategic Services. They included such people as Captain John Hamilton, USMCR, better known as actor Sterling Hayden, and screenwriter Peter Viertel, Captain, USMCR. . . .

But that's still another story. . . .

CALL TO ARMS

Preface

The first surrender of United States military forces in World War II—the first time, in fact, since the Civil War that American military forces went forward under a white flag to deliver American soil over to an enemy—took place on a tiny but militarily useful dot of volcanic rock in the Pacific Ocean, Wake Island, shortly after the Japanese struck the U.S. Pacific Fleet at Pearl Harbor, Hawaii.

In 1939, with war on the horizon, the U.S. Navy began to pay particular attention to the tiny atoll in the middle of the Pacific. This almost infinitesimal U.S. possession was 450 miles from the Bikini atoll; 620 miles from the Marshalls, which the Japanese would certainly use for military purposes; 1,023 miles from Midway Island; and 1,300 miles from Guam. The USS *Nitro* was ordered to Wake to make preliminary engineering studies with a view to turning the atoll into a base for land (which of course included carrier-based) aircraft and submarines, and to fortify the island against any Japanese assault.

In 1940, Congress appropriated the funds. On 19 August 1941, 6 officers and 173 enlisted men of the 1st Defense Battalion, USMC, were put ashore on Wake Island from the

1

USS *Regulus*. The first of what would be about 1,200 construction workers landed a few days later, and in October, Major James P. S. Devereux, USMC, arrived from Hawaii to take command.

Devereux brought with him two five-inch Naval cannon (which had been removed from obsolescent and scrapped battleships); four three-inch antiaircraft cannon (only one of which had the required fire-control equipment); twenty-four .50-caliber machine guns; and a large number (probably about one hundred) of air- and water-cooled .30-caliber Browning machine guns. And, of course, a stock of ammunition for his ordnance.

Nine Marine officers and two hundred enlisted men from the Navy base at Pearl Harbor arrived on 2 November 1941, bringing the strength of the 1st Defense Battalion to approximately half of that provided for in the table of organization and equipment. On 28 November 1941, Commander Winfield Scott Cunningham, USN, was detached from the aircraft tender USS *Wright* (after the Wright Brothers) with nine Navy officers and fifty-eight sailors to Wake to take control of the air station already under construction.

As senior officer, Cunningham replaced Devereux as Commander of United States Forces, Wake Island.

A five-thousand-foot runway was completed, and U.S. Army B-17 aircraft began to use Wake Island as a refueling stop en route to Guam, although it was necessary to fill the aircraft tanks by hand-pumping avgas from fifty-five-gallon barrels.

On 3 December 1941, the USS *Enterprise* launched at sea twelve Grumman F4F fighters, of Marine Fighter Squadron VMF-211, under Major Paul Putnam, USMC. They landed on the Wake Island landing strip that afternoon, and steps were immediately taken to begin bulldozing revetments for the aircraft.

On Sunday, 7 December 1941 (Saturday, 6 December 1941 in Hawaii) Major Devereux gave his command the day off. His Marines swam in the surf, played softball, and many of them—most of the young, recently recruited enlisted men—hurried to complete letters home. The letters would be carried to civilization aboard the Pan American *Philippine Clipper* moored in the lagoon, which would take off at first light for Guam.[1]

[1]Pan American had been using Wake as a refueling stop.

Reveille sounded at 0600, 8 December 1941. While the Marines had their breakfast, the Pan American crew prepared the *Philippine Clipper* for flight.

At 0650, the radio operator on duty at the air station communications section, attempting to establish contact with Hickam Field, Hawaii, began to receive uncoded messages, which did not follow established message-transmission procedures, to the effect that the island of Oahu was under attack. He informed the duty officer, who went to Major Devereux.

At 0655, the *Philippine Clipper* rose from the lagoon and gradually disappeared from sight in the bright blue morning sky.

When he was told of the "Oahu under attack" message, Major Devereux attempted to contact Commander Cunningham by telephone, but there was no answer.

When he hung up the telephone, it immediately rang again. It was the communications shack; there was an urgent message from Hawaii, now being decoded.

"Has the *Clipper* left?"

"Yes, sir."

"Call it back," Devereux ordered, and then sent for his field music—his bugler.

"Yes, sir?"

"Sound 'call to arms,' " Major Devereux ordered.

Admiral Husband Kimmel's Pacific Fleet, and the navy base at Pearl Harbor, had been grievously wounded by the Japanese attack on December 7, 1941, but that is not the same thing as destroyed. The battleship force of the Pacific Fleet had been essentially wiped out at its moorings ("Battleship Row") at Pearl Harbor, together with a number of other men-of-war and supply ships, and there had been great loss of aircraft and matériel.

But the Fleet was not totally lost, nor were its supplies.

There were three aircraft carriers available—the *Saratoga,* the *Enterprise,* and the *Lexington*—as well as a number of cruisers, plus a large number of smaller men-of-war.

On December 13, 1941, Admiral Kimmel (who expected to be relieved at any minute as the Navy, and indeed the nation, searched for somebody on whom to blame the Pearl Harbor disaster) ordered Rear Admiral Frank Jack Fletcher to reinforce Wake Island.

Fletcher put out the same day from Pearl Harbor with the

aircraft carrier *Saratoga;* the cruisers *Minneapolis, Astoria,* and *San Francisco;* nine destroyers; a fleet oiler; and the transport *Tangier.*

Marine Fighter Squadron VMF-211, equipped with Grumman F4F-3 Wildcats, was aboard the *Saratoga* (in addition to *Saratoga*'s own aircraft), and the 4th Defense Battalion, USMC, was aboard the *Tangier.* The relief force carried with it nine thousand shells for Devereux's old five-inch battleship cannon, twelve thousand three-inch shells for his antiaircraft cannon, and three million rounds of belted .50-caliber machine-gun ammunition.

The aircraft carrier *Enterprise,* and its accompanying cruisers and destroyers, was ordered to make a diversionary raid on the Japanese-held Marshall Islands. The carrier *Lexington* and its accompanying vessels put to sea to repel, should it come, a second Japanese attack on the Hawaiian Islands.

At 2100 hours, 22 December 1941, a radio message was flashed from Pearl Harbor, ordering the *Saratoga* Wake Island relief force back to Hawaii. It had been decided at the highest echelons of command that Wake Island was not worth the risk of losing what was in fact one third of U.S. Naval strength in the Pacific. When the message was received, the *Saratoga* was five hundred miles (thirty-three hours steaming time) from Wake.

At shortly after one in the morning of December 23, 1941, Japanese troops landed on Wake, near the airstrip.

That afternoon, his ammunition gone, his heavy weapons out of commission, and greatly outnumbered, Major Devereux was forced to agree with Commander Cunningham that further resistance was futile and that surrender was necessary to avoid a useless bloodbath.

Major Devereux had to roam the island personally to order the last pockets of resistance to lay down their arms.

Four hundred seventy officers and men of the Marine Corps and Navy and 1,146 American civilian workmen entered Japanese captivity.

I

(One)
Wake Island
1200 Hours, 18 December 1941

Ensign E. H. Murphy, USN, had planned the flight of his Consolidated Aircraft PBY5 Catalina to Wake Island with great care. It wasn't a question only of finding the tiny atoll, which of course required great navigational skill, but of reaching Wake when there was the least chance of being intercepted by Japanese aircraft.

His Catalina was a seaplane (though the PBY5-A, fitted with retractable gear, was an amphibian) designed for long-range reconnaissance. Its most efficient cruising speed was about 160 MPH, so it had little chance of running away from an attacker. The high-winged, twin-engine Catalina had three gun ports, one on each side of the fuselage mounting a single .50-caliber machine gun, and one in the nose with a .30-caliber machine gun.

If Ensign Murphy's Catalina encountered one of the Japanese bombers that had been attacking Wake on an almost daily basis, all the Japanese would have to do was slow down to his speed, and, far out of range of his .50-caliber machine guns, shoot him down at his leisure with his 20-mm machine cannon.

It was a five-hour flight from Guam. Murphy took off at first light in the hope that he could be at Wake before the Japanese began their "scheduled" bombing attack.

Hitting Wake on the nose was skill; finding it covered with a morning haze was good luck. He landed in the lagoon and taxied to the Pan American area. Commander Cunningham's requisition of Pan American's *Philippine Clipper* had been almost immediately overridden by Pacific Fleet, which had plans for the use of the aircraft itself, and it had flown on to Guam, carrying hastily patched Japanese bullet holes in its fuselage.

Marine Fighter Squadron VMF-211 was down to two Wildcats, although Major Putnam told Ensign Murphy that he hoped to get a third Wildcat back in the air within hours with parts scavenged from wrecked airplanes.

Murphy carried with him official mail for Commander Cunningham and Major Devereux, including the last known position of the *Saratoga* relief force, but the Navy had not risked one of its precious few Catalinas solely to deliver messages. Many Catalinas had been destroyed on December 7, and what planes were left were in almost constant use.

But there was on Wake one of the Marine Corps' few highly skilled communications officers, Major Walter L. J. Bayler, USMC, who had previously been assigned to the USS *Wright* and had come to Wake with Commander Cunningham. Bayler's services were desperately needed on Midway Island and the decision had been made to send for him, even at the great risk of losing him, and the Catalina carrying him, in the attempt.

Bayler spent the afternoon of December 20 collecting official documents (including casualty lists) from Cunningham and Devereux, and then personal messages from the Marines of the garrison, for delivery, when it could be arranged, to their families.

The next morning, Ensign Murphy lifted the Catalina from the Wake lagoon and pointed the nose toward Pearl Harbor, eight hours and 1,225 miles distant. The Catalina was the last American aircraft to visit Wake Island until the war was over.

At Pearl Harbor, mechanics swarmed over the Catalina to ready it for another flight. Three hours after it landed, it was airborne again with another flight crew, this time bound for the Philippines, where the Japanese were approaching Manila, and demolition at the Cavite U.S. Navy Base had already begun.

The Catalina remained in the Philippines only long enough to drop off its passengers—a Navy petty officer who was a Japanese linguist, and an Army Ordnance Corps major, a demolitions expert—and its mail bags. It loaded aboard the outgoing cargo, mail bags, and its Pearl Harbor–bound passengers while it was taking on fuel. These were a U.S. Foreign Service officer, an Army colonel of Artillery, and a Marine Corps second lieutenant.

Manila Bay was choppy, and the Catalina smashed heavily into unyielding water several times before the pilot was finally able to get it into the air. When they'd reached cruising altitude, he went back into the fuselage to see if any damage had been done to the aircraft—in particular to the floats—and to the passengers. He found the Army colonel and the Foreign Service officer doing what they could to bandage the Marine Corps second lieutenant.

Although it had not been visible under the lieutenant's uniform when he boarded the Catalina, his body was bandaged. The bone-jarring bounces of the Catalina as it had taken off had ripped loose four or five of the two dozen or so stitches holding an eight-inch gash in the young Marine officer's side together. There was some bleeding, and he was obviously in pain, but he refused, rather abruptly, the pilot's offer of a syringe of morphine.

They rigged a sort of bed for him out of life preservers and blankets, but that was all that could be done for him until the seaplane reached Pearl Harbor.

An hour out of Pearl, the young Marine went forward to the cockpit. The pilot was surprised to see him.

"Feeling better?" he asked.

The young Marine nodded.

"In a couple of minutes, I'll radio ahead, and they'll have medics meet us," the pilot said.

"I thought maybe you'd do that," the young Marine said. "That's why I came up here. Don't."

"Why not?"

"Because, unless I get put in a hospital, my orders will carry me to Washington," he said. "I can get myself rebandaged there."

"You may not make it to Washington, in your shape."

"Then in San Francisco, or Diego, wherever they land me. Do me a favor, just don't say anything."

"Suit yourself," the pilot said, after a moment's thought.

"Thank you," the young Marine officer said, and he went back into the fuselage.

Curious, the pilot took his flight manifest out and looked at it. It gave no identification beyond, "McCoy, Kenneth J. 2nd Lt USMCR," but then the pilot noticed that Second Lieutenant McCoy was listed first on the manifest. Passengers were listed in order of their travel priority, which meant that McCoy had a higher priority than even the Foreign Service big shot.

The pilot was curious about that, and said so to the copilot.

"He's a courier," he said. "Didn't you see the briefcase?"

The pilot shook his head. "No."

"He had it when he came on board, chained—actually handcuffed—to his wrist."

"I didn't notice," the pilot said.

"And when he took off his jacket, he had a .45 stuck in his belt, and a knife strapped to his arm."

"I wonder what's in the briefcase?" the pilot said.

"I don't know," the copilot replied, adding, "but I don't think I'd want to try to take it away from him."

(Two)
The Willard Hotel
Washington, D.C.
1215 Hours, 26 December 1941

"Peacock Alley," which ran through the Willard Hotel from Fourteenth Street to Pennsylvania Avenue, was where, since before the Civil War, the elegant ladies of the nation's capital (and, some said, the more expensive courtesans) and their elegant gentlemen had strutted . . . like peacocks.

It was ornately decorated, still with Victorian elegance, and along the alley were small alcoves, furnished with tables and chairs where conversations could be held in private. The cynics said that more politicians had been bought and sold in the alcoves of Peacock Alley than in all the smoke-filled rooms in the United States combined.

Thomas C. Wesley, a tall, fifty-year-old, portly, ruddy-faced full colonel of Marines, got out of a 1941 Chevrolet staff car on Pennsylvania Avenue and entered the building. He removed his overcoat and hat and put them in care of the cloakroom. He tugged at the skirt of his blouse and checked the position of his Sam Browne leather belt, and then walked slowly down Peacock Alley all the way to the stairs leading down into the lobby, obviously looking for someone. When he didn't find him, he stationed himself halfway along the corridor and waited.

At just about the same time, a tall, thin, somehow unhealthy-looking man entered the Willard from Fourteenth Street. He was wearing a gray snap-brim felt hat, which he removed (exposing his balding head) as he came through the revolving door. He headed across the old and battered, but still elegant, lobby toward Peacock Alley shrugging awkwardly out of his gray topcoat. By the time he saw Colonel Wesley, he had it draped none too neatly over his left arm.

Colonel Wesley nodded stiffly, perhaps even disapprovingly, when he saw the tall, thin, unhealthy-looking man in the badly fitting blue pinstripe suit.

"Rickabee," he said.

"Colonel," Rickabee said, then looked around Peacock Alley until he found an empty table and two chairs in one of the alcoves and made a gesture toward it. Lieutenant Colonel F. L. Rickabee was carried on the Table of Organization of Headquarters, USMC, as "special assistant to the Public Affairs Officer," although his real duties had nothing to do with public relations.

Colonel Wesley marched to the alcove and sat down, leaving to Rickabee the other chair, which faced the wall. Rickabee moved the chair so that he, too, could look out into Peacock Alley.

"It's been some time, Rickabee, hasn't it?" Colonel Wesley said, and then, before Rickabee had a chance to reply, said what was actually on his mind: "Are you people exempt from the uniform requirements?"

"It's left to General Forrest's discretion, sir, who wears the uniform and who doesn't. The general feels I'm more effective in mufti."

Brigadier General Horace W. T. Forrest, USMC, was Assistant Chief of Staff, Intelligence, USMC.

"General Forrest explained the situation to you?" Colonel Wesley asked.

"He said that you and General Lesterby had been handed a

very delicate problem by the Major General Commandant, and that I was to do what I could to help. How can we help you, sir?"

"*He* thought you might be interested in this," Colonel Wesley said, taking an envelope from his lower blouse pocket and handing it to Rickabee.

There was no question in Lieutenant Colonel Rickabee's mind who "He" was. Colonel Thomas C. Wesley was one of a handful of officers at the absolute upper echelon of the Marine Corps. They were somewhat derisively known as "the Palace Guard," because of their reputation for doing the bidding of, and protecting from all enemies, foreign and domestic, the Commandant of the U.S. Marine Corps.

"Captain James Roosevelt has been good enough to offer some suggestions on how he believes the Marine Corps should organize its own version of a Communist Route Army," Colonel Wesley said dryly.

"I thought he was working for Colonel Wild Bill Donovan," Rickabee said.

"Not any longer," Wesley said. "He now works for Lieutenant Colonel Evans Carlson."

Rickabee took from the envelope a thin sheath of carbon sheets. They were the fifth or sixth carbon, he concluded. They were just barely readable.

A waiter appeared.

"Nothing for me, thank you," Colonel Wesley said.

"I'll have a Jack Daniel's," Lieutenant Colonel Rickabee said. "No ice, and water on the side."

He sensed Colonel Wesley's disapproval.

"The way I handle drinking on duty, Colonel," Rickabee said, "is that for the first twenty-four consecutive hours I have the duty, I don't touch alcohol. After that . . ."

"Do what you like, Rickabee," Colonel Wesley said.

Rickabee returned to reading, very carefully, the sheath of carbon copies Wesley had given him. Finally, he finished and looked at Wesley.

"Very interesting," he said. "Where did you get this?"

"I'm not at liberty to say," Wesley said.

"You think he's actually going to submit it?"

"Yes, I do."

"And apparently you don't think that General Vogel is going to call him in for a little chat and point out that it's just a touch pushy for a reserve captain to tell him, much less the Commandant, how the Corps should be run?"

"I believe the letter will be forwarded to the Commandant," Wesley said. "I'm interested in your reaction to it."

"You are, or He is? Does He know you're showing this to me?"

Colonel Wesley nodded his head, signifying, Rickabee decided, that Wesley was running an errand.

"I would really like to know where you got this, where He got it," Rickabee said.

"I can assure you, Colonel," Wesley said, "that it is authentic."

"I'd still like to know how it came into His hands," Rickabee insisted. "That could be very important."

"The document was typed, from a handwritten draft, by a clerk, a corporal, who thought the sergeant major should see it. He made six, instead of five carbons. The sergeant major sent it on to . . . sent it on here."

"To you or to Him?" Rickabee asked.

"To Him," Wesley said.

The waiter, an elderly black man, delivered Rickabee's bourbon on a silver tray.

"I believe I will have one," Colonel Wesley said. "The same, with ice. . . . This is obviously a very delicate situation," he continued, when the waiter had gone.

"Well, there's one way to handle it," Rickabee said. "I know several people at San Diego who would be happy to run Carlson over with a truck. Better yet, a tank."

Wesley was not amused; it showed on his face.

"Then you think that Colonel Carlson has a hand in this?" he asked.

"That seems pretty obvious," Rickabee said. "Have you read his reports, Colonel? Or his books?"

"As much as I could stomach," Colonel Wesley said.

"That 'leaders' and 'fighters' business," Lieutenant Colonel Rickabee said, "has appeared before. That's pure Carlson. So is the business about everybody being treated equally, officers, noncoms, and privates. He got all that from the Chinese Eighth Route Army . . . and the term 'column,' too, meaning 'battalion.' That's pure Chinese Red Army."

"Well then, let's get right to that," Wesley said. "Did he get himself infected by them when he was with them? Is he a Communist?"

Rickabee sipped at his bourbon, and then took a sip of water before replying.

"No, I don't think so," he said. "He's been investigated. When he applied to get his commission back, the FBI investigated him, and came up with nothing we didn't already know."

"You've seen the FBI reports?" Wesley asked.

"Of course not," Rickabee said, dryly. "FBI reports are confidential and never shown to outsiders. What agencies requesting an investigation get is a synopsis of what the FBI thinks it found out."

He clearly meant, Wesley decided, that he had indeed seen the FBI reports on Lieutenant Colonel Evans Carlson, USMCR.

"What's your personal opinion of him?" Wesley said.

"I think he's a good Marine gone off the deep end," Rickabee said. "That he's a zealot, quite eccentric, perhaps even unbalanced. He might have gotten Roosevelt to sign this, but the Major General Commandant will know he was behind it."

Wesley grunted his agreement.

"But on the other hand," Rickabee said after taking a sip of his drink, "they said very much the same things about Jesus Christ, you will recall. *'What's happened to that nice Nazarene carpenter? Why is he attacking the established order?'*"

"I don't think that's funny, Colonel," Wesley said, coldly.

"It wasn't intended to be, Colonel. There is even the parallel between Christ being able to talk to his heavenly, all-powerful father. . . ."

What could have been a faint smile crossed Wesley's lips.

"And what about Roosevelt . . . the son, I mean?" he asked.

"Everything I know about him is positive. He's smarter than hell, hard working, everything a good reserve officer should be. After seeing this, I would suggest that he's fallen in with evil companions . . . *an* evil companion."

"You know him, personally?"

Rickabee nodded. "Not well. Great big guy. Getting bald. Has to wear glasses. Nice guy, from the little I know him. What I would like to know is why they gave Carlson his commission back."

"Isn't that obvious, Colonel?" Colonel Wesley replied, sarcastically. "He came highly recommended. He has the Navy Cross. And, as they say, 'friends in high places.'"

"A little backbone then would have kept this from happening," Rickabee said, and raised the sheets of paper.

"*He* made that decision," Wesley said.

"That was the big mistake," Rickabee said, undaunted.

"You say your mind, Colonel, don't you?" Colonel Wesley said, coldly.

"That's what I'm paid for," Rickabee said. "I would prefer to be at Camp Elliott myself. Believe it or not, I'm qualified to command an infantry battalion."

"Obviously, the Corps feels that what you're doing now is of greater importance," Colonel Wesley said.

"What does the Corps want me to do about this?" Rickabee asked, holding up the sheaf of paper again. "How does my run-him-over-with-a-truck suggestion sound?"

"As if you don't understand the seriousness of the problem," Wesley said. "Otherwise you wouldn't be joking."

"You seem to be very sure that I *was* joking," Rickabee said.

Colonel Thomas C. Wesley was furious with himself when he realized that he did not in fact know for sure that Rickabee was being flip. He met Rickabee's eyes for a long moment, and learned nothing.

"What I was hoping—" he said, finally.

"Was that I could give you proof positive," Rickabee interrupted him, "proof that He could take to at least Frank Knox, and/or to the White House, that Evans Carlson is in fact a Communist and/or certifiably out of his mind. I can't do that, Colonel. I can't even manufacture any evidence to that effect. It wouldn't stand up in the light."

"But you do see the problem," Wesley said.

"Would you like to hear how I see it?" Rickabee asked.

"Of course," Wesley said, impatiently.

"The Corps is in a no-win situation," Rickabee said. "When this document reaches His desk, He's going to have to approve it, at least on a trial basis. Carlson's Eighth Communist Route Army, also known as the Marine Commandos or Rangers or whatever, will have to be employed. That will result in one of two things: They will get wiped out on the beach of some Pacific island, and He will find Himself explaining why He approved such a nutty idea, resulting in such a terrible waste of young American life. Or, Carlson's private army will do what Carlson says it will do, which, by the way, is very likely to happen. Carlson has proved that he's a skilled, courageous officer. If Carlson succeeds—and to repeat, he damned well may—the Commandant will find himself turning the Corps into the U.S. Commandos, with at least full Colonel Carlson—and possibly General Carlson—at his side while the rules are written."

"It could mean the end of the Corps," Wesley said.

"Yes, it could," Rickabee said. "After the war, when there was no need for Commandos, or for more than a few of them, the Marine Corps could become an Army regiment. A lot of people would like to see that happen."

"If you were charged with stopping this, Rickabee," Colonel Wesley asked, "how would you go about it?"

"Is that what this little chat is all about, Colonel? He sent you here to order me to stop it?"

"I said nothing of the kind," Wesley said quickly. "Just answer the question, please."

"I would look for proof positive that Carlson is crazy or a Communist, or both," Rickabee said. "That's the only chance I see to scuttle this."

"And, how would you do that?"

"I would put someone close to him, telling him what to look for, and to make sure he had witnesses . . . unimpeachable witnesses."

"A spy, you mean."

"An *undercover operative*," Rickabee said.

"Have you such a man available?" Wesley asked.

"Not off the top of my head," Rickabee said, then changed his mind. "I might. He's a bright young shavetail—"

Wesley interrupted him. "I don't want to know the details," he said. "Not yet."

"Then where are we?" Rickabee said.

"I want you to think this through," Wesley said. "Come up with a plan, including the name of the man you intend to employ, and a synopsis of his background. When you have that, as soon as you have it, call me."

"Yes, sir," Rickabee said. He motioned to someone standing in Peacock Alley to come to the table.

"What are you doing?" Colonel Wesley asked, confused.

A good-looking young man in a camel's hair sports coat and gray flannel trousers came to the table.

"Colonel Wesley, Lieutenant Frame," Rickabee said.

"How do you do, sir?" Lieutenant Frame asked politely.

"Lieutenant," Colonel Wesley said.

"Bill, take this to the office and have it photographed," Rickabee ordered, handing Frame the sheaf of carbon copies. "Stick around until you have the negatives, then bring this back here. I have just accepted Colonel Wesley's kind invitation to lunch, and we'll be in the dining room."

"Aye, aye, sir," Lieutenant Frame said. He looked at Colonel Wesley, said, "It was a pleasure to meet you, sir," and then walked down Peacock Alley toward Fourteenth Street.

"And what's his reason for being in mufti?" Colonel Wesley asked. He was annoyed that Rickabee had, without asking, turned the carbon of Captain James Roosevelt's proposal for Marine Commandos over to Frame to be photographed.

"He'd look a little strange following a civilian around in uniform, don't you think, Colonel?" Rickabee replied, smiling.

"And that's necessary? His following you around?"

"That was the general's idea, Colonel," Rickabee said, and stood up. "Shall we have our lunch? He won't be long, and I've got a busy afternoon."

From Colonel Wesley's silence during lunch, Lieutenant Colonel Rickabee decided that Wesley was displeased with him. He had probably been a little too flip for the colonel, failed to display the proper respect for a senior member of the Palace Guard. But there was nothing that could be done about that now.

He was wrong. When Colonel Wesley returned to Headquarters, USMC, and to the office of Major General Lesterby, he told Lesterby that Rickabee might just be the answer to "the Carlson problem."

"He had a specific suggestion?"

"Yes, sir, that he arrange to have Carlson run over with a truck."

"You think he was serious?"

"Sir, I don't know."

"It may come down to that, Tom."

(Three)
The Brooklyn Navy Yard
Brooklyn, New York
0400 Hours, 6 January 1942

Two noncommissioned officers of the United States Marine
Corps, Staff Sergeant C. (for Casimir) J. Koznowski and
Sergeant Ernst W. "Ernie" Zimmerman, stood on the cobble-
stone street before an old brick barracks, shifting their feet and
slapping their gloved hands against the cold. Koznowski was
twenty-seven, tall, and slim. Zimmerman was stocky, muscular, round faced, and twenty-three. There were two "hash
marks"—red embroidered diagonal bars each signifying the
satisfactory completion of four years' service—on the sleeve of
Koznowski's overcoat, and one hash mark on Zimmerman's.

Sergeant Zimmerman's face was pale, and his uniform
seemed just a hair too large for him. Sergeant Zimmerman had
two days before been released from the St. Albans Naval
Hospital where he had been treated for malaria. He had been
certified as fit for limited service and was being transferred to
Parris Island for duty in his military specialty of motor
transport sergeant.

Two corporals came around the corner of the brick barracks
building, and when they saw Koznowski and Zimmerman,
broke into a trot to join them.

"Where the fuck have you two been?" Staff Sergeant
Koznowski demanded. It was not really a question, but rather
an expression of disapproval, and no answer was expected or
given.

"Go get 'em," Staff Sergeant Koznowski said to one of the
corporals, and threw a clipboard at the other.

Both corporals ran into the building. There was the blast of a
whistle, and lights were on, and the sound of muffled shouts.

Less than a minute later, encouraged by curt shouts of
"Move it! Move it! Move it!" the first of 106 young men
began to pour out of the building. They were in civilian
clothing. The day before, or two days before, they had been
civilians. They were now recruits of the United States Marine
Corps. And they were about to be transported, under the
command of Staff Sergeant Koznowski, Sergeant Zimmerman,
and the two corporals, to the United States Marine Corps

Recruit Depot, Parris Island, South Carolina, for basic training.

One of the corporals stood on the street. He grabbed the first four men to reach him by the shoulders and placed them one behind the other. Then he got the others to form ranks on them, sometimes by pointing, sometimes by shoving them into place.

Finally, they were all lined up in four ranks.

"Ah-ten-hut!" the corporal with the clipboard barked.

One hundred and five of the 106 young men stood as stiff as they knew how. The 106th young man continued to try to tie the laces of his right shoe.

Staff Sergeant Koznowski walked quickly to him, standing before him until the shoe was tied and the young man stood erect.

"Got it all tied now?" Koznowski asked.

"Uh-huh," the young man replied. He was now wearing a nervous smile.

"When you are in ranks, and someone calls 'ah-ten-hut,' you come to attention right *then*," Koznowski said. "Not when it's convenient for you. You think you can remember that?"

"My shoe—"

"I asked, can you remember that?" Koznowski snapped.

"Yeah, sure."

"And you never, never, never say 'yeah, sure' to a sergeant," Koznowski said.

The young man was clever enough to sense that whatever he said next was going to be the wrong thing, so he said nothing.

"Take off the shoe," Koznowski said, conversationally.

The young man looked at him in disbelief.

"Take off the fucking shoe!" Koznowski shouted, his face two inches from the young man's face, spraying him with spittle.

The young man did as he was ordered, and finally stood up again, holding the shoe in his hand.

"Call the roll, Corporal," Staff Sergeant Koznowski ordered.

"Listen up, you people," the corporal with the clipboard said. "I will call off your last name, and you will respond with your first."

The roll was called.

The corporal turned and saluted. "The recruit draft is formed, sir," he reported.

Koznowski returned the salute, and then barked, "At ease."

Next he delivered a short speech. He told them that there was clear proof that God did not love him, for he had been assigned the unpleasant task of moving their miserable asses from the Brooklyn Navy Yard to Parris Island, South Carolina, where an attempt would be made to turn their miserable asses into something resembling Marines.

Before they could leave the Navy Yard, Staff Sergeant Koznowski announced, four things had to be done. First, they would be fed. After which they would run, not walk, back to the barracks. Second, their blankets, sheets, pillow cases, and mattress covers would have to be turned in. Third, the barracks and the head which they had managed to turn into a fucking pig sty in a remarkably short time would have to be returned to the immaculate state in which they had found it. Finally, they would have to wash and shave and do whatever else they could to make themselves as presentable as possible for the walk between the buses at the entrance to Pennsylvania Station and the train itself.

It was going to be humiliating enough, Staff Sergeant Koznowski said, for himself and Sergeant Zimmerman and Corporals Hayworth and Cohn to be seen shepherding so many assholes around without the assholes looking like they had just crawled out of the fucking sewer.

They had, he informed them, precisely twenty-eight minutes and twenty seconds to accomplish breakfast and get back here.

"Are there any questions?" Staff Sergeant Koznowski asked.

A tall, rather thin young man in the rear rank had raised his hand above his shoulders.

Koznowski looked at him. "Anyone tell you to put your hand up? You want permission to leave the room so you can take a piss?"

"Sergeant," the tall thin young man said, nervously, "you asked if there were questions."

"I didn't mean it," Staff Sergeant Koznowski said, pleased with himself. "Sergeant Zimmerman, take over."

With that, Staff Sergeant Koznowski marched off in the direction of the mess hall, leaving Sergeant Zimmerman in charge.

Like many—perhaps most—Marines, Zimmerman was ambivalent about the hoary Marine Corps tradition of shitting all over recruits until they had passed through either the Parris Island or San Diego Recruit Depots. He understood the philosophy, which was to break a man down and then rebuild him as a Marine; and he knew that it worked. It had turned him into a Marine. But he was personally uncomfortable with shitting on people; he could not have been a drill instructor himself, and he had been made uncomfortable when he had learned that he would be taking a draft of recruits to Parris Island.

When Koznowski had turned the corner, Zimmerman said, "Finish buttoning your clothes."

The young man holding his shoe in his hand looked at him questioningly. Zimmerman shook his head no.

When they had time to tuck their trousers in their pants and button their jackets and overcoats, Zimmerman called them to attention and marched them to the mess hall.

He watched the line until the young man with his shoe tucked under his arm passed through it, and then told him he could now put his shoe on. Then he had his own breakfast.

Afterward, he walked back to the barracks as the recruits ran past him. And there he supervised the turning in of the bed clothes and the cleaning of the barracks. He did not find it necessary to jump anybody's ass while doing so.

When Staff Sergeant Koznowski returned from the staff NCO mess he found the draft of recruits lined up on the street before the barracks waiting to be loaded onto the chartered buses for the trip into Manhattan and Pennsylvania Station.

II

(One)
Rocky Fields Farm
Bernardsville, New Jersey
O605 Hours, 6 January 1942

Second Lieutenant Malcolm S. Pickering, USMCR, stood in the bay window of the breakfast room, holding a cup and saucer in his hand. Pickering was a tall, erect young man of twenty-two, ruggedly handsome, with sharp features, and eyes that appeared experienced beyond his years. In his superbly tailored uniform, he looked, Elaine (Mrs. Ernest) Sage thought, like an advertisement in *Town & Country* magazine. Or a Marine Corps recruiting poster.

Elaine Sage was a striking, trim, silver-haired woman in her middle forties. She was wearing a pleated plaid skirt, a simple white blouse, and a pink sweater. There was an antique gold watch hanging from a gold chain around her neck, and a three-carat emerald-cut diamond engagement ring next to her wedding ring. She crossed the room to Pickering, surprising but not startling him, and kissed him on the cheek.

"Good morning, Pick," she said, and then she put her arm around his waist and leaned her head against his arm.

20

It was a motherly gesture. Elaine Sage had known "Pick" Pickering all his life; she had been at Sarah Lawrence with his mother; and she had taken the Twentieth-Century Limited to California and waited in Doctor's Hospital with his father for Patricia Foster Pickering to deliver her first and only child.

Just over a year later, Patricia Pickering had come to Elaine's room at Presbyterian Hospital and cooed and oohed over precious little Ernestine.

"Well," Patricia had said then, "the next thing we have to do is get the two of them together." That had been a running joke over the years, but not wholly a joke or a preposterous idea. It would have been nice, but it wasn't going to happen.

What Pick Pickering had been looking at from the bay window of the breakfast room was Ernestine Sage standing by the duck pond at the far side of the wide lawn. She was standing with another Marine officer, and he had his arm around her. Twice, they had kissed.

"What rouses you from bed at this obscene hour?" Pick Pickering asked Ernie Sage's mother.

"You could say I am just being a gracious hostess," she replied.

Pick Pickering snorted.

"When I went to bed last night," Elaine Sage said, "I went to Ernie's room. I was going to tell her . . . following the hoary adage that the best way to get rid of your daughter's undesirable suitor is to praise him to the skies . . . how much I liked your friend out there." She bent her head in the direction of the Marine who was holding her daughter.

Pickering looked down at her, his eyebrows raised.

"She wasn't in her bed," Elaine Sage said.

"If she wasn't, Aunt Elaine," Pick Pickering said, "it was her idea, not his."

"Ken McCoy frightens me, Pick," Elaine Sage said. "He's not like us."

"That may be part of his attraction," Pickering said.

"I'm not sure he's good for Ernie," Elaine Sage said.

"*I* think he's very good for her," Pickering said. When she looked at him, he added: "Anyway, I think it's a moot point. *She* thinks he's good for her. She thinks the sun comes up because he wants it to."

Ernestine Pickering and Second Lieutenant Kenneth J.

McCoy had turned from the duck pond and were walking back to the house. He had unbuttoned his overcoat and she was half inside it, resting her face on his chest.

"You will forgive me for not being able to forgive you for introducing them at your party," Elaine Sage said.

"I *didn't* introduce them," Pickering said. "Ernie picked him up. She saw in him someone who was as bored with my party as she was. She walked up to him, introduced herself, and shortly thereafter they disappeared. I found out the next morning that he'd taken her to a Chinese restaurant in Chinatown. Where, apparently, he dazzled her by speaking to the proprietor in Chinese, and then won her heart with his skill with chopsticks."

Elaine Sage chuckled.

"For what it's worth, Aunt Elaine," Pickering went on, "he didn't know she had a dime."

"Love at first sight?" she said. "Don't tell me you believe that's possible?"

"Take a look," he said. "You have a choice between love at first sight or irresistible lust. I'm willing to accept love at first sight."

"They have nothing in common," she protested.

"I don't have a hell of a lot in common with him, either," Pickering said. "But I realized some time ago he's the best friend I've ever had. If you've come looking for an ally in some Machiavellian plot of yours to separate the two of them, you're out of luck. *I* think they're good for each other. My basic reaction is jealousy. I wish someone like Ernie would look at me the way she looks at McCoy."

"I wish *Ernie* would look at you the way she looks at McCoy," Elaine Sage said.

There was a rattling sound behind them. They turned and saw a middle-aged, plump woman in a maid's uniform rolling a serving cart into the breakfast room.

"Do you suppose that she was looking out the window, too, for the return of Romeo and Juliet?" Pickering asked dryly. "Will it be safe for him to eat the scrambled eggs?"

"I am placing what hope I have left in the 'praise him to the skies' theory," Elaine Sage said. "Poison will be a last desperate resort."

Ernestine Sage and Second Lieutenant Kenneth J. McCoy,

USMCR, walked onto the broad veranda of the house, disappeared from sight, and a moment later came into the breakfast room. Their faces were red from the cold. McCoy was not quite as large as Pickering, nor as heavily built. He had light brown hair, and intelligent eyes.

Ernie Sage was wearing a sweater and a skirt, and she wore her black hair in a pageboy. She was, both her mother and Pick Pickering thought, a truly beautiful young woman, healthy, and wholesome.

"Mother," Ernie Sage said, "you didn't have to get up."

"All I *have* to do is die and pay taxes," Elaine Sage said. "I'm up because I want to be up. Good morning, Ken. Sleep well?"

"Just fine, thank you," McCoy said. His intelligent eyes searched her face for a moment, as if seeking a reason behind the "sleep well?" question.

"I'm starved," Ernie Sage said. "What are we having?"

"The cold air'll do that to you every time," Pickering said dryly.

"We'd better start eating," Elaine Sage said. "I asked Tony to have the car ready at half-past six. The roads may be icy."

Ernestine Sage looked at McCoy.

"If we're really ahead of time at Newark," she said, "you can ride into Manhattan with us and catch the train there."

"What time is your plane?" Elaine Sage asked Pickering.

"Half-past eleven," he said. "I've plenty of time."

"He said he'll catch the bus at the airlines terminal," Ernie Sage said.

"Don't be silly," Elaine Sage said. "You might as well use the Bentley."

"The bus is easier," Pickering said, as he went to the serving cart and started lifting silver covers. "Thanks anyway." He lifted his eyes to Elaine Sage. "Take a look at these scrambled eggs," he said. "Don't they have a funny color?"

Both mother and daughter went to examine the eggs.

"There's nothing wrong with the eggs," Elaine Sage said.

"Well, if you're sure," Pickering said. "There's supposed to be lot of poisoned eggs around."

"Honey," Ernie Sage said. "You just sit, and I'll serve you."

"'Honey'?" her mother parroted. McCoy flushed.

"It's a sticky substance one spreads on bread," Pickering said.

"It's also what I call him," Ernie Sage said. "It's what they call a 'term of endearment.'"

"Gee, Aunt Elaine," Pickering said. "Ain't love grand?"

"Ginger-peachy," Elaine Sage said. "I understand it makes the world go round." She smiled at Ken McCoy. "We get the sausage from a farmer down the road," she said. "I hope you'll try it."

McCoy looked at her; their eyes met.

"Thank you," he said.

Intelligent eyes, she thought. And then she amended that: *Intelligent and wary, like an abused dog's.*

(Two)
Pennsylvania Station
New York City
0925 Hours, 6 January 1942

When the buses from the Navy Yard reached Penn Station, the recruits had been formed into two platoon-sized groups and marched into the station and down to the platform by the corporals. Koznowski and Zimmerman walked to one side. Commuters coming off trains from the suburbs had watched the little procession with interest. Some had smiled. The nation was at war; these were the men who would fight the war.

Two coach cars had been attached to the Congressional Limited, immediately behind the blue-painted electric locomotive and in front of the baggage car and railway post office, so that they were effectively separated from the rest of the train.

On the platform there, Staff Sergeant Koznowski had delivered another little lecture, informing the group that under the Regulations for the Governance of the Naval Service, to which they were now subject, anyone who "got lost" between here and Parris Island could expect to be tried by court-martial not for AWOL (Absence Without Leave) but for "missing a troop movement," which was an even more severe offense.

They were to sit where they were told to sit, Staff Sergeant Koznowski said, and they were not to get out of that seat for any reason without specific permission from one of the corporals. He also said that there had been incidents embarrassing the Marine Corps where recruits had whistled at young civilian women. Any one of them doing that, Staff Sergeant Koznowski said, would answer to him personally.

He had then stood by the door and personally checked the names of the recruits off on a roster as they boarded the cars. When the last was aboard, he turned to Sergeant Zimmerman.

"Let's you and me take a walk," he said. "Fucking train ain't going anywhere soon."

It was more in the nature of an order than a suggestion, so Sergeant Zimmerman nodded his agreement, although he would have much preferred to get on the car and sit down and maybe put his feet up. The malaria had got to him, and while he no longer belonged in the hospital, he was still pretty weak.

What Koznowski wanted to do, it immediately became apparent, was look at the young women passing through the station. Zimmerman had nothing against young women, or against looking at them, but if you were about to get on a train, it seemed futile. And he was tired.

They had been standing just to the right of the gate to the platform on which the Congressional Limited of the Pennsylvania Railroad was boarding passengers for about twenty minutes when Koznowski jabbed Zimmerman, painfully, in the ribs with his elbow.

"Look at that candy-ass, will you?" he said softly, contemptuously, barely moving his lips.

A Marine officer, a second lieutenant, was approaching the gate to the Congressional Limited platform. He was very young, and there was a young woman hanging on to his right arm, a real looker, with her black hair cut in a pageboy.

The customs of the Naval Service proscribed any public display of affection. The second lieutenant was obviously unaware of this proscription, or was ignoring it. The good-looking dame in the pageboy was hanging on to him like he was a life preserver, and the second lieutenant was looking in her eyes, oblivious to anything else.

Zimmerman was uncomfortable. It was his experience that the less you had to do with officers, the better off you were. And what the hell, so he had a girl friend, so what? Good for him.

Staff Sergeant Koznowski waited until the second lieutenant was almost on them, if oblivious to them.

"Watch this," he said softly, his lips not moving. Then he raised his voice. "Ah-ten-hut!" he barked, and then saluted crisply. "Good morning, sir!"

He succeeded in his intention, which was to shake up the candy-ass second lieutenant. First, the second lieutenant was rudely brought back to the world that existed outside the eyes of the good-looking dame in the black pageboy. Then, his right arm moved in Pavlovian reflex to return Staff Sergeant Koznowski's gesture of courtesy between members of the profession of arms, knocking the girl on his arm to one side and causing her to lose her purse.

Staff Sergeant Koznowski coughed twice, very pleased with himself.

But the second lieutenant did not then, as Staff Sergeant Koznowski firmly expected him to do, continue through the gate mustering what little dignity he had left, and possibly even growing red with embarrassment.

"I'll be goddamned," the second lieutenant said, as he looked at Staff Sergeant Koznowski and Sergeant Zimmerman. And then he walked toward them.

"Oh, shit!" Staff Sergeant Koznowski said softly, assuming the position of "attention."

The second lieutenant had his hand extended.

"Hello, Ernie," he said. "How the hell are you?"

Sergeant Zimmerman shook the extended hand, but he was speechless.

The good-looking dame in the black pageboy, having reclaimed her purse, walked up, a hesitant smile on her face.

"Honey," the second lieutenant said, "this is Sergeant Ernie Zimmerman. I told you about him."

There was a moment's look of confusion on her face, and then she remembered.

"Of course," she said, and smiled at Zimmerman, offering her hand. "I'm Ernie, too, Ernie Sage. Ken's told me so much about you."

"Yes, ma'am," Zimmerman said, uncomfortably.

"Stand at ease, Sergeant," the second lieutenant said to Staff Sergeant Koznowski.

The conductor called, "Bo-aard!"

"You're on the train?" the second lieutenant asked.

"Yes, sir," Zimmerman said.

"Save me a seat," the second lieutenant said. "I'm going to be the last man aboard."

The good-looking dame chuckled.

"We had better get aboard, sir," Staff Sergeant Koznowski said.

"Go ahead," the second lieutenant said.

Staff Sergeant Koznowski saluted; the second lieutenant returned it. Then, with Zimmerman on his heels, Koznowski marched through the gate and to the train.

"Where'd you get so chummy with the candy-ass, Zimmerman?" Koznowski asked, contemptuously.

"You ever hear of Killer McCoy, Koznowski?" Zimmerman asked.

"Huh?" Staff Sergeant Koznowski asked, and then, "Who?"

"Forget it," Zimmerman said.

When they were on the train, and the train had rolled out of Pennsylvania Station and through the tunnel and was making its way across the wetlands between Jersey City and Newark, Staff Sergeant Koznowski jabbed Zimmerman in the ribs again.

"Hey," he said. "There was a story going around about some real hardass in the Fourth Marines in Shanghai. That the 'Killer McCoy' you were asking about?"

Zimmerman nodded.

"Story was that he cut up three Italian marines, killed two of them."

"Right."

"And then he shot up a fucking bunch of Chinks," Koznowski said.

Zimmerman nodded again.

"True story?" Koznowski asked, now fascinated.

"True story," Zimmerman said.

"What's that got to do with that candy-ass second lieutenant?" Koznowski asked.

"That's him," Zimmerman said.

"Bullshit," Koznowski said flatly.

"No bullshit," Zimmerman said. "That was Killer McCoy."

"Bullshit," Koznowski said, "How the hell do you know?"

"I was there when he shot the Chinks," Zimmerman said. "I shot a couple of them myself."

Koznowski looked at him for a moment, and finally decided he had been told the truth.

"I'll be goddamned," he said.

(Three)

Tony, the Sages' chauffeur, had parked the Bentley on Thirty-fourth Street, in a NO PARKING zone across from Pennsylvania Station in front of George's Bar & Grill. Ten minutes after Ernestine Sage had gone into the station with Second Lieutenant Kenneth J. McCoy, a policeman walked up to the car, rapped on the window with his knuckles, and gestured with a jerk of his thumb for Tony to get moving.

On the second trip around the block, they saw Ernestine Sage standing on the curb. Tony tapped the horn twice, quickly, and she saw the car and ran to it and got in.

"Just so you won't feel left out," Ernie Sage said to Second Lieutenant Malcolm Pickering, "I will now put you on your airplane."

"Where to, Miss Ernie?" Tony asked, cocking his head to one side in the front seat.

"My apartment, please, Tony," Ernie Sage said, and turned to Pickering. "I'll make you a cup of coffee."

"The Foster Park, Tony," Pickering ordered. "She makes a lousy cup of coffee."

They were stopped in traffic. There was a chance for Tony to turn to look into the backseat. Ernestine Sage nodded her approval.

Tony made the next right turn and pointed the Bentley uptown.

"You're not going to work?" Pickering asked. When she shook her head no, he asked, "What happened to Nose to the Grindstone?"

"When we get there," Ernie Sage said, "I will call in. I will say that I have just put my boyfriend-the-Marine on a train, that I am consequently in a lousy mood, and will be in later this afternoon."

"Patriotism," Pickering said solemnly, "is the last refuge of the scoundrel."

She laughed, and took his arm.

"He's only going to Washington, Ernie," Pickering said.

"He ever tell you about a Marine named Zimmerman?" Ernie asked. "When he was in China?"

Pickering shook his head. "No."

"The one who had a Chinese wife and a bunch of children?"

"Yeah," Pickering said, remembering. "Why?"

"He was in the station, by the gate," Ernie said. "With another Marine. A sergeant. Another sergeant."

"Really?"

"They looked like Marines, Pick," she said. "I mean, they *were* Marines. And they saluted Ken and stood stiff . . . what do they call it?"

"At attention," he furnished. "And?"

"I can't really understand that he's really a Marine officer . . . or you either, for that matter."

"I'm not so sure about me," Pickering said, "but you better get used to the idea that that's what Ken is. Hell, he's already been in the war, and it's hardly a month old."

"He was shot *before* the war, when he was in China, with Zimmerman," she said. "He told me about it. It's not that I didn't believe him, but it wasn't *real* until just now, when I saw Zimmerman. It wasn't at all hard to imagine Zimmerman with a gun in his hands, shooting people."

"The fact of the matter, Ernie, is that your boyfriend is one tough cookie. He may look like he's up for the weekend from Princeton, but he's not. What are you doing, having second thoughts about the great romance? Are you just a little afraid of him?"

"*For* him," she said, and then corrected herself. "No. For me. Oh, God, Pick, I don't want to lose him!"

"For the moment, Ernie, you can relax," Pickering said. "He's only going to Washington."

"Yeah, but where does he go from Washington?" she replied.

The Bentley turned right again onto Fifty-ninth Street, and halfway down the block pulled to the curb before a canvas marquee with THE FOSTER PARK HOTEL lettered on it.

A tall, florid-faced doorman in a heavy overcoat festooned with gold braid scurried quickly across the sidewalk and opened the door.

"Oh, good morning, Mr. Pickering," he said, as Pickering got out. "Nice to see you again, sir."

"Nice to see you, too, Charley," Pickering said, shaking his hand, "but it's 'Lieutenant Pickering.' We second lieutenants are very fussy about that."

"I was glad to hear your folks are all right," the doorman said. "And you're Miss Sage, right?"

"Hello," Ernie Sage said.

Pickering opened the front door of the Bentley.

"No sense you hanging around, Tony," he said. "I'll catch a cab to the airlines terminal."

"I don't mind, Mr. Pick," the chauffeur said.

"You go ahead," Pickering insisted.

The chauffeur leaned across the seat and offered his hand.

"You take care of yourself, young fella," he said. "We want you back in one piece."

"Thank you, Tony," Pickering said. "And keep your eye on Whatsername for me, will you?"

The chauffeur chuckled, and then Pickering closed the door.

When the bellman spun the revolving glass door, passing first Ernie Sage and then Pickering into the lobby of the Foster Park Hotel, an assistant manager was waiting for them.

"Mr. Pickering, I'm Cannell, the assistant manager. How can I be of service?"

"I've got to be at the airlines terminal at half-past ten," Pickering said. "Will you make sure there's a cab outside at quarter-past?"

"Why don't we just run you out to the airport in the limousine, Mr. Pickering?"

"Because the limousine is for paying guests," Pickering said. "A cab will do fine."

Pickering took Ernie Sage's arm and steered her across the lobby of the luxury-class hotel to the coffee shop, and then to a red leather banquette in the rear.

"Just coffee, please," Pickering ordered when a waitress appeared.

His order was ignored. With the coffee came toast and biscuits and slices of melon and an array of preserves.

The Foster Park Hotel was one of forty-one hotels in the Foster chain. Mr. Andrew Foster, the Chairman of the Board of the closely held Foster Hotels Corporation, who made his home in the penthouse atop the Andrew Foster Hotel in San Francisco, had one child, a daughter; and his daughter had one child, a son; and his name was Malcolm Pickering.

"Oh, nice!" Ernie Sage said, pulling a slice of melon before her and picking up a spoon.

"Amazing, isn't it," Pickering said, "what romance does for the appetite?"

"Meaning what?" Sage asked.

"Meaning that your mother went to your room last night to have a little between-us-girls tête-à-tête," Pickering said.

"Oh, my God!" Ernie Sage said, and then challenged: "You're sure? How do you know?"

"She told me," Pickering said. "As we watched you and Ken billing and cooing down by the duck pond."

"Okay," Ernie Sage said. "So she knows. I don't care."

"And if she tells Daddy?" Pickering asked.

Ernie Sage thought that over.

"She won't tell him," she announced. "She knows how he would react."

"You being his precious little girl and such?"

"She knows it would change nothing," Ernie Sage said. She spread strawberry preserve on a slice of toast and handed it to him. "My mother is a very level-headed woman."

"Her tactic for the moment is to praise your boyfriend to the skies," Pickering said. "If that fails, she's considering poison."

"Your goddamned Marine Corps may solve the problem for her," Ernie Sage said.

"For the third time, Ernie, he's only going to Washington."

"Yeah, and for the third time, where's your damned Marine Corps going to send him from Washington?"

"I probably shouldn't tell you this, Ernie," Pickering said. "But I don't think there's much chance that the Corps is going to hand Ken a rifle and send him off to lead a platoon onto some exotic South Pacific beach."

"Tell me more about that," she said sarcastically.

"It's true. He's an intelligence officer," Pickering said. "He speaks and reads Chinese and Japanese. That's why they sent him to Quantico to officer candidate school. And that's why

they're not going to hand him a rifle and tell him to go forth
and do heroic things. There are very few Marines who speak
Chinese or Japanese, much less both, and they are far too
valuable to send off to get shot up."

"That's how come he got wounded in the Philippines,
right?" she challenged.

"He wasn't supposed to be where he was when he was hit,"
Pickering said.

"You know that wound is still . . . what's the word? He's
still bleeding."

"Suppurating," Pickering furnished. "They'll take care of
him, Ernie. Really."

"I got that speech, too," she said. "They give you a thirty-
day convalescent leave, not chargeable against your regular
leave. And then ten days later, they call you up, and say,
'Come back, otherwise we lose the war.'"

"On the other hand, there is an adequate supply of people
like myself," Pickering said, "who are—in the hoary Naval
Service phraseology—available to be *'put in harm's way.'*"

She looked at him for a moment, her face serious.

"You're afraid, aren't you, Pick?" she asked. When he
didn't reply, she went on. "Did I make you mad by asking?"

"Shitless, Ernie," Pickering said. "In the quaint cant of the
Marine Corps, I am scared shitless. Not only do I have a very
active imagination, but I have been associated with your
boyfriend long enough to understand from him that there is
very little similarity between war movies and the real thing."

She reached across the table and took his hand.

"Oh, Pick!" she said sympathetically.

"I have volunteered for flight training," he went on, "not
with any noble motive of sweeping the dirty Jap from the sky,
but because, cold-bloodedly, I have decided it will be a shade
safer than being a platoon leader. And because, presuming no
one will see that I have been wetting my pants in the airplane,
it will keep me out of the war, with any luck, for six months,
maybe longer. Just about all the guys in our class in Quantico
are getting ready to go overseas. Some of them have already
gone."

"Then why the hell did you enlist?" she asked.

"Daddy was a Marine," he said, dryly. "Could I disappoint
Daddy?"

She leaned forward and kissed him on the cheek.

"You're a nice guy, Pick," she said.

"I can't imagine why I told you this," he said.

"I'm glad . . . proud . . . you did," Ernie Sage said.

"Wasted effort," he said. "I should have saved it for some female who would be moved to inspire the coward in the time-honored way."

"You sonofabitch," Ernie Sage said, chuckling. And she freed her hand. But only after she had kissed his knuckles tenderly.

(Four)

When the Congressional Limited stopped at Newark, Second Lieutenant Kenneth J. McCoy, USMCR, got off and walked up to the platform to the two cars immediately behind the locomotive.

The doors to the cars had not been opened, and he had some trouble figuring out how to open them himself before he could get on.

The moment he stepped into the car itself, one of the corporals saw him, jumped to his feet, and bellowed, "Attention on deck!"

"As you were," McCoy said quickly. Fifty-odd curious faces were looking at him.

"Who's in charge?" McCoy asked.

"Staff Sergeant Koznowski, sir," the corporal said. "He's up in front."

It had been Lieutenant McCoy's intention to find the man in charge and "borrow" Ernie Zimmerman, to take him back to the dining car and buy him breakfast, or at least a cup of coffee. His motive was primarily personal; Ernie Zimmerman was an old buddy whom he had last seen in Peking. But there was, he realized, something official about it. He knew where the Corps could put Zimmerman to work, doing something more important than he was now, escorting boots to Parris Island: Zimmerman spoke Chinese.

But before he had made his way down the aisle of the first car, the Congressional Limited began to roll out of the station, and McCoy knew he would be stuck in these coaches until the train stopped again.

Zimmerman saw him passing between the cars, and by the time McCoy had entered the second car, the boots were standing up. Or most of them. There were half a dozen, McCoy saw, who were confused by the order, "Attention on deck!" and were looking around in some confusion.

"As you were!" McCoy said loudly, and smiled when he saw that that command, too, was not yet imbedded in the minds of the boots.

A fleeting thought ran through his mind: He, too, had taken this train on his way to boot camp at Parris Island, but by himself, not with a hundred others to keep him company.

And then the staff sergeant he had seen with Zimmerman walked up to him.

"Staff Sergeant Koznowski, sir," he said.

"I wanted a word with Sergeant Zimmerman, Sergeant," McCoy said. "If that would be all right with you."

"Yes, sir," Koznowski said.

"Zimmerman and I were in the Fourth Marines," McCoy said, as Zimmerman walked up to them.

"Yes, sir," Koznowski said. "Zimmerman told me."

And then Staff Sergeant Koznowski took a good look at Second Lieutenant McCoy and decided that Zimmerman had been bullshitting him. There *was* a Killer McCoy in the Corps, a tough China Marine who had killed two Eye-talian Marines when they had gone after him during the riots and who had left dead slopeheads all over the Peking Highway when they had been foolish enough to try to rob a Marine truck convoy Killer McCoy had been put in charge of.

Stories like that moved quickly through the Corps. Koznowski had heard it several times. And Koznowski now recalled another detail. It had been *Corporal* Killer McCoy. And nobody got to make corporal with the 4th Marines in China on the first hitch. This pleasant-faced, boyish-looking second lieutenant wasn't old enough to have been a corporal in the China Marines, and he sure as hell didn't look tough enough to have taken on three Eye-talian marines by himself with a knife.

"Zimmerman was telling me, sir," Staff Sergeant Koznowski said, with a broad, I'm-now-in-on-the-joke smile, "that you was Killer McCoy."

Second Lieutenant McCoy's face tightened, and his eyes turned icy. "You never used to let your mouth run away with you, Zimmerman," he said, coldly furious.

Zimmerman's face flushed. "Sorry," he said. Then he raised his eyes to McCoy's. "I didn't expect to see you in an officer's uniform."

Very slowly, the ice melted in McCoy's eyes. "I didn't expect to see you on a train in New Jersey," he said. "How'd you get out of the Philippines?"

"Never got there," Zimmerman said. "I come down with malaria and was in sick bay, and they never put me off the ship. It went on to Diego after Manila, and I was in the hospital there for a while. Then they shipped me here."

"You all right now?" McCoy asked.

"Yeah, I'm on limited duty. They're shipping me to the motor transport company at Parris Island."

"The story I heard," Koznowski said, "was that Killer McCoy was a corporal."

The ice returned to McCoy's eyes. He met Koznowski's eyes for a long moment until Koznowski, cowed, came to a position of attention.

Then he turned to Zimmerman and said something to him in Chinese. Zimmerman chuckled and then replied in Chinese. Koznowski sensed they were talking about him.

McCoy looked at Koznowski again. "I was a corporal in the Fourth Marines, Sergeant," he said. "Any other questions?"

"No, sir."

"In that case, why don't you go check on your men?" McCoy said.

"Aye, aye, sir," Staff Sergeant Koznowski said. *Fuck you!* he thought. He walked down the aisle. Then he thought, *I'll be a sonofabitch. He really is Killer McCoy. I'll be goddamned!*

"What about your family, Ernie?" McCoy asked, still speaking Chinese.

"Had to leave them in Shanghai," Zimmerman said. "I gave her money. She said she was going home."

"I'm sorry," McCoy said.

"I wasn't the only one," Zimmerman said. "Christ, even Captain Banning couldn't get his wife out. You heard he married that White Russian?"

McCoy nodded.

Captain Edward J. Banning had been the Intelligence Officer of the 4th Marines in Shanghai. Corporal Kenneth J. McCoy had worked for him. McCoy thought that Banning was everything a good Marine officer should be.

And he had heard from Captain Banning himself that Banning had married his longtime mistress just before the 4th Marines had sailed from Shanghai to reinforce the Philippines, and that she hadn't gotten out before the war started. He had heard that from Banning as they lay on a bluff overlooking the Lingayen Gulf watching the Japanese put landing barges over the sides of transports. But this was not the time to tell Ernie Zimmerman about that.

"How'd you get to be an officer?" Zimmerman asked.

"They got what they call a platoon leader's course at Quantico," McCoy said. "It's like boot camp all over again. You go through it, and you come out the other end a second lieutenant."

"You look like an officer," Zimmerman said. It was more of an observation than a compliment, and there was also a suggestion of surprise.

"With what I had to pay for these uniforms," McCoy said, "I damned well better."

Zimmerman chuckled. "It got you a good-looking woman, at least," he said.

McCoy smiled and nodded. But he did not wish to discuss Miss Ernestine Sage with Sergeant Ernie Zimmerman.

"Ernie," he said. "If you like, I think I can get you a billet as a translator."

"What I want to do is figure out some way to get back to China," Zimmerman said.

"It'll be a long time before there are any Marines in China again," McCoy said.

"I have to try," Zimmerman said. "That what they got you doing, McCoy? Working as a translator?"

"Yeah, something like that."

"I'm a motor transport sergeant, McCoy," Zimmerman said.

"The Corps got a lot of those," McCoy said. "But not many people speak two kinds of Chinese."

Zimmerman paused thoughtfully.

"What the hell," he said finally. "If you can fix it, why not? I'd be working for you?"

"I don't know about that," McCoy said. "But it would be a better billet than fixing carburetors at Parris Island would be."

III

III

(One)
Corregidor Island
Manila Bay, Island of Luzon
Commonwealth of the Philippines
2115 Hours, 5 January 1942

The United States submarine *Pickerel*, a 298-foot, fifteen-hundred-ton submersible of the Porpoise class, lay two hundred yards off the fortress island of Corregidor. There was a whaleboat tied alongside, from which small and heavy wooden crates were being unloaded and then taken aboard through the fore and aft torpedo-loading hatches. A second whaleboat could just be made out alongside a narrow pier on the island itself, where it was being loaded with more of the small, heavy wooden crates.

Lieutenant Commander Edgar F. "Red" MacGregor, USN, commander of the *Pickerel*, was on the sea bridge of her conning tower. MacGregor was a stocky, plump-faced, red-headed thirty-five-year-old graduate of the United States Naval Academy at Annapolis, and he was wearing khaki shirt and trousers, a khaki fore-and-aft cap bearing the shield-and-fouled-anchor insignia of the U.S. Navy, and a small golden oak leaf indicating his rank.

When the last of the crates had been removed from the whaleboat alongside, and it had headed for the pier again, Commander MacGregor bent over a small table on which he had laid out two charts. One of them was a chart of Manila Bay itself, with the minefields marked, and the other was a chart of the South China Sea, which included portions of the islands of Luzon and Mindoro. On the "Luzon" chart was marked with grease pencil the current positions of the Japanese forces that had landed on the beaches of Lingayen Gulf on the morning of December 10, 1941, and were now advancing down the Bataan Peninsula.

To prevent its destruction, Manila had been declared an open city on December 26, 1941. Japanese troops had entered the city, unopposed, on January 2, 1942.

Meanwhile, General Douglas MacArthur had moved his troops, Philippine and American, to Bataan, where it was his announced intention to fight a delaying action until help reached the Philippines from the United States.

As Commander MacGregor observed the loading of his vessel, it was necessary again and again to force from his mind the thoughts that inevitably came to him. As a professional Naval officer, of course, he was obliged to view the situation with dispassionate eyes.

The Japanese had, almost a month before, destroyed the United States' battleship fleet. The only reason the Japs hadn't sent the aircraft carriers to the bottom of Pearl Harbor as well was that the aircraft carriers had been at sea when they had attacked.

The professional conclusion he was forced in honesty to draw was that the U.S. Pacific Fleet had taken a hell of a blow, one that very easily could prove fatal, and that the "help" MacArthur expected—the reinforcement of the Philippine garrison—was wishful thinking. The United States was very close to losing the Philippines, including the "impregnable, unsinkable 'Battleship' Corregidor."

The proof was that if anyone in a senior position of authority really believed that Corregidor could hold out indefinitely until "help" arrived, the *Pickerel* would at this moment be out in the South China Sea trying to put her torpedos into Japanese bottoms.

Instead, she was sitting here, for all intents and purposes an unarmed submersible merchantman, taking aboard as much of the gold reserves of the Philippine Commonwealth as she could carry, to keep them from falling into Japanese hands when Corregidor fell.

Commander MacGregor once again reminded himself that there was good reason for what the U.S. Navy had ordered him to do. And that he was a professional Naval officer. And that when he was given an order, he was obliged to carry it out, not to question it, or to entertain doubts about the ability of senior Naval officers. *They* had to bear the responsibility for getting the Navy into the kind of goddamned mess where a submarine was stripped of its torpedoes and turned into a merchantman because control of the seas was in the hands of the enemy.

He did not take his eyes from the chart of Manila Bay again until the second whaleboat had tied up alongside again. Then he looked down from the conning tower.

"Christ!" he muttered. "Now what?"

"Sir?" his exec asked politely.

Commander MacGregor gestured impatiently downward.

Two ladders, lashed edge to edge, had been put over the side. The wooden crates carrying the gold reserves of the Philippine Commonwealth were heavy, too heavy to be carried aboard by one man. They had been taken from sailors in the whaleboat by two husky sailors, each grasping one rope handle, who had then together climbed the slanting ladders, carefully, grunting with the effort, one rung at a time.

What was coming aboard now was not a crateful of gold bars but a man in khaki uniform. He was being helped up the side-by-side ladders by another man in khaki uniform. He needed the help. His left shirt sleeve was empty. Commander Mac-Gregor could not see whether the man had lost his arm or whether it was in a sling under his shirt. He could see that the man had bandages on his head, bandages covering his eyes.

When the one-armed man with the bandaged head reached the deck, he was helped to his feet. After having received the necessary permission to come aboard, he tried to observe the Naval custom of saluting the officer of the deck and then the national colors.

A Naval officer, Commander MacGregor decided.

The attempt to adhere to Naval tradition failed. The blinded man's salute of the officer of the deck and the colors was directed into the bay.

Commander MacGregor went quickly down from the conning tower to the deck. He could now see that the officer with the blinded man wore the silver eagle of a Navy captain. The blinded officer (MacGregor could not see that his arm was strapped against his chest, under his khaki shirt) was also a captain, but a captain of the United States Marine Corps, the equivalent of a U.S. Navy full lieutenant.

MacGregor saluted the Navy captain.

"Commander MacGregor, sir," he said. "I'm the skipper."

The Navy captain returned the salute. "Captain," he replied, acknowledging Commander MacGregor's role as captain of his vessel, "this is Captain Banning. He will be sailing with you. Captain Banning, this is Captain MacGregor."

The blinded Marine officer put out his hand.

"How do you do, sir?" he said. "Sorry to inflict myself on you."

"Happy to have you aboard, Captain," MacGregor said, aware that it was both inane and a lie. He certainly felt sorry for the poor bastard, but the *Pickerel* was not a hospital ship, it was a crowded submarine, with only a pharmacist's mate aboard. No place for a man who was not only wounded but incapable of feeding himself—or of seeing.

"Captain Banning," the Navy captain said, "*will* sail with you. I now ask you how many other men in his condition you are prepared to take aboard."

"Sir, I have only a pharmacist's mate aboard," MacGregor replied.

The Navy captain said, "There are nine others suffering from temporary or permanent loss of sight. They will require no special medical attention beyond the changing of their bandages."

"I'll have to bed them down on the deck," Commander MacGregor said.

"You can, without jeopardizing your mission, take all of them?" the Navy captain asked.

"Yes, sir."

"They will come out with the next whaleboat," the Navy captain said. "Thank you, Captain. Have a good voyage."

"Thank you, sir," MacGregor said.

"Permission to leave the ship, sir?" the Navy captain asked.

"Granted," MacGregor said.

The Navy captain saluted MacGregor, then the colors, and then backed down the ladder into the whaleboat.

"Chief!" Commander MacGregor called.

"Yes, sir?" the chief of the boat, the senior noncommissioned officer aboard, said. He had been standing only a few feet away, invisible in the darkness.

"Take this officer to the wardroom," MacGregor said. "See that he's comfortable, and then tell Doc to prepare to take aboard nine other wounded. Tell him they are . . . in the same condition as Captain Banning."

"The 'same condition' is blind, Chief," Captain Banning said matter-of-factly. "Once you face it, you get used to it in a hurry."

"Aye, aye, sir," the chief of the boat said to MacGregor, then put his hand on Captain Banning's good arm. "Will you come this way, please, sir?"

MacGregor noticed for the first time that Captain Banning was wearing a web belt, and that a holstered Colt .45 automatic pistol was hanging from the belt.

A blind man doesn't need a pistol, MacGregor thought. *He shouldn't have one. But that guy's a Marine officer, blind or not, and I'm not going to kick him when he's down by taking it away from him.*

The chief torpedoman, who had been supervising the storage of the gold crates in the fore and aft torpedo rooms, came onto the deck.

"All the crates are aboard and secure, sir," he said.

"Let's have a look, Chief," MacGregor said, and walked toward the hatch in the conning tower.

The substitution of gold for torpedos had been on the basis of weight rather than volume. The equivalent weight of gold in the forward torpedo rooms was a small line of wooden boxes chained in place down the center line. The torpedo room looked empty with the torpedoes gone.

"We're taking nine blinded men with us, Chief," Commander MacGregor said. "Ten, counting that Marine captain. I said they would have to bed down on the deck. But we can do better than that, with all this room, can't we?"

"I'll do what I can, Skipper," the chief torpedoman said.

"Let's have a look aft," MacGregor said.

Ten minutes later, the *Pickerel* got underway, her diesels throbbing powerfully.

Launched at the Electric Boat Works in Connecticut in 1936, the *Pickerel* had been designed for Pacific Service; that is, for long patrols. Since she was headed directly for the Hawaiian Islands, fuel consumption was not a problem. With at least freedom from the concern, Commander MacGregor ordered turns made for seventeen knots. Although this greatly increased fuel consumption, he believed it was justified under the circumstances. The farther he moved away from the island of Luzon into the South China Sea, the less were the chances he would be spotted by the Japanese.

There was time, until dawn—too much time—for Commander MacGregor to consider that he was now what he trained all his adult life to be, master of a United States warship at sea, in a war; but that, instead of going in harm's way, searching out the enemy, to close with them, to send them to the bottom, what he was doing was sailing through enemy-controlled waters, doing his very best to make sure the enemy didn't see him.

The one thing he could not do was fight.

He hated to see night begin to turn into day. He had been running at seventeen knots for seven hours. And he had thus made—a rough calculation, not taking into consideration the current—about 120 nautical miles. But as he had been on a north-northwest course, heading into the South China Sea as well as up the western shore of Luzon, he wasn't nearly as far north as he would have liked to be.

He was, in fact, very near the route the Japanese were using to bring supplies and reinforcements to the Lingayen Gulf, where they had made their first amphibious landing in the Phillipines three days after they had taken out almost all of the Pacific Fleet at Pearl Harbor.

There would be Japanese ships in the area, accompanied by destroyers, and there would be at least reconnaissance aircraft, if not bombers. This meant he would have to spend the next sixteen hours or so submerged. Since full speed submerged on batteries was eight knots, he would not get far enough on available battery power to make it worthwhile; for it would not get him out of the Japanese shipping lane to the Lingayen Gulf. But he had to hide.

"Dive," Commander MacGregor ordered.

"Dive! Dive! Dive!" the talker repeated.

The lookouts, then the officer of the deck, then the chief of the boat, dropped quickly through the hatch.

The captain took one last look through his binoculars as water began to break over the bow, and then dropped through the hatch himself.

The roar of the diesels had died; now there was the whine of the electric motors.

MacGregor issued the necessary orders. They were to maintain headway, that was all; as little battery energy as possible was to be expended. They might need the batteries to run if they were spotted by a Japanese destroyer. He was to be called immediately if Sonar heard anything at all, and in any event fifteen minutes before daylight. Then he made his way to his cabin.

Captain Banning was sitting on a Navy-gray metal chair before the fold-down desk. MacGregor was a little surprised that the Marine officer was not in a bunk.

"Good morning," MacGregor said. "You heard? We're submerged."

"And you want to hit the sack," Banning said. "If you'll point me in the direction of where you want me, I'll get out of your way."

"Coffee keeps most people awake," MacGregor said. "Perverse bastard that I am, I always have a cup before I go to bed. You're not keeping me up."

"I'm not sleepy," Banning said. "I've been cat-napping. I did that all the time ashore, but I thought that was because it was quiet. I thought the noises on here would keep me awake, but they haven't."

"I think it would be easier for both of us if you used my bunk," MacGregor said. "Whenever you're ready . . ."

"I could use a cup of coffee," Banning said. "Yours is first rate. And it's in short supply ashore."

"I'll get us a pitcher," MacGregor said. "Cream and sugar?"

"Black, please," Banning said.

When he returned with the stainless steel pitcher of coffee, MacGregor filled Banning's cup three-quarters full.

"There's your coffee, Captain," he said.

"I heard," Banning said. "Thank you."

He moved his hand across the table until his hand touched the mug.

"I issued, earlier on tonight, an interesting order for a Marine officer," Banning said. "'Piss like a woman.'"

"Excuse me?" MacGregor said.

"I went to the head," Banning said. "Ashore, you learn to piss by locating the target with your knees, then direct fire by sound. I learned that won't work with your toilet, and, to keep your head from being awash with blind men's piss, went and passed the word to the others."

He's bitter, MacGregor thought. Then, *Why the hell not?*

"How did it happen?" MacGregor blurted.

"The U.S. Army done it to me," Banning said, bitterly. "The one thing they did right over here was lay in adequate stocks of artillery ammunition."

"I don't quite follow you, Captain Banning," Commander MacGregor said.

Banning very carefully raised his coffee mug to his lips and took a swallow before replying.

"I was at Lingayen Gulf, when the Japs landed," he said. "I got the arm there"—he raised his arm-in-a-sling—"and took some shrapnel in the legs. Naval artillery from their destroyers. The kid with me . . . I shouldn't call him a kid, I suppose, a mustang second lieutenant, and one hell of a Marine . . ." (A mustang is an officer commissioned from the ranks.) "Anyway, he got me to a school, where a Filipino nurse took care of me and hid me from the Japanese until I was mobile. Then she arranged to get me through the Japanese lines. We'd almost made it when the U.S. Army artillery let fly."

"Shrapnel again?" MacGregor asked gently.

"No. Concussion," Banning said. "*'There is no detectable damage to the optic nerves,'*" he went on, obviously quoting a doctor. "*'There is no reason to believe the loss of sight is permanent.'*"

"Well, that's good news," MacGregor said.

"On the other hand," Banning said bitterly, "there's no reason to believe it isn't. Permanent, I mean." His hand was tight around the cup, like a vise.

"When will you find out?" MacGregor asked.

Banning shrugged. "If they really thought it was temporary, I would not have been sent home with you," Banning said. "The official reason seemed a little flimsy."

"What was the official reason?"

"I was the Intelligence Officer for the Fourth Marines,"

Banning said. "They said they were under orders to do whatever they could to keep intelligence officers from falling into Japanese hands."

"That makes sense," MacGregor said.

"Not if most of my knowledge is about China, and the Japanese have already taken Shanghai. And not if your regiment has been just about wiped out, as mine was. I think they wanted us out of the Philippines because we were just too much trouble to care for. The real pain in the ass about being blind is that people are very gentle with you, as if a harsh word, or the truth, will make you break into tears."

He raised his coffee cup and took another careful sip.

"You piss on the deck in my head, Banning," Commander MacGregor said, "and I'll have your ass."

Banning smiled.

"Aye, aye, sir," he said, lightly, and then seriously: "Thank you, Captain."

(Two)
The Foster Peachtree Hotel
Atlanta, Georgia
1630 Hours, 6 January 1942

Flagship Dallas, a twenty-one-passenger Douglas DC-3 of Eastern Airlines' Great Silver Fleet, touched down at Atlanta on time, after a 775-mile, four-hour-and-twenty-five-minute flight from New York's LaGuardia Field.

Second Lieutenant Malcolm Pickering, USMCR, was no stranger to aerial transportation. He could not remember— even after some thought—when he had made his first flight, only that he had been a little boy. He could also recall several odd details about that airplane: The seats had been wicker, like lawn furniture, and the skin of the fuselage had been corrugated like a cardboard box.

There had been God only knew how many flights since then.

His grandfather, Andrew Foster, had leapt happily into the aviation age, for it permitted him to move between his hotels far faster than traveling by rail. He crisscrossed the country in commercial airliners, and there was even a company aircraft, a six-passenger, stagger-wing single-engine Beechcraft, which the Old Man had christened *Room Service*.

Once the Old Man had led the way, Fleming Pickering, Pick's father, had been an easy convert to aerial travel. Pacific

& Far East Shipping, Inc., used ports all up and down the West Coast, from Vancouver, British Columbia, to San Diego. It made a lot more sense to hop aboard a Northwest DC-3 in San Francisco and fly the eight hundred–odd miles to Vancouver at three miles a minute than it did to take the train, which traveled at a third of that speed. Very often his father and grandfather had taken him with them.

And Pick and his parents had been aboard one of the very first Pan American flights from San Francisco to Honolulu, an enormous, four-engined Sikorsky seaplane, the *China Clipper*.

But airplanes had just been there, part of the scenery, like the yellow locomotives of the Southern Pacific Railroad and the white steamships of Pacific & Far East Shipping, Inc. It had never entered his mind that he would personally fly an airplane, any more than he would have thought about climbing into the cab of a locomotive, or marching onto the bridge of the *Pacific Conqueror* and giving orders.

There were people who did that sort of thing, highly respected, well-paid professionals. But he wasn't going to be one of them. He had known from the time he had first thought of things like that that he was going to follow in the Old Man's footsteps into the hotel business, rather than in his father's into the shipping business.

By the time he was in his third year at Harvard, he got around to wondering if he hadn't hurt his father's feelings, perhaps deeply, by avoiding the shipping business. But then it had been too late. He'd gone to work for Foster Hotels at twelve, in a starched white jacket stripping tables for thirty-five cents an hour and whatever the waiter had chosen to pay him (usually a nickel a table for a party of four) out of his tips.

Before he was a junior at Harvard, Pickering had been a salad chef, a fry cook, a bellman, an elevator operator, a bartender, a broiler chef, a storekeeper, a night bookkeeper, a waiter, and an assistant manager. He had spent the summer between his junior and senior years in six different Foster Hotels, filling in for vacationing bell captains.

His motive for that had been pure and simple avarice. A bell captain took home a hell of a lot more money than everybody in a hotel hierarchy but the top executives. It was not corporate benevolence; bell captains earned every nickel they made. And it was a position of prestige within the hierarchy, especially within Foster Hotels Corporation, where the Old Man devoutly believed that bell captains made more of an impression on guests than any other individual on the staff, impressions that would either draw them back again or send them to Hilton or Sheraton.

He had been proud that the Old Man had okayed his working as a bell captain . . . and he had driven to Cambridge that fall in an all-paid-for black 1941 Cadillac convertible.

That had been the last of the easy money. From the day of his graduation until he'd gone off to the Marine Corps, Pick Pickering had been carried on the payroll of the Andrew Foster Hotel, San Francisco, as a supernumerary assistant manager. And he'd been paid accordingly, which came out to a hell of a lot less than he'd made as a bell captain. What he'd really been doing was learning what it was like to run a chain of luxury hotels from the executive suite.

He's spent a lot of time traveling with the Old Man, and a lot of that in airliners or the *Room Service,* but he had paid no more attention to the way those airplanes had worked than he had to what made the wheels go around on a locomotive.

That was now all changed. A Marine brigadier general, a pilot, who had been in the trenches in France as an enlisted man with Corporal Fleming Pickering, USMC, had saved his old buddy's son from a Marine Corps career as a club officer by arranging to have him sent to flight school.

As the passengers were escorted from the terminal at LaGuardia Field to board *Flagship Dallas,* Second Lieutenant Malcolm Pickering, USMCR, stepped out of the line and took a good close look upward at the engine mounted on the wing, then studied the wing itself. For the first time he noticed that the front of the wing was made out of rubber (and he wondered what that was for), and that the thin back part of the wing was movable, and that on the back part of the part that moved there was another part that moved. And that there were little lengths of what looked like clothesline attached to the wing.

A stewardess finally went to him, took his arm, and loaded him aboard, eyeing him suspiciously.

He did not have his usual scotch and soda when they were airborne. The stewardess seemed relieved. He sat in his single aisle seat and watched the movable parts of the wing move, and tried to reason what function they performed.

They flew above the clouds. His previous reaction to a cloud cover, viewed from above, had been *"How pretty! It looks like cotton wool."*

He now wondered for the first time how the pilot knew when it was time to fly back down through the cloud cover; how he knew, specifically, when Atlanta was going to be down there, since obviously he couldn't see it.

Before today, before he was en route to Florida to learn how to fly airplanes himself, he would have superficially reasoned that pilots flew airplanes the way masters of ships navigated across the seas. They used a compass to give them the direction, and clocks (chronometers) to let them know how long they had been moving. If they knew how fast they were going, how much time they were taking, and in what direction, they could compute where they were.

Now he saw the differences, and they were enormous and baffling. The most significant of these was that a ship moved only across the surface of the water, whereas an airplane moved up and down in the air as well as horizontally. And if things were going well, a ship moved at about fifteen miles an hour; but an airplane—the airplane he was now on—moved something like twelve times that fast. And if it was lost, an airplane could not simply stop where it was, drop its anchor, sound its foghorn, and wait for the fog to clear.

When the *Flagship Dallas* touched down at Atlanta, Pick Pickering waited until all the other passengers had made their way down the steeply slanting cabin floor and debarked, and then he went forward to the cockpit.

The door was open, and the pilot and copilot were still in their seats, filling out forms before a baffling array of instruments and controls—what looked like ten times as many instruments and controls as there were on the *Room Service*.

"Excuse me," Pickering said, and the pilot turned around, a look of mild annoyance on his face. The annoyance vanished when he saw that Pickering was in uniform.

"What can I do for you, Lieutenant?"

"You can tell me how you knew Atlanta was going to be down here when you started down through the clouds."

The pilot chuckled and looked at his watch. The watch caught Pickering's attention. It was stainless steel and had all sorts of dials and buttons.

A pilot's watch! Pickering thought.

"We just took a chance," the pilot said. "We knew it had to be down here somewhere."

"So could a mountain have been," Pickering replied.

The pilot saw that he was serious.

"We fly a radio beam," he said, pointing to one of the dials on the control panel. "There's a radio transmitter on the field. The needle on the dial points to it. When you pass it, the needle points in the other direction, and you know you've gone too far."

"Fascinating!" Pickering said. "And the altimeter tells you when you're getting close to the ground, right?"

The pilot suppressed a smile.

"Right," he said. "What the altimeter actually does is tell you how far you are above sea level. We have charts—maps— that give the altitude above sea level of the airports."

"Uh-huh," Pickering grunted his comprehension.

"There is a small problem," the pilot said. "The altimeter tells you how high you were seven seconds ago. Seven seconds is sometimes a long time when you're letting down."

"Uh-huh," Pickering grunted again.

"Let me ask you a question," the pilot said. "This isn't just idle curiosity on your part, is it."

"I'm on my way to Pensacola," Pickering said. "To become a Marine aviator."

"Are you really?" the pilot said. "Watch out for Pensacola, Lieutenant. Dangerous place."

"Why do you say that?"

"They call it the mother-in-law of Naval aviation," the pilot said. "Blink your eyes, and you'll find yourself standing before an altar with some Southern belle on your arm."

"You sound as if you speak from experience," Pickering said.

"I do," the pilot said. "I went to Pensacola in 'thirty-five, a happy bachelor. I left with wings of gold and a mother-in-law."

"I suppose I sound pretty stupid," Pickering said.

"Not at all," the pilot said. "You seem to have already learned the most important lesson."

"Excuse me?"

"If you don't know something, don't be embarrassed to ask questions."

He smiled at Pickering and offered his hand.

"Happy landings, Lieutenant," he said. "And give my regards to the bar in the San Carlos hotel."

Pickering walked down the cabin aisle and got off the plane. The stewardess was standing on the tarmac, again looking at him with concern and suspicion in her eyes.

"I noticed that the Jensen Dynamometer was leaking oil," Pickering said, very seriously, to explain his visit to the cockpit. "I thought the pilot should know before he took off again."

He saw in her eyes that she believed him. With a little bit of luck, he thought, she would ask the pilot about the Jensen Dynamometer, and the pilot would conclude his stewardess had a screw loose.

The airlines limousine, a Checker cab that had been cut in half and extended nine feet, was loaded and about to drive away without him when he got to the terminal.

Thirty minutes later, it deposited him before the Foster Peachtree Hotel in downtown Atlanta. It was one of the smaller Foster hotels, an eight-story brick building shaped like an "E" lying on its side. The Old Man had bought it from the original owners when Pickering was in prep school, retired the general manager, built a new kitchen, installed a new air-conditioning system, and replaced the carpets and mattresses. Aside from that, he'd left it virtually untouched.

"People don't like change, Pick," the Old Man had explained to him seven or eight months ago, when they had been here on one of the Old Man's unannounced visits. "The trick to get repeat customers is to make them think, subconsciously, of the inn as another home. You start throwing things they're used to away, they start feeling like intruders."

A very large, elderly black man, in the starched white jacket of Peachtree bellmen, recognized him as he got out of the Checker limousine.

"Well, nice to see you again, Mr. Pickering," he said. "We been expecting you. You just go on inside, I'll take care of your bags."

The Old Man is right, Pickering thought as he walked up to a door being opened by another white-jacketed black man, *if we dressed the bellmen in red uniforms with brass buttons, people would wonder what else was changed in the hotel, and start looking for things to complain about.*

The resident manager spotted him as he walked down the

aisle of shops toward the lobby, and moved to greet him. He was a plump, middle-aged man, who wore what hair he had left parted in the middle and slicked down against his scalp. Pickering knew him. L. Edward Locke had been resident manager of the Foster Biscayne in Miami when Pick had worked a spring vacation waiting tables around the pool during the day and tending bar in the golf course clubhouse at night.

"Hello, Mr. Pickering," Locke said. "It's good to see you."

"When did I become 'Mr. Pickering'?" Pick said, as he shook his hand.

"Maybe when you became a Marine?" Locke said, smiling.

"I'd rather, in deference to my exalted status as a Marine officer, prefer that you stop calling me 'Hey, you!'" Pick said. "But aside from that, 'Pick' will do fine."

"You look like you were born in that uniform," Locke said. "Very spiffy."

"It's supposed to attract females like moths to a flame," Pick said. "I haven't been an officer long enough to find out for sure."

"I don't think you'll have any worries about that at all," the resident manager said. "Would you like a drink? Either here"—he gestured toward the bar off the lobby—"or in your room? I've put you in the Jefferson Davis Suite." And then Locke misinterpreted the look in Pickering's eyes. "Which we cannot fill, anyway."

"I wasn't planning to stay," Pick said. "Unless my car hasn't shown up?"

"Came in two days ago," Locke said. "I had it taken to the Cadillac dealer. They serviced it and did whatever they thought it needed."

"Thank you," Pick said. "Then all I'll need is that drink and a road map."

They started toward the bar, but Pickering stopped when he glanced casually into a jewelry store. There was a display of watches laid out on velvet. One of them, in gleaming gold, band and all, had just about as many fascinating buttons and dials and sweeping bands as had the watch on the wrist of the Eastern Airlines pilot.

"Just a second," Pick said. "I have just decided that I am such a nice fellow that I am going to buy myself a present."

The price of the watch was staggering, nearly four hundred dollars. But that judgment, he decided, was a reflection of the way he had come by money—earning it himself or doing, by and large, without—until his twenty-first birthday. On his majority, he had come into the first part of the Malcolm Pickering Trust (there would be more when he turned twenty-five, and the balance when he turned thirty) established by Captain Richard Pickering, founder of Pacific & Far East Shipping, Inc., for his only grandson.

The first monthly check from the Crocker National Bank had been for four times as much money as he was getting as a supernumerary assistant manager of the Andrew Foster Hotel. He could afford the watch.

"I'll take it," he said. "If you'll take a check."

"I'll vouch for the check," Locke said quickly, as a cloud of doubt appeared on the face of the jewelry store clerk.

"That's a fascinating watch," Locke said, as Pick strapped it on his wrist. "What are all the dials for?"

"I haven't the foggiest idea," Pick said. "But the Eastern Airlines pilot had one like it. It is apparently what the well-dressed airplane pilot wears."

Locke chuckled, and then led Pickering into the lobby bar. They took stools and ordered scotch.

"I really can't offer you the hospitality of the inn for the night, Pick?"

"I want to get down there and look around," Pick said. "What we Marine officers call 'reconnoitering the area.'"

"Not even an early supper?"

"Ah understand," Pick said, in a thick, mock Southern accent, "that this inn serves South'ren fried chicken that would please Miss Scarlett O'Hara herself."

"That we do," Locke said. "Done to a turn by a native. Of Budapest, Hungary."

Pickering chuckled. He looked over his shoulder and nodded at a table in the corner of the bar.

"You serve food here?"

"Done," Locke said. He reached over the bar and picked up a telephone.

"Helen," he said. "Edward Locke. Would you have the garage bring Mr. Pickering's car around to the front? And then ask my secretary to bring the manila envelope with 'Mr. Pickering' on it to the bar? And give me the kitchen."

The manila envelope was delivered first. It contained a marked road map of the route from Atlanta to Pensacola,

Florida. It had been prepared with care; there were three sections of road outlined in red, to identify them as speed traps.

"There's a rumor that at least some of the speed traps are passing servicemen through, as their contribution to the war effort," Locke said. "But I wouldn't bank on that. And on the subject of speed traps, they want cash. You all right for cash?"

"Fine, thank you," Pickering said. "What about a place to stay once I get there?"

"All taken care of," Locke said. "An inn called the San Carlos Hotel. Your grandfather tried to buy it a couple of years ago, but it's a family business and they wouldn't sell. They're friends of mine. They'll take good care of you."

"Just say I'm a friend of yours?"

"I already called them," Locke said. "They expect you."

"You're very obliging," Pick said. "Thank you."

"Good poolside waiters are hard to find," Locke said, smiling.

IV

(One)
Temporary Building T-2032
The Mall
Washington, D.C.
1230 Hours, 6 January 1942

There was a sign reading ABSOLUTELY NO ADMITTANCE on the door to the stairway of the two-floor frame building.

Second Lieutenant Kenneth J. McCoy pushed it open and stepped through it. Inside, there was a wall of pierced-steel netting, with a door of the same material set into it. On the far side of the wall, a Marine sergeant sat at a desk, in his khaki shirt. His blouse hung from a hanger hooked into the pierced-steel-netting wall.

The sergeant stood up and pushed a clipboard through a narrow opening in the netting. When he stood up, McCoy saw the sergeant was armed with a Colt Model 1911A1 .45 ACP pistol, worn in a leather holster hanging from a web belt. Hanging beside his blouse was a Winchester Model 1897 12-gauge trench gun.

"They've been looking for you, Lieutenant," the sergeant said.

McCoy wrote his name on the form on the clipboard and pushed it back through the opening in the pierced-metal wall.

"Who 'they'?" he asked, smiling.

"The colonel, Captain Sessions," the sergeant said.

"I was on leave," McCoy said, "but I made the mistake of letting them know where they could find me."

The sergeant chuckled and then pressed a hidden button. There was the buzzing of a solenoid. When he heard it, McCoy pushed the door in the metal wall open.

"They said it was important," McCoy said. "Since I am the only second lieutenant around here, what that means is that they need someone to inventory the paper towels and type-writer ribbons."

The sergeant smiled. "Good luck," he said.

McCoy went up the wooden stairs two at a time. Beyond a door at the top of the stairs was another pierced-steel wall. There was another desk behind it, but there was no one at the desk, so McCoy took a key from his pocket and put it to a lock in the door.

He pushed the door open and was having trouble getting his key out of the lock when a tall thin officer saw him. The officer was bent over a desk deeply absorbed with something or other. He was in his shirtsleeves (with the silver leaves of a lieutenant colonel pinned to his collar points), and he was wearing glasses. Even in uniform, and with a snub-nosed .38-caliber Smith & Wesson Chief's Special revolver in a shoulder holster, Lieutenant Colonel F. L. Rickabee, USMC, did not look much like a professional warrior.

He looked up at McCoy with an expression of patient exasperation.

"The way it works, McCoy," Lieutenant Colonel Rickabee said, as if explaining it to a child, "is that if you're unavoidably detained, you call up and tell somebody. I presume you were *unavoidably* detained?"

"Sir," McCoy said, "my orders were to report no later than oh-eight-hundred tomorrow morning."

Rickabee looked at Second Lieutenant McCoy for a moment. "Goddamn it," he said. "You're right."

"The sergeant said you were looking for me, sir," McCoy said.

"Uh-huh," Colonel Rickabee said. "I hope you haven't had lunch."

"No, sir," McCoy said.

"Good," Rickabee said. "The chancre mechanics flip their lids if you've been eating."

"I had breakfast," McCoy said.

"Don't tell them," Rickabee said.

"I had a physical when I came back, sir," McCoy said. "That was just a week ago."

"You're about to have another," Rickabee said.

He bent over the desk again, shuffled the papers he had been looking at into a neat stack, and then put them into a manila envelope stamped with large red letters SECRET. He put the envelope into a file cabinet, then locked the cabinet with a heavy padlock.

"Wait here a moment, McCoy," Lieutenant Colonel Rickabee said. "I'll fetch Captain Sessions."

He went down the corridor and into an office. A moment later, Captain Sessions, USMC, appeared. He was a tall, well-set-up young officer, whose black hair was cut in a crew cut. His brimmed officer's cap was perched on the back of his head, and he was slipping his arms into his blouse and overcoat. He had obviously removed the blouse and overcoat together.

"Hey, Killer," he said, smiling, revealing a healthy set of white teeth. "How was the leave?"

"As long as it lasted, it was fine, thanks," McCoy replied. Captain Sessions was about the only man in the Corps who could call McCoy "Killer" without offending him. Anyone else who did it seldom did it twice. It triggered in McCoy's eyes a coldness that kept it from happening again.

Captain Sessions was different. For one thing, he said it as a joke. For another, he had proved himself on several occasions to be McCoy's friend when that had been difficult. Perhaps most importantly, McCoy believed that if it had not been for Captain Sessions, he would still be a corporal somewhere—in a machine-gun section or a motor transport platoon. McCoy looked on Sessions as a friend. He didn't have many friends.

"Major Almond," Captain Sessions said as they went back down the stairs, referring to the Administrative Officer, "is looking forward to jumping your ass for reporting back in late. If he sees you before I see him, or Colonel Rickabee does, you tell him to see one of us."

"Yes, sir," McCoy said.

"With a little bit of luck, you'll be out of here before you run into him, and he won't learn that I made a fool of myself again. I really thought you were due back at oh-eight-hundred this morning."

"Yes, sir," McCoy repeated. He didn't understand the "you'll be out of here" business, but there was no time to ask. Captain Sessions was already at the foot of the stairs, reaching for the sergeant's clipboard to sign them out.

"The car's outside?" Sessions asked.

"No, sir," the sergeant said. "Major Almond took it, sir. He went over to the Lafayette Hotel, looking for Lieutenant McCoy."

"My car's in the parking lot, sir," McCoy said.

"Why not?" Sessions said, smiling. He turned to the sergeant. "When Major Almond returns, Sergeant, tell him that Lieutenant McCoy was not AWOL after all, and that I have him."

"Yes, sir," the sergeant said, then pushed the hidden switch that operated the door lock.

McCoy's car, a 1939 LaSalle convertible coupe, was covered with snow, and the windows were filmed with ice.

"I hope you can get this thing started," Captain Sessions said as he helped McCoy chip the ice loose with a key.

"It should start," McCoy said. "I just put a new battery in it."

"You didn't take it on leave?" Sessions asked.

"I went to New York City, sir," McCoy said. "You're better off without a car in New York."

"You didn't go home?" Sessions asked. He knew more about Second Lieutenant McCoy than anyone else in the Marine Corps, including the fact that he had a father and a sister in Norristown, Pennsylvania.

"No, sir," McCoy said.

Sessions found that interesting, but didn't pursue it.

The car cranked, but with difficulty.

"I hate Washington winters," McCoy said as he waited for the engine to warm up. "Freeze and thaw, freeze and thaw. Everything winds up frozen."

"You may shortly look back on Washington winters with fond remembrance," Captain Sessions said.

"Am I going somewhere, sir?"

"Right now you're going to the Bethesda Naval Hospital," Sessions said. "You know where that is?"

"Yes, sir."

The outpatient clinic at the hospital was crowded, but as soon as Sessions gave his name, the Navy yeoman at the desk summoned a chief corpsman, who took them to an X-ray room, supervised chest and torso and leg X rays, and then led them to an examining room where he ordered McCoy to remove his clothing. He weighed him, took his blood pressure, drew blood into three different vials; and then, startling McCoy, pulled off the bandage that covered his lower back with one quick and violent jerking motion.

"Jesus," McCoy said. "Next time, tell me, Chief!"

"You lost less hair the way I done it," the chief said, unrepentant, and then examined the wound.

"That's healing nicely," he said. "But there's still a little suppuration. Shrapnel?"

McCoy nodded.

"That's the first wound like that I seen since World War I," the chief said.

A younger man in a white medical smock came in the room. The silver railroad tracks of a Navy full lieutenant were on his collar points.

"I'm sure there's a good reason for doing this examination this way," he said to Sessions.

"Yes, Lieutenant, there is," Sessions replied.

The Naval surgeon examined McCoy's medical records, and while he was listening to his chest, the chief corpsman fetched the X rays. The surgeon examined them, and then pushed and prodded the line of stitches on McCoy's lower back.

"Any pain? Any loss of movement?"

"I'm a little stiff sometimes, sir," McCoy said.

"You're lucky you're alive, Lieutenant," the surgeon said, matter-of-factly. Then he grunted and prodded McCoy's upper right thigh with his finger. "Where'd you get that? That's a small-arm puncture, isn't it?"

"Yes, sir."

"Not suffered at the same time as the damage to your back? It looks older."

"No, sir," McCoy said.

"Not very talkative, is he, Captain?" the surgeon said to Sessions. "I asked him where he got it."

"In Shanghai, sir," McCoy said.

"That's a Japanese twenty-five caliber wound?" the surgeon asked doubtfully.

"No, sir," McCoy said. "One of those little tiny Spanish automatics . . . either a twenty-five or maybe a twenty-two rimfire."

"A twenty-five?" the surgeon asked curiously, and then saw the look of impatience in Session's eyes. He backed down before it.

"That seems to have healed nicely," he said, cheerfully. "You don't have a history of malaria, do you, Lieutenant?"

"No, sir."

"Nor, according to this, of social disease," the surgon said. "Have you been exposed to that, lately?"

"No, sir."

"Well, presuming they don't find anything when they do his blood, Captain, he should be fit for full duty in say, thirty days. I think he should build up to any really strenuous exercise, however. There's some muscle damage, and—"

"I understand," Sessions said. "Thank you, Doctor, for squeezing him in this way."

"My pleasure," the surgeon said. "You can get dressed, Lieutenant. It'll be a couple of minutes before the form can be typed up. I presume you want to take it with you?"

"If we can," Sessions said.

When they were alone in the treatment room, McCoy put his blouse back on and fastened his Sam Browne belt in place. Then he looked at Sessions.

"Are you going to tell me what's going on?" he asked.

"Well, from here we go to my place," Captain Sessions said. "Where my bride at this very moment is preparing a sumptuous feast to honor the returned warrior, and where there is a bottle of very good scotch she has been saving for a suitable occasion."

"In other words, you're not going to tell me?"

"Not here, Ken," Sessions said. "At my place."

McCoy nodded.

"Colonel and Mrs. Rickabee will be there," Sessions said.

McCoy's eyebrows rose at that, but he didn't say anything.

(Two)
Chevy Chase, Maryland

"The second house from the end, Ken," Captain Sessions said. "Pull into the driveway."

McCoy was surprised at the size of the house, and at the quality of the neighborhood. The houses were large, and the lots were spacious; it was not where he would have expected a Marine captain to live.

"Well, thank God that's home," Sessions said when McCoy had turned into the driveway. "Jeannie's getting a little large to have to drive me to work."

McCoy had no idea what he was talking about, but the mystery was quickly cleared up when Jean Sessions, a dark-haired, pleasant-looking young woman, came out of the kitchen door and walked over to the car. She was pregnant.

She kissed her husband, and then pointed at a 1942 Mercury convertible coupe.

"Guess what the Good Fairy finally fixed," she said. "He brought it back five minutes ago."

"I saw," Sessions said, dryly. " 'All things come to him who waits,' I suppose."

Jean Sessions went around to the driver's side as McCoy got out. She put her hands on McCoy's arms, and kissed his cheek, and then looked intently at him.

"How are you, Ken?" she asked.

It was more than a ritual remark, McCoy sensed. She was really interested.

"I'm fine, thanks," Ken said.

"You look fine," she said. "I'm so glad to see you."

She took his arm and led him to the kitchen. There was the smell of roasting beef, and a large, fat black woman in a maid's uniform was bent over a wide table wrapping small pieces of bacon around oysters.

"This is Jewel, Ken," Jean said, "whose hors d'oeuvres are legendary. And this is Lieutenant McCoy."

"You must be somebody special, Lieutenant," Jewel said, with a smile. "I heard all about you."

McCoy smiled, slightly uncomfortably, back at her.

"Colonel Rickabee called and said you were to call him when you got here," Jean Sessions said to her husband. "So you do that, and I'll fix Ken a drink."

She led him into the house to a tile-floored room, whose wall of French doors opened on a white expanse that after a moment he recognized to be a golf course.

"This is a nice house," Ken said.

"I think it is," Jean said. "It was our wedding present." She handed him a glass dark with scotch.

"How was the leave?" she asked.

"As long as it lasted, it was fine," he said.

"I heard about that," Jean said. "You were cheated out of most of it, weren't you?"

"I made the mistake of telling them where they could find me," he said.

"How'd the physical go?" she asked. "You going to be all right?"

"It's fine," he said. "The only time it hurts is when they change the bandage. Most of the time it itches."

"Curiosity overwhelms me," Jean said. "Ed says you've got a girl. Tell me all about her."

The answer didn't come easily to McCoy's lips.

"She's nice," he said finally. "She writes advertising."

He thought: *Ernie would like Mrs. Sessions, and probably vice versa.*

Jean Sessions cocked her head and waited for amplification.

"For toothpaste and stuff like that," McCoy went on. "I met her through a guy I went through Quantico with."

"What does she look like?" Jean asked.

McCoy produced a picture. The picture surprised Jean Sessions. Not that McCoy had found a pretty girl like the one hanging on to his arm in the picture, but that he'd found one who wore an expensive full-length Persian lamb coat, and who had posed with McCoy in front of the Foster Park Hotel on Central Park South.

"She's very pretty, Ken," Jean said.

"Yeah," McCoy said. "She is."

"The colonel will be here in half an hour," Captain Ed Sessions announced from the doorway.

"So soon?" Jean asked.

"He wants to talk to Ken before his wife gets here," Sessions said. "And he asked if we could set a place for Colonel Wesley."

McCoy saw that surprised Jean Sessions.

"Certainly," she said. "It's a big roast."

"I told him we could," Sessions said.

"Ken was just showing me a picture of his girl," Jean said, changing the subject. "Show her to Ed, Ken."

Sessions said that he thought Ernestine Sage was a lovely young woman.

Lieutenant Colonel Rickabee arrived almost exactly thirty minutes later. He was followed into the room by Jewel, who carried a silver tray of bacon-wrapped oysters. Jean Sessions left after making him a drink. She explained that she had to check the roast, and she closed the door after her.

"I was sorry to have to cheat you out of the rest of your recuperative leave, McCoy," Rickabee said. "I wouldn't have done it if it wasn't necessary."

"I understand, sir," McCoy said.

"The decision had just about been made to send you over to COI, after you'd had your leave," Rickabee said.

"Sir?"

"You've never heard of it?" Rickabee asked, but it was a statement rather than a question. "You ever hear of Colonel Wild Bill Donovan?"

"No, sir."

"He won the Medal of Honor in the First World War," Rickabee explained. "He was in the Army. More important, he's a friend of the President. COI stands for 'Coordinator of Information.' It's sort of a clearinghouse for intelligence information. A filter, in other words. They get everything the Office of Naval Intelligence comes up with, and the Army's G-2 comes up with, and the State Department, us, everybody . . . and they put it all together before giving it to the President. Get the idea?"

"Yes, sir," McCoy said.

"Donovan has authority to have service personnel assigned to him," Rickabee said, "and General Forrest got a call from the Commandant himself, who told him that when he got a levy against us to furnish officers to the COI, he was not to regard it as an opportunity to get rid of the deadwood. The Commandant feels that what Donovan is doing is worthwhile, and that it is in the best interest of the Corps to send him good people. Despite your somewhat childish behavior in the Philippines, you fell into that category."

McCoy did not reply. And Rickabee waited a long moment,

staring at him hard in order to make him uncomfortable—without noticeable effect.

"Let me get *that* out of the way," Rickabee said finally, with steel in his voice. "You were sent there as a courier. Couriers do *not* grab BARs and go AWOL to the infantry. In a way, you were lucky you got hit. It's difficult to rack the ass of a wounded hero, McCoy, even when you know he's done something really dumb."

"Yes, sir," McCoy said, after a moment.

"Okay, that's the last word on that subject. You get the Purple Heart for getting hit. But no Silver Star, despite the recommendation."

He reached into his briefcase and handed McCoy an oblong box. McCoy opened it and saw inside the Purple Medal.

"Thank you, sir," McCoy said. He closed the box and looked at Rickabee.

Rickabee was unfolding a sheet of paper. Then he started reading from it: ". . . ignoring his wounds, and with complete disregard for his own personal safety, carried a grievously wounded officer to safety through an intensive enemy artillery barrage, and subsequently, gathered together eighteen Marines separated from their units by enemy action, and led them safely through enemy-occupied territory to American lines. His courage, devotion to duty, and . . . et cetera, et cetera . . .'"

He folded the piece of paper and then dipped into his briefcase again, and came up with another oblong box.

"*Bronze* Star," Rickabee said, handing it to him. "If the Corps had *told* you to go play Errol Flynn, you would have got the Silver. And if you hadn't forgotten to duck, you probably wouldn't have got the Bronze. But, to reiterate, it's hard to rack the ass of a wounded hero, even when he deserves it."

McCoy opened the Bronze Star box, glanced inside, and then closed it.

"For the time being, McCoy, you are not to wear either of those medals," Rickabee said.

"Sir?"

"Something has come up which may keep you from going to COI," Rickabee said. "Which is why I was forced to cancel your recuperative leave."

McCoy looked at him curiously, but said nothing.

"You're up, Ed." Rickabee said to Captain Sessions.

"When you were in China, McCoy," Sessions began, "did you ever run into Major Evans Carlson?"

"No, sir," McCoy said. "But I've seen his name." And then memory returned. "And I read his books."

"You have?" Rickabee asked, surprised.

"Yes, sir," McCoy said. "Captain Banning had them. And a lot of other stuff that Carlson wrote. Letters, too."

"And Captain Banning suggested you read the books?" Sessions asked.

"Yes, sir, and the other stuff."

"What did you think?" Rickabee asked, innocently.

McCoy considered the question, and then decided to avoid it. "About what, sir?"

"Well, for example, what Major Carlson had to say about the Communist Chinese Army?" Rickabee asked.

McCoy didn't immediately reply. He was, Sessions sensed, trying to fathom why he was being asked.

"Just off the top of your head, Ken," Sessions said.

McCoy looked at him, and shrugged. "Out of school," McCoy said. "I think he went Chink."

"Excuse me?" Rickabee said.

"It happens," McCoy explained. "People spend a lot of time over there, China gets to them. That 'thousands of years of culture' crap. They start to think that we don't know what we're doing, and that the Chinks have everything figured out. Have had it figured out for a thousand years."

"How does that apply to what Carlson thinks of the Chinese Communists?" Rickabee asked.

"That's a big question," McCoy said.

"Have a shot at it," Rickabee ordered.

"There's two kinds of Chinese," McCoy said. "Ninety-eight percent of them don't give a damn for anything but staying alive and getting their rice bowl filled for that day. And the other two percent try to push the ninety-eight percent around for what they can get out of it."

"Isn't that pretty cynical?" Rickabee asked. "You don't think that, say, Sun Yat-sen or Chiang Kai-shek—or Mao Tse-tung—have the best interests of the Chinese at heart?"

"I didn't mean that all they're interested in is beating them out of their rice bowls," McCoy said. "I think most of them want the power. They like the power."

That's simplistic, of course, Sessions thought. *But at the same time, it's a rather astute observation for a twenty-one-year-old with only a high school education.*

"Then you don't see much difference between the Nationalists and the Communists?" Rickabee asked.

"Not much. Hell, Chiang Kai-shek was a Communist. He even went to military school in Russia."

I wonder how many of his brother officers in the Marine Corps know that? Rickabee thought. *How many of the colonels, much less the second lieutenants?*

"What about the Communist notion that there should be no privileges for officers?" Rickabee went on.

"They got that from the Russians," McCoy said. "Everybody over there is 'comrade.' Chiang Kai-shek's copying the Germans. The Germans were in China a long time, and the Germans think the way to run an army is to really separate the officers from the enlisted men, make the officers look really special, so nobody even thinks of disobeying an officer."

"And the Communists? From what I've heard, they almost elect their officers."

"I heard that, too," McCoy said. "We tried that, too, in the Civil War. It didn't work. You can't run an army if you're all the time trying to win a popularity contest."

Sessions chuckled. "And you don't think it works for the Chinese Communists, either?"

"You want to know what I think the only difference between the Chinese Nationalists and the Communists is?" McCoy asked. "I mean, in how they maintain discipline?"

"I really would," Sessions said.

"It's not what Carlson says," McCoy said. "Carlson thinks the Communists are . . . hell, like they got religion. That they think they're doing something noble."

"What is it, then?" Rickabee asked.

"Somebody gets an order in the Nationalists and fails to carry it out, they form a firing squad, line up the regiment to watch, and execute him by the numbers. Some Communist doesn't do what the head comrade tells him to do, they take him behind a tree and shoot him in the ear. Same result. Do what you're told, or get shot."

"And the Japanese?"

"*That's* another ball game," McCoy said. "The Japs *really believe* their emperor is God. They do what they're told because otherwise they don't get to go to heaven. Anyway, the

Japs are different than the Chinese. Most of them can read, for one thing.''

"Very interesting," Rickabee said. "You really are an interesting fellow, McCoy."

"You going to tell me why all the questions?" McCoy asked, after a moment.

Rickabee dipped into his briefcase again and came up with a manila envelope stiff with eight-by-ten inch photographs of the Roosevelt letter. He handed it to McCoy.

"Read that, McCoy," Rickabee said.

McCoy read the entire document, and then looked at Rickabee and Sessions.

"Jesus!" he said.

"If the question in your mind, McCoy," Rickabee said, "is whether the Marine Corps intends to implement that rather extraordinary proposal, the answer is yes."

McCoy's surprise and confusion registered, for just a moment, on his face.

"Unless, of course, the Commandant is able to go to the President with proof that the source of those extraordinary suggestions is unbalanced, or a Communist," Rickabee added, dryly. "The source, of course, being Evans Carlson and not the President's son. I don't know about that—about the unbalanced thing or the Communist thing—but I think there's probably more to it than simply an overenthusiastic appreciation of the way the Chinese do things."

"I'm almost afraid to ask, but why are you showing me all this stuff?" McCoy asked.

"It has been proposed to the Commandant that the one way to find out what Colonel Carlson is really up to is to arrange to have someone assigned to his Raider Battalion who would then be able to make frequent, and if I have to say so, absolutely secret reports, to confirm or refute the allegations that he is unbalanced, or a Communist, or both."

"Named McCoy," McCoy said.

"The lesser of two evils, McCoy," Rickabee said. "Either intelligence—which I hope means you—does it, or somebody else will. There's a number of people close to the Commandant who have already made up their minds about Carlson, and whoever they arranged to have sent would go out there looking for proof that he is what they are convinced he is."

"So I guess I go," McCoy said.

"There are those in the Marine Corps, McCoy," Rickabee

said dryly, "who do not share your high opinion of Second Lieutenant McCoy; who in fact think this is entirely too much responsibility for a lowly lieutenant. What happens next is that a colonel named Wesley is coming to dinner. He will examine you with none of what I've been talking about entering into the conversation. He will then go home, call a general officer, and tell him that it would be absurd to entrust you with a job like this. Meanwhile, General Forrest, who is one of your admirers, will be telling the same general officer that you are clearly the man for the job. What I think will happen is that the general will want to have a look at you himself and make up his mind then."

"Sir, is there any way I can get out of this?"

"You may not hear drums and bugles in the background, McCoy," Rickabee said, "but if you will give this a little thought, I think you'll see that it's of great importance to the Corps. I don't want to rub salt in your wound, but it's a lot more important than what you were doing in the Philippines."

(Three)
Temporary Building T-2032
The Mall
Washington, D.C.
1230 Hours, 7 January 1942

McCoy's encounter with Colonel Wesley was not what he really expected. The meeting was clearly not Wesley's idea; he had simply been ordered to have a look at the kid. Thus at dinner Wesley practically ignored him; what few questions he asked were brief and obviously intended to confirm what he had decided about McCoy before he met him.

Despite what Rickabee had said about the importance to the Corps of checking on Carlson, McCoy didn't want the job. Even the COI seemed like a better assignment. With a little bit of luck, McCoy decided, Colonel Wesley would be able to convince the unnamed general officer that McCoy was not the man for it.

He was a mustang second lieutenant. The brass would not entrust to a mustang second lieutenant a task they considered very important to the Corps.

But just before he went to sleep in a bedroom overlooking the snow-covered golf course, he had another, more practical, thought. He could get away with spying on this gone-Chink lieutenant colonel for the same reasons Colonel Wesley didn't think he could carry it off: because he *was* a mustang second lieutenant. Wesley would send some Palace Guard type out there, some Annapolis first lieutenant or captain. If Colonel Carlson was up to something he shouldn't be, he sure wouldn't do it with an Annapolis type around. Carlson would not be suspicious of a mustang second lieutenant; but if he hadn't really gone off the deep end, he would wonder why an Annapolis-type captain was so willing to go along with his Chinese bullshit.

In the morning, Captain Sessions told him to stick around the house until he was summoned, and then Sessions drove to work.

He tried to keep out of the way, but Mrs. Sessions found him reading old *National Geographic* magazines in the living room, and she wanted to talk. The conversation turned to Ernie Sage and ended with him calling her on the phone, so Mrs. Sessions could talk to her.

They had no sooner hung up than the phone rang again. It was Captain Sessions. He told McCoy to meet him outside Building T-2032 at half-past twelve.

When he got there, five minutes early, Captain Sessions was waiting for him. He was wearing civilian clothing.

"Would it be all right if we used your car again, Killer?" Sessions asked.

"Yes, sir, of course." McCoy said.

When they were in the car, McCoy looked at Sessions for directions.

"Take the Fourteenth Street Bridge," Sessions ordered.

Twenty-five minutes later, they turned off a slippery macadam road and drove through a stand of pine trees, and then between snow-covered fields to a fieldstone farmhouse on top of a hill. As they approached the house, McCoy saw that it was larger than it appeared from a distance. And when, at Sessions's orders, he drove around to the rear, he saw four cars: a Buick, a Ford, and two 1941 Plymouth sedans, all painted in Marine green.

"It figures, I suppose," Sessions said dryly, "that the junior member of this little gathering has the fanciest set of wheels."

McCoy wasn't sure whether Sessions was just cracking

wise, or whether there was an implied reprimand; second lieutenants should not drive luxury convertibles. He had bought the LaSalle in Philadelphia when he had been ordered home from the 4th Marines in Shanghai. He had made a bunch of money in China, most of it playing poker, and he had paid cash money for the car. He'd bought it immediately on his return, as a corporal, before he had had any idea the Corps wanted to make him an officer.

He parked the LaSalle beside the staff cars, and they walked to the rear door of the farmhouse. A first lieutenant, wearing the insignia of an aide-de-camp, opened the door as they reached it.

"Good afternoon, sir," he said to Sessions, giving McCoy a curious look. "The general is in the living room. Through the door, straight ahead, last door on the left."

"Thank you," Sessions said, and added, "I've been here before."

In the corridor leading from the kitchen, they came across a row of Marine overcoats and caps hanging from wooden pegs. They added theirs to the row.

Then Sessions signaled for McCoy to knock on a closed sliding door.

"Yes?" a voice from inside called.

"Captain Sessions, sir," Sessions called softly.

"Come in, Ed," the voice called. McCoy slid the door open. Then Sessions walked into the room and McCoy followed him. There was five officers there: a major general and a brigadier general, neither of whom McCoy recognized; Colonel Wesley; Lieutenant Colonel Rickabee, in civilian clothing; and a captain wearing aide-de-camp's insignia. There was also an enlisted Marine wearing a starched white waiter's jacket.

The brigadier general shook Session's hand, and then offered his hand to McCoy.

"Hello, McCoy," he said. "Good to see you again."

McCoy was surprised. So far as he could remember, he had never seen the brigadier general before. And then he remembered that he had. *Once* before, in Philadelphia, after he had just returned from China, they had had him at the Philadelphia Navy Yard, draining his brain of everything he could recall about China and the Japanese Army. Two men in civilian clothing had come into the third-floor room where he was "interviewed." One of them, he realized, had been this brigadier general. And with that knowledge, he could put a name to him: He was Brigadier General Horace W. T. Forrest, Assistant Chief of Staff for Intelligence, USMC.

"Thank you, sir," McCoy said. *What did Rickabee mean when he said Forrest was "one of my admirers"?*

"I don't believe you know General Lesterby?" General Forrest said, gesturing to the major general.

"No, sir," McCoy said. He looked at General Lesterby and saw that the general was examining him closely, as if surprised at what he was seeing.

Then General Lesterby offered his hand.

"How are you, Lieutenant?" he said.

"How do you do, sir?" McCoy said.

"And you've met Colonel Wesley," General Forrest said.

"Yes, sir," McCoy said.

Wesley nodded, and there was a suggestion of a smile, but he did not offer his hand.

"Tommy," General Lesterby said, "make one more round for all of us. And two of whatever they're having for Captain Sessions and Lieutenant McCoy. And that will be all for now."

"Aye, aye, sir," the orderly said.

"And I think you should go keep General Forrest's aide company, Bill," General Lesterby said.

"Aye, aye, sir," General Lesterby's aide-de-camp said quickly. McCoy saw that he was surprised, and even annoyed, at being banished. But he quickly recovered.

"Captain Sessions, what's your pleasure, sir?"

"Bourbon, please," Sessions said. "Neat."

"Lieutenant?" the aide asked.

"Scotch, please," McCoy said. "Soda, please."

Not another word was spoken until the drinks had been made and the aide-de-camp and the orderly had left the room.

General Lesterby picked up his glass.

"I think a toast to the Corps would be in order under the circumstances, gentlemen," he said, and raised his glass. "The Corps," he said.

The others followed suit.

"And under the circumstances," Lesterby said, "to our oath of office, especially the phrase 'against all enemies, foreign and domestic.'" He raised his glass again, and the others followed suit.

Then he looked at McCoy.

"Obviously, you're a little curious, McCoy, right? Why I sent my aide-de-camp from the room?"

"Yes, sir," McCoy admitted.

"Because if he is ever asked," General Lesterby said, "as he very well may be asked, what happened in this room today, I want him to be able to answer, in all truthfulness, that he was sent from the room, and just doesn't know."

McCoy didn't reply.

"The rest of us, McCoy," General Lesterby said, "if we are asked what was said, what transpired, in this room this afternoon, are going to lie."

"Sir?" McCoy blurted, not sure he had heard correctly.

"I said, we're going to lie," General Lesterby said. "If we can get away with it, we're going to deny this meeting ever took place. If we are faced with someone's knowing the meeting was held, we are going to announce we don't remember who was here, and none of us is going to remember what was said by anyone."

McCoy didn't know what to say.

"And we are now asking you, McCoy, without giving you any reasons to do so, to similarly violate the code of truthfulness incumbent upon anyone privileged to wear the uniform of a Marine officer," General Lesterby said, looking right into his eyes.

When McCoy didn't reply, Lesterby went on: "As perverse as it sounds—as it *is*—I am asking for your word as a Marine officer to lie. If you are unable to do that, that will be the end of this meeting. You will return to your duties under General Forrest and Colonel Rickabee, neither of whom, obviously, is going to hold it against you for living up to a code of behavior you have sworn to uphold."

McCoy didn't reply.

"Well, Sessions," General Forrest said, "you're right about that, anyway. You can't tell what he's thinking by looking at him."

"Yes, sir," McCoy said.

"'Yes, sir,' meaning what?" General Lesterby asked.

"You have my word, sir, that . . . I'll lie, sir."

"And now I want to know, Lieutenant McCoy—and I want

you to tell me the first thing that comes to your mind—why you are willing to do so."

"Colonel Rickabee and Captain Sessions, sir," McCoy said. "They're in on this. I'll go with them."

General Lesterby looked at McCoy for a moment.

"Okay," he said. "You're in. I really hope you don't later have cause—that none of us later has cause—to regret that decision."

McCoy glanced at Captain Session. He saw that Sessions had just nodded approvingly at him.

"I presume Colonel Rickabee has filled you in at some length, McCoy, about what this is all about?"

"Yes, sir," McCoy said.

"Just so there's no question in anyone's mind, we are all talking about a brother Marine officer, Lieutenant Colonel Evans F. Carlson, who is about to be given command of a Marine Raider battalion. We are all aware that Colonel Carlson was awarded the Navy Cross for valor in Nicaragua, and that he was formerly executive officer of the Marine detachment assigned to protect the President of the United States at Warm Springs, Georgia. We are all aware, further, that he is a close friend of the President's son, Captain James Roosevelt. Because we believe that Colonel Carlson's activities in the future may cause grievous harm to the Corps, we see it as our distasteful duty to send someone—specifically, Lieutenant McCoy here—to spy on him. This action is of questionable legality, and it is without question morally reprehensible. Nevertheless, we are proceeding because we are agreed, all of us, that the situation makes it necessary." He looked around the room and then at General Forrest. "General Forrest?"

"Sir?" Forrest replied, confused.

"Is that your understanding of what is taking place?"

Forrest came to attention. "Yes, sir."

"Colonel Wesley?"

"Yes, sir," Wesley mumbled, barely audibly.

"A little louder, Wesley, if you please," General Lesterby said. "If you are not in agreement with us, now's the time to say so."

"Yes, sir!" Colonel Wesley said, loudly.

"Rickabee?"

"Yes, sir."

"Captain Sessions?"

"Yes, sir."

General Lesterly looked at McCoy. "I understand, son," he said, "that you're very unhappy with this assignment. That speaks well for you."

Then he walked out of the room.

V

(One)
Pensacola, Florida
0500 Hours, 7 January 1942

Pick Pickering pulled the Cadillac convertible up before the San Carlos Hotel in Pensacola at a quarter to five in the morning. The car was filthy, covered with road grime, and Pickering himself was tired, unshaven, dirty, and starved.

From Atlanta, it had been a two-hour drive down U.S. 85 to Columbus, Georgia. Pickering saw a sign reading COLUMBUS, HOME OF THE INFANTRY, which explained why the streets of Columbus were crowded with soldiers; he was close to the Army Infantry Center at Fort Benning.

He crossed a bridge and found himself in Alabama. There he found a small town apparently dedicated to satisfying the lusts of Benning's military population. Its businesses seemed limited to saloons, dance halls, hock shops, and tourist cabins.

The next 250 miles were down a narrow, bumpy macadam road through a series of small Alabama towns and then across the border to Florida. Twenty miles inside Florida he came to U.S. 90 and turned right to Pensacola, a 125-mile, two-and-a-half-hour drive.

He had grown hungry about the time he'd passed through Columbus, Georgia, and had told himself he would stop and get something to eat, if only a hamburger, at the first place that looked even half decent. But he had found nothing open, decent or otherwise, between Columbus and Pensacola. He dined on Cokes and packages of peanut butter crackers bought at widely spaced gas stations where he took on gas.

He was grateful to find the open gas stations, and he filled up every time he came upon one. This was not the place to run out of gas.

When he opened the door of the Cadillac at the hotel, he was surprised at how cold it was. This was supposed to be sunny Florida, but it was foggy and chilly, and the palm trees on the street in front of the San Carlos Hotel looked forlorn.

The desk clerk was a surly young man in a soiled jacket and shirt who said he didn't know nothing about no reservation. When pressed, the desk clerk did discover a note saying the manager was to be notified when a Mr. Pickering showed up.

"I'm here," Pick said. "You want to notify him?"

"Don't come in until eight-thirty, Mr. Davis don't," the desk clerk informed him. "Don't none of the *assistant* managers come in till seven."

"Is there a restaurant?" Pick asked.

"Coffee shop," the desk clerk said, indicating the direction with a nod of his head.

"Thank you for all your courtesy," Pick said.

"My pleasure," the desk clerk said.

Pickering crossed the lobby and pushed open the door to the coffee shop.

It was crowded, which surprised him, for five o'clock in the morning, until he realized that nearly all the male customers were in uniform—officer's uniforms, Marine and Navy. They are beginning their day, Pick thought, as I am ending mine.

He found a table in a corner and sat down.

A couple of the officers glanced at him—with, he sensed, disapproval.

He needed a shave, he realized. But that was impossible without a room with a wash basin.

He studied the menu until a waitress appeared, and then ordered orange juice, milk, coffee, biscuits, ham, three eggs, and home fries; and a newspaper, if she had one.

The newspaper was delivered by a Marine captain in a crisp uniform.

"Keep your seat, Lieutenant," he said, as Pickering—in a Quantico Pavlovian reaction—started to stand up, "that way as few people as possible will notice a Marine officer in a mussed uniform needing a shave."

"I've been driving all night, Captain," Pick said.

"Then you should have cleaned up, Lieutenant, before you came in here, wouldn't you say?"

"Yes, sir. No excuse, sir," Pickering said.

"Reporting in, are you?"

"Yes, sir."

"Then we shall probably have the opportunity to continue this embarrassing conversation in other surroundings," the captain said. Then he walked off.

Pickering, grossly embarrassed, stared at the tableware. As he pretended rapt fascination with the newspaper, he became aware that the people in the coffee shop were leaving. He reasoned out why: Officers gathered here for breakfast before going out to the base. The duty day was about to begin, and they were leaving.

When his breakfast was served, he folded the newspaper. As he did that he glanced around the room. It was indeed nearly empty.

But at a table across the room was an attractive young woman sitting alone over a cup of coffee. She was in a sweater and skirt and wore a band over her blond hair. And she was looking at him, he thought, with mingled amusement, condescension, and maybe even a little pity.

Pick, with annoyance, turned his attention to his breakfast.

A moment later, the blonde was standing by his table. He sensed her first, and then smelled her perfume—or her cologne, or whatever it was—a crisp, clean, feminine aroma; and then as he raised his eyes, he saw there was an engagement ring and a wedding band on her hand.

"That was Captain Jim Carstairs," she said, "and as a friendly word of warning, his bite is even worse than his bark."

Pick stood up. The blonde was gorgeous. He was standing so close to her than he could see the delicate fuzz on her cheeks and chin.

"And you, no doubt, are Mrs. Captain Carstairs?" he said.

"No," she said, shaking her head. "Just a friendly Samaritan trying to be helpful. I wouldn't let him catch me needing a shave again."

"The last time he caught you needing a shave, it was rough, huh?" Pick said.

"Go to hell," she said. "I *was* trying to be helpful."

"And I'm very grateful," Pick said.

She nodded at him, smiled icily, and went back to her table.

What the hell was that all about? Pick wondered. *Obviously, she wasn't trying to pick me up. Then what? There was the wedding ring, and she knew the salty captain with the mustache. She was probably some other officer's wife, drunk with his exalted rank. Well, fuck her!*

He sat down again and picked up a biscuit and buttered it.

The blonde, whose name was Martha Sayre Culhane, returned to her table wondering what had come over her; wondering why she had gone over to the second lieutenant she had never seen before—much less met—in her life; wondering if she was drunk, or just crazy.

That he was good-looking and attractive never entered her conscious mind. What *had* entered Martha Sayre Culhane's conscious mind was that the second lieutenant looked very much like Greg, even walked like him. And *that* resemblance made her throat catch and her breathing speed up.

Greg was—had been—First Lieutenant Gregory J. Culhane, USMC (Annapolis '38), a tall, lanky, dark-haired young man of twenty-four. A Navy brat, he was born in the Navy hospital in Philadelphia. His father, Lieutenant (later Vice Admiral) Andrew J. Culhane, USN (Annapolis '13), was at the time executive officer of a destroyer engaged in antisubmarine operations off the coast of Ireland. He first saw his son six months later, in December of 1917, after the War to End All Wars had been brought to a successful conclusion, and he had sailed his destroyer home to put it in long-term storage at Norfolk, Virginia.

Admiral Culhane's subsequent routine duty assignments sent him to Pearl Harbor, Hawaii; Guantanamo Bay, Cuba; San Diego, California; and to the Navy Yards at Brooklyn and Philadelphia.

Two weeks after his graduation from Philadelphia's Episcopal Academy in June of 1934, Greg Culhane, who had earned letters in track and basketball at Episcopal, traveled by train to

Annapolis, Maryland, where he was sworn into the United States Navy as a midshipman.

On his graduation from Annapolis in June 1938 (sixty-fifth in his class) he was commissioned at his request—and against the advice of his father—as second lieutenant, USMC, and posted to the Marine detachment aboard the battleship USS *Pennsylvania,* the flagship of the Pacific Fleet, whose home port was Pearl Harbor, Hawaii.

He immediately applied for training as a Naval aviator, which may have had something to do with his relief from the *Pennsylvania* four months later and his transfer to the Marine Detachment, Peking, China, for duty with troops.

Second Lieutenant Culhane traveled from Pearl Harbor to Tientsin, China aboard the USS *Chaumont,* one of two Navy transports that endlessly circled the world delivering and picking up Navy and Marine personnel from all corners of the globe.

In Peking, Greg Culhane served as a platoon leader for eighteen months, along with the additional duties customarily assigned to second lieutenants: He was mail officer; athletic officer; custodian of liquor, beer, and wine for the officer's mess; venereal disease control officer; and he served as recorder and secretary of various boards and committees formed for any number of official and quasi-official purposes.

In April 1939, he boarded the *Chaumont* again and returned to the United States via the Cavite Navy Base in the Philippines; Melbourne, Australia; Port Elizabeth, South Africa; Monrovia, Liberia; Rio de Janeiro and Recife, Brazil; and Guantanamo, Cuba.

Second Lieutenant Greg Culhane reported to the United States Navy Air Station, Pensacola, Florida, on June 10, 1939, nine days after the date specified on his orders. His class had already begun their thirteen-month course of instruction.

The personnel officer brought the "Culhane Case" to the attention of the deputy air station commander, Rear Admiral (lower half[1]) James B. Sayre, USN, for decision.

---

[1]The Navy rank structure provides four grades of "flag" officers corresponding to the four grades of "general" officers of the Army and Marine Corps. The lowest of these grades, corresponding to brigadier general, is rear admiral (lower half). But where brigadier generals wear only one star, rear admirals (lower half) wear two silver stars, as do rear admirals (upper half) and major generals. The result of this inconsistency is a good deal of annoyance on the part of brigadier and major generals of the Army and Marine Corps.

When he had not shown up, the training space set aside for the young Marine officer had been filled by one of the standby applicants. There were two options, the personnel officer explained. One was to go by the book and request the Marine Corps to issue orders returning Lieutenant Culhane to the Fleet Marine Force. The second option was to keep him at Pensacola and enroll him in the next flight course, which would commence 1 September.

"There's a third option, Tom," Admiral Sayre said. "For one thing, it's not this boy's fault that the *Chaumont* was, as usual, two weeks late. For another, I notice that he came here just as soon as he could after the *Chaumont* finally got to Norfolk; he didn't take the leave he was authorized. And finally, he's only nine days late. What I think is in the best interests of the Navy, as well as Lieutenant Culhane, is for me to have a word with Jim Swathley and ask him to make the extra effort to let this boy catch up with his class."

"I'll be happy to talk to Captain Swathley, sir, if you'd like," the personnel officer said.

"All right then, Tom, you talk to him. Tell him that's my suggestion."

"Aye, aye, sir."

Admiral Sayre had not considered it necessary to tell the personnel officer that he had been a year behind Greg Culhane's father at the academy, nor that in 1919–20 (before he had volunteered for aviation) he had served under Admiral Culhane with a tin-can squadron.

But as soon as the personnel officer had left his office, he had asked his chief yeoman to get Mrs. Sayre on the line, and when she came to the phone, he told her that Andy Culhane's boy had just reported aboard, and from the picture in his service jacket as well as from the efficiency reports in the record, Greg Culhane was a fine young Marine officer.

"I wonder why he went in the Marines?" Jeanne Sayre said absently, and then without waiting for a reply, she asked, "I wonder if Martha remembers him? They were just little tykes the last time . . . Well, we'll just have to have him to dinner. I'll write Margaret Culhane and tell her we're keeping an eye on him."

The engagement of Martha Ellen Sayre, the only daughter of Rear Admiral and Mrs. James B. Sayre, USN, to First

Lieutenant Gregory J. Culhane, USMC, elder son of Vice Admiral and Mrs. Andrew J. Culhane, USN, was announced at the traditional Admiral's New Year's Day Reception.

It was a triple celebration, Admiral Sayre announced jovially at midnight when he was getting just a little flushed in the face: It was the new year, 1941, and that was always a good excuse for a party; he had finally managed to unload his daughter, who was getting to be at twenty-one a little long in the tooth; and her intended, even if he was a Marine, could now afford to support her, because as of midnight he had been made a first lieutenant.

Greg and Martha Culhane were married in an Episcopal service at the station chapel at Pensacola on July 1, 1941, the day after he was graduated as a Naval aviator. It was a major social event for the air station, and indeed for the Navy. Seventeen flag and general officers of the Navy and Marine Corps (and of course their ladies) were in the chapel for the ceremony. And twelve of Greg's buddies (nine Marines and three swabbies) from flight school, in crisp whites, held swords aloft over the couple as they left the chapel.

Despite secret plans (carefully leaked to the enemy) that the young couple would spend their wedding night in Gainesville, they actually went no farther than a suite in Pensacola's San Carlos Hotel. And the next morning, they drove down the Florida peninsula to Opa-locka, where Greg had been ordered for final training as a fighter pilot.

That lasted about two months. They had a small suite in the Hollywood Beach Hotel, which was now a quasi-official officers' hotel. Martha spent her days playing tennis and golf and swimming, and Greg spent his learning the peculiarities of the Grumman F4F-3 fighter.

In September, Greg was ordered to San Diego on orders to join Marine Fighter Squadron VMF-211. Martha drove to the West Coast with him, and she stayed until he boarded ship for Pearl Harbor. Then she left their car in storage there and returned to Florida by train. She didn't want a fight with her parents about driving all the way across the country by herself, and besides, it would be nice to have the Chevrolet Super Deluxe coupe there when Greg came back to San Diego.

Greg flew his brand-new Grumman F4F-3 Wildcat off the *Enterprise* to Wake Island on December 3, 1941. He wrote her that night, quickly, because he had to make sure the letter left aboard a Pan American *China Clipper*. Among other things, he told her that Wake had been unprepared for them, and that Marine and civilian bulldozer operators were working from first light until after dark to make revetments.

Greg also wrote that he loved her and would write again just as soon as he had the chance.

The next news she had about Greg was a letter to her father from Commander Winfield Scott Cunningham, the senior Naval officer on Wake Island. Cunningham had once worked for Admiral Sayre at Guantanamo Bay in Cuba.

Commander Cunningham wrote his old commanding officer that as soon as word of the Japanese attack on Pearl Harbor had reached Wake Island, he had ordered Major Paul Putnam, VMF-211's commanding officer, to lead a flight of four F4F-3s on a scouting mission for Japanese naval forces. The remaining eight fighter planes and the squadron itself prepared for combat.

This had posed some problems, he continued; there was more to that job than simply filling the aircraft fuel tanks and loading ammunition for the guns. Aviation fuel, presently in large tanks, had to be put into fifty-five-gallon drums and the drums dispersed. And much of the .50-caliber machine-gun ammunition had to be linked, that is to say removed from its shipping containers and fitted with metal links to make belts of ammunition.

All hands had then gone to work, officers and enlisted men alike, bulldozing revetments and taxiways; filling sandbags; pumping fuel; and working the .50-caliber linking machines.

At 0900, Putnam's four-plane patrol returned to Wake for refueling. At about 0940, immediately after the tanks of their Grumman Wildcats had been topped off, Commander Cunningham wrote, Putnam and three others took off again, taking up a course to the north and climbing to twelve thousand feet, as high as they could fly without using oxygen.

At 1158, First Lieutenant Wallace Lewis, USMC, an experienced antiaircraft artilleryman whom Major James P. S. Devereux, the senior Marine on Wake Island, had placed in charge of antiaircraft defenses, spotted a twelve-plane V of aircraft approaching Wake Island from the north at no more than two thousand feet.

The three-inch antiaircraft cannon, and the dozen .50-caliber

Browning machine guns on Wake, brought the attacking formation under fire.

The pilots of the eight Grumman F4F-3 Wildcats ran for their aircraft as crew chiefs started the engines.

There were now thirty-six Japanese aircraft, three twelve-plane Vs, in sight. One-hundred-pound bombs fell from the leading V, but instead of turning away from the target once their bomb load had been released, which was the American practice, the Japanese aircraft continued on course, and began to strafe the airfield with their 20-mm machine cannon.

The projectiles were mixed explosive and incendiary. One of them, Commander Cunningham wrote Admiral Sayre, had struck Lieutenant Gregory J. Culhane, USMC, in the back of the head as he ran toward his Grumman F4F-3 Wildcat. It exploded on impact.

"I'm not even sure, Admiral," Commander Cunningham concluded, "if there will be an an opportunity to get this letter out. They're supposed to be sending a Catalina in here, and we are supposed to be reinforced by a task force from Pearl, but in view of the overall situation, I'm not sure that either will be possible.

"Please offer my condolences to Martha and Mrs. Sayre."

(Two)

Pickering had just about finished with the paper when a man came into the coffee shop, looked around, and then walked to his table.

"Lieutenant Pickering?"

Pickering looked up and nodded. The man was plump and neatly dressed in a well-cut suit. He looked to be in his early thirties.

"I understand you're an innkeeper yourself," the man said.

Pickering nodded.

"Then you'll understand that no matter how hard you try, sometimes the wrong guy gets behind the desk," the man said. He put out his hand. "I'm Chester Gayfer, the assistant manager. Much too late, let me welcome you to the San Carlos. May I join you?"

Pickering waved him into a chair. A waitress appeared with a cup of coffee.

"Put all this on my chit, Gladys," Gayfer said, and then

looked at Pickering and smiled. "Unless you'd rather have a basket of fruit?"

"Breakfast is fine," Pickering said. "Unnecessary, but fine."

"We didn't expect you until later today," Gayfer said.

"I drove straight through," Pickering said.

"I think you may be able to solve one of our problems for us," Gayfer said. "If we extended a very generous innkeeper's discount, would you be interested in a penthouse suite? A large bedroom, a small bedroom, a sitting room, and a tile patio covered with an awning? There's even a butler's pantry."

"It's a little more than I had in mind," Pickering said.

"We have trouble renting something like that during the week," Gayfer said. "On weekends, however, it's in great demand by your brother officers at the air station. Two of them rent it. Eight, sometimes more, of their pals seem to extend their visits overnight. And they have an unfortunate tendency to practice their bombing—"

"Excuse me?"

"Among other youthful exuberances, your brother officers amuse themselves by filling balloon-type objects with water," Gayfer said, "which they then, cheerfully shouting 'bombs away,' drop on their friends as they pass on the sidewalk below."

Pickering chuckled.

"The management has authorized me to say that if the San Carlos could recoup just a little more by the week than it now gets for Friday and Saturday night," Gayfer said, "it would be delighted to offer the penthouse suite on a weekly basis. How does that sound to you?"

"I'm always willing to do what I can to help out a fellow hotelier," Pickering said. "That sounds fine."

They ceremoniously shook hands.

The good-looking blonde who had come to Pickering's table with the unsolicited Good Samaritan warning about Captain Carstairs stood up and walked out of the coffee shop. She had nice legs, and her skirt revealed much of the shape of her derriere. Pickering thought of himself, by and large, as a derriere man. This was one of the nicer derrieres he'd come across lately, and he gave it the careful study an object of beauty clearly deserved. Pity the owner was impressed with her role as an officer's wife.

And then he became aware that Gayfer was watching him stare.

"Some things do tend to catch one's eye, don't they?" Pick said.

There was not the understanding smile on Gayfer's face that he expected.

"I saw the wedding ring," Pick said. "No offense intended. Just a statement of appreciation."

"She's a widow," Gayfer said.

Pickering's eyebrows rose in question.

"Her name is Martha Culhane," Gayfer said. "Martha *Sayre* Culhane."

"Is that name supposed to mean something to me?" Pickering asked.

"Her father is Admiral Sayre," Gayfer said. "He's the number-three man at the Naval air station. Her husband is . . . was . . . a Marine pilot. He was killed at Wake Island."

"Oh, God!" Pickering said softly.

"She's not the only service wife around here to suddenly find herself a widow," Gayfer said. "This is a Navy town. But when she went home to her family, it was back into admiral's quarters on the base. I think that made it tougher for her. If she was back in Cedar Rapids or someplace, she wouldn't be surrounded by uniforms."

"What was she doing here this time of morning?"

"She hangs around the Marine fliers. The ones who were friends of her husband. They sort of take care of her."

Pickering would have liked an explanation of "hangs around" and "take care of her," but he suppressed the urge to ask for one.

No wonder, he thought, *that she looked at me with such amused contempt.*

"When you're through, I'll show you the suite," Gayfer said.

"I'm through," Pickering said, and stood up.

"Where's your car?" Gayfer asked as they entered the lobby.

The widow was standing, sidewards to him, by a stack of newspapers on the marble desk. *Nice legs,* Pickering thought idly, again, and then he saw how her skirt was drawn tight against her stomach, and his mind's eye was suddenly filled with a surprisingly clear image of her naked belly.

Goddamn you! You sonofabitch! She's a widow, for Christ's sake. Her husband was shot down!

"Out in front," he replied to Gayfer.

"The Cadillac with the California plates?"

Pickering nodded.

"Give me the keys," Gayfer said, and Pickering handed them to him.

There was a new clerk behind the desk. Gayfer walked over to him, gave him the keys, told him to have the bellman bring the bags in the Cadillac convertible outside up to the penthouse, and then to put the Cadillac in the parking lot.

The widow (*Martha Sayre Culhane*, Pickering remembered), who couldn't help but overhear what Gayfer said, looked at Pickering with unabashed curiosity.

Gayfer, smiling, led Pickering to the elevator. When Pickering turned and faced front, Martha Sayre Culhane was still looking at him.

(Three)

Second Lieutenant Malcolm Pickering, USMCR, had learned from Second Lieutenant Kenneth J. McCoy, USMCR, a number of things about the United States Marine Corps that were not taught in the Platoon Leader's Course at United States Marine Corps' Schools, Quantico.

One of them was that a commissioned officer of the United States Marine Corps was not required to use rail tickets issued to move officially from one place to another. Such rail tickets, Pickering had learned from McCoy, were issued for the officer's convenience.

"There's two ways to do it, Pick," McCoy had explained. "The best way, if you know they're going to issue orders, is to request TPA—Travel by Private Auto—first. If they give you that, they also give you duty time to make the trip . . . four, five hundred miles a day. Three days, in other words, to get from Washington to Pensacola. Then they pay you so much a mile.

"But even if you don't have TPA on your orders, you can take your car. You don't get any extra travel time, all you get is what it would have taken you to make the trip by train. But when you get there, you can turn in your ticket, and tell them you traveled TPA, and they'll still pay you by the mile."

There was more: "The duty day runs from oh-oh-oh-one to twenty-four hundred."

That had required explanation, and McCoy had furnished it.

"Whether it's one minute after midnight in the morning when you leave, or half-past eleven that night, that's one day. And whether you report in after midnight or twenty-three-and-a-half hours later, so far as the Corps is concerned, it's the same day. So the trick is to leave just after midnight, and report in just before midnight."

And there had been a final sage word of advice from McCoy: "And never report in early. You report in early, they'll find something for you to do between the time you reported in and when they expected you. Something nobody else wants to do, like counting spoons, or inspecting grease pits."

Second Lieutenant Pickering's orders, transferring him from U.S. Marine Barracks, Washington, D.C., to Navy Air Station, Pensacola, Florida, for the purpose of undergoing training as a Naval aviator, had given him a ten-day delay en route leave, plus the necessary time to make the journey by rail. The schedule for rail travel called for a forty-nine-hour journey. Since forty-nine hours was one hour more than two days, he had three full days to make the rail trip.

He had flown from his Authorized Leave Destination—in other words, New York City—to Atlanta, and then driven through the night to Pensacola. He had two days of travel time left when he got to Pensacola; and taking McCoy's advice as the Gospel, he had no intention of reporting in early and finding himself counting spoons or inspecting grease pits.

He went to bed in the penthouse suite of the San Carlos and slept through the day, rising in time for the cocktail hour. He had a couple of drinks at the bar, then dinner, and then a couple of more drinks. He looked for, but did not see, the Widow Culhane, and told himself this was idle curiosity, nothing more.

Suspecting that if he stayed in the bar, he would get tanked up, which would not be a smart thing for a just-reporting-in second lieutenant to do, he left the bar and wandered around downtown Pensacola.

It was, as Chester Gayfer had told him, a Navy town. Every third male on the streets was in Navy blue. There were fewer Marines, though, and most of them seemed to be officers. There were more service people on the streets of Pensacola, Pickering decided as he saluted for the twentieth or thirtieth time, than there were in Washington.

He went into the Bijou Theatre, taking advantage of the price reduction for servicemen, and watched Ronald Reagan playing a Naval aviator in a movie called *Dive Bomber*. He was fascinated with the airplanes, and with the notion—truth being stranger than fiction—that he might soon be flying an airplane himself.

When the movie was over (he had walked in in the middle) and the lights went up, he kept his seat and stayed for the Bugs Bunny cartoon and *The March of Time*, much of which was given over to footage of the "Arsenal of Democracy" gearing up its war production.

When *Dive Bomber* started up again, he walked out of the theater and back to the San Carlos Hotel bar.

This time the Widow Culhane (*Martha Sayre Culhane*, her full name came to him) was there, in the center of a group of Marine officers and their wives and girl friends. All wore the gold wings of Navy aviators. Among them was Captain Mustache Carstairs, the one who had objected to his unshaven chin and mussed uniform the day before.

As Pickering had his drinks, both of them looked at him, the Marine captain with what Pick thought was a professional curiosity (*"Has that slovenly disgrace to the Marine Corps finally taken a shave?"*) and Martha Sayre Culhane with a look he could not interpret.

Pick had two drinks, and then left. He went to the penthouse suite and took off his uniform, everything but his shorts, and sat on the patio looking up at the stars and smoking a cigar until he felt himself growing sleepy. Then he went to bed.

VI

(One)
420 Lexington Avenue
New York City
1135 Hours, 8 January 1942

When her telephone rang, Miss Ernestine Sage was sitting pushed back in her chair with her hands—their fingers intertwined—on top of her head, looking at the preliminary artwork for a Mint-Fresh Tooth Paste advertisement, which would eventually appear in *Life, The Saturday Evening Post*, and sixteen other magazines; and on several thousand billboards across the nation.

The preliminary artwork showed a good-looking, wholesome blonde with marvelous teeth saying something. A balloon was drawn on the preliminary drawing. When Miss Sage decided exactly what Miss Mint-Fresh was going to say (and after that had been approved by her senior copywriter; her assistant account executive; her vice president and account executive; the vice president, creative; and, of course, the client) it would be put inside the balloon.

Right now the balloon was empty. The preliminary artwork gave the impression, Miss Sage had just been thinking, that someone had just whispered an obscenity in Miss Mint-Fresh's ear, and Miss Mint-Fresh had been rendered speechless.

Miss Ernestine Sage took one hand from the top of her head and reached for the telephone.

"Mint-Fresh," she said to the telephone. "Ernie Sage."

"Hello, honey," her caller said. "I'm glad I caught you."

"Hello, Daddy," Ernie Sage said. She had been expecting the call. She had, in fact, expected it yesterday.

She spun in her chair so that she could rest her feet on the windowsill. The window in Miss Ernestine Sage's closet-sized office at J. Walter Thompson Advertising, Inc. offered a splendid view of the roof of a smaller building next door, and then of the windows of the building next to that.

Miss Sage was a copywriter, which was a rank in the J. Walter Thompson hierarchy as well as a description of her function. In the Creative Division, the low man on the corporate totem pole was a "trainee." Next above that came "editorial assistant," then "junior copywriter." Above "copywriter" came "senior copywriter." Beyond that, one who kept one's nose to the grindstone could expect to move upward over the years to "assistant account executive" and "account executive" and possibly even into the "vice president and account executive" and plain "vice president" categories.

It had taken Miss Sage about three weeks to figure out that JWT, as it was known to the advertising cognoscenti, passed out titles in one or both of two ways. The first was in lieu of a substantial increase in salary, and the other was with an eye on JWT's clients. Just as JWT sold a myriad of products to the public by extolling their virtues, so it sold itself to its clients with manifestations of the degree of importance in which it held them.

A very important client, "a multimillion biller," for example, such as American Personal Pharmaceutical, Inc., who the previous year had spent "12.3 mil" in bringing its array of products before the American public, had one JWT vice president, four JWT vice presidents and account executives, eight JWT account executives, and God only knew how many JWT assistant account executives and senior copywriters devoting their full attention to American Personal Pharmaceutical's products.

Miss Sage was in the "Mint-Fresh" shop. Mint-Fresh was the third best-selling of American Personal Pharmaceutical's family of five products intended to brighten America's (and for that matter, the world's) teeth.

Miss Sage was one of three copywriters reporting to a senior copywriter, who reported to the Mint-Fresh account executive, who reported to the vice president and account executive, APP Dental Products. There were three other vice presidents and account executives, one for APP Cosmetic Products (shampoos, acne medicines, hair tonics, et cetera); one for APP Health Products (cold remedies, cough syrups, et cetera); and one for APP Personal Products (originally nostrums for feminine complaints, but now—after APP had acquired controlling interest in the companies involved in their manufacture—including three brands of sanitary napkins and eleven brands of rubber prophylactics).

Each of the vice presidents and account executives had his own empire of account executives, assistant account executives, and so on through the hierarchy, under him.

Miss Sage knew more than just about any other copywriter about the upper echelons of the "APP Family" for the same reason that she had had very little trouble getting herself hired by JWT. That was not, as the vice president, creative personnel had publicly announced, because she had proved herself to be a very bright girl, indeed, by coming out of Sarah Lawrence with a summa cum laude degree (BA, English), just the kind of person JWT was always on the lookout for. Rather it was because the grandson of the founder of American Personal Pharmaceuticals (Ezekiel Handley, M.D., whose first product was "Dr. Handley's Female Elixir") was now chairman of the board and chief executive officer. His name was Ernest Sage, and he was Ernie's father.

This is not to suggest that Ernie Sage regarded her job as a sort of hobby, a socially acceptable, even chic, way to pass the time until she made a suitable marriage and took her proper place in society. She had decided in her freshman year at Sarah Lawrence that she wanted to make (as opposed to inherit) a lot of money. And after an investigation of the means to do that open to females, she had decided the way to do it was in advertising.

She had learned as much about the business as she could while in college, and she had taken courses she thought would be of value to that end. When she graduated, she had two choices. The summa cum laude would have been enough to get her a job on Madison Avenue if her name hadn't been Sage. But she decided two things about JWT. First, that they were arguably the best and biggest of all the large agencies and would thus offer her the opportunity to learn all facets of the business; and, second, with APP as their next-to-largest client, she would have certain privileges, while learning her chosen profession, that she would not have elsewhere.

It was her intention—once she felt secure, once she had learned the way things worked in the real world, once she had a portfolio of work she had done—to open her own agency. Just her, and an artist, and a secretary. She would find some small manufacturer of something who was bright enough to figure out that he wasn't getting JWT's full attention with billings under a hundred thou and convince him that she could give him more for his money than he would get elsewhere. She would build on that; she grew more and more convinced that she could.

Everything had gone according to plan, including the exercise of special privilege. She had almost bluntly told the vice president and account executive, APP Personal Products, that, substantial jump in pay or not, promotion to senior copywriter or not, she would not want to "move over into his shop" and put her now-demonstrated talents to work there.

There were a number of nice things about being rich, she told herself, and one of them was not needing a job so badly that she would have to spend her time thinking up appealing ways to sell Kotex-by-another-name and rubbers.

And then Ken McCoy had come along. And the best-laid plans of mice and men, et cetera.

The call she was taking from her father right now came about as a result of a call he had made to her the day after Thanksgiving. You were not supposed to make or receive personal calls at JWT, and rumor had it that there was official eavesdropping to make sure the rule was obeyed. No one had ever said anything to Ernie Sage about her personal calls.

"Honey, am I interrupting anything?" he'd said that Thanksgiving Friday.

"Actually, I'm flying paper airplanes out the window," she'd told him, truthfully. The way the air currents moved outside her window, paper airplanes would fly for astonishingly long periods of time.

"Has Pick called?"

"Any reason he should?" she'd replied. "I didn't even know he was in town."

Malcolm "Pick" Pickering had grown up calling her father "Uncle Ernie." Ernie Sage knew that sometimes her father wished she had been born a boy, since there was to be only one child. But since she *was* a girl, there was little secret that everybody concerned would be thrilled to death if Pick suddenly looked at her like Clark Gable had looked at Scarlett before carrying her up the stairs.

"He is," Ernest Sage had said. "He's at the Foster Park."

"He called you?" she had asked.

"He left a message on the bulletin board at the Harvard Club," her father had said.

"Why didn't he just call?" she had asked. "Wouldn't that have been easier?"

"He didn't leave a message for *me*," her father had said, as realization dawned that he was having his leg pulled. "Don't be such a wise-ass. Nobody likes a wise-ass in skirts."

"Sorry," she'd laughed.

"He's having a party."

"I thought he was in Virginia playing Marine," she'd replied.

"I don't think he's *playing* Marine," her father had said, more than a little sharply.

"Sorry," she'd said again, this time meaning it.

"He's giving a party," her father had said. "Cocktails. I think you should go."

"I haven't been invited," she'd replied, simply.

"The thing on the bulletin board said 'all friends and acquaintances.' You would seem to qualify."

"If Pick wanted me, he knows my phone number," she'd said.

"I just thought you might be interested," her father had said, and from the tone of his voice and the swiftness of his getting off the line, she knew that she had hurt his feelings. Again.

Several hours later, sitting in the Oak Room of the Plaza Hotel with two girls and three young men as they debated the monumental decision where to have dinner and go afterward, she had remembered both Pick's party and her father's disappointment. And the Foster Park Hotel was only a block away.

Doing her duty, she had taken the others there. Penthouse C, overlooking Central Park, had been crowded with people, among them Ken McCoy, in a uniform like Pick's. He'd been sitting on a low brick wall on the patio, twenty-six floors above Fifty-ninth Street, looking as if he was making a valiant effort not to spit over the side.

That had turned into a very interesting evening, far more interesting than it had first promised to be. Instead of catching a cab uptown to some absolutely fascinating restaurant Billy had discovered, she'd ridden the subway downtown with Platoon Leader Candidate, McCoy, K. After he had taken her to a tiny Chinese restaurant on the third floor of a building on a Chinatown alley, she had taken him to her apartment, where she gave him a drink and her virtue.

Quite willingly. This was all the more astonishing because she had ridden downtown on the subway a virgin. *More* than willingly given it to him, she subsequently considered quite often; she'd done everything but put a red ribbon on it and hand it to him on a silver platter.

And he had not been humbly grateful, either. He'd been astonished and then angry, and she'd thought for a moment that he was about to march out of the apartment in high moral outrage. He didn't in the end. He stayed.

But as he and Pick drove back to Quantico, Pick had told him about her family. Until Pick opened his fat mouth, Ken McCoy had thought she lived in the small apartment in the Village because that was all she could afford.

The result was that her letters to him had gone unanswered. And when she sent him a registered letter, it had came back marked REFUSED. At the time, she'd been firmly convinced he was ignoring her because he was a Marine officer, and Marine officers do not enter into long-term relationships with young women who enthusiastically bestow upon them their pearl of great price two hours after meeting them.

"Wham, bang, thank you, Ma'am," of course. But nothing enduring. The Marine Corps equivalent of "We must lunch sometime. I'll call you."

At first she'd been angry, then ashamed, then angry and ashamed, and then shameless. And on The Day That Will Live In Infamy, after hearing from her mother, who'd heard it from Pick's mother, that Pick had been commissioned and was in Washington, she'd gone down there to ask Pick to help.

There Pick had explained that it was not her freedom with her sexual favors that was bothering Ken McCoy; it was her money.

"What's that got to do with anything?"

"After a lot of solemn thought," Pick had replied, "I have concluded that he is afraid that you regard him as an interesting way to pass an otherwise dull evening."

"That's just not so!"

"That the minute he lets his guard down, you're going to make a fool of him. There was a woman in China who did a pretty good job on his ego."

"A Chinese woman?"

"An American. Missionary's wife. He had it pretty bad for her, the proof being that he was going to get out of the Marine Corps to marry her. For him, the supreme sacrifice."

"What happened? What did she do to him?"

"What he's afraid you're going to do to him," Pick told her. "Humiliate him."

"Goddamn her," Ernie had said. And then: "Pick, it's not that way with me. I've got to see him."

"It'll be a little difficult at the moment," Pick had said. "He's in Hawaii right now, on his way to the Philippines."

"Oh, God!" she'd wailed.

"But he'll be back," Pick had said. "He's a courier. Sort of a Marine Corps mailman."

"When?"

"A week, maybe. Ten days."

"You'll let me know when he's back?"

"I will even arrange a chance meeting under the best possible circumstances," Pick had said. "Here. He's living here with me. You can be waiting for him, soaked in perfume, wearing something transparent, with violin music on the phonograph."

"You tell me when," she'd said. Things were looking up.

When she'd walked through the lobby of the hotel, on her way to the station, NBC was broadcasting the bulletin that the Japanese had attacked the U.S. Naval Station at Pearl Harbor.

And a week after that, Pick had called her and told her that there had been word from the Philippines that Second Lieutenant Kenneth J. McCoy, USMCR, was missing in action and presumed dead.

Ernestine Sage's reaction to that was not what she would have thought. She had not screamed and moaned and torn her hair. She hadn't even cried. She'd just died inside. Gone completely numb.

And then, a week later, Pick had called again, his voice breaking. "I thought you might like to know that our boy just called from San Francisco. As Mark Twain said, the report of his death is somewhat exaggerated."

She'd been waiting in Pick's suite at the Foster Lafayette Hotel when McCoy returned. Not soaked in My Sin, or wearing a black negligee, which had been her intention; but, because he was an hour early, she was in a cotton bathrobe with soap in her ears and her hair shower-plastered to her head.

He hadn't seemed to notice. They'd turned the Louis XIV bedroom into the Garden of Eden, and she'd wept with joy when she felt him in her. And as perverse as it sounded, with joy again when she'd changed his bandages, for it seemed proof that she was a woman who had found her mate and was caring for him.

That had been the result of her father's phone call on Thanksgiving Friday. Now he was on the line again, and there was no doubt in Miss Ernestine Sage's mind that he had on his mind now the relationship between his daughter and her Marine officer; her mother had gone to him and told him that she knew for a fact that their daughter had left her own bed in the middle of the night so that she could get in bed with Ken McCoy.

"Are you free for lunch?" Ernest Sage asked his daughter.

"Sure," she said.

"Could you come here?" he asked. "It would be better for me."

She wondered how he meant that; was his schedule tight? Or did he just want to have his little talk with her on his own ground?

He picked up on her hesitation.

"Anywhere would be fine, honey," her father said.

"Twelve-fifteen?" Ernie Sage said.

"Would you like anything in particular?" her father asked. "I think Juan's making medallions of veal."

"That'll be fine, Daddy," she said.

"Look forward to it," he said, and hung up.

The hell you do, Daddy.

At five minutes to twelve, Miss Ernestine Sage put on her overcoat and galoshes and left her office. She walked the two blocks from JWT to Madison Avenue and then the half block to the American Personal Pharmaceutical Products Building. This was a nearly new (1939) fifty-nine-story, sandstone-sheathed structure, the upper twenty floors of which housed the executive offices of APP.

She walked across the marble floor and entered an elevator.

"Fifty-six," she told the operator.

The APP building's top formed a four-sided cone, with each floor from fifty-nine down to fifty-two somewhat smaller than the floor below, from which point the walls descended straight to the street level. The fifty-sixth floor was the highest office floor, the top three floors being dedicated to various operating functions for the building itself.

Her father's office was on fifty-five. Fifty-six was the Executive Dining Room, something of a misnomer as there were actually four dining rooms on that floor, plus the kitchen and a bar. APP, like JWT, had a hierarchy. Individuals attaining certain upper levels of responsibility received with their promotions permission to take their lunch on fifty-six, on the company, or to stop by fifty-six for a little nip, also on the company, at the end of the business day.

Fully two-thirds of the floor was occupied by the Executive Dining Room itself. That establishment looked like any good restaurant in a club. And then, in addition to the Executive Dining Room, there were Dining Rooms A, B, and C. Of these, Dining Room C was the smallest, containing but one table and a small serving bar. Its use was controlled by Mrs. Zoe Fegelbinder, executive secretary to the chairman of the board of APP. And it was reserved for special occasions.

When Ernie Sage got off the elevator, the maître d'hotel spotted her right away and walked quickly to her.

"Good afternoon, Miss Sage," he said. "How nice to see you again. You're in 'C.'"

She was not surprised. This was a special occasion. The chairman of the board of APP did not want to show off his daughter in the Executive Dining Room today.

Today, the chairman of the board wanted to be alone with his daughter, so that he could talk to her about her screwing a Marine, or words to that effect.

As the maître d' ushered her across the lobby, a path was

made for her and people smiled, and she heard herself being identified. She had often thought that it must be like this for Princess Elizabeth; for around here, she was sort of like royalty.

Her father was not in 'C,' but Juan was, in his chef's whites.

"Hallo, Miss Ernie," he said, smiling, apparently genuinely pleased to see her.

"Hello, Juan," she said.·

She remembered now that Juan was a Filipino. As in invaded by the Japanese. As in the place where Japanese artillery had damned near killed Ken.

"Your poppa say veal medallions," Juan said. "But I think maybe you really like a little steak . . . with *marchand de vins* sauce?"

"Yes, I would," she said. "Thank you, Juan."

"*Pommes frites? Haricots verts?* And I find a place sells Amer'can Camembert, not bad. You try for dessert?"

"Sounds fine," she said.

"You wanna little glass wine, while you wait? Got a real nice Cal'fornia Cabernet sauvignon?"

What I really would like to have is a triple shot of cognac.

"Thank you, Juan," she said, smiling at him. "That sounds fine."

He opened the bottle and poured a glass for her.

"You wanna try?" he asked, as he gave it to her.

She took a healthy sip.

"Fine," she said. "Thank you."

"You think your poppa want a steak, too?" Juan asked.

"I thought we were having medallions of veal," Ernest Sage said, as he walked into the room.

He was a tall and heavyset man, with a full head of curly black hair, gray only at the temples. Her father, Ernie Sage often thought, looked like a chairman of the board is supposed to look, and seldom does.

"Miss Ernie," Juan said, "really wanna steak. You wanna steak, too?"

"I'll have the veal, thank you, Juan," Ernest Sage said, "with green beans and oven-roasted potatoes, if you have them. And a sliced tomato."

"Yes, sair," Juan said, and left the room.

Ernest Sage looked at his daughter as if he was going to say something, and then changed his mind. He flashed her a smile, somewhat nervously, Ernie thought, and then picked up the telephone on the table.

"No calls," he announced. "I don't care who it is."

"Said the hangman, as he began to knot the rope," Ernie Sage said.

Her father looked at her, and smiled. "Conscience bothering you?"

"Not at all," Ernie said.

"What are you drinking?" he asked.

She walked to him and handed her glass. When he'd taken a sip and nodded his approval, she stood on her tiptoes and kissed him.

"So what's new in advertising?" he asked.

She poured him a glass of wine.

"Everyone is all agog with '*Lucky Strike Green Has Gone to War*,'" Ernie said.

"What does that mean?"

"Nothing, that's why everyone is all agog," she said.

"Not that I really give a damn, but you've aroused my curiosity."

"They changed the color on the package," she said. "It used to be predominantly green. Now it's white, with the red Lucky Strike ball in the middle. The pitch is, with appropriate trumpets and martial drums, '*Lucky Strike Green Has Gone to War*.'"

"Why'd they do that?"

"Maybe they wanted a new image. Maybe they wanted to save the price of the green ink. Who knows?"

"What's that got to do with the war?"

"Nothing," she said. "That's why everyone is all agog. It's regarded as a move right up there with '*Twice as Much for a Nickel Too, Pepsi-Cola Is the Drink for You*,' which was the jingle Pepsi-Cola came onto the market with. Better even. Pure genius. It makes smoking Lucky Strike seem to be your patriotic duty."

"You sound as if you disapprove," he said.

"Only because I didn't think of it," she said. "Whoever thought that up is going to get rich."

Juan entered the room with shrimp cocktails in silver bowls on a bed of rice.

"Appetizer," he announced. "Hard as hell to get."

He walked out of the room.

Ernest Sage chuckled, and motioned for his daughter to sit down.

He ate a shrimp and took a sip of wine.

"I was sorry to have missed Pick's friend at the house. Your mother was rather taken with him."

"Was that before or after she found out I was sleeping with him?" Ernie Sage asked.

Ernest Sage nearly choked on a shrimp. "Good God, honey!" he said.

"I'm a chip—maybe a chippie?—off the old block," Ernie said, "who is frequently prone to suggest that people 'cut the crap.'"

"Whatever you are—and that probably includes a fool," Ernest Sage said, "you're not a chippie."

"Thank you, Daddy," Ernie said. "I'm sorry you missed him, too. I think you would have liked him."

"At the moment, I doubt that," he said. "I wonder what the penalty is for shooting a Marine?"

"In this case, the electric chair, plus losing your daughter," Ernie said.

"That bad, eh?" her father said, looking at her.

She nodded.

"God, you're only twenty-one."

"So's he," she said. "Which means that we're both old enough to vote, et cetera, et cetera."

"Okay, so tell me about him," Ernest Sage said.

"Mother hasn't?" Ernie asked, as she finished her last shrimp.

"I'd rather hear it from you," he said.

"He's very unsuitable," Ernie Sage said. "We have nothing in common. He has no money and no education."

"That's the debit side," her father said. "Surely there is a credit?"

"Pick likes him so much he almost calls him 'sir,'" Ernie said.

Her father nodded. "Well, that's something," he said.

"He speaks Chinese and Japanese . . . and some others."

"I'm impressed," her father said.

"No, you're not," Ernie said. "You're looking for an opening. I'm not going to give you one. Not that it would matter if I did. You're just going to have to adjust to this, Daddy."

"You're thinking of marriage, obviously?"

"I am," she said. "He's not."

"Any particular reason? Or is he against marriage on general principles?"

"He's against girls marrying Marine officers during wartime," she said. "For the obvious reasons."

"Well, there's one other point in his favor," her father said. "He's right about that. There's nothing sadder than a young widow with a fatherless child."

"Except a young widow without a child," Ernie Sage said.

"That doesn't make any sense, Ernie," he said sternly. "And you know it."

"I'm tempted to debate that," she said. "It's not as if I would have to go rooting in garbage cans to feed the little urchin. But it's a moot point. Ken agrees with you. There will be no child. Not now."

He looked at her for a long moment before he spoke again.

"You have to look down the line, honey," he said. "And you have to look at things the way they are, not the way you would wish them to be. Have you considered, really considered, what your life with this young man would be, removed from this initial flush of excitement, without the thrill . . . ?"

"I had occasion to consider what my life would be like without him," Ernie said. "He was reported missing and presumed dead. I died inside."

He looked at her with curiosity on his face.

"He's an intelligence officer," she said. "He was in the Philippines when the Japanese invaded. For a week they thought he was dead. But he wasn't, and he came home, and I came back to life."

Ernest Sage looked at his daughter, his tongue moving behind his lip as it did when he was in deep thought. "There seems to be only one thing I can do about this situation, honey," he said finally. "I go see your young man, carrying a shotgun, and demand that he do right by my daughter. Would you like me to do that?"

She got up and bent over her father and put her arms around him and kissed him. And laughed. "Thank you, Daddy," she said. "But no thanks."

"Why is that funny?" he asked.

"There is one little detail I seem to have skipped over. He

didn't tell me. Pick did. They call him 'Killer' McCoy in the Marine Corps."

"Because of the Philippines? What he did there?"

"What he did in China," Ernie said. "I think I'll skip the details, but I think threatening him with a shotgun, or anything else, would be very dangerous."

"I'd love to hear the details," her father said.

"He was once attacked by four Italian Marines," Ernie said, after obviously thinking it over. "He killed two of them."

"My God!"

"And, another time, he was attacked by a gang of Chinese bandits," she went on. "He killed either twelve or fourteen of them. Nobody knows for sure."

"I think we can spare your mother those stories," her father said.

"You asked," she said simply.

"Have you considered, honey, that just maybe—considering your background—"

She interrupted him by laughing again. "That I am thrilled by close association with a killer?" she asked.

He nodded.

"I fell in love with him, Daddy," she said, "the first time I saw him. When I thought he was some friend of Pick's from Harvard. He was sitting on the patio wall of one of the penthouse suites at the Foster Park. The very first thought I had about Ken was that the Marine Corps was crazy if they thought they could take someone so gentle, so sweet, so vulnerable, and turn him into an officer."

"And when you found out what he's really like?"

"I found that out the same day," Ernie Sage said. "I didn't find out about the Italians and the Chinese until later."

Her father looked at her (she met his eyes, but her face did blush a little) until he was sure he had correctly taken her meaning, then asked, "When do I get to meet Mr. Wonderful?"

"Soon," she said. "Now that he's back in Washington, he doesn't think they'll be sending him anywhere else. Not soon, anyway."

Twenty minutes after Miss Ernestine Sage returned to her office at J. Walter Thompson, she received a telephone call from Second Lieutenant Kenneth J. McCoy, USMCR, from Washington, D.C.

Lieutenant McCoy told Miss Sage that he had been transferred to a Marine base near San Diego, California. He would write. Or call, if he had access to a phone. He was sorry, but there would be no chance for him to come to New York; he was getting in the car the moment he got off the phone.

If he was going by car, Miss Sage argued, there was no reason he couldn't go to the West Coast by way of New York. If not New York, then Philadelphia. If she left right now from New York, she could be at the Thirtieth Street Station in Philadelphia just about the time he could get there by car from Washington.

"Honey, goddamnit," Miss Sage argued. "You can't go without saying good-bye."

Lieutenant McCoy agreed to meet Miss Sage at the Thirtieth Street Station of the Pennsylvania Railroad in Philadelphia.

"But that's it, baby," Lieutenant McCoy said. "There won't be any time for anything else."

"I'll be standing on the curb," Ernie Sage said, and hung up.

VII

(One)
The San Carlos Hotel
Pensacola, Florida
8 January 1942

When Pick Pickering woke in the morning, he decided he would not go to the coffee shop for breakfast. It was entirely possible that Captain Mustache would be there. And Pick was not anxious to run into Carstairs again, not after the captain had eaten his ass out for being sloppy and unshaven. And there was a good chance that *Martha Sayre Culhane* would be there as well. He couldn't quite interpret them, but he saw danger flags flying in the territories occupied by the blond widow with the flat tummy and the marvelous derriere.

Discretion was obviously the better part of valor, Pick decided. *If* he decided to find some gentle breast on which to lay his weary head while he was in Pensacola, he would find one that did not belong to the widow of a Marine aviator who was not only the daughter of an admiral but who was also surrounded by noble protectors of her virtue. There was no reason at all to play with fire.

He called room service and had breakfast on his patio,

surprised and disappointed that the orange juice had come from a can. This was supposed to be Sunny Florida—with orange trees. He tasted the puddle of grits beside his eggs and grimaced. There must be two Floridas, he decided, the one he knew and the one he was condemned to endure now. On Key Biscayne, which was the Florida he knew, the Biscayne Foster would not dream of serving canned orange juice or, for that matter, grits.

He called the valet and ordered them to press his uniforms, and then he dressed in the one least creased and rumpled. After that, he went down to the lobby barbershop for a haircut and a shave and a shoeshine. Then he got in the Cadillac (which, he noticed, had been washed and serviced) and put the top down.

Three blocks from the hotel, he pulled to the curb and put the top back up. Even in his green woolen blouse, he was cold. Obviously, there *were* two Floridas. This one was a thousand miles closer to the Artic Circle.

He drove more or less aimlessly, having a look around. After a while, he found himself on a street identified as West Garden Street. And then the street signs changed, and he was on Navy Boulevard. That sounded promising, and he stayed on it, driving at the 35-MPH speed limit for five or six miles.

Here were more signs of the Navy: hock shops, Army-Navy stores, and at least two dozen bars.

Then he heard the sound of an airplane engine. Close. He leaned forward and looked up and out of the windshield.

To his right, a bright yellow, open-cockpit, single-engined biplane was taking off from a field hidden by a thick, though scraggly, stand of pine. NAVY was painted on the underside of one wing.

Pickering slowed to watch it as it sort of staggered into the air, and he was still watching when an identical plane followed it into the air. Pick pulled onto the shoulder of the road, stopped, and got out. At what seemed to be minute or minute-and-a-half intervals, more little open-cockpit airplanes flew over his head, taking off.

He was awed at the number of airplanes the Navy apparently had here, until, feeling just a little foolish, he realized he was watching the same planes over and over. After they staggered into the air, they circled back and landed, and then took off again. There were really no more than a dozen or so, he realized, and they were using two runways.

He climbed back in his car and started up again, looking for a road he could take to where he could watch the actual takeoffs and landings. But no road appeared. Instead, he came to a low bridge across some water. On the other side of the bridge was a sign, UNITED STATES NAVY AIR STATION, PENSACOLA, and immediately beyond that a guardhouse.

A Marine guard saluted crisply, waving him past the gate and onto the reservation. A few hundred yards beyond the Marine guard, he saw to his right a red, triangular flag. It bore the number "8," and its flagstaff was in the center of what looked like a very nicely tended golf green.

It had been some time since he had gone a round of golf. Much too long. He missed bashing golf balls. And then he remembered that he had found his clubs in the Cadillac's trunk when he had loaded his luggage in Atlanta. Were lowly second lieutenants permitted on Navy base golf courses? he wondered. Or was that privilege restricted to high-ranking officers? He would, he decided, find out.

He drove around the enormous base, finding barracks and headquarters and the Navy Exchange, and finally an airfield. He parked the convertible by a chain-link fence and watched small yellow airplanes endlessly take off and land, take off and land. He found this fascinating, almost hypnotic, and he lost track of time.

Eventually, his stomach told him it was time to eat; and his new wristwatch told him that it was ten minutes after twelve. Earlier he had driven past the Officers' Club. The question was, could he find it again?

The answer was yes, but it took him twenty mintues. He went inside, and for thirty-five cents was fed a cup of clam chowder, pork chops, and lima beans.

The hotelier in him told him that there was no way the Navy could afford to do this without some kind of a subsidy, and then he realized what the subsidy was. The building and the furnishings were owned by the Navy. There was no mortgage to amortize, and it was not necessary to provide for maintenance or painting. And the cooks were on the Navy payroll.

He drank a second cup of coffee and then left the dining room. Near the men's room was a map of the air station mounted on the wall. He studied it, and after a few moments he realized that with the exception of several off-the-main-base training airfields, he had covered in his aimless driving just about all of Pensacola NAS that there was to cover.

Next, he decided to leave the base, drive back into Pensacola, and ask Gayfer where he could find a good place to take a dip in the Gulf of Mexico. And then, after a swim and dinner, and maybe a couple of drinks, he would put his uniform back on and return out here and report in.

He didn't make it off the base. On the way out, he saw an arrow pointing to the officers' golf course and decided he would really rather play golf than swim. He recalled additionally that this was the arctic end of Florida and that there would probably be icebergs in the water.

He found the clubhouse without trouble. There he asked a middle-aged Navy petty officer how one arranged to play a round. Shoes and clubs were available for fifty cents in the locker room, he was told, and the greens fee was a dollar.

"And do I have to play in uniform?"

"Uniform regulations are waived while you are physically on the golf course proper, sir," the petty officer told him. "You can take off your hat and blouse and tie."

Pickering fetched his clubs and a pair of golf shoes from the trunk of the convertible and then went to the locker room and paid the fees. After that he hung his blouse, hat, Sam Browne belt, and field scarf in a locker and went outside. A lanky teen-aged Negro boy detached himself from a group of his peers, offered his services as a caddy, and led him to the first tee.

A middle-aged woman was already on the tee. A woman who took her golf seriously, he saw. She was teed up, but had stepped away from the ball and was practicing her swing. He at first approved of this (his major objection to women on the links was that most of them did not take the game seriously); but his approval turned to annoyance when the middle-aged woman kept taking practice swings.

How long am I supposed to wait?

And then she saw him standing there and smiled. "Good afternoon," she said.

"Hello," he said politely.

"I didn't see you," she said. "I'm really sorry."

"Don't be silly," Pickering said.

"I was waiting for my daughter," the woman said. And then, "And here, at long last, she is."

Pickering followed her gesture and found himself looking at

Martha Sayre Culhane. She was wearing a band over her blond hair, a cotton windbreaker on top of a pale blue sweater, and a tight-across-the-back khaki-colored gabardine skirt. That sight immediately urged into his mind's eye another image of her. In that one she was in her birthday suit.

Martha Sayre Culhane's eyebrows rose when she saw him; she was not pleased.

"If you don't mind playing with women," Martha Sayre Culhane's mother said. "They really discourage singles."

"I would be delighted," Pick said.

"I'm Jeanne Sayre," Martha Sayre's Culhane's mother said. "And this is Martha. Martha Culhane."

In turn, they offered their hands. Martha Sayre Culhane's hand, he thought, was exquisitely soft and feminine.

"My name is Malcolm Pickering," he said. "People call me Pick."

"I thought your name was Foster," Martha Sayre Culhane said, matter-of-factly.

"Oh, you've met?" Jeanne Sayre asked.

"The desk clerk at the San Carlos, almost beside himself with awe, pointed him out to me," Martha Sayre Culhane said.

That's not true, Pickering thought, with certainty. *She asked him who I was. She was curious.*

"Oh?" her mother said, her tone making it clear that her daughter was embarrassing and annoying her.

"According to the desk clerk," Martha Sayre Culhane said, "we are about to go a round with the heir apparent to the Foster Hotel chain, now resident in the San Carlos penthouse."

"He told me about you, too," Pickering blurted.

Jeanne Sayre looked uncomfortably from one to the other. And then she looked between them, avoiding what she did not want to look at.

"But your name isn't Foster?" Martha challenged. "What about the rest of the story? How much of that is true?"

"Martha!" Jeanne Sayre snapped.

"Andrew Foster is my mother's father," Pickering said.

He saw surprise on Jeanne Sayre's face. But he didn't know what was in Martha Sayre Culhane's eyes.

"And what brought you to honor the Marine Corps with your presence?" Martha Sayre Culhane challenged.

"An old family custom," Pick snapped. "My father—my father is Fleming Pickering, as in Pacific & Far East Shipping—was a Marine in the last war. Whenever the professionals need help to pull their acorns out of the fire, we lend a hand. I am twenty-two years old. I went to Harvard, where I was the assistant business manager of the *Crimson*. I am unmarried, have a polo handicap of six, and generally can get around eighteen holes in the middle seventies. Is there anything else you would like to know?"

"Good for you, Lieutenant!" Jeanne Sayre said. "Martha, really—"

"If there's no objection," Martha Sayre Culhane interrupted her mother, "I think I'll go first."

She stepped to the tee and drove her mother's ball straight down the fairway.

Whoever had taught her to play golf, Pickering saw, had managed to impress upon her the importance of follow-through. At the end of her swing, her khaki gabardine skirt was skintight against the most fascinating derriere he had ever seen.

"If you would rather not play with us, Lieutenant," Jeanne Sayre said, "I would certainly understand."

"If it's all right with you," Pick said, "I'll play with you."

She met his eyes for a moment. Her eyes, Pick saw, were gray, and kind, and perceptive.

"You go ahead," Jeanne Sayre said. "I'll bring up the rear."

Martha Sayre Culhane hated him, Pick was aware, because *he* was here. Alive. And her husband—the late Lieutenant Whatever-his-name-had-been Culhane, USMC—had died in the futile defense of Wake Island.

Pick was ambivalent about that. Shamefully, perhaps even disgustingly ambivalent. He was sorry that Lieutenant Culhane was dead. He was sorry that Martha Sayre Culhane was a widow. *And glad that she was*.

By the time they came off the course, there was no doubt in Pick Pickering's mind that he was in love. There was simply no other explanation for the way he felt when—however briefly—their eyes had met.

(Two)
Thirtieth Street Station
Philadelphia, Pennsylvania
1820 Hours, 8 January 1942

The weather was simply too cold and nasty for Ernie Sage to wait on the curb outside the Thirtieth Street Station as she had promised.

But she found, inside the station near one of the Market Street doors, a place where she could look out and wait for him. It was hardly more comfortable than the street: Every time the door opened, there was a blast of cold air, and she desperately needed to go to the ladies' room. But she held firmly to her spot; she was afraid she would miss him if she left.

And finally he showed up. Except for the path the wipers had cleared on the windshield, the LaSalle convertible was filthy. The bumper and grill were covered with frozen grime, and slush had packed in the fender wells.

Ernie picked up her bags and ran outside; and she was standing at the curb when he skidded to a stop.

She pulled open the door and threw her bags into the car.

"If they won't let you wait, go around the block," Ernie ordered. Then she ran back inside the Thirtieth Street Station to the ladies' room.

He wasn't there when she went back outside, but he pulled to the curb a moment later, and she got in.

She had planned to kiss him, but he didn't give her a chance. The moment she was inside, he pulled away from the curb. She slid close to him, put her hand under his arm, and nestled her head against his shoulder.

"Hi," she said.

"What's with all the luggage?" McCoy asked, levelly.

"I thought you'd probably be going through Harrisburg," Ernie said. "I thought I would ride that far with you, and then catch a train."

He looked at her for a just a moment, but said nothing.

"I'm lying," Ernie Sage said. "I'm going with you. All the way."

"No you're not," he said flatly.

"I knew that was a mistake," Ernie said. "I should have

waited until we were in the middle of nowhere before I told
you. Somewhere you couldn't put me out."

"You can't come with me," he said.

"Why not? 'Whither thou goest . . .' Book of Ruth."

When there was no reply to that, Ernie said, "I love you."

"You think you love me," he said. "You don't really know a
damn thing about me."

"I thought we'd been through all this," Ernie said, trying to
keep her voice light. "As I recall, the last conclusion you came
to was that I was the best thing that ever happened to you."

"Oh, Jesus Christ!"

"Well, am I or ain't I?" Ernie challenged.

"You ever wondered if . . . what happened . . . is what
this is really all about?"

"You mean," she said, aware that she was frightened, that
she was close to tears, "because we fucked? Because you
copped my cherry?"

"Goddamn it, I hate it when you talk dirty," he said
furiously.

Her mouth ran away with her. "Not always," she said.

He jammed his foot on the brakes, and the LaSalle slid to the
curb.

"Sorry," Ernie said, very softly.

There was something in his eyes that at first she thought was
anger, but after a moment she knew it was pain.

"I love you," Ernie said. "I can't help that."

He was breathing heavily, as if he had been running hard.

Then he put the LaSalle in gear and pulled away from the
curb.

"I was afraid you were going to put me out," Ernie said.

"Do me a favor," McCoy said. "Just shut up."

When she saw a U.S. 422 highway sign, Ernie thought that
maybe she had won, maybe that he even would reach across
the seat for her and take her hand, or put his arm around her
shoulder. U.S. 422 was the Harrisburg highway. If she got that
far, if they spent the night together . . .

In Norristown, ten miles or so past the western outskirts of
Philadelphia, he turned off the highway and pulled into an
Amoco station.

A tall, skinny, pimply-faced young man in a mackinaw and
galoshes came out to the pump. McCoy opened the door and
got out.

"Fill it up with high test," McCoy ordered. "Check the oil. And can you get the crap off the headlights?"

"Yes, sir," the attendant said.

"Dutch around?" McCoy asked.

"Inna station," the attendant said.

McCoy turned and looked through the windshield at Ernie, and then gestured for her to come out.

By the time she had put her feet back in her galoshes, McCoy was at the door of the service station. Ernie ran after him.

There was no one in the room where they had the cash register and displays of oil and Simoniz, but there was a man in the service bay, putting tire chains on a Buick on the lift.

"Whaddasay, Dutch?" McCoy greeted him. "What's up?"

The man looked up, first in impatience, and then with surprised recognition. He smiled, dropped the tire chains on the floor, and walked to McCoy.

"How're ya?" he asked. "Ain't that an officer's uniform?"

"Yeah," McCoy said. "Dutch, say hello to Ernie Sage."

"Hi ya, honey," Dutch said. "Pleased to meetcha."

"Hello," Ernie said.

"How's business?" McCoy asked.

"Jesus! So long as we got gas, it's fine," Dutch said. "But there's already talk about rationing. If that happens, I'll be out on my ass."

"Maybe you could get on with Budd in Philly," McCoy said. "I guess they're hiring."

"Yeah, maybe," Dutch said doubtfully. "Well, I'll think of something. What brings you to town? When'd you get to be an officer?"

"Month or so ago," McCoy said.

"Better dough, I guess?" Dutch asked.

"Yeah, but they make you buy your own meals," McCoy said.

"You didn't say what you're doing in town?"

"Just passing through," McCoy said.

"But you will come by the house? Anne-Marie would be real disappointed if you didn't."

"Just for a minute," McCoy said. "She there?"

"Where else would she be on a miserable fucking night like this?" Dutch asked. Then he remembered his manners. "Sorry, honey," he said to Ernie. "My old lady says I got mouth like a sewer."

Ernie smiled and shook her head, accepting the apology. She had placed Dutch. His old lady, Anne-Marie, was Ken McCoy's sister. Dutch was Ken's brother-in-law.

"Gimme a minute," Dutch said, "to lock up the cash, and then you can follow me to the house."

Anne-Marie and Dutch Schulter and their two small children lived in a row house on North Elm Street, not far from the service station. There were seven brick houses in the row, each fronted with a wooden porch. The one in front of Dutch's house sagged under his and McCoy's and Ernie's weight as they stood there while Anne-Marie came to the door.

She had one child in her arms when she opened the door, and another—with soiled diapers—was hanging on to her skirt. It looked at them with wide and somehow frightened eyes. Anne-Marie was fat, and she had lost some teeth, and she was wearing a dirty man's sweater over her dress, and her feet were in house slippers.

She was not being taken home by Ken McCoy to be shown off, Ernie Sage realized sadly, in the hope that his family would be pleased with his girl. Ken had brought her here to show her his family, sure that she would be shocked and disgusted.

Dutch went quickly into the kitchen and returned with a quart of beer.

Ernie reached for McCoy's hand, but he jerked it away.

To Dutch's embarrassment, Anne-Marie began a litany of complaints about how hard it was to make ends meet with what he could bring home from the service station. And her reaction to Ken's promotion to officer status, Ernie saw, was that it meant for her a possible source of further revenue.

In due course, Anne-Marie invited them to have something to eat—coupled with the caveat that she didn't know what was in the icebox and the implied suggestion that Ken should take them all out for dinner.

"Maybe you'd get to see Pop, if we went out to the Inn," Anne-Marie said.

"What makes you think I'd want to see Pop?" McCoy replied. "No, we gotta go. It's still snowing; they may close the roads."

"Where are you going?" Anne-Marie asked.

"Harrisburg," McCoy said. "Ernie's got to catch a train in Harrisburg."

"Going back to Philly'd be closer," Dutch said.

"Yeah, but I got to go to Harrisburg," McCoy said. He looked at Ernie, for the first time meeting her eyes. "You about ready?"

She smiled and nodded.

When they were back in the LaSalle and headed for Harrisburg, McCoy said, "A long way from Rocky Fields Farm, isn't it?"

A mental image of herself with McCoy in the bed in what her mother called the "Blue Guest Room" of Rocky Fields Farm came into Ernie's mind. The Blue Guest Room was actually an apartment, with a bedroom and sitting room about as large as Anne-Marie and Dutch Schulter's entire house.

And it didn't smell of soiled diapers and cabbage and stale beer.

"When you're trying to sell something, you should use all your arguments," Ernie said.

"What's that supposed to mean?" McCoy asked, confused.

"You asked your sister why she thought you would want to see Pop," Ernie said. "What did that mean?"

"We don't get along," McCoy said, after hesitating.

"Why not?" Ernie asked.

"Does it matter?" McCoy asked.

"Everything you do matters to me," Ernie said.

"My father is a mean sonofabitch," McCoy said. "Leave it at that."

"What about your mother?" Ernie asked.

"She's dead," McCoy said. "I thought I told you that."

"You didn't tell me what she was like," Ernie said.

"She was all right," McCoy said. "Browbeat by the Old Man is all."

"And I know about Brother Tom," Ernie said. "After he was fired by Bethlehem Steel for beating up his foreman, he joined the Marines. Is that all of the skeletons in your closet, or are we on our way to another horror show?"

There was a moment's silence, and then he chuckled. "Anyone ever tell you you're one tough lady?"

"You didn't really think I was going to say how much I liked your sister, did you?"

"I don't know," he said.

"I didn't like her," Ernie said. "There's no excuse for being dirty or having dirty children."

"That the only reason you didn't like her?"

"She was hinting that you should give her money," Ernie said. "She doesn't really like you. She just would like to use you."

"Yeah, she's always been that way," McCoy said. "I guess she gets it from Pop."

"Daughters take after their fathers," Ernie said. "I take after mine. And I think you should know that my father always gets what he goes after."

"Meaning?"

"That we're in luck. Our daughter will take after you."

There was a long moment before McCoy replied. "Ernie, I can't marry you," he said.

"There's a touch of finality to that I don't like at all," Ernie said. "What is it, another skeleton?"

"What?"

She blurted what had popped into her mind: "A wife you forgot to mention?"

He chuckled. "Christ, no," he said.

"Then what?" she asked, as a wave of relief swept through her.

"You've got a job," he said. "A career in advertising. You're going places there. What about that?"

"I'd rather be with you. You know that. And you also know that when it comes down to it, I need you more than I need a career in advertising. . . . And besides, I don't think that's what is bothering you either."

"There's a war on," McCoy said. "I'm going to be in it. It wouldn't be right to marry you."

"That's not it," Ernie said surely.

"No," he said.

"I don't give a damn about your family," Ernie said.

"That's not it, either," he said.

"Then what? What's the reason you are so evasive?"

"I can't tell you," he said. "It's got to do with the Corps."

"What's it got to do with the Corps?" she persisted.

"I can't tell you," he said.

Now, she decided, *he's telling the truth.*

"Military secret?" she asked.

"Something like that," he said.

"*What,* Ken?"

"Goddamnit, I *told* you I can't tell you!" he snapped. "Jesus, Ernie! If I could tell you I would!"

"Okay," she said, finally. "So don't tell me. But for God's sake, at least between here and Harrisburg, at least can I be your girl?"

McCoy reached across the seat and took her hand. She slid across the seat, put his arm around her shoulders, and leaned close against him.

"And when we get to Harrisburg, instead of just putting me on the train, can I be your mistress for one more night?"

"Jesus!" he said. The way he said it, she knew he meant yes.

"I'm not hard to please," Ernie said. "I'll be happy with whatever I can have, whenever I can have it."

(Three)
Room 402
The Penn-Harris Hotel
Harrisburg, Pennsylvania
0815 Hours, 9 January 1942

Second Lieutenant Kenneth J. McCoy, USMCR, was so startled when Miss Ernestine Sage joined him behind the white cotton shower curtain that he slipped and nearly fell down.

"I hope that means you're not used to this sort of thing," Ernie said.

"I didn't mean to wake you," he said.

"I woke up the moment you ever so carefully slipped out of bed," Ernie said. "It took me a little time to work up my courage to join you."

"Oh, Jesus, Ernie, I love you," McCoy said.

"That's good," she said, and then stepped closer to him, wrapped her arms around him, and put her head against his chest. His arms tightened around her, and he kissed the top of her head. She felt his heartbeat against her ear, and then he grew erect.

She put her hand on him and pulled her face back to look up at him.

"Well," she said, "what should we do now, do you think?"

"I suppose we better dry each other off, or the sheets'll get wet," he said.

"To hell with the sheets," she said.

When she came out of the bathroom again twenty minutes later, he was nearly dressed. Everything but his uniform blouse.

When he puts the blouse on, and I put my slip and dress on, she thought, *that will be the end of it. We will close our suitcases, send for the bellboy, have breakfast, and he will put me on the train.*

"Don't look at me," Ernie said. "I'm about to cry, and I look awful when I cry."

She went to her suitcase and turned her back to him and pulled a slip over her head.

"I'm on orders to Fleet Marine Force, Pacific," McCoy said, "for further assignment as a platoon leader with one of the regiments."

She turned to look at him. "I thought you were an intelligence officer," Ernie said.

"Early next month, the Commanding General, Fleet Marine Force, Pacific," McCoy went on in a strange tone of voice, ignoring her question, "will be ordered to form the Second Separate Battalion. It will be given to Lieutenant Colonel Evans F. Carlson—"

"What's a separate battalion?" Ernie interrupted. "Honey, I don't understand these terms. . . ."

"You heard about the English Commandos?" McCoy asked. Ernie nodded. "The Corps's going to have their own. Two battalions of them."

"Oh," Ernie said, somewhat lamely. She was frightened. Her mind's eye was full of newsreels of English Commandos. There were shock troops, sent to fight against impossible odds.

"Colonel Carlson is going to recruit men from Fleet Marine Force, Pacific," McCoy went on. "He has been given authority to take anybody he wants. He's an old China Marine. I'm an old China Marine. He's probably—almost certainly—going to try to recruit me. He is not recruiting married men."

"And that's why you won't marry me?" Ernie said, suddenly furious. "So you can be a commando? And get yourself killed right away? Thanks a lot."

"Carlson's a strange man," McCoy went on, ignoring her again. "He spent some time with the Chinese Communists. There is some scuttlebutt that he's a Communist."

"Scuttlebutt?" Ernie asked.

"Gossip, rumor," McCoy explained. "And there is some more scuttlebutt that he's not playing with a full deck."

Ernie Sage had never heard the expression before, but she

thought it through. Now she was confused. And still angry, she realized, when she heard her tone of voice.

"You're telling me . . . let me get this straight . . . that you're going to volunteer for the Marine commandos, which are going to be under a crazy Communist?"

"You can only volunteer after you're asked," McCoy said. "My first problem is to make sure I'm asked."

"And *then* you can go get yourself killed?"

"I didn't ask for this job," he said.

"What the *hell* are you talking about?"

"Nobody knows for sure whether Carlson is either a Communist or crazy," McCoy said.

"If there seems to be some question, why are they making him a commando?"

"When he was a captain, he was commanding officer of the Marine detachment that guards President Roosevelt at Warm Springs, Georgia. He and the President's son, who is a reserve captain, are good friends."

"Oh," Ernie said. "But what has this got to do with you? Common sense would say, stay away from all of this."

"Somebody has to find out, for sure, if he's crazy, or a Communist, or both," McCoy said.

Ernie suddenly understood. Ken McCoy had told her the military secret he wouldn't talk about in the car. But it was so incredible she needed confirmation.

"And that's you, right?"

He nodded.

"They made up a new service record for me," he said. "It says that after I graduated from Quantico, they assigned me to the Marine Barracks in Philadelphia, where I was a platoon leader in a motor transport company. There's nothing in it about me being assigned to intelligence."

"And this is what you wouldn't tell me yesterday?"

He nodded. "I'm trusting you," he said. "Even Pick doesn't know. I don't know what the hell they would do to me if they found out I told you. Or what Carlson and the nuts around him would do to me if they found out I was there to report on them."

Ernie smiled at him. "So why did you tell me?" she asked, very softly.

"I figured maybe, if you're still crazy enough to want to

drive across the country with me, that is, it would be easier to put you on the train once we get there if you knew."

"That's not the answer I was looking for," Ernie said. "But it's a start."

"What answer were you looking for?" McCoy asked.

"That you love me and trust me," Ernie said.

"That, too," he said.

VIII

VIII

(One)
U.S. Navy Air Station
Pensacola, Florida
9 January 1942

Second Lieutenant Richard J. Stecker, USMC, was an eager-faced, slightly built young man of something less than medium height who looked even younger than his twenty-one years and who was wearing a uniform that looked every bit as fresh off the rack as it in fact was.

It was not surprising, therefore, that the Marine corporal behind the desk at the Marine Detachment, Pensacola Naval Air Station, imagined that he was dealing with your standard candy-ass second john who couldn't find his ass with both hands.

"Yes, sir?" the Marine corporal said, with exaggerated courtesy. "How may I be of assistance to the lieutenant, sir?"

"They sent me over here for billeting, Corporal," Stecker said, and laid a copy of his orders on the desk.

The corporal read the orders, and then looked at Stecker, now more convinced than ever that his original assessment was correct.

"Lieutenant," he said tolerantly, "your orders say that you are to report to Aviation Training. This is the Marine detachment. We only billet permanent party."

"An officer wearing the stripes of a full commander told me to come here," Stecker said. "Do you suppose he didn't know what he was talking about?"

The corporal looked at Stecker in surprise. It was not the sort of self-assured response he expected from a second lieutenant. The tables had been turned on him; *he* was being treated with tolerance.

And then he saw the door swing open again behind the slight, boy-faced second john, and another Marine second lieutenant walked in. Taller, larger, and older-looking than the first one, but still—very obviously—a brand-new second john.

"Excuse me, sir," the corporal said to Stecker, then: "Can I help you, Lieutenant?"

"I was sent here for billeting," Second Lieutenant Malcolm S. Pickering, USMCR, said.

"Be right with you," the corporal said, then left his desk and went into the detachment commander's officer.

"Hello," Pick said to Stecker. "My name is Pickering."

"How are you?" Stecker said, offering his hand. "Dick Stecker."

"Have you been getting the feeling that you, too, are unexpected around here?" Pickering asked. "Or, if expected, unwelcome."

"We are screwing up their system," Stecker said. "I think what's happened—"

He stopped in mid-sentence as the corporal returned with a staff sergeant, who picked up the copy of Stecker's orders and read them carefully. Then he raised his eyes to Pickering, who understood that he was being asked for a copy of his orders. He handed them over.

"You've been over to Aviation Training Reception?" the staff sergeant asked.

"And they sent us here," Stecker said.

"We only billet permanent party here, Lieutenant," the staff sergeant said.

"Far be it from me, a lowly second lieutenant," Stecker said, "aware as I am that there is nothing lower, or dumber, in the Corps, to suggest that either you or the commander who sent me here doesn't know what he's talking about, Sergeant, but that would seem to the case, wouldn't you say?"

Pickering chuckled. Stecker looked at him and winked.

"Just a moment, please, sir," the staff sergeant said, and went back into the detachment commander's office. In a moment, a captain came out.

Pickering and Stecker came to attention. Pickering winced inwardly. He had met the captain before . . . unpleasantly, in the San Carlos Hotel. His name was Carstairs . . . Captain Mustache.

And obviously, from the way the captain looked at him, he remembered the incident, too.

"As you were," the captain said, and picked up the orders and glanced at them.

"The both of you were sent here from Aviation Reception?" the captain asked.

"Yes, sir," Pickering and Stecker said, together.

The captain looked for a number in a small, pamphlet-sized telephone book and dialed it up on the phone.

"Commander," he said, "this is Captain Carstairs at the Marine detachment. I have two second lieutenants here with orders for flight training who tell me that you sent them here for billeting."

Whatever the commander replied, it took most of a minute, after which Captain Carstairs said, "Aye, aye, sir," and hung up. Then he turned to the sergeant. "Put them somewhere, two to a room."

Finally he turned to them.

"Gentlemen," he said, "when you are settled, I would be grateful if you could spare me a few minutes of your valuable time. Say in forty-five minutes?"

"Aye, aye, sir," Stecker said, popping to attention. Pickering was a half second behind in following his lead.

Captain Carstairs walked out of the room.

The sergeant consulted a large board fixed to the wall. When Pickering looked at it, he saw it represented the assignment of rooms in the Bachelor Officers' Quarters.

"Put them in one-eleven-C," the sergeant ordered, and then he walked out of the room.

The corporal took a clipboard from a drawer in his desk and then said, "Please follow me, gentlemen."

They followed him out of the building over to what looked

to be a brand-new, two-story frame barracks building. Inside he led them upstairs and down the corridor, stopping before a door.

He ceremoniously handed each of them a key.

"There is a dollar-and-a-quarter charge if you lose the key," he announced.

He waited for one of them to unlock the door; Stecker was the first to figure out what was expected of him.

Inside they found that the room was not finished; unpainted studs were exposed. Between them could be seen the tar-paper waterproofing and the electrical wiring. The floor was covered with Navy gray linoleum.

Otherwise, the place was furnished with two bunks, two desks, two upholstered armchairs, two side tables, and four lamps, one on each of the desks and side tables. A wash basin with a shelf and mirror shared one wall with a closet. A curtain, rather than a door, covered the closet entrance, but a real door led to a narrow room equipped with a water closet and a stall shower.

The corporal walked around the room, touching each piece of furniture as he announced, "One bunk, with mattress and pillow; one desk, six-drawer; one chair, wood, cloth-upholstered; one table, side, with drawer; and two lamps, reading, with bulb. There are two curtains on the closet, you each sign for one of them."

He handed Stecker the clipboard and a pencil. Stecker signed his name on the receipt for the room's furnishings and handed it back. The corporal then handed the clipboard to Pickering, who did the same.

The corporal nodded curtly at them and left them alone.

"What do you think?" Pickering asked, glancing around the room.

"I think I'm going to find someplace off base to live," Stecker said, "and leave you to wallow in all this luxury all by yourself."

"Can you do that?"

"I think I have figured out what's going on around here," Stecker said.

"Which is?"

"Let me ask you a question first," Stecker replied. "How come you're going to flight school?"

"I applied, and they sent me," Pickering said.

"You get passed over for first lieutenant?"

"Excuse me?"

"You're supposed to have two years' troop duty before they send you to flight school," Stecker said. "If you had two years' service, unless you really fucked up, you'd be a first john."

"I was commissioned just after Thanksgiving," Pickering said.

"I was commissioned second January," Stecker said.

"Last week?"

"Right."

"Quantico?"

"Actually, at West Point," Stecker said.

"I thought West Point graduated in June?"

"Not this year," Stecker said. "They needed second lieutenants, so they commissioned us right after the Christmas leave. Six months early."

"I have no idea what this conversation is all about," Pickering confessed.

"We are discussing how and where we are going to live for the next six months," Stecker said.

"That implies there is an alternative to this," Pickering said, gesturing at the bare studs and the crowded room. "One that we can *legally* take advantage of."

"I think there is," Stecker said. "Would you care to hear my assessment of the situation? I have reconnoitered the area, and carefully evaluated the enemy's probable intentions."

Pickering chuckled again. "You remind me of my buddy at Quantico," he said. "He knew his way around, too. He'd done a hitch as an enlisted man in China before they sent him to the Platoon Leader's course."

"A China Marine," Stecker said. "I did a hitch with the Fourth Marines myself."

"Bullshit," Pickering blurted. "You're not that old."

"I was eleven when we went there," Stecker said, smugly. "I was born in the Corps. My father was the master gunnery sergeant of the Fourth Marines."

"And now he's a captain, right?" Pick demanded, suddenly. "He won the Medal of Honor in the First World War?"

"How'd you know that?" Stecker asked.

"They were sticking it to my buddy when we went through Quantico," Pick said. "*Captain Jack NMI Stecker* showed up like the avenging angel of the Lord, banged heads together, boomed, 'go and sin no more,' and left in a cloud of glory.''

"That sounds like my old man," Stecker said. "He's one hell of a Marine. I'm surprised you know about the Medal, though. He never wears it."

"He wasn't wearing it," Pick said. "But I asked my buddy who he was, and he told me about him."

"How did he find out?"

"I told you, he's another China Marine," Pickering said.

"They stick together," Stecker said. "The Medal got me in the Point. Sons of guys who won it get automatic appointments to service academies if they want one. My brother went to Annapolis, but I was sick of being the little brother following him everywhere, so I went to West Point."

"How come you didn't go in the Army, then?" Pick asked.

"I will consider how recently you have been a Marine, and forgive you for asking that question," Stecker said. "The *Army?*" he added incredulously.

"You said you had reconnoitered the area?" Pickering asked, chuckling.

"Would you like the full report, or just the conclusions I have drawn?" Stecker asked.

"I think I'd better hear the full report," Pickering said. "I don't want to do anything that will get me thrown out of flight school."

"Okay," Stecker said. "It does not behoove a second lieutenant to act impulsively."

Pickering chuckled again. He liked this boy-faced character.

"The lecture begins with a history of Naval aviation," Stecker said solemnly. "Which carries us back to 1911, which was six years before my father joined the Corps, and ten years before I was born."

Pickering was aware that he was giggling.

"The flight school was established here, with two airplanes . . . and if you keep giggling, I will stop—''

"Sorry," Pickering said.

"We career Marines do not like to be giggled at by reservists," Stecker said. "Keep that in mind, Pickering."

Pickering laughed, deep in his throat.

"As I was saying," Stecker said, "flight training has continued here ever since. Pensacola is known as the Mother-in-Law of Naval Aviation."

"I heard that," Pickering said.

"You do keep interrupting, don't you?" Stecker said, in mock indignation.

Pickering threw his hands up in a gesture of surrender.

"Between wars, Pensacola trained three categories of individuals as Naval aviators," Stecker went on, seriously. "Commissioned officers of the Navy and Marines; enlisted men of the Navy and Marines; and Naval aviation cadets."

"Enlisted men? As pilots, you mean?"

"Since the question is germane, I will overlook the interruption," Stecker said. "Yes, enlisted men. There was argument at the highest levels whether or not flying airplanes required the services of splendid, well-educated, young officers such as you and me, Pickering, or whether a lot of money could be saved by having enlisted men drive them. The argument still rages. For your general fund of Naval information, there are a number of Naval aviation pilots—petty officers—in the Navy, and 'flying sergeants' in the Corps. And while we are off on this tangent, most Japanese pilots, and German pilots, and a considerable number of Royal Air Force pilots, are enlisted men."

"I didn't know that," Pickering said.

"Much as I would like to add to your obviously dismally inadequate fund of service lore by discussing the pros and cons of enlisted pilots," Stecker said, "we have to face that salty captain with the mustache in"—he looked at his watch—"thirty-two minutes, and I respectfully suggest you permit me to get on with my orientation lecture."

"Please do," Pickering said, unable to contain a chuckle.

"Marine and Navy officers who applied for flight training had to have two years of service before they could come here. Since promotion to lieutenant junior grade or first lieutenant was automatic after eighteen months of service, this meant that even the junior officer flight student wore a silver bar, and there were some who were full lieutenants—or captains, USMC—and even a rare lieutenant commander or major.

"*Rank hath its privileges,* and it is presumed that anyone with two years of service as a commissioned officer does not need round-the-clock off-duty supervision. Officer flight students are given their training schedule and expected to be at the proper place at the appointed time. What they do when they are off duty is their own business."

"And that includes us?" Pickering asked.

Stecker put his index finger in front of his mouth and said, "Sssh!" Then he went on: "The enlisted flight students are selected from the brightest sailors and Marines in the fleet. They pose virtually no disciplinary problems for Pensacola. And, like the officers, it is not necessary for Pensacola to teach them that a floor is a deck in the Navy, or that patting the admiral's daughter's tail is not considered nice."

A remarkably detailed image of Martha Sayre Culhane's tail popped into Pickering's mind.

"The third category, Naval aviation cadets, is a horse of an entirely different hue. In addition to teaching them how to fly, Pensacola must also teach them what will be expected of them once they graduate and are commissioned. Actually, before they come here, they have been run through an 'elimination program' at a Naval air station somewhere, during which they have been exposed to the customs and traditions of the Naval service, including close-order drill, small-arms training, and things of this nature; and, importantly, they are given enough actual flight training to determine that they were physically and intellectually capable of undergoing the complete pilot training offered at Pensacola."

"As fascinated as I am by your learned discourse," Pickering said, "so what? What has this got to with this cell they've put us in?"

"There *was* a fourth category of students," Stecker said. "Newly commissioned ensigns and second lieutenants. Such as we, Pickering. Since it came down from Mount Sinai graven on stone that ensigns and second lieutenants cannot find their ass with both hands, they were run through courses intended to teach them not to piss in the potted palms at the Officers' Club and otherwise to behave like officers and gentlemen."

" 'Was'?" Pickering asked.

"For a number of reasons, including complaints from the fleet and the Fleet Marine Force that Aviation was grabbing all the nice, bright ensigns and second lieutenants the fleet and the Fleet Marine Force needed, they stopped sending new second lieutenants here. If you want to become a Naval aviator in the future, you will have to start as an aviation cadet, or have completed two years with the fleet or with troops in the Corps."

"But *we're* here," Pickering asked, now genuinely confused.

"That's precisely the point of my lecture," Stecker said. "We have fallen somehow through the cracks; there has been a hole in the sieve. I know why I'm here . . . I qualified for aviation training last fall, before they decided to send no more second lieutenants through Pensacola. My guess is that the word didn't reach the Navy liaison officer at West Point. All he knew was that there was a note on my record jacket that I was to be sent here when I got my commission. And when I got my commission, he cut the orders. But what about you? How'd you manage to get here? You should be running around with an infantry platoon in the boondocks at Quantico, or at Camp Elliott."

Pickering decided it was the time and place to be completely truthful.

"I should be working in the Officers' Club at the Marine Barracks in Washington," he said. "That's where they sent me when I graduated from the Platoon Leader's Course at Quantico."

"Why?" Stecker asked.

"I grew up in the hotel business," Pickering said. "I worked for Foster Hotels. I know how to run a restaurant-bar operation."

"That would seem to be pretty good duty."

"I didn't join the Corps to run a bar for the brass," Pickering said.

"How'd you get out of it? And manage to get yourself sent here?"

"I had some influence," Pickering said. "With a general."

"Which general?" Stecker asked. Pickering sensed disapproval in Stecker; his eyes were no longer smiling.

"McInerney," Pickering said. "Brigadier General McInerney. You know who he is?"

"As a matter of fact, I do," Stecker said. "He and my father were in France together in the First World War. Belleau Wood."

"Then maybe my father knows your father," Pickering said. "That's where my father met McInerney. They were both corporals. McInerney got me assigned as his aide to keep me out of the Officers' Club, and then he sent me down here."

Stecker nodded absently, and Pickering sensed that he was making a decision.

"This is how I see it," Stecker said, finally. "They don't know what to do with us. The easiest thing is what they've done, nothing. Let us go to flight school, which is easier than writing letters to Headquarters, USMC, and asking what to do with us. And since there are probably just the two of us, and one of us is a regular, I don't think they're going to start up a series of 'don't piss in the potted palms' classes just for us. Because it's easier for them, they'll treat us as if we were officers sent here as first lieutenants or captains from the Fleet Marine Force."

"All of which means what?"

"Until somebody tells us we're restricted to post, as officers and gentlemen we can assume we're *not* restricted to the post. And I don't think they're going to appoint somebody to come all the way over here at midnight every night to see if we're in our bunks."

"You mean, we just go tell that corporal 'thanks but no thanks, you can keep your room'?"

"How are you fixed for money?" Stecker asked.

"All right," Pickering replied.

"If we try to check out of the BOQ," Stecker said, "Captain Mustache is likely to think it over and order us to stay here. And if he does that, it's also going to start him thinking about 'don't piss in the potted palms' lectures and sending the OD over to see if we're in bed. The whole Boy Scout routine. You follow my reasoning?"

"Yes," Pickering said.

"We'll just have to forget collecting the allowance in lieu of quarters," Stecker said.

"I understand," Pickering said.

"One other potential problem," Stecker said. "Have you got a car?"

Pickering nodded.

"Well, let's go hear what Captain Mustache has to say. He can blow this whole idea out of the water. But if he says what I think he'll say, I think we can pass the next six months in relative comfort. We started drawing flight pay the moment we reported in . . . why not spend it?"

On the walk back to the Marine detachment office, Stecker saw Pickering's Cadillac convertible.

"How'd you like to have that to use for pussy bait?" he asked.

Pickering smiled, but said nothing about the ownership of the car.

Captain Mustache put them at ease before his desk when they reported to him, but he did not offer them seats.

"I've been on the phone about you two," he said. "What you are are exceptions to the rule, pebbles that shouldn't have dropped through the sieve but did. Both of you should be running around in the boondocks at Quantico with a rifle platoon. But you're here, and it has been decided that it's easier to leave you here."

He's even using the same words that Stecker did, Pickering thought.

"When you are addressed by a superior officer," Captain Mustache said, "it is the custom to acknowledge that by saying something like 'Yes, sir.' That lets the superior officer know you're alive."

"Yes, sir," Pickering and Stecker said.

"There was a price for my curiosity," Captain Mustache said. "I presume you are familiar with the term 'in addition to his other duties'?"

"Yes, sir," Pickering and Stecker said in chorus.

"My primary duty here is as a flight instructor," Captain Mustache said. "In addition to that duty, I am the Marine detachment commander. And as of about twenty minutes ago, in addition to *that* duty, I have been given the responsibility for you two. Someone has to be responsible for your well-being and to answer for it if you misbehave. For example, if you should disturb the peace and tranquillity of Pensacola by getting drunk and having yourselves thrown into jail, I will be the officer who will get you out of jail, prepare court-martial charges, and arrange to have your asses shipped out of here. Do I make my point, or will a more detailed explanation be necessary?"

"Yes, sir," they chorused.

"Which, gentlemen? Do you understand me? Or would you like a more detailed explanation?"

"I understand you, sir," Stecker said.

"You make your point, sir," Pickering said.

"Splendid," Captain Mustache said. "Getting through this course is going to be hard," he went on. "A year ago it was thirteen months. We're going to try in six months to teach you everything that was taught in that course. And what that means is that you'll have to work your asses off. And what that means is that there will be very little time for you to carouse and make whoopee. Do I make my point?"

"Yes, sir," Pickering and Stecker said in chorus.

"Splendid! I will not belabor the point," Captain Mustache said. "Take the rest of the day getting settled. If you have personal automobiles, get them registered. Take a ride around the base and orient yourselves. Report at oh-six-thirty tomorrow at Aviation Reception; the uniform is greens."

"Yes, sir," they chorused.

"That will be all, gentlemen," Captain Mustache said.

"Yes, sir, thank you, sir," the two of them said, did an about-face, and marched out of the room.

"We're home free," Stecker said. "And we have all day to find us someplace decent to live."

"I've already got a place," Pickering said, as he headed toward his car.

"Big enough for the both of us?" Stecker asked.

"Two bedrooms, a living room, a patio," Pickering said.

"On Pensacola's world-famous snow-white beaches, no doubt?"

"Actually, it's on the roof of the San Carlos Hotel," Pick said. "The penthouse."

Stecker's eyebrows rose, but he said nothing. He walked to the Cadillac, bent over, and looked inside.

"And this, it would follow, is yours?"

"Yeah," Pickering said.

"I don't suppose that it's run through your mind that a second lieutenant driving a new Cadillac convertible and living in a penthouse is going to stand out like a syphilitic pecker at a short-arm inspection?" Stecker asked.

"Seven months from now, if I don't kill myself between now and then, I will be living in a tent on some Pacific Island. At that time some people will be trying to kill me. A phrase from classic literature occurs to me: 'Live today, for tomorrow we die.'"

"You're a man after my own heart, Pickering," Stecker said. "Let's go register our cars and then go have a look at our penthouse."

"I told you, I was in the hotel business," Pickering said.

"I've got a deal on the penthouse . . . a professional discount. It doesn't cost as much as you might think."

"I don't give a damn what it costs," Stecker said. "I recently came into some money."

Pickering didn't reply.

Stecker took out his wallet, and from it a folded sheet of paper. He unfolded the paper and handed it to Pickering. It was a short, typewritten note.

Dear Twerp,

If at some time in the future, you should get a large check from Uncle Sam, I would be highly pissed if you did anything foolish with it . . . like putting it in the bank. Drink all the whiskey and screw all the girls while you have the chance.

Love,
Jack.

Pickering read the short note and then looked at Stecker.

"That's from my big brother," Stecker said. "Ensign Jack NMI Stecker, Jr. Annapolis '40. He went down with the *Arizona*."

"I'm sorry," Pickering said, very softly.

"Yeah," Stecker said. "Me, too. He was one of the good guys."

Their eyes met for a moment.

"You did say our penthouse has *two* bedrooms, didn't you?" Stecker asked. "Plus a living room? And a patio? What about a bar?"

"Two bars," Pickering said. "One in the living room, and another one, a wet bar, on the patio."

"I think that's just the sort of thing Jack had in mind," Stecker said.

IX

(One)
Headquarters, 2nd Joint Training Force
Camp Elliott, California
O815 Hours, 9 January 1942

Captain Jack NMI (No Middle Initial) Stecker, USMCR, was a large man, tall and erect. His uniform was perfectly tailored and sharply creased. It bore the insignia of his grade, the double silver bars of a captain, both on the epaulets of the blouse and on his shirt collar. His high-topped dress shoes were highly polished. But there were no ribbons pinned to the breast of the blouse. For what he considered good reason, Captain Stecker had put his ribbons in one of the bellows pockets of his blouse.

Captain Stecker was quite surprised that the technical sergeant functioning as Colonel Lewis T. Harris's sergeant major apparently had no idea who he was. Equally surprising was that he could not recall having ever seen the technical sergeant before.

The technical sergeant wore the diagonal hash marks of sixteen years of satisfactory enlisted service on the sleeve of his blouse. Captain Jack NMI Stecker had worn a Marine uniform since 1917. It bordered on the incredible that they had never run into each other before someplace. The Marine Corps, between major wars, was a small outfit. By the time someone had put in a couple hitches, he knew practically everybody else in the Corps.

There was supposed to be an exception to every rule, Stecker decided, and this was apparently it.

"The colonel will see you now, sir," the technical sergeant said.

"Thank you, Sergeant," Stecker said, and rose up out of his chair. He tugged on the skirt of his blouse and walked to the door with a red sign on it, lettered, "LEWIS T. HARRIS, COL, USMC, COMMANDING."

He rapped his knuckles on the jamb of Colonel Harris's door.

"Come!" Colonel Harris ordered.

Stecker marched into the office, stopped three feet from the desk, came to attention; and, looking six inches over Colonel Harris's head, barked, "Sir, Captain Stecker reporting for duty, sir."

Colonel Lewis T. Harris, a stocky, bald-headed, barrel-chested officer, looked up at Stecker without smiling. Then he stood up, walked to his office door and closed it, and returned to his desk.

"Well, you old sonofabitch, how the hell are you?" Colonel Harris asked.

"Very well, thank you, sir," Captain Stecker said.

"I'm always right, Jack," Colonel Harris said. "Some people don't understand that, but I hope this proves that to you."

"Sir?"

"If you had taken a commission when I wanted you to, you'd be sitting here with a chicken pinned to *your* collar, and I'd be reporting to you."

For the first time, Stecker met Colonel Harris's eyes.

"I'm still a little uncomfortable with the railroad tracks," he said.

"Shit!" Colonel Harris said. "Where the hell are your ribbons, Jack?"

"In my pocket," Stecker said.

"I figured," Colonel Harris said. "The Medal's something

to be ashamed of, like some bare-teated dame in a hula skirt tattooed on your arm?"

"It makes people uncomfortable," Stecker said.

"Suit yourself, Jack, you can stand there at attention like some second lieutenant fresh out of Quantico, or you can sit down over there while I pour you a drink."

Stecker walked to the small couch and sat down.

"I didn't know how to handle this, Lew," he said. "So I did it by the book."

"And that's why you didn't call when you got in last night, right?" Colonel Harris said. "And spent the night on a cot in a BOQ, instead of with Marge and me?"

Captain Stecker did not reply. Colonel Harris went to a metal wall locker and took a bottle of scotch and two glasses from a shelf. He handed the glasses to Stecker and then poured an inch and a half of scotch in each glass.

He took one of the glasses and touched it against Stecker's.

"I'm glad to see you, Jack," he said. "Personally and professionally."

"Thank you," Stecker said. He started to add something, stopped, and then went on: "I was about to say, 'like old times,' but it's not, is it?"

"It never is," Harris said.

They solemnly sipped at the whiskey.

"*I* don't know how to handle this, Jack," Harris said. "I'm sorry about your boy."

"Thank you," Stecker said.

"He passed through here on his way to Pearl," Harris said. "He looked like a fine young man."

"He was," Stecker said. "Sixteenth in his class."

"I didn't hear how it happened," Harris said. "Just that it had."

"He was in the Marine detachment on the *Arizona*," Stecker said. "I understand they got at least one of the Marine-manned antiaircraft cannon into operation before she went down. I hope Jack at least got a chance to shoot back."

"How's Elly?" Colonel Harris said.

Stecker shrugged. There was no way to put the reaction of his wife to the loss of their oldest son into words.

"And the other boy? Richard? He's in the class of 'forty-two at West Point, right?"

"He was supposed to be," Stecker said.

"Supposed to be?" Harris asked.

"They commissioned them early," Stecker said. "Dick reported to Pensacola today. Or he reports tomorrow. For aviation training."

"You don't sound pleased."

"I don't know if I am or not," Stecker said. "Elly's afraid of airplanes."

"Hell, so am I," Harris said.

Stecker looked at him and smiled. "The only thing in the world you're afraid of is your wife," he said.

"And airplanes," Harris said. "I went to Pensacola in 'thirty, when I came back from Haiti. I did fine until they actually put me in the front seat of an airplane and told me to drive. I broke out in a cold sweat and was so scared I couldn't find my ass with both hands. Once I tilted the wings, I really didn't know which way was up. Somewhere in my jacket is a remark that says 'this officer is wholly unsuited for aviation duty.'"

"I didn't know you tried it," Stecker said.

"I was afraid when I went," Harris said. "I knew I was no Charles Lindbergh. But I was a brand-new captain with three kids, and I needed the flight pay. If your boy can't hack it, Jack, he'll find out in a hurry. Nothing to be embarrassed about if he can't. Some people are meant to soar like birds, and others, like you and me, to muck around in the mud."

Stecker chuckled.

"You know Evans Carlson, Jack?" Colonel Harris asked.

The question was asked lightly, but Stecker sensed that Harris was not playing auld lang syne.

"Sure," Stecker replied.

"China?" Harris pursued.

"I was on the rifle team with him," Stecker said.

"I forgot about that," Harris said. "You're one of those who thinks the Garand's the answer to a maiden's prayer."

The U.S. Rifle, Caliber .30, M1, a self-loading weapon fed by an eight-round en bloc clip, was invented by John C. Gerand, a civilian employee of the Springfield Arsenal. It was adopted as standard for the U.S. military in 1937 to replace the U.S. Rifle, Caliber .30, M1903, the Springfield, a bolt-operated rifle with an integral five-shot magazine.

"I don't know about a 'maiden's prayer,'" Stecker said. "But it's a fine weapon. It's a better weapon than the Springfield."

"I'm surprised to hear you say that," Harris said.

"You ever fire it?" Stecker asked.

"Familiarization," Harris said. "I had trouble keeping it on the target. I rarely got close to the black." (The eight, nine, and ten scoring rings of the standard rifle target are printed in black; the "bull's-eye.")

"I was on the troop test at Benning," Stecker said. (The U.S. Army Infantry Center was at Fort Benning, Georgia.) "And I had an issue piece out of the box. I had no trouble making expert with it. More important, neither did twelve kids fresh from Parris Island."

Harris grunted. A lesser man, he thought, would have quickly detected his disapproval of the Garand rifle and deferred, as is appropriate for a captain, to the judgment of a colonel. But Jack NMI Stecker, until recently Master Gunnery Sergeant Stecker, was not a lesser man. He spoke his mind.

"I've got one," Stecker went on, "that was worked over by an Army ordnance sergeant at Benning. It shoots into an inch and a half at two hundred yards."

"I've got a Springfield that'll do that," Harris argued.

"Your Springfield won't put eight shots in the black at three hundred yards as fast as you can pull the trigger," Stecker said.

"You're like a reformed drunk, Jack," Harris said. "Nothing worse than a reformed drunk. They have seen the goddamn light."

"Sorry," Stecker said.

"Maybe I'm wrong," Harris said. "I've been wrong before."

"The last time was May 13, 1937, right?" Stecker said.

Harris laughed, heartily, deep in his chest. "Moot point, anyway," he said. "This war'll be over long before the goddamned Army gets around to giving your wonderful Garand to the Corps."

"Probably," Stecker agreed, chuckling. The Marine Corps received all of its small arms through the Ordnance Corps of the U.S. Army. It was accepted as a fact of life that the Army supplied the Corps only after its own needs, real and perceived, were satisfied.

"We were talking about Evans Carlson," Harris said. "You get along with him all right, Jack?"

"Isn't *that* a moot point? I heard he resigned a couple of years ago. Actually, what I heard is that he was asked to resign. I heard he went Asiatic and annoyed some very important people."

"I don't know about that, but he's back. He applied for a reserve commission as a major, and they gave it to him. And then they promoted him. He knows some very important people."

"I hadn't heard that," Stecker said, thoughtfully. "Well, hell, why not? He's a good Marine. And here I sit wearing captain's bars."

"You didn't answer my question, Jack," Colonel Harris said.

"Do I get along with him? Sure. Is he here?"

Colonel Harris did not reply to the question directly.

"From this point, what I tell you is between us girls, Jack. I don't want it repeated."

"Yes, sir," Stecker said.

"Within the next couple of weeks, maybe the next month, the Corps is going to establish two separate battalions. One of them here. The one here will be commanded by Lieutenant Colonel Carlson."

"What do you mean, separate battalions? To do what?"

"Commando battalions," Harris said.

"I'm lost," Stecker confessed.

"A reserve captain wrote the Commandant a letter," Harris said, "in which he recommended the establishment of Marine units to do what the English Commandos do. Raids by sea on hostile shores."

"A reserve *captain* wrote the Commandant?" Stecker asked, incredulously.

"And the Commandant has decided to go along," Harris said.

Stecker didn't reply, but there was wonderment and disbelief all over his face.

"The captain who wrote the letter has friends in high places," Harris said.

"He must," Stecker said.

"His name is Roosevelt," Colonel Harris said.

"*Captain* Roosevelt," Stecker said, suddenly understanding.

"You know him?"

"I saw him a couple of times at Quantico," Stecker said. "I don't know him."

"Captain James Roosevelt will be the executive officer of the Second Separate Battalion, under Lieutenant Colonel Carlson, when it is activated," Harris said.

Stecker's eyebrow rose but he said nothing.

"I have been directed to do whatever can be done to grease the ways for Colonel Carlson and his separate battalion. He will have the authority to recruit for his battalion anywhere within the Corps. And simultaneously he will be able to transfer out from his battalion anybody he doesn't want. He will have the authority to equip and arm his battalion as he sees fit, and funds will be provided to purchase whatever he wants that can't be found in the warehouse. If there is a conflict between Carlson's battalion and some other unit for equipment, or the use of training facilities, Carlson will get what he thinks he needs. You getting the picture, Jack?"

"Yes, sir."

"Good, because as of this minute, it's your job to take care of Colonel Carlson and his separate battalion for me."

"I had hoped to get a company," Stecker said.

"No way, Jack," Harris said. "Even without Carlson, there would be no company for you. We have company commanders. We're damned short of people like you. Once you get Carlson formed and trained and he's gone from here, I've got a spot from you in S-Three. If you handle Carlson right, there'll probably be a major's leaf to go with it."

"And if not?"

"Carlson has to be handled right, period," Colonel Harris said. "Or you and me will both be doing things we won't like."

Stecker frowned thoughtfully. Finally he said, "Aye, aye, sir."

"There's more, Jack," Colonel Harris said. "And if this goes outside the walls of this room, we're both in trouble."

"I understand," Stecker said.

"Carlson not only wants to have a commando outfit, he has some very strange ideas about how it should be run."

"That I don't understand," Stecker said. "How do you mean, 'run'?"

"Well, for one thing, the original proposal would do away with the rank structure. Instead of officers and noncoms and privates, there would be 'leaders' and 'fighters.' There would be no officers' mess. Everybody would 'cooperate.'"

"You're serious," Stecker said, after a moment. "That's crazy."

"Odd that you should use that word," Harris said, dryly. "There are some very important people who think that Carlson is crazy."

"You mean *really* crazy, don't you?"

Harris nodded. "And the same people think that he may have been turned into a Communist," he added.

"Then why are they giving him a battalion?"

"Because the President of the United States has got a commando bee up his ass, and he thinks Carlson is the man to come up with American commandos," Harris said.

He waited for that to sink in, and then went on: "The Commandant is worried about three things, Jack. First and foremost, that Carlson has gone off the deep end, and after he's picked the cream of the crop for his Raiders, he'll get a bunch of them wiped out on some crazy operation. Or worse: that he'll be successful on a mission, and the entire Corps will be converted to the U.S. Commandos."

"What's wrong with that?" Stecker asked, thoughtfully. "We do what I understand the commandos do, invest hostile enemy shores."

"The British Commandos have neither aviation nor artillery," Harris said. "If the Marine Corps is turned into the U.S. Commandos, there would be no need for the Corps to have either aviation or artillery either. And after the war, Jack? What would the Corps become? A regiment, maybe two, of Commandos."

"I hadn't thought about that," Stecker admitted.

"The Commandant has had this commando idea shoved down his throat," Harris said. "And like the good Marine he is, he has said 'aye, aye, sir,' and will do his best to carry out his orders. There are some other people, close to the Commandant, who are not so sure they should go along with it."

"I don't understand that," Stecker said. "What do you mean, not go along with it?"

"There's some interesting scuttlebutt that Intelligence is going to get an officer assigned to Carlson with the job of coming up with proof that he is a Communist, or crazy, or preferably both. Proof that they could hand the Commandant, proof that he could take to the President."

"Jesus!"

"Jack," Harris said carefully. "If something out of the ordinary, something you believe would be really harmful to the Corps, comes to your attention when you are dealing with Colonel Carlson, I expect you to bring it to my attention. But don't misunderstand me. I want you to do the best job you can in supporting him."

Stecker met his eyes. After a moment, he said, almost sadly, "Aye, aye, sir."

(Two)
The USS Pickerel
178 Degrees 35 Minutes West Longitude
21 Degrees 20 Minutes North Latitude
0405 Hours, 14 January 1942

Captain Edward J. Banning, USMC, awake in his bunk in the captain's cabin of the *Pickerel,* knew that it was a few minutes after 0400. He had heard the sounds of the watch changing, and that happened at percisely 0400.

He also knew that it was Wednesday, 14 January.

Not quite six hours before, the *Pickerel* had crossed the international date line; and Thursday, 15 January, had become Wednesday, 14 January, once again. From 180 degrees (which was both west and east longitude, exactly halfway around the world from Greenwich, England, which was at 0 degrees, east and west longitude), it was 22 degrees and some seconds—say 675 nautical miles—to the U.S. Navy Base at Pearl Harbor, on the Island of Oahu, Territory of Hawaii.

Captain Edward T. Banning, USMC, was aware that there was a very good chance that this Wednesday, 14 January 1942, would be the last day in his life. After a good deal of what he believed was careful, unemotional thought, he had decided that he did not want to continue living if that meant he had to live blind. And after reaching that decision, he had calmly concluded that today was the day he should do what had to be done.

He would remove the bandages from his eyes, open his lids, and if he saw nothing but black, he would use the .45 on himself.

With a little luck and a lot of careful planning, this could be accomplished with a minimum of disruption to anyone else's life. And that was important—not to make a spectacle of himself. It would be much better to go out here and now with a bullet fired through the roof of the mouth into the brain and to be buried immediately at sea than it would be, say, to jump out of a window in a VA hospital somewhere, or to swallow a handfull of pills. A .45 pistol was the answer, and today was the day.

The *Pickerel* was sailing on the surface now, making sixteen or seventeen knots, and it would thus arrive at Pearl Harbor sometime between thirty-nine and forty-two hours from the time it had crossed the international date line.

Captain Banning had done the arithmetic in his head. Not without effort, for without seeming unduly curious, it was necessary to acquire the data on which to base his calculations from Captain Red MacGregor and others. And then he had to do the work in his head. There was plenty of time to do it, of course, which was fortunate, for Banning had learned that he was far less apt with mental arithmetic than he would have believed.

But he was reasonably sure that the *Pickerel* would be off Pearl Harbor waiting for the antisubmarine nets across the mouth of the harbor to be opened sometime between 1900 and 2200 hours on 16 January 1942. In other words, less than two full days from now. The antisubmarine nets would probably not be opened at night, which meant that the *Pickerel* would not actually be able to sail into Pearl until first light on 17 January.

From his observations of Captain Red MacGregor (Banning was aware of the incongruity of a blind man making observations, but he could think of no more accurate word), he had concluded that the closer the *Pickerel* came to Pearl, the more according to the book MacGregor would run his command.

Earlier, after Banning had very carefully asked if it would be possible for the blind men aboard to be given some fresh air, MacGregor had had no problem breaking the rules for him.

This meant allowing them up on the conning tower, where there was really no room for them, and where they would not only be in the way, but would pose a hazard if a crash dive was necessary.

When Banning asked him, shortly after they had entered the Philippine Sea at the upper tip of Luzon, MacGregor had considered the request and denied it.

"A little later, Ed," he said then. "Maybe when we get past the Marianas."

MacGregor had meant what he said. Two days later, when Banning had still been wondering if the time was ripe to ask again, the chief of the boat had come to him, and with rather touching formality said, "The captain's compliments, sir, and will you join him on the bridge?"

Getting up the ladders to the conning tower hadn't been as difficult as Banning had thought it would be.

And the smell of the fresh salt water had been delightful after breathing nothing but the smell of unwashed bodies, paint, and diesel fuel.

Thereafter, the blind men aboard were permitted to get a little air on the conning tower once a day, for half-hour periods. And even though the time they spent on the conning tower cut into the time set aside for that for the crew of the *Pickerel*, there were no complaints. Only a real sonofabitch would deny blind men whatever pleasure they could find.

After this had been going on awhile, Captain Red MacGregor noticed (as Banning hoped that he would; the manipulation shamed him, but he considered it necessary) that Banning himself never came to the conning tower, and he asked him about it.

"I think my 'troops' need it more than I do," Banning said.

MacGregor snorted at the time, but said nothing. At that evening's meal, however, he announced, "Henceforth, Captain Banning has the privilege of the bridge."

What that meant was that Banning could go to the conning tower whenever he wished. He could then ask for permission to "come onto the bridge." If there was no good reason for him not to, permission was more or less automatic.

In practice, others with the "privilege of the bridge" (the officers and chief petty officers) quickly left the bridge to make room for Banning when he put his head through the hatch and asked for permission.

Banning was careful not to abuse his privilege. He went to the conning tower often, but never stayed long. His intent (and he was sure he succeeded) was to make his presence there routine. The officers and crew thus grew used to him coming to the bridge at all hours. And once there he kept out of the way, cleared his lungs, sometimes accepted a cigarette, and then went quickly below again.

Banning was sure, however, that as the *Pickerel* came closer to Pearl, MacGregor would tighten his command, and conning-tower privileges would be revoked. Maybe not for him, but he couldn't take the chance.

Now was the time. Twenty-four hours later the opportunity would more than likely be gone.

Banning's "observation" of Captain Red MacGregor had taught him that MacGregor woke up whenever the watch was changed. Just for a minute or two, but he was awake.

And he had wakened when the watch had changed to 0400. He hadn't moved or gotten out of his bunk, but his breathing pattern had changed, and Banning knew that he was awake and waiting to see if something would require his attention. Only when he was satisfied things were going as they should would he go back to sleep.

Banning had acquired a good deal of admiration for Red MacGregor. He was a fine officer. He hoped that what he had in mind would not appear as a derogatory remark in MacGregor's service jacket. That had been an important consideration while he was making his plans. It was unfortunate that he could not think of anything that would get MacGregor completely off the hook. He could only hope that in the circumstances it would not be a really important black mark against him.

Banning, as stealthily as he could, slipped down from the narrow upper bunk and lowered himself carefully to the deck.

He sensed that he had not been as stealthy as he had hoped, even before MacGregor spoke.

"You all right, Ed?"

"I'm going to take a piss and then get a breath of air," Banning replied, hoping that there was nothing in his voice that would betray him to MacGregor. Banning had "observed" that MacGregor, like most good commanders, was both sensitive and intuitive.

"We crossed the date line just after twenty-two-hundred," MacGregor said. "It's yesterday."

"The chief of the boat told me," Banning replied, as he felt around for the drawer in which he knew he could find freshly washed khakis.

"I had a hell of a time with that at the academy," MacGregor said. "My mind just doesn't accept that you can lose, or gain, a day just because somebody drew a line on a chart."

Banning chuckled.

He heard sounds he interpreted as the kinds MacGregor would make as he rolled over in his bunk.

Banning put on his shirt, and then his trousers, and finally socks and shoes. He did so slowly, both because he wanted to make sure that he had the right button in the right hole, and because he wanted to give MacGregor time to go back to sleep.

When he had finished tieing his shoes, he felt behind him on the bulkhead for the gray metal locker MacGregor had turned over to him. He opened it as quietly as he could and then took from it a khaki-colored rubber-lined canvas foul-weather jacket. Sometimes the wind carried spray as high as the conning tower, even in relatively calm seas.

When he had the jacket on and had finished closing its metal hooks, Banning took something else from his closet where it had been concealed under a stack of skivvy shirts. He jammed it quickly in his waistband, and then pulled the foul-weather jacket down over it.

He went to the hatch and felt his way through it, and then he moved down the passageway to the head. He sensed that two crew members had flattened themselves against the sides of the passageway to make room for him to pass, but neither of them spoke to him.

He found the door to the head, and then the doorknob. He pushed down on it, and it moved. This meant the head was unoccupied. If the head was in use, the door handle would not move.

He went inside and threw the latch, and then sat down on the head. He pulled the foul-weather jacket out of the way, and then took the Colt .45 automatic from his waistband.

Banning had thought this through, too, very carefully, going over it again and again in his mind. If he actually had to do the thing, he had to do it right. That meant very quickly pulling the pistol out from under the jacket and placing the muzzle into his mouth, so that even if someone on the conning tower bridge did happen to be looking in his direction, they wouldn't have time to stop him. He thought that even if someone did happen to be looking at him when he took the Colt out, they would be so astonished that there would be a couple of seconds' delay before they would try to take it away from him. A couple of seconds would be all he needed.

That was presuming there was a cartridge in the chamber when he pulled the trigger. If the firing pin flew forward into an empty chamber, there would be no time to take the pistol out of his mouth and work the action again. If it didn't fire the first time, that would be it. They would take the pistol away from him with whatever force was necessary, and they'd never take their eyes off him until they docked at Pearl. After that he would be turned over to the men in white coats from the psychiatric ward at the Naval hospital.

There weren't that many ways to end your life aboard a submarine at sea. You couldn't just jump over the side, for example. The bulkheads on the conning tower were almost shoulder high and would be difficult to climb over even if you could see. And even if he managed to jump off the conning tower without being stopped, then what? He would probably break his leg on the fall to the deck, or else knock himself out. The best he could hope for in that circumstance would be to be able to scurry across the deck like a crippled crab and bounce off the hull into the sea, then try to swim away from the hull before the suction of the propellers sucked him down to where the blades could slice him up.

It would also be a dirty trick on Red MacGregor to blow his brains all over his cabin. Or to do it in the head where, every time one of the Pickerel's crew took a leak, he would remind himself that this was where that poor, blind jarhead captain blew his brains out.

The place to do it was on the conning tower. His brains would be blown off the conning tower, and there would only be a little blood on the conning-tower deck when the body fell, easily washed away.

After Banning did it, the captain would be called to the bridge. He would probably be thoroughly pissed at the officer of the deck for not seeing what the poor, crazy, blind jarhead captain had been up to, and for not stopping it. But once that passed, MacGregor would start to think clearly, like the good commander he was. There would be no point in getting the crew upset. Then someone would be sent below for a mattress cover and some line, and something heavy (probably a couple of shells for the five-inch cannon), and the body would be tied into the mattress cover with the shells, and then lowered to the deck.

MacGregor would probably even go so far as ordering a flag placed over the mattress cover (it would be tied to the deck so it wouldn't be lost). And more than likely, he would read the Episcopal service for the burial of the dead at sea.

And then he would order the *Pickerel* submerged.

There would be a note in the log, *Captain Edward J. Banning, USMC, buried at sea 0500, 14 January 1942,* and the coordinates.

There was a school of thought, of course, that felt that suicide was the coward's way out of a tough situation. Banning had spent much time pondering that line of reasoning, and he had come to the conclusion that in his case, it just didn't wash.

The main pain in the ass for him in being blind had not turned out to be the inconvenience. The inconveniences—the difficulties of just living without sight: spilling food all over his chin, not knowing if he had been able to properly wipe his ass, the constant bumping painfully into things—he could probably get used to, in time.

What was wrong with being blind was that it gave you so much time to think. That was really driving him crazy.

Thinking about Ludmilla, for instance.

Ludmilla, "Milla," was the only woman he had ever loved in his life. And he had left her on the wharf in Shanghai when he'd been flown to Cavite with the advance party of the 4th Marines. The Japs were in Shanghai now, and it was entirely possible that Milla had already done to herself what he was going to do if it was black when he took the bandages off.

He knew that she had thought about it. Once in bed, she had told him that she had been close to it before she met him, that she just didn't think she had it in her to become a whore, and that death wasn't all that frightening to her. Certainly, she would have thought of that again when the Japanese drove down the Bund. There weren't very many options open to a

White Russian woman in Shanghai besides turning herself into a whore for some Japanese officer. Milla still thought seriously about such things as honor and pride and shame, and she was very likely to have concluded that death was far preferable to the dishonor of being a Japanese whore.

And Milla had been around the block. She'd already gone through one revolution, and what she had told him about what she had experienced in St. Petersburg—the complete breakdown of society as she had known it—couldn't have been much different from what the breakdown of society in Shanghai must have been once the Japanese had come in.

Milla was practical. She would have understood that the chances of her ever again getting to be with her husband of eighteen hours—her American, Marine officer husband, gone off to fight what looked to be a losing war—were practically nil.

And she would have concluded that the eleven good months that they had had together before they had made it legal had been a brief happy interval in a miserable, frightening life.

And she didn't know, of course, that he was blind.

"The trauma to your optical nerves, Captain, is one of those things, I'm afraid, we don't know a hell of a lot about. Obviously, the trauma was of such severity to cause loss of sight, but on the other hand, it isn't as if anything in there had been severed or destroyed, in which case there would be no hope. I really can't offer an opinion whether your impaired condition will in time pass, or whether the damage is permanent. We just don't have the experience in this area. I would not be surprised, either way. In any event, we should have some indication in two or three weeks."

If the sonofabitch thought there was any real chance the "impaired condition" would "in time pass," they would not have sent him out on the *Pickerel*. The 4th Marines had been given the responsibility for defending Fortress Corregidor. They needed the regimental intelligence officer, presuming of course that he could see.

He had been sent out, with the colonel's permission, on the *Pickerel*. Q.E.D.

Banning knew what would come next. They would get him stateside, most likely to the Naval hospital at San Diego. And there they would do whatever was humanly possible for him.

Following which he would be handed a white cane, his retirement orders, and a one-hundred-percent disability pension. They would then turn him over to the Veterans Administration until he learned how to maneuver with the white cane, or maybe with a seeing-eye dog.

He could handle that, too, if he didn't have all this time to think about Milla and wonder what she was doing.

The final conclusion he had drawn was that he could live without Milla, or the Corps, or his sight; but he could not give up all three at once.

If he could see when he went to the conning tower and took the bandage off, then there was something. He wouldn't be with the regiment, but he would be what he had trained all of his adult life to be, a serving Marine officer in a war. Which meant he could do *something* about Milla, too—though he had no idea how.

Banning pressed the checkered round steel magazine-release button on the Colt .45 automatic. The magazine slipped out of the butt into his hand. He laid the pistol carefully on his lap, then thumbed the cartridges from the magazine, putting them one at time into the side pocket of the canvas foul-weather jacket. There were seven.

He loaded one cartridge back into the magazine, slipped the magazine into the pistol until he felt it click in place, and then worked the action. He pulled the slide back all the way, and then, still hanging on to it, let the spring move it forward into the battery.

He didn't think it had completely chambered the cartridge. He ran his thumb over the rear of the pistol where the slide mated with the frame. It was uneven. He pushed on the slide and it clicked into place.

He put the safety on and then stood up and put the pistol back in his waistband and pulled the foul-weather jacket to cover it.

Banning made his way very carefully from the head to the conning-tower ladder. When his hand found it, he gripped it firmly. He had learned that if there was someone on the ladder, there would be vibrations on the steel framework.

There were none, and he climbed the ladder into the upper compartment.

"Good morning, sir," someone said to him.

"Morning," Banning replied, smiling, as he felt for the ladder to the conning-tower bridge.

This time, there were vibrations in the steel frame. Banning stood to one side of the ladder.

"Sorry, Captain," a voice tinged with embarrassment said in his ear. "I would have—" The kid's breath smelled of peppermint chewing gum.

"It's all right, son," Banning said, reassuringly. He had recognized the voice as one of the enlisted men.

He moved in front of the ladder and went up it, until his head was through the hatch and he could smell the fresh salt air.

"Permission to come on the bridge, sir?" he asked.

"Come ahead, Captain," a voice he recognized as belonging to one of the young JG's said.

Banning went through the hatch, got to his feet, and put his hand out in search of the after bulkhead. When his fingers touched it, he went to it, turned and rested his back against it, and took a deep breath of the fresh, clean air.

"Good morning," Banning said.

Three voices replied. They were in front of him. With a little bit of luck, they would be looking forward, too, when the time came.

Banning took off his fore-and-aft cap and put it in the pocket of his foul-weather jacket.

Then he took a razor blade from his trousers pocket, got a good grip on it, and moved the hand that held it to the back of his head.

Sawing through the gauze bandage and the adhesive tape that held it in place was easier than he thought it would be. He felt the gauze slip off and fall across his face. He caught it, balled it up in his hand, and then reached his hand over the bulkhead and dropped it.

There now remained two pads of gauze, liberally greased with petroleum jelly, over his closed eyelids. The idea, the surgeon had told him, was to keep all light from the optic nerves, in the hope this might facilitate natural recovery from the trauma to the nerves.

Once a day the *Pickerel*'s pharmacist mate had replaced the Vaseline-soaked pads, and then wrapped Banning's head with gauze and adhesive tape to keep them in place.

Banning put both hands to his eyes and jerked the pads away.

He felt a cold chill and heard himself grunt.

The pads were gone, and there was no light.

He was blind.

He felt faint, weak in his knees, and shivered.

All I have to do is put my hands over my face and go below and say I must have caught the bandage on something, and jerked it off.

Fuck it! Don't turn chicken at the last minute. You took a chance and you lost.

He put his hand under the foul-weather jacket and found the butt of the .45 Colt automatic. Following the U.S. Marine Corps' near-sacred tradition that one does not put one's finger on the trigger of a loaded firearm until one is prepared to fire, he took it in his hand, the trigger finger extended along the slide rather than on the trigger, and flicked the safety off.

Then he put his finger on the trigger.

Our Father Who art in Heaven, give me the balls to go through with this . . .

Banning became aware that his eyelids were squinted closed, as they were habitually whenever the Vaseline-soaked pads were removed.

He forced them open.

Shit! Nothing. Nothing more, anyway, than a glow to one side. If I'm not blind, I'm the next fucking thing to it.

Our Father Who art in—

That's the fucking luminous dial of a wristwatch! That's what that glow is!

Captain Banning removed his finger from the trigger of his pistol.

Captain Banning could now make out the upper edge of the forward bulkhead, and rising above that three vague but unmistakable silhouettes: the officer of the deck, the talker, and somebody else, another officer, with binoculars to his eyes.

Captain Banning snapped the safety of the Colt back on, took his hand from under the foul-weather jacket, and then leaned, weak and faint, against the bulkhead.

He had a sudden terrible necessity to void his bladder.

"Permission to leave the bridge, sir?"

"Granted," the officer of the deck said automatically, and then, remembering that Banning had only minutes before come onto the bridge, asked, "Is there something wrong, Captain Banning?"

"No, thank you," Banning said. "Everything's just fine."

The light inside the conning tower hurt his eyes. He felt tears, and he closed them. He knew how to get down the ladder with his eyes closed.

With a little luck, he would go down both ladders and get to the head before his bladder let go and he pissed his pants. And then he would go to the captain's cabin and wake Red MacGregor and tell him. With a little more luck, he would be able to get the pistol back into the cabinet before MacGregor woke up.

X

San Francisco, California
0915 Hours, 14 January 1942

The office of the chairman of the board of Pacific & Far East Shipping, Inc., occupied the southwest corner of the top (tenth) floor of the P&FE Building. Its tinted plate-glass windows overlooked the harbor and the bridge; and an eight-by-twelve-foot map of the world was mounted on one wall. Every morning at six A.M., just before he went off duty, the night operations manager came up from the third floor and laid a copy of the more important overnight communications on the huge, near-antique (which is to say post-1800) mahogany desk of the chairman of the board. Then he went to the map and moved small devices on it.

The devices, mounted on magnets, were models of the vessels of Pacific & Far East Shipping. They represented tankers, bulk carriers, passenger liners, and freighters of all sizes. There were seventy-two of them, and they were arranged on the map to correspond with their last-reported position around the world. Just over a month before, there had been eighty-one ship models scattered around the map.

Now nine models—representing six small interisland freighters ranging in size from 11,600 to 23,500 tons, two identical 39,400-ton freighters, and one 35,500-ton tanker—were arranged in the lower left-hand corner of the map as if anchored together in the Indian Ocean off Australia. Eight of them had been lost to Japanese submarines. The ninth, the tanker *Pacific Virtue*, had been offloading aviation gasoline at Pearl Harbor when the Japanese struck.

In a mahogany gimbal mount near Fleming Pickering's desk, there was a globe, five feet in diameter, crafted in the 1860s. And two glass cases holding large, exquisitely detailed ship models had been placed against the wall behind the desk. One of the models was of the clipper ship *Pacific Princess* (Hezikiah Fleming, Master), which had held the San Francisco–Shanghai speed record in her day; and the second was of the 51,000-ton *Pacific Princess*, a sleek passenger ship that was the present speed-record holder for the same run.

According to the wall map, the *Pacific Princess* was sailing alone somewhere between Brisbane and San Francisco, trusting in her maximum speed of 33.5 knots to escape Japanese torpedos.

Fleming Pickering looked up from his desk with mingled annoyance and curiosity when he heard the sound of high heels on the small patches of parquet floor exposed here and there beneath fine antique (seventeenth-century) Oriental rugs. He knew it was not his secretary, the only person permitted to come into his office unannounced when he was there. Mrs. Florian wore rubber heels. All the facts considered, his visitor had to be either his wife or a very brazen total stranger.

It was his wife.

After twenty-four years of marriage, Fleming Pickering was still of the belief that he was married to one of the world's most beautiful women. And she was one of the smartest, too. Smart enough to avoid waging a losing battle against growing older than thirty. Her hair was silver, and if she was wearing makeup (which seemed likely), it didn't appear to be layered on her face with a shovel.

She sat down in one of the chairs facing his desk and crossed her legs, giving him a quick glance of thigh and black petticoat.

"'Come into my parlor,' the spider leered at the fly," Fleming Pickering said. "To what do I owe the honor?"

"God!" Patricia Foster Pickering groaned.

"Really?" Flem Pickering joked. "The clouds opened, and a suitably divine voice boomed, *'Go to thy husband!'?"*

She shook her head, but had to chuckle, even though she didn't want to under the circumstances.

"I hate to bother you," Patricia Pickering said. "You know I wouldn't come here unless—"

"Don't be silly," he said. "Would you like some coffee?"

"I would really like a double martini," she said.

"That bad, huh?" he said.

"I'll settle for the coffee," Patricia Pickering said.

Fleming Pickering tapped three times with his toe on a switch under his desk. It was a code message to Mrs. Florian. One tap summoned her. Two taps meant *"get this idiot out of here by whatever means necessary,"* and three meant *"deliver coffee."*

"I just had a call from Ernie Sage," Patricia Pickering said.

"And? What did he want?"

"Little Ernie," she corrected him.

"And what did *she* want?"

"She's out here. In San Diego."

He looked at her curiously, waiting for her to go on.

"She wanted me to get a check cashed for her," Patricia said. "And to see if I knew someone in Diego who could find her someplace to stay."

"I hate to tell you this, honey," he said. "But the way you're presenting this, it's not coming across as a serious problem."

"She's out here with McCoy," Patricia said. "You remember him? Pick's friend from Quantico? You met him?"

"I remember him very well," Flem said. "What did they do, elope?"

"That's part of the problem," she said. "No. They are not married."

"A real Marine, that boy," Flem said. "I could tell the moment I saw him."

"Flem, this is not funny," Patricia said.

"Well, it's not the end of the world, either," he said. "She is not the first nice young woman in history to go to bed with a Marine before their union was solemnized before God and the world."

She glared at him. And her face colored. "That was a cheap shot, damn you!" she said. But she smiled.

"There's something about a Marine, you know," Flem Pickering went on. "My response to this situation is that I hope whatever it is Marines have will work for Pick, too. That he gets somebody as nice as Ernie. Let her who is without sin cast the first stone."

"Well, thanks a lot," she snapped.

"Honey, this is none of our business," Flem said.

Mrs. Florian came into the office, pushing a serving cart with a silver coffee service on it.

"I like your dress, Mrs. Pickering," she said.

"I will not tell you it's an old rag I found in the back of my closet," Patricia said. "I bought it yesterday, and made them alter it right away. Surprising absolutely no one, Guess Who hasn't seemed to notice."

"The way to catch my attention is to come in here not wearing a dress," Flem said.

"I'd sock him for that," Mrs. Florian said, and left the office.

"It *is* our business, Flem," Patricia said.

"How do you figure that?"

"Elaine is my best friend," Patricia said. "And Ernie's the closest thing I have to a daughter."

"Does Elaine know about this?" he asked.

"No. I asked Ernie, and she told me she was going to call her. And she went on to ask me to please not say anything until she works up the courage to do it."

"Then don't say anything," he said.

"I think I'm going to go to Diego and talk like a Dutch aunt to her," Patricia said.

"All that would do would be to piss her off," Flem said.

"I love your language," Patricia snapped.

"It caught your attention, didn't it?" he replied, unrepentant.

She met his eyes, raised her eyebrows, and then shifted her gaze and sat up in the chair to pour coffee. She handed him a cup and then slumped back in her chair, holding her cup with both hands.

"I think it's entirely possible that Ernie may need a friend," Flem said. "If she thinks you're going to say exactly the same thing her mother would say, she won't come to you."

She looked at him again but said nothing.

"I seem to recall when I was a handsome young Marine just home from France, that your own mother had a long talk with you about not letting me get you alone—in case I tried to kiss you. I gather she was afraid I'd give you trench mouth."

"I never should have told you that," Patricia said.

"You remember where you told me?" he asked.

"Damn you!" she said.

"In a ne'er-to-be-forgotten bed in the Coronado Beach Hotel in San Diego."

"All right," she said, just a little sharply.

"Never did get trench mouth, did you?" he asked. "And neither will Ernie. And you can no more talk her out of what she has decided to do than your mother could talk you out of seducing me."

"You bastard!" she said. "*Me* seducing you!"

But their eyes met and she smiled.

"So what do we do, Flem?" she asked after a moment.

"That will depend on what you've already done," he said.

"I told her to go to the San Diego office, and we'd arrange for her to cash a check."

"That's all?"

"That's all," she said.

Fleming Pickering picked up one of the three telephones on his desk and told the operator to patch him through to San Diego.

When J. Charles Ansley, General Manager, San Diego Operations, Pacific & Far East Shipping, Inc., came on the line, Fleming Pickering told him that a Miss Ernestine Sage was on her way to see him. She needed a check cashed. He should cash it; and then he should arrange something with the Bank of America branch in San Diego so that she could cash checks whenever she wanted in the future.

"The second thing I need from you, Charley," Fleming Pickering went on, "is to find someplace for her to live. A little house, preferably on the beach, or at least with a view of it."

"Jesus, Flem," the general manager protested. "That's going to be hard. This town is full of sailors and Marines, and most of them, the officers anyway, brought their wives and their families."

"A little house on the beach, or with a view of it, and someplace where the lady can entertain an overnight guest on a regular basis without any embarrassing questions being asked."

"It's a good thing I know you're a straight arrow, Flem," the general manager said. "Or otherwise—"

"The young lady, you dirty-minded old man, you, is the closest thing Patricia and I have to a daughter. She is visiting a young Marine officer. I don't know for how long."

"It's going to be hard finding a place."

"Do whatever has to be done, Charley," Fleming Pickering said. "And with your well-known tact and finesse. And get back to me."

When he put the phone back in its cradle, he looked at his wife. She was sitting back in the chair, tapping the balls of her extended fingers together.

"Done," he said.

"I hope we know what we are doing," Patricia Pickering said.

"Me, too," he said.

She shrugged and rose out of the chair.

"Where are you going to be at, say, one?"

"Here, probably," he said.

"I've got a few things to do," she said. "After which I thought I would drop by the apartment. Say about one?"

"Oh," he said.

"I would hate to drag you away from something important," she said.

He picked up another of the telephones on his desk.

"Mrs. Florian," he said. "If I have anything scheduled between one and three, reschedule it."

He put the phone back in its cradle.

"There was a time," Patricia Pickering said, "when you would have taken the whole afternoon off."

"I can always call back," he said.

"Braggart," Patricia Pickering said, and went through the door.

(Two)
Pensacola Navy Air Station
18 January 1942

If they are asked, aviators will tell you there is no such thing as a "natural" or "born" pilot. The human animal, they will explain, is designed to move back and forth and sideways with one foot planted on something firm. But aircraft move in a medium that is more like an ocean than solid ground; and they move more like a fish swimming than a man walking. Controlling an aircraft, consequently, does not come naturally; a pilot has to be *taught* how to move around in the sea of air.

Aviators will also modestly point out that while it is not really much more difficult than riding a bicycle, flying requires a certain degree of hand-eye coordination. And this must be taught and learned. It is for instance often necessary for one hand to do one thing, while the other does something else. And meanwhile, the feet might be doing still another thing.

Making a climbing turn, for example, requires both rearward and sideward pressure on the control stick (or as the originally scatological term, now grown respectable, has it, the "joystick") between the legs, while the feet apply the appropriate pressure to the rudder pedals. And while he makes these movements, the pilot's eyes must take into consideration where the aircraft is relative to the horizon; and at the same time he must monitor the airspeed, vertical speed, and all the gauges indicating engine function and condition.

Almost without exception, pilots will relate that the first time they were given the controls by their instructor pilot (IP), they were all over the sky.

They will often add by way of explanation that fledgling birdmen usually "overcontrol," which is to say that they apply far more pressure to the controls than should be applied. What results is that the plane goes into a steep dive, or a steep climb, or veers sharply off to one side or the other. . . . It goes all over the sky.

This condition is made worse by the fledgling birdman's lack of experience operating with his body on its side, and/or tipped steeply upward or downward.

One's first flight at the controls, aviators will all agree, is a traumatic experience. But over a period of time—long or short, depending almost always on the skill of the instructor pilot—those student pilots who ultimately make it (there are many who simply cannot learn) gradually pick up the finesse that permits them to smoothly control their aircraft. And their bodies. They no longer are quite so dizzy, or disoriented, or nauseous.

Like riding a bicycle, aviators will affirm, piloting an aircraft is something you have to be *taught* to do—*always* under the watchful eye of a skilled instructor pilot. The way you learn to do it well is with a great deal of practice, slowly growing a little better.

And then, after they have gone through all this explanation, a puzzled look will very often come onto their faces, and there will be a caveat:

"Yeah, but I remember a guy at Pensacola [or Randolph Field, or wherever] *. . . the IP just didn't believe him. He thought he'd come to basic with at least a couple of hundred hours and was being a smart ass . . . who just got in the sonofabitch and could fly it like he really had three, four hundred hours in it. No problem at all, not even when the IP did his best to disorient him. Looped it, whatever. When he gave him the controls, he just straightened it out. And he knew where he was.*

"Just that one guy, though. Little [or Great big, or Perfectly ordinary] *guy. I forget his name. But he just knew how to fly. All they had to do was explain to him what the propeller was doing, spinning around like that."*

Captain James L. Carstairs, USMC, had heard all the stories himself, of course, about that one character in ten thousand—or a hundred thousand—whom Mother Nature in her infinite wisdom had elected to equip naturally with a feeling for the air that others could acquire only after much time and great effort.

But until he took Second Lieutenant Malcolm S. Pickering, USMC, up for his orientation flight in an N2S[1] he had never personally met one.

Captain Carstairs had been annoyed, but not surprised, when he learned from the records of Lieutenants Pickering and Stecker that neither had been afforded the opportunity of an "orientation flight" before they had been ordered to Pensacola.

The "orientation flight" was something of a misnomer. It was designed primarily to disqualify would-be Naval aviators from the training program. If the SOP (Standing Operating Procedure) had been followed, the two second johns whom a cruel fate had placed in his hands would have been given their "orientation flights" before they came to Pensacola. And

---

[1] The Stearman N2S, an open, twin-cockpit training biplane, painted yellow for visibility, was officially called the 'Cadet.' But like the other basic training aircraft, the Navy-manufactured N3N, it was rarely called anything but the "Yellow Peril."

they'd have passed them; otherwise they would not have been sent to Pensacola at all.

It made much more sense to take would-be birdmen up for a ride—a ride in which the IP would do his very best to frighten and/or sicken his passenger—to determine before the kid was actually sent to Pensacola that he *really* wanted to be a pilot and was physically able to endure the physical and mental stresses of flight. They would thus eliminate before they began training those who had second thoughts about becoming aviators, or who proved unfit for flight. In that way time and money were saved.

His two second johns had slipped through that hole in the sieve, too. Neither of them should have been sent to Pensacola in the first place, so it made a certain perverted sense that they had been sent without having taken the required orientation flight. Captain Carstairs realized there were two ways the omission could be rectified. He could write a memorandum outlining the facts and requesting that the two officers named above be scheduled for an orientation flight. He could then have a clerk type it up and send it over to Mainside and let it work its way through the bureaucracy. This would take at least a week, and probably two. Or he could load his second johns in his Pontiac coupe and drive them to Saufley Field right then and take them for a ride in a Yellow Peril himself.

Second Lieutenant Stecker went first. Captain Carstairs loaded him into the backseat, carefully adjusted his mirror so that he could see Stecker's face, and then took off. He left the traffic pattern at Saufley and flew up to U.S. 98 in the vicinity of the Florida-Alabama border. There, climbing to eight thousand feet, he put the Yellow Peril through various aerobatic maneuvers, frequently glancing in his mirror to examine the effect on Second Lieutenant Stecker.

Stecker was a picture of grim determination. From time to time, his face grew deathly pale, and he frequently swallowed and licked his lips. He otherwise stared grimly ahead, as if afraid of what he would see if he looked over the side of the cockpit.

But he neither closed his eyes to shut out the horror, nor did he get sick to his stomach. Just about the reaction he expected, Captain Carstairs realized when he thought about it. Stecker was young and in superb physical condition. And, significantly, he was a West Pointer. Himself an Annapolis graduate,

Carstairs was willing to grant that the U.S. Military Academy probably did nearly as a good a job as the U.S. Naval Academy to instill self-discipline in its students. That meant that by pure willpower, Stecker was able to keep his eyes open and stop himself from being sick.

Forty minutes into the flight, after just about half an hour of violent aerobatics, Captain Carstairs put the Yellow Peril into straight and level flight. He then conveyed via the speaker tube that Second Lieutenant Stecker was to put his feet on the rudder pedals and his hand on the joystick and "follow through" as Carstairs maneuvered the airplane, so that he would acquire some sense of what control motions were required to go up and down and side to side.

Second Lieutenant Stecker's orientation flight lasted one minute less than an hour. When Carstairs taxied the Yellow Peril to the place where Second Lieutenant Pickering was waiting for his turn, he saw that Pickering was eating.

Enterprising merchants from Pensacola had been given permission to roam the edges of the parking aprons at Saufley, Correy, and Chevalier fields, selling box lunches to civilian mechanics and service personnel. Pickering had obviously bought himself a snack.

When he came closer, Captain Carstairs saw that what Pickering was eating an oyster loaf. This consisted of maybe eight fried-in-batter oysters in a highly Tabasco-flavored barbecue sauce on a long, soft roll. It was not the sort of thing someone about to experience violent aerobatic maneuvers in an airplane should put in his stomach. And Pickering, he saw, was about to make a bad situation worse. He was washing the oyster loaf down with a pint bottle of chocolate milk.

There was no question whatever in Captain Carstairs's mind that Second Lieutenant Pickering was going to throw up all over the Yellow Peril. But there was a silver lining in that black cloud, Carstairs decided. For one thing, the student rode aft of the instructor. None of what erupted from Pickering's stomach would reach Carstairs.

Getting sick, moreover, would teach Pickering the important lesson that an aviator must consider what he eats or drinks before flight. And cleaning up what he threw up from the aircraft would serve two additional purposes. It would emphasize the importance of lesson one, and it would serve as a test of Pickering's determination to become a Naval aviator.

"If you have finished your snack, Pickering, get in," Captain Carstairs said.

Second Lieutenant Pickering stuffed the rest of his oyster loaf in his mouth, then washed it down with the rest of his chocolate milk, after which he climbed into the rear seat of the Yellow Peril.

Captain Carstairs flew the same course he had flown with Stecker. And once he was near the Florida-Alabama border, to start things off, he rocked the Yellow Peril from side to side. In his mirror, he saw Lieutenant Pickering's eyebrows raise in surprised delight.

Next Carstairs pulled back on the joystick and put the Yellow Peril in a climb. Eventually inertia overcame velocity and the airspeed fell below that necessary to provide lift. The Yellow Peril stalled, which is to say, it suddenly started falling toward the earth.

In his mirror, Captain Carstairs saw that Pickering's face now reflected happy surprise at this new sensation.

Carstairs recovered from the stall by pushing the nose forward until sufficient airspeed had been regained to permit flight. He pulled it straight and level for a moment, and then peeled off into a steep dive to the left.

Pickering's stomach was stronger than Carstairs would have believed. But there would be an eruption soon, either when he pulled out of the dive, or when he rolled the Yellow Peril: The aircraft would turn upside down as he reached the apex of his climbing maneuver.

When, in inverted flight, Captain Carstairs looked in his mirror at his passenger, his passenger's face bore the enchanted look of a little boy finding an unexpected wealth of presents under the Christmas tree. He was smiling from ear to ear and gazing in pure, excited rapture all around this strange and wonderful inverted world he was seeing for the first time.

An additional fifteen minutes of intricate aerobatics not only failed to make Second Lieutenant Pickering sick to his stomach, but it failed to wipe the smile of joyous discovery off his face. Indeed, if possible, each more exotic maneuver seemed to widen proportionally his ecstatic grin of delight.

Captain Carstairs was willing to admit that he was capable of making an error in judgment, and fair was fair. He put the Yellow Peril into straight and level flight and conveyed the order that Pickering was to follow him through on the controls. In a moment he felt a slight resistance to both joystick and rudder movement. This told him that Pickering had his feet on the pedals and his hand on the joystick.

. Carstairs moved the aircraft up and down, and from side to side, and then made a sweeping turn. Then his own very sensitive hand on the controls told him that Pickering had let go of the controls. There was no longer any resistance when he moved them.

The arrogant sonofabitch is bored; he's taken his hands off the controls. He thinks I'm up here to take him for a ride!

He set the Yellow Peril up in a steep climbing turn to the left, and then took his own feet off the rudder pedals and his hand off the joystick.

The Yellow Peril would continue in the attitude that he had placed it in until it ran out of airspeed, whereupon it would stall. And since it would be moving leftward when it stalled, it would not fall straight through, but would slide in a sickening skid to the left. With just a little bit of luck, it would enter a spin.

That would catch Second Lieutenant Pickering's attention.

He watched the airspeed indicator as it moved downward toward stall speed, so that he would be prepared. And he frequently glanced at Second Lieutenant Pickering's face for the first glimmer of concern. This would be shortly followed by bewilderment, and then terror.

When the airspeed indicator needle showed about five miles above stall speed, Captain Carstairs sensed first that the angle of climb was diminishing, and then that the aircraft was coming out of its turn. He looked at the joystick between his legs. It was moving. And when he looked at the rudder pedals, so were they.

In a moment, the airspeed indicator began to rise again, and shortly after it did that, the control stick moved again, returning the aircraft to its turn and to a climbing attitude. But in a more shallow climb than before, one that it could maintain more or less indefinitely.

This wiseass sonofabitch is a pilot, and not too bad a pilot. That was the natural, practiced reflex action of somebody who feels in the seat of his pants that he's about to stall. He did what had to be done to recover.

Captain Carstairs put his mouth to the speaking tube. "Okay, Pickering, take us back to the field and land it," he ordered.

For the first time, a look of confusion and concern appeared on Second Lieutenant Pickering's face.

"When I give you a command, you say 'Aye, aye, sir,' " Carstairs ordered.

"Aye, aye, sir," Lieutenant Pickering responded.

The Yellow Peril entered a 180-degree turn.

Steep, Carstairs thought, *but smooth.*

Ten minutes later, after an arrow-straight flight, the traffic pattern over Saufley Field came into view. Eight or nine other Yellow Perils were waiting their turn to make their approach to the runway.

"Sir," Pickering's voice came over the tube to Carstairs's ears, "what do I do now?"

"Sit it down, Pickering."

There was a moment's pause, then, "Aye, aye, sir."

Pickering moved the Yellow Peril to a position behind the last Yellow Peril in the stack.

Carstairs finally found something to fault in Pickering's flying technique. They were a little too close to the Yellow Peril before them before Pickering retarded the throttle.

And then it was their turn to land.

"Sir," Pickering's voice came over the tube, "I've never landed an airplane before."

"Do the best you can, Lieutenant," Carstairs replied.

Pickering aimed the Yellow Peril at the runway.

When he was over the threshold, he chopped the throttle and skewed the Yellow Peril from side to side as he tried to line it up with the runway.

Carstairs made a quick decision. While it was entirely possible that Pickering was going to be able to get it safely on the ground the way he was doing it, he was coming in way too high.

"I've got it," Carstairs said over the speaking tube. He shoved the throttle forward and put his hands and feet on the controls, and they went around.

Carstairs put the Yellow Peril at the tail of the stack of Yellow Perils, and then spoke again.

"The way this is supposed to be done," he said, "is that you run out of lift the moment you level the wings. We like you to do that about ten feet off the runway, not one hundred."

Pickering shook his head to signal his understanding.

On his next attempt to land, Pickering greased the Yellow Peril in two hundred feet from the threshold. The Yellow

Peril's main gear touched, and then a moment later, it settled gently onto its tail wheel.

And then, for the first time, there was terror in Pickering's voice. "I can't see to steer!"

"I've got it," Captain Carstairs responded. He braked, turned onto a taxiway, and taxied the Yellow Peril back to where Second Lieutenant Stecker waited for them.

Captain Carstairs hoisted himself out of his cockpit ahead of Pickering, and then he stood on the wing root in a position where he could look directly into Second Lieutenant Pickering's face.

"Am I to believe, Pickering, that this has been your first opportunity to attempt to fly aircraft?"

"Yes, sir," Pickering said. "Captain, I realize I screwed up. But I really think I can learn how to do it."

Carstairs looked directly into Pickering's eyes for a long moment before he spoke.

"Actually, Pickering, you didn't do too badly," he said, and a smile of relief appeared on Pickering's face. "I would, in fact, go so far as to say I saw a suggestion—faint, but a suggestion—that you may have a natural talent for flying."

The smile of relief turned into one of joy.

"Thank you, sir."

"You're going to have to work a little harder than your friend Stecker," Captain Carstairs said. "But if you apply yourself, there's really no reason why you can't get through the course."

"Thank you, sir," Pickering said, absolutely seriously. "I'll really try to do my best, sir."

Carstairs nodded at Pickering and then jumped off the wing root.

Second Lieutenant Malcolm Pickering surprised Captain James L. Carstairs a second time that same day.

At half-past six, Captain Carstairs was at the bar of the San Carlos Hotel in the company of Captain and Mrs. Lowell B. Howard, USMC, and Mrs. Martha Sayre Culhane. They were waiting for a table in the dining room; they had reserved a table for eight.

There were two empty stools beside them at the bar.

Second Lieutenant Pickering, trailed by Second Lieutenant Stecker, obviously freshly showered and shaved, crossed the room to them.

"Good evening, sir," Pickering said.

"Pickering."

"Sir, are these stools occupied?"

"No. Help yourself. We're about to leave."

"Thank you, sir," Pickering said. "Hello, Martha."

"Hello, Pick," Martha Sayre Culhane said.

"May I present Lieutenant Dick Stecker?" Pickering said.

"Hello," Martha Sayre Culhane said, and gave him her hand.

"I'm a little surprised that you know Mrs. Culhane, Pickering," Captain Carstairs said.

"My mother introduced us on the golf course," Martha said.

Captain and Mrs. Howard were introduced.

"You two here to have dinner?" Carstairs asked, to make conversation.

"Yes, sir," Pickering said.

The headwaiter appeared, and beckoned to Carstairs.

"There's our table," Carstairs said. And then he gave in to a generous impulse. "Listen, we've reserved a larger table than it looks like we're going to need. Would you like to have dinner with us? It's sometimes hard to get a table. . . ."

"Thank you, sir, but no," Second Lieutenant Stecker said.

"Shut up," Pickering said. "Yes, sir. Thank you very much."

The invitation did not seem to please Martha Sayre Culhane.

"They can probably get a table of their own without too much trouble," she said. "They live here. In the penthouse."

It was a rude thing for Martha to say, Carstairs thought. He wondered how long she had been waiting in the bar; how much she'd had to drink.

"Well, it must be nice to have a rich father," Carstairs joked.

"No, sir, we're just a pair of payday-rich second johns," Dick Stecker said. "My father's a captain at Camp Elliott."

"But *his* father," Martha Sayre Culhane said, inclining her head toward Pickering, "owns Pacific and Far East Shipping."

Martha really doesn't like Pickering, Carstairs thought. *I wonder why. I wonder what happened on the golf course.*

"I think," Pickering said, "that on reconsideration, we had best decline with thanks your kind invitation, Captain."

Carstairs could think of no other way to get out of what had become an awkward situation.

He nodded at Pickering and Stecker and, taking Martha's arm, led her away from the bar.

But at the entrance to the dining room, she shook loose from his hand and walked back to the bar. Carstairs, now sure that she was in fact drunk and about to make a scene, hurried after her.

Martha put her hand on Pickering's arm, and he turned to look at her.

"For some reason," she said, "you bring out the bitch in me. I'm sorry. Come and have dinner."

Pickering hesitated.

"Please, Pick," Martha said. "I said I'm sorry."

Carstairs saw the look on Pickering's face and knew that he was absolutely incapable of refusing anything Martha Sayre Culhane asked. And then he had a sure, sudden insight why Pickering brought out the bitch in Martha. She was attracted to him, strongly attracted to him, and under the circumstances she didn't know how to handle it.

As Captain Carstairs had recently come to realize, he himself didn't know how to handle Martha Sayre Culhane.

Carstairs had known Greg Culhane at Annapolis, where Greg had been three years behind him. They had become closer when Greg had come to Pensacola. And Carstairs had been at Admiral Sayre's quarters when Greg's engagement to Martha had been announced, and he had been the best man at their wedding.

And he had been considered part of the family after the telegram from the Secretary of the Navy had made official what Admiral Sayre had been told personally over the phone days before the Deputy Chief of Naval Operations. And he had sat with the family during the memorial service in the chapel where she and Greg had been married.

And then Martha had started to hang around with him and his friends. The polite fiction was that Martha took comfort from the company of the other officers' wives. That wasn't true. Martha took comfort from the officers, and from Captain James L. Carstairs, USMC, in particular.

This had not escaped the attention of Admiral Sayre, who had spoken to Carstairs about it: *"Mrs. Sayre and I appreciate the time and consideration you're giving Martha. She needs a friend right now, someone she can trust when she is so vulnerable, emotionally."*

Carstairs was aware then that the admiral might well mean exactly what he said. But he also thought that the admiral might well be saying, *"It would not especially displease Mrs. Sayre and myself if something developed between the two of you,"* or the reverse of that: *"I'm sure that a bright young man like you, having received a word to the wise, knows what somebody like me could and would do to you if I ever found out you had taken advantage of my widowed daughter's emotional vulnerability to get into her pants."*

Carstairs had not laid a hand on Martha Sayre Culhane. At first it had been unthinkable. He was, after all, a Marine officer, and she was the widow of a brother officer. But lately he had become very much aware of the significant difference between the words *wife* and *widow,* and he had been equally aware of her beauty. It was too soon, of course, for him to make any kind of a move. But eventually, inevitably, he had concluded (wondering if it made him some kind of a sonofabitch), time would put a scar on her wound, and nature would take over again, and there would be room in her life for a man.

Martha's behavior toward Lieutenant Pickering—that handsome, rich sonofabitch—made him now realize that even if she didn't know it, there was already a thick layer of scar tissue covering her wound.

Pickering slid off his bar stool. For a moment Martha held his hand, and then, as if she realized what she was doing, quickly let go of it.

Captain Carstairs stepped out of the way, and then followed the two of them into the dining room.

XI

(One)
Machine Gun Range #2
Camp Elliott, California
1030 Hours, 19 January 1942

The pickup truck was a prewar Chevrolet. It had a glossy paint job, and on each door a representation of the Marine Corps insignia was painted above the neatly painted letters "USMC" It even had chrome hubcaps.

The pickup trucks issued currently (and for several months before the war started) were painted with a flat Marine-green paint; and none of these had chrome hubcaps or the Marine emblem on the door. They did have USMC on the door, but that had been applied with a stencil, using black paint.

The driver of the pickup, seen up close, was even more unusual than the truck. He was a thin—even gaunt—man not quite forty-two years old. He was dressed in dungarees; and the letters USMC and a crude representation of the Marine Corps insignia had been stenciled in black paint on the dungaree jacket. The jacket was unpressed, and the silver oak leaves of a lieutenant colonel were half-hidden in the folds of the collar.

The lieutenant colonel parked the Chevrolet in line with the

other vehicles—an ambulance, two other pickups, and two of
the recently issued and still not yet common trucks, 1/4-ton, 4
× 4, General Purpose, called "Jeeps"—and got out. There
were a captain, several lieutenants, and four noncoms standing
in the shade of a small frame building, an obviously newly
erected range house.

It was two story. The second story was an observation
platform, only half framed-in. A primitive flagpole of two-by-
fours rose above the observation platform. Flying from this
was a red "firing in progress" pennant.

There were what the lieutenant colonel judged to be two
companies of infantry (somewhere in the neighborhood of four
hundred men) sitting on the ground twenty-five yards away
from the firing line. It was already getting hot, and the sun was
shining brightly. Shortly, the lieutenant colonel decided, they
would grow uncomfortable.

The captain glanced at the newcomer and looked away. He
had seen the man's face, and guessed his age, and concluded
that he was probably a gunnery sergeant. It did not enter the
captain's mind that the newcomer might be an officer, much
less a lieutenant colonel. Officers were provided with drivers,
and field-grade officers were customarily provided with Ford or
Chevrolet staff cars.

The captain's ignorance was not surprising. This was the
first time the lieutenant colonel had come to Machine Gun
Range #2. He walked to the front of the pickup, leaned
casually against the hood, studied the setup carefully.

He saw that there were twelve machine-gun positions, each
constructed more or less as a machine-gun position would be
set up in a tactical situation. That is to say, a low semicircle of
sandbags had been erected at each position, in the center of
which sat a Browning machine gun, placed so that it would fire
over the sandbags.

Three different types of machine gun had been set up. Each
of the four sandbag positions on the right of the firing line held
a Browning Model 1919A4 .30-caliber weapon. This version
of the Browning was "air cooled," with a perforated jacket on
the outside of its barrel intended to dissipate the heat generated
by bullets passing through the barrel. The gun was mounted on
a low tripod, a single, short leg forward, and two longer legs,
forming a V, to the rear. There was a steel rod between the two
rearward legs. Elevation of the weapon was controlled by a
threaded rod connected to and rising upward from the steel rod

to the rear action of the weapon. Traverse of the weapon was limited by the length of the steel rod connecting the two rear legs of the tripod.

Four M1917A1 .30-caliber "water-cooled" Brownings had been set up in the center four firing positions. A jacket through which water was passed encased the barrel of the '17A1s. And the mounting, otherwise identical to that of the '19A4s, was different in one important respect: Traverse of the weapon was restricted only by the length of the hose connecting the water jacket to the water reservoir. In theory, the '17A1 could be fired through 360 degrees. Elevation was controlled by curved steel plates connected to the machine gun itself and the top of the tripod.

The four firing positions on the left of the firing line each held an M2 Browning. This was the .50-caliber[1] version of the Browning. And it was essentially an enlargement of the .30-caliber '19A4. The perforated steel cooling device on the barrel, however, ran only a short distance out from the receiver. The quick-replaceable barrel was fitted with a handle, for ease in handling; the cocking lever was enlarged and fitted with a wooden handle; and the "pistol grip" behind the trigger of the '19A4 was replaced with a dual wooden-handled trigger mechanism.

The lieutenant colonel found nothing wrong with the placement of the machine guns. And he saw why the weapons were silent; there was some sort of trouble with one of the 1917A1s. He saw an armorer on his knees with the '17A1 in pieces before him. He was being watched by its fascinated two-man crew.

The range was new, and consequently primitive. There was neither a target pit (a below-ground trench at the targets) or a berm (a mound of earth used as a bullet trap) behind the targets. The targets were constructed of two-by-fours, with target cloth stretched between them. The targets themselves were approximately life-size silhouettes of the human torso, rather than the expected bull's-eye targets.

The bullets fired from the machine guns impacted on low, sandy hills the lieutenant colonel judged to be a mile and a half from the firing line. He presumed that whoever had laid out the range was perfectly familiar with the ballistics of .30- and

[1]Caliber is expressed in decimal portions of an inch. For example, the .50-caliber machine gun projectile has a diameter of one-half inch.

.50-caliber machine-gun projectiles and that a large area behind the hills had been declared an impact area and thus *Off Limits*.

When he had seen what he wanted to see (and he was not here to judge machine-gun training; only professionally curious) the lieutenant colonel pushed himself off the hood of the pickup and walked toward the officers gathered in the shade of the range office.

He was almost on them, as they chatted quietly together before one of the noncoms, when a staff sergeant glanced in his direction and saw the glitter of silver on his dungaree jacket collar points. He inclined his head toward the captain, who looked quickly in his direction.

When the lieutenant colonel drew close, the officers and the noncoms came to attention, and the captain saluted and smiled.

"Good morning, sir," the captain said.

"Good morning," the lieutenant colonel said, with a salute that was far short of parade-ground perfect. "Are you in charge here, Captain?"

"I'm the senior officer, sir," the captain said.

"That's what I asked," the lieutenant colonel said, reasonably, with a smile. He examined the lieutenants and picked one out. "Are you Lieutenant McCoy?"

The lieutenant came to attention. "No, sir," he said.

"I was told I could find Lieutenant McCoy here," the lieutenant colonel said.

"He's on the line, sir," the captain said. "There's a stoppage on one of the weapons." He gestured in the direction of the pit where the lieutenant colonel had seen the armorer working on the machine gun.

The lieutenant colonel started to walk toward it. The captain followed him. When they were out of hearing of the group in the shade of the range house, the lieutenant colonel stopped and turned to the captain.

"I think I can find Lieutenant McCoy myself, Captain," he said softly. "What I suggest you do is put one officer and one noncom in the observation tower, and then send the others over to the troops. If I were, say, a PFC, I would resent being ordered to sit in the sun while my sergeant stood in the shade. Much less my officers."

The captain came to attention, with surprise on his face.

"Aye, aye, sir," he said.

The lieutenant colonel walked to the machine-gin pit where there was a malfunctioning weapon.

One of the two troops saw him coming and said something to the third man, who was, the lieutenant colonel saw, just about finished reassembling the weapon. The man started to straighten up. The lieutenant colonel saw the gold bars of a second lieutenant on his dungaree shirt. The two Marines came to attention.

"Finish what you're doing," the lieutenant colonel said, in Chinese.

"Yes, sir," McCoy replied in English, and went on with his work.

"You two can stand at ease," the lieutenant colonel ordered, and then switched to Chinese: "What was wrong with it?"

"Dirt," McCoy replied, again in English. "We just drew these guns. They've been in storage since the First World War. What stopped this one was petrified Cosmoline. It was too hard to wash out with gasoline, but then firing shook it loose. It jammed the bolt as it tried to feed."

"Your record, Lieutenant, says that you are fluent in Cantonese," the lieutenant colonel said in Chinese.

"I don't speak it as well as you do, sir," McCoy said, in Cantonese. He got the machine gun back together, opened the action, and stood up. "Is there something I can do for you, sir?"

The lieutenant colonel ignored the question.

"Isn't there an armorer out here?" he asked.

"Yes, sir," McCoy said. "But I like to explain what went wrong, instead of just fix it."

"Where did you learn about machine guns?"

"I was in a heavy-weapons company with the Fourth Marines in Shanghai, sir," McCoy said.

The lieutenant colonel was pleased with what he had found. The service record of Second Lieutenant McCoy had said that he was an Expert with a .30- and a .50-caliber Browning machine guns and that he was fluent in Cantonese. He was now satisfied that both were the case.

"You're the range officer, I understand?" the lieutenant colonel said.

"Yes, sir."

"If you would feel comfortable in turning over that responsibility to one of the other officers, I'd like to talk to you for a few minutes."

"I'll ask one of the other officers to take over for me, sir," McCoy said.

"I'll wait for you in the pickup," the lieutenant colonel said, smiling and pointing toward the Chevrolet.

When McCoy got to the pickup truck, the lieutenant colonel was inside. He signaled for McCoy to get in. After McCoy was inside, he put out his hand. His grip was firm.

"My name is Carlson, McCoy," he said. "I'm pleased to meet you. I'm an old China Marine myself."

"Yes, sir." McCoy said.

"How'd you get your commission, McCoy?" Carlson asked.

"When I came home from China, I applied for officer school and they sent me," McCoy said.

"You like being an officer?"

"It pays better," McCoy said.

Carlson chuckled.

"Most second lieutenants, faced with a malfunctioning Browning, would get a an armorer to fix it," Carlson said. "Not dirty their hands on it themselves."

"Most second lieutenants wouldn't have known what was wrong with it," McCoy said.

"I was hoping you would say you don't mind getting your hands dirty if that's the quickest solution to a problem."

"Yes, sir," McCoy said. "That, too."

"I've been given command of a special battalion, McCoy," Carlson said. "What we'll be doing is something like the British Commandos. Amphibious raids on Japanese-held islands; probably, later, working behind Japanese lines. I'm recruiting officers for it."

"I heard something about that, sir," McCoy said.

"What did you hear?"

"I heard suicide troops, Colonel," McCoy said. "That you didn't want married men."

"Well, let me correct that," Carlson said. "*Not* suicide troops. Only a fool would volunteer to commit suicide, and the one thing I *don't* want is fools. I don't want married men because I don't want people thinking about wives and children . . . because that would raise their chances of getting killed. I want them to think of nothing but the mission. If they do that, they stand a much better chance of staying alive. You follow the reasoning?"

"Yes, sir," McCoy said.

"And the training is going to be tough, and there's going to be a lot if it, and a married man would get trouble from his wife because he didn't come home at night and on weekends. My philosophy is that well-trained men stand a better chance of staying alive. You follow me?"

"Yes, sir."

McCoy had seen enough of Lieutenant Colonel Evans F. Carlson to make a fast judgment, but one he was sure of. He judged that Carlson was a good officer. McCoy had noticed, for instance, that the officers and noncoms were now doing what they were supposed to be doing, instead of standing around bullshitting in the shade of the range building; and he was sure that Carlson had straightened them out. And McCoy was impressed with Carlson, the man. There was a quiet authority about him. He didn't have to wave his silver lieutenant colonel's leaf in somebody's face to command respect.

His eyes were soft, but intelligent. He certainly didn't look crazy. Or even like he'd gone Chink. McCoy had no idea what a Communist looked like.

McCoy was worried about the intelligent eyes. They made him think that there was very little that got by Lieutenant Colonel Carlson. He wondered how long it would be before Carlson began to suspect—if he didn't already suspect—that the big brass would send somebody to keep an eye on him, to see if he was crazy, or a Communist, or whatever. And once he figured that out, it wouldn't be a hell of a jump for him to figure out that the spy was Second Lieutenant McCoy.

Shit! Why didn't they send somebody else? I like this guy.

(Two)
Pearl Harbor, Hawaii
17 January 1942

The blind men evacuated from Corregidor aboard the *Pickerel* were taken from the wharf to the Naval hospital by ambulance.

There they were given thorough physical examinations to determine if they had any medical condition that required immediate attention. None did. One of them—who had for some unaccountable reason regained his sight—even demanded immediate return to duty, but that was out of the question. He was told that because his shrapnel wounds had not completely healed, he would be evacuated to the United States with the others.

Actually, it had been decided that this man's case indicated the necessity of a psychiatric examination. His temporary blindness was psychosomatic in nature, and that was sometimes an indication of psychiatric problems. But telling him that was obviously not the thing to do; it might even aggravate the problem.

The nine blind men and the one who had regained his sight were placed in the medical holding detachment for transport (when available) to the United States for further medical evaluation and treatment.

The first available shipping space turned out to be aboard a civilian freighter under contract to the Navy. When this came to the attention of a senior medical officer, a Navy captain, he found the time to examine the ship, and he saw that its berthing space was temporary. Its number-two and number-three holds had been temporarily rigged with bunks consisting of sheets of canvas stretched between iron pipe. The head available to the sightless men was primitive, the ladders steep, and there were many places where a blind man could smash against sharp objects.

The Navy doctor then went to see the personnel shipment officer on the staff of the Commander in Chief, Pacific Fleet, to ask him if they couldn't do a little better for the blind men in the way of accommodation.

The personnel shipment officer was also a Navy captain. Aware that the doctor might actually outrank him, he didn't stand him tall as he would have liked to do, but rather contented himself with a lecture, which touched on the fact that he was a busy man, that there was a war on, and that medical officers should really stick to medicine and leave the conduct of the Navy to line officers.

This encounter was followed, as soon as the doctor could find a telephone, by a call to the Chief of Staff to the Commander in Chief, Pacific Fleet. The doctor had a little trouble getting the Commander in Chief onto the phone, but eventually he heard the familiar voice.

"Did you really tell my aide," the admiral asked, "that you'd boot his ass from here to Diego if he didn't get me on the horn?"

"Or words to that effect," the doctor said.

"What's the problem, Charley?" the admiral said, suppressing a chuckle. The admiral had known the doctor for twenty years; they had once shared a cabin as lieutenants on the *Minneapolis*.

"One of your chickenshit part-time sailors wants to send those poor bastards, the blind guys the *Pickerel* brought here from Corregidor, to the States on a cargo ship. The pasty-faced, candy-ass sonofabitch told me with a straight face there's a war on and everyone has to make sacrifices."

"I gather you are referring to my personnel shipping officer?" the admiral asked, dryly.

"I think his name is Young," Paweley said. "Tall, thin sonofabitch. Came in the Navy the day before yesterday, and thinks he's Bull Halsey, Junior."

"I'll take care of it, Charley," the admiral said. "How many of them are there?"

"Ten."

"I'll take care of it, Charley," the admiral repeated. "Now you calm down."

"Sorry to bother you with this, Tom. I know you're busy—"

"Never too busy for something like this," the admiral said.

The next afternoon, the departure of the regularly scheduled courier flight to the United States was delayed for almost an hour. Already loaded and in the water, the Martin PBM-1 was ordered back to the seaplane ramp, where its seven passengers and six hundred pounds of priority cargo were offloaded.

Nine blind men were loaded aboard under the supervision of a Marine captain. All of the seven passengers removed from their seats were senior in grade to the captain, and all had urgent business in the United States, and protest was made to the personnel shipment officer.

It was to no avail. The personnel shipment officer, the previous afternoon, had had a brief chat with the Chief of Staff to the Commander in Chief, Pacific Fleet. No one had ever talked to him like that before in his life.

(Three)
USMC Recruit Training Depot
Parris Island, South Carolina
0845 Hours, 19 January 1942

The motor transport officer, the officer charged with operating the fleet of trucks and automobiles for the recruit depot, was First Lieutenant Vincent S. Osadchy. A lithe, deeply tanned twenty-eight-year-old, he was a mustang with eleven years in the Corps. He had been an officer three months, and the motor transport officer nine days. The previous transport officer, a major, as the TO&E (Table of Organization & Equipment) called for, had been transferred. He knew what he was doing. Osadchy, who didn't, had been given the job until such time as an officer of suitable grade and experience could be found.

Lieutenant Osadchy drove himself in a jeep from the motor pool to the brick headquarters building, not sure of his best plan of attack. Should he make a display of anger? Or should he get down on his knees before the personel officer and weep?

The personnel officer was a major, a portly, natty man completely filling his stiffly starched khaki shirt. He wasn't bulging out of it, nor really straining the buttons; but, Osadchy thought, there would not be room inside the shirt for the major and, say, a hand scratching an itch.

"Hello, Vince," the major said, smiling. "Can I offer you some coffee?"

"Yes, sir," Osadchy said. "Thank you. And if you have one, how about a weeping towel?"

The major chuckled. He poured coffee from a thermos into a china cup and handed it to Osadchy.

"I thought maybe you'd drop by," he said.

"Can I deliver a lecture on what it takes to operate a motor pool?"

"By all means," the major said.

"Aside from vehicles," Osadchy said, pronouncing the word *"vee*-hic-els," "and tools and POL [petrol, oil and lubricants], it requires five or six good noncoms, corporals, or sergeants who know the difference between a spark plug and a transmission, and at least one, but preferably two or three, officers who know at least half as much as the noncoms."

"That sounds reasonable," the major said, smiling warmly at him.

"A month ago, our motor pool had both," Osadchy went on. "And then the Corps transferred out all—not some, all—the non-coms who could find their ass with both hands without a map."

"Very colorful," the major said, chuckling.

"And then the Corps, in its wisdom, sent us *one* sergeant

who had previously seen a truck with the wheels off. Actually a pretty good man, even if he just got out of the hospital. But then—the Corps giveth and the Corps taketh away—the Corps transferred the motor transport officer out."

"The Corps is having a few little personnel problems, Vince," the major said. "It's supposed to have something to do with there being a war on."

Osadchy had to smile, although he didn't want to. He was afraid this would happen, that the major would hear him out, be as pleasant as hell, and give him no help whatsoever.

"Which left the motor pool in the hands of an officer who knows as much about operating a motor pool as he does about deep-sea fishing. And of course the one sergeant who does know what he's doing."

"And now the Corps says promote the sergeant to gunnery sergeant and transfer him, right? Is that the source of your unhappiness, Vince?"

"Yes, sir," Osadchy said. "Sir, don't misunderstand me. Sergeant Zimmerman is a good man. I'd like to see him as a staff sergeant, or a technical sergeant. But gunny? I was a gunny. Zimmerman is not the gunny type."

"In other words, if you could have your way, Zimmerman would be promoted, but not to gunnery sergeant, and kept here?"

"Yes, sir."

"I know, Vince," the major said, "that you really believe that what I do here all day is think up ways to torment people like you—"

"No, sir," Osadchy protested.

"So, you will doubtless be surprised to hear that when the TWX"—a message transmitted by teletype—"came down, and I reviewed both your situation and Sergeant Zimmerman's record jacket, I came to the same conclusion. I TWX-ed back the day before yesterday, asking for reconsideration of the transfer. I said Zimmerman is critical here."

"And?" Osadchy asked.

"And when there was no reply, I got the Old Man's permission to call up and ask."

"And?" Osadchy asked.

"Pay attention, Lieutenant," the major said. "See for yourself how field-grade officers at the upper echelons of command are willing to grovel before the feet of their betters for the good of the command."

He picked up his telephone.

"Sergeant Asher," he said, "get a control number and then put in a call for me to Enlisted Assignment, G-One, Headquarters, Marine Corps. I want to speak to the officer in charge."

He put the telephone back in its cradle.

"Sometimes, Vince," he said, "it works. And sometimes it doesn't. I haven't called lately. Maybe we'll get lucky."

It took a minute or two to put the call through. The conversation itself took just over a minute.

"I understand, sir. Thank you very much," the major said, then hung up and turned to Lieutenant Osadchy.

"This time we weren't lucky," he said. "Both the decision to make Zimmerman a gunnery sergeant and to transfer him came from 'higher authority.' Since he carefully avoided saying *what* higher authority, I'm pretty sure he meant Intelligence. That make any sense to you?"

"No, sir," Lieutenant Osadchy said. "Zimmerman . . . Zimmerman's *not* an *intelligence* type. He's just a good China Marine motor sergeant."

"Well, that's it, Vince," the major said, "There's nothing else I can do. I'm sorry."

"Thanks for the try, sir."

The major called in his clerk and told him to cut orders promoting Sergeant Zimmerman to gunnery sergeant with date of rank 31 December 1941, and then to cut orders transferring Gunnery Sergeant Zimmerman to the 2nd Separate Battalion, USMC, at Quantico, Virginia; effective immediately.

(Four)
San Diego, California
0830 Hours, 19 January 1942

The Martin PBM-1 flying boat made its approach to San Diego harbor straight in from the Pacific Ocean. Her twin sixteen-hundred-horsepower Wright R-2600-6 engines had been droning steadily for nearly eighteen hours. It was three thousand miles from Pearl to Diego, a long way in an airplane that cruised at 170 knots.

When she was down to two thousand feet, and her speed retarded, her pilot ordered "floats down," and the copilot operated the lever that caused wing-tip floats to be lowered from the high, gull-shaped wings.

"Navy Four Two Four," the tower called, "be on the lookout for one or more small civilian vessels east end landing area."

"Roger," the copilot said. "We have them in sight. Four Two Four on final."

The Martin came in low and slow, touched down in a massive splash, bounced airborne, and then touched down again in an even larger splash and stayed down.

"Four Two Four down at three-one past the hour," the copilot reported.

"Four Two Four, steer zero-thirty degrees, a follow-me boat will meet you and direct you to the seaplane ramp."

"Roger."

A gray Navy staff car and two ambulances, one a glistening Packard with chrome-plated flashing lights and siren on the roof, and the other a Dodge 3/4-ton, painted olive drab and with large red crosses painted on the sides and roof, waited for the PBM to taxi across the bay to the seaplane ramp.

The PBM got as close to the seaplane ramp as her pilot intended to take her under her own power. He cut the engines. A sailor walked down the ramp into the water until it was chest high. He reached over his head and hooked a cable to a ring in the nose of the PBM. An aircraft tractor at the end of the ramp pulled the PBM out of the water by the cable far enough up the ramp so that it could back up to the PBM and hook up a rigid tow bar. Then it pulled it into the parking area.

The doors of the ambulances opened, and doctors and corpsmen went to the hatch on the side of the flying boat's fuselage. A doctor and two corpsmen entered the fuselage. And then Captain Ed Banning climbed out.

A technical sergeant, a stocky man in his thirties, got out of the staff car and walked to him, saluted, and asked, "Captain Banning?"

Baning returned the salute.

"I'll go with the men in the ambulances," Banning said.

The technical sergeant handed him a sheet of teletype paper.

PRIORITY
SECRET
HQ USMC WASH DC X 16 JANUARY 1942 X COMMANDING
GENERAL X MARINE BARRACKS PEARL HARBOR HAWAII X INFO
COMMANDING GENERAL MARINE BARRACKS SAN DIEGO X

REFERENCE YOUR TWX SUBJECT ARRIVAL PEARL HARBOR CAPT
EDWARD J BANNING USMC X PHYSICAL CONDITION PERMITTING
SUBJECT OFFICER WILL PROCEED HQ USMC BY FIRST AVAILABLE AIR
TRANSPORTATION X PRIORITY AAA2 AUTHORIZED X COMMGEN
MARBAR PEARL WILL ADVISE COMMGEN MARBAR DIEGO AND HQ
USMC ATTN G2 ETA CONUS AND ETA WASH X

BY DIRECTION X

H W T FORREST BRIG GEN USMC

"How'd you know it was me, Sergeant?" Banning asked.

"They called—a Captain Sessions called—this morning,
after they heard you'd left Pearl, sir. Captain Sessions
described you. And he said to tell you 'Welcome home,' sir."

Banning nodded.

"We've got you a seat on the two thirty-five Western flight to
Los Angeles, sir, connecting at five oh-five with a United flight
to Washington. That's if you feel up to it."

Banning nodded again, but didn't reply. He didn't trust his
voice to speak.

"It's up to you, sir. We can reschedule you later, if you're
tired. My orders are to stick with you and do whatever has to
be done."

Banning looked at the sergeant for a long moment, until he
was reasonably sure that when he spoke he would display no
more emotion than is appropriate for a Marine officer.

"What has to be done, Sergeant," he said, "if I am to get on
civilian airplanes without disgracing the Corps, is to acquire a
decent-looking uniform. And to do that, I'm going to have to
get some money. How do I do that?"

"That's all laid on, sir," the technical sergeant said.
"Captain Sessions suggested that there might be a problem
with your pay and luggage."

XII

(One)
San Diego, California
0830 Hours, 19 January 1942

The first time Miss Ernestine Sage noticed the young woman was when she drove the LaSalle into the parking lot of the Bay-Vue Super Discount Super Market. The young woman was attractive, if harried-looking, and in what appeared to be the eighth month of her pregnancy. The pregnant young woman seemed to be examining her, or maybe the car, with more than ordinary interest.

But then, as she got out of the car, Ernie's attention was distracted by a Navy airplane, an enormous, twin-engine seaplane, coming in over the ocean and then landing in the bay with two enormous splashes. The sun was shining (it shined just about all the time here), and the bay was blue, and the airplane landing, Ernie thought, was beautiful. It made her think of Pick Pickering, who was learning to fly.

The pregnant young woman was standing in front of the plate-glass windows of the supermarket when Ernie grabbed a shopping cart and headed for the door. She smiled—shyly—at Ernie, and Ernie returned the smile.

Inside the supermarket, Ernie took her shopping list from her purse and went first to the dairy cooler for eggs and milk and butter. As they were driving across the country, and since they had arrived here, she had been astonished at Ken's enormous breakfast appetite. He regularly wolfed down four eggs and as much bacon or ham as she put before him. Once, for the hell of it, she had cooked a whole pound of bacon, and, with the exception of her own three slices, Ken had eaten all of it.

Next she went to the meat cooler and bought bacon and ham and sausage. And then she had the most extraordinary feeling that she was being followed by the pregnant young woman.

Ernie moved from the bacon and sausage display case into one of the aisles. Halfway down it, the pregnant young woman appeared, coming the other way.

Without doing anything that would suggest she was trying to lose the pregnant young woman, Ernie tried to do just that. Fixing an *"ooops, I forgot paprika"* look on her face, she twice reversed direction, and pushed her shopping cart into another aisle.

And both times the pregnant young woman, whose shopping cart held a loaf of bread and a quart bottle of ginger ale and nothing else, appeared behind her in the same aisle. The second time Ernie reversed direction she moved three aisles away, to the beef section, where she bought a half a dozen T-bone steaks; but that move didn't shake loose the pregnant woman either.

Ken never tired of steak. Which was a good thing, for her culinary skills were just about limited to frying eggs and bacon and broiling steak.

As she maneuvered her cart, Ernie had managed to glance at the young woman (even to study her for a long moment in a curved mirror apparently installed to discourage shoplifters). And by now she was convinced that she had never seen the young woman before. But she was also convinced that whatever the young woman was—and she looked like a nice young woman—she was not a threat.

But she unnerved Ernie. And feeling a little foolish, Ernie cut short her shopping trip. She had steaks for dinner and stuff for breakfast in the shopping cart. She could pick up bread and toilet tissue on the way to the checkout counter. What else she needed she would get tomorrow. Or maybe even later today, if Ken called up and said he would be a little late again.

Ernie didn't see the young woman as she went through the checkout line, but when she pushed the shopping cart out of the supermarket, the young woman was in the parking lot, between Ernie and the LaSalle.

Ernie pushed the shopping cart off the concrete sidewalk onto the macadam and toward the car. The pregnant young woman was now looking at her. Ernie put on a faint smile (the only explanation for her behavior, she suddenly concluded, was that the young woman mistakenly believed that she knew her) and headed for the car.

"Excuse me," the pregnant young woman said, "you're an officer's wife, aren't you?"

Ernie hesitated.

"I saw the Camp Elliott sticker," the pregnant young woman said, making a vague gesture toward a sticker on the LaSalle's windshield. It identified the car as having been registered on the post by a Marine officer.

"The car belongs to a friend," Ernie said.

"Oh," the pregnant young woman said, obviously disappointed, and then added, "I am. A Marine officer's wife, I mean."

"Right now," Ernie blurted, "that's the great ambition of my life. To be a Marine officer's wife."

The young woman smiled. It was a nice smile, Ernie thought, and the young woman was obviously a nice young woman.

"Is there something I can do for you?" Ernie asked.

The pregnant young woman dipped into her purse and came up with a wallet. She took from it a dependent's identification card, which she thrust at Ernie. There was a photograph on it, which made the pregnant young woman look all of sixteen years old. Her name was Dorothy Burnes and she was the dependent wife of Martin J. Burnes, 1st Lt., USMCR.

"Can I talk to you?" Dorothy Burnes said.

"Sure," Ernie said. "Mine is a second lieutenant."

"I've been following you around the supermarket," Dorothy said.

"I noticed," Ernie said. A look of embarrassment crossed Dorothy Burnes's face. "Why don't you sit in the car?" Ernie added.

"Thank you," Dorothy said. She got in the passenger seat. Then Ernie unloaded the groceries from the shopping cart into the LaSalle and pushed the basket to a steel-pipe enclosure. When that was done she walked back to the convertible. The roof was down and the boot snapped in place. The car glistened. Ernie had waxed it, with Simoniz, partly because she had come to understand how important the car was to Ken, and partly because there wasn't much to do with him gone all day.

Ernie got behind the wheel, pulled the door closed, and turned to Dorothy Burnes.

"I'm desperate," Dorothy said. "They put me out of the motel today, and unless I find someplace to stay between now and half-past five, my husband's going to put me on the Lark at half-past six."

"The Lark?"

"The train to Los Angeles," Dorothy explained. "Where you can connect with trains to Kansas City. We're from Kansas City."

"Oh," Ernie said.

"I really thought if I offered them twice as much money, they'd let me stay," Dorothy said. "But the lady said that wouldn't be 'fair to the other girls,' and that I would have to check out."

"Oh, hell," Ernie said.

"So," Dorothy said, trying and failing to sound amusing, "I got this clever idea that maybe if I asked some other officer's wife, who looked like she had some place to stay, maybe she'd know of something. And then I decided the best place to find some officer's wife who had a place to stay was at a supermarket. If she was buying groceries, she would have a place to cook them. So I came here and you came in."

"Good thinking, anyway," Ernie said.

She's just like me. Or, there but for the grace of God and Pick's father, go I.

"But I suppose you're living with your folks," Dorothy said, "and have no idea where I could find a place . . . anyplace out of rain?"

"I'm living on a boat," Ernie said. "And I don't, I'm afraid, know of any place for rent."

"A boat?" Dorothy asked.

Ernie nodded. "One of those things that goes up and down in the water," she said.

"And you don't have any idea—" Dorothy said.

Ernie shook her head.

"Damn," Dorothy said, and then started to sniffle.

The tears, Ernie knew, were genuine, not a pitch for sympathy. Dorothy Burnes was at the end of her rope. She was pregnant and didn't have a place to stay, and her Marine was about to send her home.

"Sorry," Dorothy Burnes said, wiping her nose with a Kleenex.

"If they threw you out, where's your luggage?" Ernie asked.

"In the motel office," Dorothy said.

"Well, you can stay with us tonight," Ernie said. "And in the morning, you and I will start looking for a place for you."

"Have you got room?"

Ernie nodded.

"I've got money," Dorothy said. "I can pay. I really thought if I offered them twice as much money . . . I wired my father for money, and I wasn't going to tell Marty—"

"Where's the motel?" Ernie interrupted, as she pushed the LaSalle's starter button.

"I don't know how to thank you," Dorothy said.

"I guess we camp followers have to stick together," Ernie said.

That made Dorothy Burnes giggle. She smiled shyly at Ernie. Ernie was pleased.

Twenty minutes later, Ernie stopped the LaSalle near Pier Four of the San Diego Yacht Club. A hundred yards out on the pier, the *Last Time* bobbed gently up and down. It was separated from the wharf by five white rubber bumpers the size of wastebaskets, and connected to it by a teak gangplank and electric service and telephone cables.

The *Last Time*, the property of a San Diego attorney whose firm did a good deal of business with Pacific & Far East Shipping, Inc., was fifty-three feet long, sixteen feet in the beam, and drew six feet. She was powered with twin General Motors Detroit diesels.

Her owner had been delighted, when approached, to offer it, via the chairman of the board of Pacific & Far East Shipping, to the daughter of the chairman of the board of the American Personal Pharmaceutical Corporation for as long as she wanted it. Not only for the obvious reasons, but also because her normal three-man crew, carried away on a wave of patriotism, had enlisted in the Coast Guard, leaving the *Last Time* untended.

"Oh, my God!" Dorothy Burnes said when she stepped down into the lounge. "I've never been on one this big. What is it, a Bertram?"

Which question indicates, Ernie decided, *that you are not entirely unfamiliar with yachts. And it follows from that, and from other things you have said, that while you obviously are a homeless and pregnant waif, you are probably not a poor homeless waif.*

"No," she said. "It's a Mitchell. It was made in Florida and sailed here."

"It's yours?"

"It belongs to a friend of a friend," Ernie said. "We're boat-sitting. The crew went off to the Coast Guard."

"I just hope I'm not dreaming," Dorothy said. "I can't tell you how grateful I am."

"I'm glad to have the company," Ernie said. And she realized then that although they would certainly look around the next day, and diligently, for some place for Dorothy Burnes and her husband to live, they almost certainly were not going to find one.

Which means they will stay here. Which, on balance, may be a pretty good idea. It'll give me company. And we are, in a sense, sisters.

"Maybe I should have told you this before," Ernie said. "I think the phrase for what my Marine and I are doing on here is 'shacking up.' "

There was a look of embarrassment in Dorothy Burnes's eyes. "You didn't have to tell me that," she said, softly. "That's none of my business."

"Ken doesn't think that Marine officers, about to be sent overseas, should be married," Ernie said.

"Do you love him?"

"Oh, yes," Ernie said.

"Isn't that all that's important? I mean, really?"

"So my reasoning goes," Ernie said.

"Maybe, when he sees Marty and me, it will be contagious," Dorothy said.

"That's a nice thought," Ernie said. "Come on, I'll show you your room . . . cabin."

By four o'clock, Ernie Page and Dorothy Burnes had become friends. They were of an age, and of roughly comparable background. Dorothy's father operated a large condiment-bottling business (pickles, relish, horseradish, et cetera) founded by his grandfather. She had gone to Emma Willard, and then on to Vanderbilt College, where, as a junior, she had married Marty, then a senior. Marty had gone to Quantico for the Platoon Leader's Course when he graduated.

"Ken went through Quantico," Ernie offered, "with my childhood sweetheart. That's how we met. And my childhood sweetheart's parents fixed it for us to live on the boat."

"They know?" Dorothy asked. The rest of the sentence, "that you and Ken are living together on this boat?" went unsaid.

"They know," Ernie said. "My parents know, too, but they pretend not to. I mean, they know I'm out here with Ken. They don't know about the boat."

"Where did Ken go to school?" Dorothy asked.

"He didn't," Ernie replied, with a sense of misgiving. "He's what they call a mustang. He came up from the ranks."

"Oh?"

"He's very bright," Ernie said. "And the Marine Corps saw it, and they sent him to officer's school."

"He must be," Dorothy readily agreed.

A clock chimed four times.

"Time to get him," Ernie said, and then, "what do we do about yours? What will he do, go to the motel?"

Dorothy nodded.

"Well, then, I'll drop you off there and go fetch Ken," Ernie said. "You bring him here."

Ken, who was wearing dungarees, looked tired when Ernie picked him up behind the orderly room at Camp Elliott. When he was tired, he looked older. Sometimes, she thought, he looked like a boy. And in his dungarees, he did not much resemble the Marine officer in the recruiting posters.

She pushed the door open and then slid halfway across the seat to let him get behind the wheel.

"Been waiting long?" she asked.

"No," he said simply.

"Don't I get a kiss?"

He graciously offered the side of his face. It wasn't what she had had in mind, but she knew that it was all she was going to get. The official excuse was that there was a Marine Corps regulation—yet another regulation—that proscribed the public display of affection by officers and gentlemen. The real reason was that *Ken* was made uncomfortable by public displays of affection; the regulation just gave him the excuse he needed to treat her, when in public, like a sister.

Sometimes, as now, this annoyed Ernie.

She moved her hand and quickly groped him.

"Jesus Christ!" Ken said, knocking her hand away.

"There's a time and place, right?" she teased. "And this isn't it?"

He looked at her and shook his head.

"You're something," he said.

"Uh-*huh*," she agreed.

For just a moment, he touched her cheek very gently with the back of his hand.

"Watch out!" she said in mock horror. "Someone will see, and they will cut your buttons off and drum you out of the Corps in disgrace!"

He laughed softly and smiled at her.

"How was your day?"

"Noisy," he said. He dug in his shirt pocket and handed her a brass cartridge case.

"What's this?"

"Look at the stamp," he said. "On the bottom."

"I'm looking," she said. "What do I see?"

"See where it says 'FA 15'?" She nodded. "That means it was made by the Frankfurt Arsenal in 1915; before the First World War."

They were at the gate then. A Marine MP saluted crisply as he waved them through.

"Do you think he'd do that if he suspected that you and I are carrying on?" Ernie said innocently after Ken had returned the salute. "Or do you think he'd turn you in? '*Sir, I saw an officer today I just know is carrying on with a female civilian.*'"

He laughed again and smiled at her.

"You just don't give up, do you?"

"Does it still work?"

"Does what still work?"

"Bullets made before the First World War," Ernie said.

"The bullet is the pointed thing that comes out the barrel," Ken said. "The round consists of the case, the powder, the primer—*and* the bullet."

"Sorry," she said, mockingly.

"And the answer is most of the time," he said. "It's really surprising."

"What happens if it doesn't work?" she asked.

"Colonel Carlson came to see me today," McCoy said, changing the subject.

"What?" she asked, confused. It wasn't the answer she expected.

"Colonel Carlson came out to the machine-gun range," McCoy said. "Looking for me."

"What did he want?"

"He spoke to me in Cantonese," McCoy said, and smiled. "You should have seen the looks on the kids' faces when he did that."

"What did he want?" Ernie repeated.

"Well, I guess he wanted to have a look at me, and to see if I really spoke Chinese."

"And?" she asked, impatiently.

"He wanted to know if I had heard of the Chinese Route Army, and if so, what I thought about them."

"What did you tell him?"

"What I thought he wanted to hear," McCoy said. "That they do a pretty good job."

"That's all?"

"Oh, he asked me the usual questions; he was feeling me out," McCoy said. "And then he told me he was forming a battalion, and asked if I was interested in joining it."

"And you, of course, said yes," Ernie said.

"That's why they sent me out here," McCoy said. "You know that. The whole idea was to get him to recruit me."

He suddenly pulled out of the line of traffic and stopped before a commercial laundry. He went in and came out a minute or two later carrying two enormous bundles of paper-wrapped laundry. He threw them in the back and got behind the wheel.

"What's for supper?" he asked.

"Steak, for a change," she said.

He nodded his approval.

"Well, are you going to tell me, or not?"

"Tell you what?"

"Did he 'recruit' you, or not?"

"He fed me a line about how he wanted to compare me against other volunteers," McCoy said. "But that was just bullshit. He'll take me. I'm a young old China Marine."

"What does that mean?"

"He wants old China Marines, people who may think like Orientals. And he wants young officers and men. He'll take either. I'm both."

"Well, is he crazy, or not?"

"I liked him," McCoy said. "Ain't that a kick in the ass?"

"He's not crazy?"

"No, he's not crazy, and he struck me as a damned good officer. He's obviously smarter than hell, and his ideas about making raids with highly trained people make sense."

"What about the other thing, his being a Communist?"

"He didn't talk politics," McCoy said. "And I could hardly ask him."

"So what happens now?"

"I call Captain Sessions and tell him," McCoy said.

"I mean, to you?"

"In a couple of days, maybe a week, I think they'll transfer me," McCoy said.

He turned off the highway through the gates of the San Diego Yacht Club and drove to the water's edge.

A Pontiac coupe with Missouri license plates was parked with its nose against the Pier Four sign. There was a Marine officer, in greens, sitting behind the wheel, and Ernie could see the back of Dorothy Burnes's head.

"Oh, good," Ernie said. "They're here."

"'Oh, good,'" Ken McCoy parroted, "*who's* here?"

Oh, my God! I should have told him before we got here!

"We have houseguests," Ernie said, as she opened the door of the LaSalle and got out.

The door of the Pontiac opened and Dorothy Burnes, grunting, pushed herself out of the car. She smiled warmly and gratefully at Ernie. Her husband got out from behind the wheel, looking a little uneasy.

Then he saluted. Ernie wondered why he had done that, and

then realized he was returning Ken's salute. And then she understood why. There were silver bars on Martin J. Burnes's epaulets; he outranked Ken, and Ken had saluted him.

"Well, I see you found each other all right," Ernie said. She turned and saw Ken walking up. "This is Ken," she said. "Ken, this is Marty Burnes."

"How do you do, sir," Ken McCoy said formally. Ernie did not like the look on Ken McCoy's face.

"And this is Dorothy," Ernie plunged ahead.

"Hi," Dorothy said.

"Dorothy and I are old pals, and she's having a hard time finding a place to stay, so they'll be staying with us for a couple of days."

"I hope we're not going to put you out too much," Marty Burnes said to McCoy.

"It's her boat," Ken said simply.

Oh, God! He doesn't like this at all. Why not? What's wrong with him? He could easily be in Marty Burnes's place. And then she understood. *He's not here as just one more lieutenant; he's going to spy on that Colonel Whatsisname, and he's afraid that the Burneses being on the boat will get in the way of that. And, damnit, maybe he's right.*

"Well, let's go aboard," Ernie said, trying to be bright and cheerful. "Dorothy and I have spent the afternoon making hors d'oeuvres."

"And then there'll be steaks," Dorothy chimed in.

"And I'm sure you both could use a drink," Ernie said. She stole a glance at Ken. His eyes were cold. But not angry, she thought. Disappointed, resigned, as if he had expected her to do something dumb like this.

McCoy forced a polite smile on his face.

"I could use a drink," he said. "After you, Lieutenant."

"Can't we forget the Marine Corps?" Ernie said. "Just for an hour or two? What I mean is can't you two use your *names?*"

"Sure," Marty Burnes said. He smiled and put out his hand to McCoy. "I'm Marty."

McCoy took the hand and forced another brief smile. "Ken," he said.

"You two unload the cars," Ernie ordered. "By the time you're finished, we'll have drinks made."

When the drinks were made, Ernie proposed a toast. "I think, for the Burneses, that this is the proverbial any old port in a storm," she said. "Welcome aboard, Burneses."

McCoy chuckled and raised his glass, and this time his smile was genuine.

"Welcome aboard," he said.

He sat slumped in the largest of the four upholstered chairs in the cabin. He was still in dungarees with his rough-side-out field shoes stretched out in front of him. And for the first time (probably because Marty Burnes was in a green uniform, she thought) she noticed how incongruous a Marine dressed that way looked in the plush cabin.

Ernie and Dorothy passed the tray of hors d'oeuvres. McCoy helped himself to several chunks of cheddar, and then gulped down his drink.

"Now that I am refueled," he said, "I think I'll scrape off some of the barnacles."

He went down the passageway to the master cabin.

In a minute, they could hear the shower start, and a moment after that, faintly, the sound of McCoy singing.

Thank God, he's over the mad.

"He does that, too," Dorothy Burnes said, nodding fondly at her husband.

Ernie made Marty Burnes another drink.

When the sound of the shower stopped and McCoy did not appear in a reasonable time, she excused herself and went to their cabin.

If there's going to be a fight, I might as well get it over with.

She got to the cabin as Ken, naked, lay back on the bed with the telephone in his hand.

He looked at her but said nothing, and he did not react to the way she raised her eyebrows approvingly at his nakedness.

"Collect for anyone, operator, from Lieutenant McCoy to Liberty seven, oh nine five six in Washington, D.C. I'll hold."

"Ken, she had no place to stay. He was going to send her home," Ernie said.

He held the telephone away from his head as if to explain why he couldn't talk to her, and then he put it back. Although she knew that it was not his intention, Ernie chose to interpret the gesture as an invitation to lie down beside him and listen to the conversation. For a moment he stiffened, and she was afraid he would roll away from her, or get up. But then he relaxed.

"Liberty seven, oh nine five six," a none-too-friendly male voice came on the line.

"I have a collect call for anyone from a Lieutenant McCoy," the operator said. "Will you accept charges?"

"We'll accept," the male voice said.

"Go ahead, sir," the operator said. "Your party is on the line."

"How are you, Sergeant?" McCoy said to the telephone. "Is Captain Sessions around?"

"I'll buzz for him. I know he wants to talk to you. How's things in the boondocks?"

"I'm looking for a sergeant who knows how to take a 'Seventeen A-Four apart," McCoy said.

The sergeant chuckled, and then another voice came on the line.

"Captain Sessions."

"Lieutenant McCoy is on the line, sir," the sergeant said.

"Oh, good. Ken?"

"Yes, sir."

"I was about to call you. I was going to wait until I was sure you were home. What's on your mind?"

"Colonel Carlson looked me up today," McCoy said. "I was on the machine-gun range, and he found me there."

"And?"

"He checked to see if I really speak Cantonese, and then pumped me for what he could get."

"What did he get?"

"He wanted to know what I thought of the Mao Tse-tung tribe of slopeheads," McCoy said. "So I told him what he wanted to hear."

"Anything about the Raiders?"

"'Raiders'? Is that what they're going to call them?"

"Yeah, it looks that way. The Commandant is going to order the formation as of four February, of the Second Separate Battalion, there at Elliott. The same day, a reinforced company—about two hundred fifty people—is going to be transferred from the First Separate Battalion at Quantico to the Second at Elliott. Our friend Zimmerman, who is now a gunnery sergeant, will be one of them. On nineteen February, the Second will be redesignated as the Second Raider Battalion. That's one of the reasons I wanted to talk to you, to tell you that.''

"Maybe you better not spread this around, sir," McCoy said. "But I think he's got a good idea."

"He talked to you about it?"

"Yes, sir. And what he said made sense."

"Did he say anything about you joining up? The reason I ask, is that unless you can get into the Second Battalion out there, Colonel Rickabee's going to transfer you back to Quantico, assign you to the First Separate Battalion, and then send you back out to Carlson when they transfer the company from the First Battalion out there."

"He gave me the usual bullshit about comparing me against other volunteers, but I would be damned surprised if he didn't have me transferred."

"Good. Then we'll leave it that way. If you're wrong, if he doesn't pick you . . . any suggestion that he questioned your neatly doctored service record?"

"No, sir."

"If he doesn't pick you, we'll worry about that then."

"Captain, can I talk to you man to man?"

"Of course not, said the officer to the officer who saved his life," Sessions said. "What's on your mind, Ken?"

"I don't like this job," McCoy said. "I feel like a real slimy sonofabitch, spying on Colonel Carlson. I like him. He's a good officer, and I think the commandos are a good idea."

"Raiders," Sessions corrected him automatically, and then fell silent.

"I went too far, huh?" McCoy said, after a long moment.

"No, no," Sessions said. "I was trying to frame my reply. I think I know how you feel, Ken. The only thing I can really say is that it has to be done, and you're the fellow to do it. I don't think anyone is going to be happy if you find out he is either unbalanced or a Communist."

"I do. I've had a chance to think about this a lot. It looks to me that a lot of the brass want to stick it to Carlson because he's got a direct line to the President."

"There's some of that, sure," Sessions said. "But I also think that if he actually goes off the deep end, he could do the Corps a lot of damage. More damage, Ken, than I think you can fully appreciate."

"Aye, aye, sir," McCoy said.

"Excuse me, Ken?" Sessions asked.

"That means I understand the order and will carry it out," McCoy said. "Didn't you ever hear that before, Captain, sir?"

"Don't be a wiseass, you're only a second lieutenant," Sessions said, and then his voice grew serious. "For what it's worth, Ken, I think what you're doing has to be done."

"I knew that," McCoy said. "It's the main reason I'm doing it."

"I just had another patriotic, flag-waving, hurrah-for-the-Corps thought," Sessions said. "You want to hear it?"

"Sure."

"When they get both of the Raider battalions up to strength and trained, Ken, I don't think there will be fifty people in them, officer or enlisted, who have ever heard the sound of a shot fired in anger. Even though nobody will know about it, with your doctored service record, you'll be one of the most experienced officers around. Certainly the most experienced lieutenant. The only test that counts for an officer is how he behaves when people are shooting at him. And you've passed that test twice, Killer, and with flying colors."

"Shit," McCoy said.

"*No* shit, Ken. I'm a living witness to how well you conduct yourself under stress. If you do nothing else with the Raiders, you'll probably be able to keep some of the kids alive."

Ernie had moved on the bed, so that she could rest her head on McCoy's shoulder while she listened to the conversation. Now she raised her head so that she could see Ken's eyes.

He shrugged his shoulders, as if embarrassed by what Captain Sessions had said.

"You said you had a couple of things to tell me," McCoy said.

"Oh, yeah. I'm glad you reminded me. One of them was about Zimmerman."

"He doesn't know what I'm doing out here, does he?"

"No, and don't tell him," Sessions said. "Let him think it's because you both speak Chinese, or because Carlson likes China Marines."

"Yes, sir," McCoy said. "What else?"

"You didn't happen to see Captain Banning, did you?"

"Captain *Banning? Our* Captain Banning?"

"Banning was evacuated from Corregidor by submarine. He passed through Diego today on his way here. There was a chance he might have bumped into you. I had to ask. The worst possible case would have been for him to greet you like a long-lost brother within Carlson's hearing. Even worse, to have him thank you for saving his life. That would have blown your new service record out of the water, and told Carlson that he's being watched."

"I didn't see him," McCoy said. "What's going to happen to him?"

"Well, for one thing, he's going to be told that he never heard of you in his life, and aside from that, I can't tell you."

"Can you give him my regards?"

"Sure, Ken," Sessions said.

"I guess that's about it," McCoy said.

"How's your love life, Ken?" Sessions asked.

"None of your business."

"I was just going to say to give her my regards."

McCoy didn't reply.

"You better check in every day from now on, either with me or Colonel Rickabee."

"Aye, aye, sir."

McCoy sat up, taking Ernie with him, and put the phone back in its cradle on the bulkhead behind him.

"He knows about us?" Ernie asked. McCoy nodded. "What did you tell him?"

McCoy smiled. "That you're the best piece of ass I ever had in my life," he said, and then put his arms up to defend himself from the blows he was sure would follow.

They did not. Ernie waited for him to put his arms down, and then said, "Well, I'm glad you told him the truth."

Then she got out of the bed and went back to the main cabin.

McCoy put on a pair of khaki trousers and a T-shirt, then went out and made himself another drink.

"I understand," Lieutenant Marty Burnes said, "that you're in a heavy-weapons company."

"That's right," McCoy said. "What do they have you doing?"

"At the moment I'm assigned to S-Three," Burnes said.

"At the moment?" McCoy asked.

"You've heard about the Raiders?" Burnes asked.

"A little," McCoy replied. He was aware that Ernie had picked up on the conversation and was watching them.

"Well, I've applied, and I think I'm going to be accepted," Burnes said. "I talked to Captain Roosevelt—the President's son?—and he said I would probably qualify."

"It's a very good way to get your ass blown away," McCoy said.

"Ken!" Ernie said.

"Sorry," McCoy said. "I shouldn't have said that."

XIII

(One)
Saufley Field
Pensacola Navy Air Station
20 February 1942

There was no doubt in the mind of Lieutenant Junior Grade Allen W. Minter, USNR, that Second Lieutenant Malcolm S. Pickering, USMCR, had a good deal more time in aircraft cockpits than his record showed; or, off the record, than he was willing to admit.

That made Pickering a liar. Not only a liar, but a good liar. Of course it was possible to put that more kindly, to say that he was a good role player. One could possibly maintain—or at least imagine—that Pickering was playing the role of someone who knew nothing about flying or aircraft, but who was eager to learn, and was a very quick learner.

From the moment Minter first took him out to the flight line, Pickering asked both the natural and the dumb questions Minter expected of a student whose flight records had "NONE" written in the "PREVIOUS FLYING EXPERIENCE" block. And he appeared to listen with rapt attention—as if he was hearing it

201

all for the first time—while Minter pointed out the parts of the N3N Yellow Peril and explained their functon.

And Minter was perfectly willing to accept that Pickering was learning for the first time that the thing that sat upright at the back of the Yellow Peril was the vertical stabilizer, and that the back part of it moved when the rudder pedals were pressed; that in the sea of air it served the same function that the rudder of a boat served in the water.

And Pickering seemed absolutely fascinated to learn that while the altimeter did indeed indicate the height of the aircraft above sea level, it did so seven seconds late. In other words, because it took some time for the change in air pressure to work upon the membrane of the barometric altimeter, the altimeter reported what the altitude had been seven seconds ago, not what it was at the moment.

It was only when he took Pickering up for the first time that Minter began to smell a rat.

Instructor pilots were given some latitude in teaching their students. Lieutenant Minter did not believe the way to turn an eager young man into a pilot was to take him up and scare the shit out of him, and/or make him sick to his stomach.

He believed that it was best to start out very simply, to show the student that a very slight rearward pressure on the stick would cause the nose of the Yellow Peril to rise, and that a very slight downward pressure would put the Yellow Peril in a nose-down attitude.

As the student understood and become familiar with one movement, he could be taught another. Eventually, he would reach the point where he would understand what coordinated control movement was necessary to make the aircraft perform any maneuver it was capable of.

Slow and easy was better, in Lieutenant Minter's professional judgment, than throwing things at a student too fast and scaring hell out of him. He would have the hell scared out of him soon enough.

On the first flight, Minter demonstrated climbing and descending, and then gentle turns to the left and right, pointing out to his new student that what one tried for was to make the turn without either gaining or losing altitude. In order to do that, one tried to keep one's eye on the vertical speed indicator, which indicated (faster than the altimeter responded) the deviation, and the rate of deviation (in thousands of feet per minute, up or down) from the altitude where the aircraft started when its needle was in the center of the instrument.

As he was demonstrating, Minter cautioned Pickering that not much movement of the controls was required to move the airplane around, and that most student pilots tended to overcontrol, to move the controls farther and more violently than was necessary.

And then when Minter turned the controls over to Pickering and told him to go up, and then down, the first thing he thought was that he had a student who paid attention to what he was told. He did not overcontrol. And he had a gentle, sure touch on the joystick and rudder pedals.

The first time Pickering tried to make a 360-degree turn to the right, for instance, the needle on the vertical speed indicator didn't even flicker. And when he came out of the turn and straightened up, he wasn't more than two degrees off the course he had been on before he began to make the turn. The whole maneuver was smooth as silk.

Much too smooth for somebody trying it for the first time. Q.E.D., Pickering knew how to fly. Ergo, Pickering was a liar, for he had told the U.S. Navy that his PREVIOUS FLIGHT EXPERIENCE was "NONE."

Viewed one way, it was an innocent little joke that Lieutenant Pickering was playing on the Navy and Lieutenant Junior Grade Allen W. Minter. Viewed another way, it was a serious breach of discipline. Pickering was a commissioned officer, and the code was quite clear: Officers told the truth. An officer's word was his bond. An officer who knowingly affixed his signature to a document he knew contained an untruth was subject to court-martial and dismissal from the service.

In the beginning, Lieutenant Minter decided that he would give Lieutenant Pickering the benefit of the doubt. Pickering seemed to be a nice enough guy, and he hadn't been in the service for very long, and he was young; and maybe he didn't understand that what he probably thought of as a little joke was something that could get his ass kicked out of Pensacola. Minter had heard that officers dismissed for cause from the service no longer got to go home, but were immediately pressed into service in the ranks. Unless it was really necessary, he didn't want to be responsible for sending Second

Lieutenant Pickering to the Marine boot camp at Parris Island
as a private.

When they landed, he conversed pleasantly with Pickering,
told him that he had done remarkably well (which caused
Pickering to beam), and gave him every opportunity to admit
that he'd had at least a little pilot training before today.
Pickering responded that Captain Carstairs had taken him for a
ride when he'd first come to Pensacola, but that was it.

Minter then went over Pickering's records very carefully. He
could have made a mistake, he told himself. But he had not.
The record said "NONE" in the "PREVIOUS FLIGHT EXPERIENCE"
block. And Pickering had signed the form.

Minter next sought out Captain James L. Carstairs, who had
the administrative responsibility for Pickering, as well as for
the other Marine second john, Stecker. Minter did not like
Carstairs, which was his natural reaction to the fact that
Carstairs did not like him. Carstairs was a Marine. Not only a
Marine but a regular, out of Annapolis. Carstairs was tall,
good-looking, and mustachioed. A regular fucking recruiting-
poster Marine.

As a class, officers like Carstairs did not particularly like
people like Minter, who joined the Navy right out of the
University of Ohio to get flight training, and who planned to
get out of the service just as soon as possible to take a job with
an airline. And who were, moreover, just a little plump, and
who did not look like the tall, erect, blue-eyed Naval aviators
in the recruiting posters.

But he made a point of finding Captain Carstairs at the bar of
the officers' club during happy hour.

"Hello, Captain," he said.

"Well, if it isn't Lieutenant Dumpling," Carstairs said.

Minter let that ride. "I took your two second lieutenants up
for the first time this morning," he said, signaling the
bartender to bring two beers.

"Did you really?"

"One of them, Pickering, seems to have a really unusual
flair."

"Does he really?"

"Either that or he's got time, bootleg or otherwise," Minter
said.

"What does his record say?"

"It says no previous flight experience," Minter said.

"Then we must presume, mustn't we, that he has none," Carstairs said.

"He tells me you had him up," Minter pursued. "What did you think?"

"Nothing special," Carstairs said. "He struck me as your typical red-blooded American boy burning with ambition to earn his wings of gold," Carstairs said.

"You don't know anything about him, except what's in his records?" Minter asked.

Carstairs looked at Minter, and then over his shoulders, as if to make sure no one could overhear him.

"I have heard," Carstairs said, confidentially, "that when Henry Ford runs a little short of cash, the first person he thinks of for a loan is Pickering. Is that what you mean?"

"Oh, come on, Carstairs, I'm serious," Minter said impatiently.

For a moment, Minter thought that Carstairs was going to jump his ass for calling him by his last name. But instead, Carstairs flashed him a broad smile.

"But my dear Dumpling, I am serious," Carstairs said. "You *do* know he lives in the penthouse of the San Carlos Hotel?"

"No, I didn't," Minter confessed, wondering if Carstairs was pulling his leg about that, too.

Carstairs shook his head in confirmation.

"If that's so," Minter blurted, "what's he doing in the Marine Corps?"

"Why, Dumpling, he's doing the same thing as you and me. Remembering Pearl Harbor, avenging Wake Island, and making the world safe for democracy. I'm really surprised that you had to ask."

Minter, not without effort, kept his temper and his mouth shut, finished his beer, and left.

The next morning, when it was time to take Pickering up again, he was just about ready to call Pickering on lying about and concealing his previous flying experience. And then he decided, fuck it.

He still wasn't sure whether or not Carstairs had been telling the truth in the officers' club bar about Pickering being rich and living in the San Carlos penthouse. It was equally credible that Carstairs was pulling his leg, making a fool of him.

What really counted was that Pickering seemed like a nice kid; and the Marines needed good pilots. Despite the black-and-white code of conduct expected of officers, what was really important was what he had been ordered to do, which was to turn Pickering into a pilot of sufficient skill to be promoted to Squadron-2. Minter told himself that he was an instructor pilot, not an FBI agent, and that saying you had no previous flying experience when you did was not a sin of the first magnitude.

He flew with Pickering for two hours, and then with Stecker for two hours. When he dismissed them to have lunch before going to ground school during the afternoon, he thought that he had proof that he was teaching Stecker, but that Pickering was just going through the motions of learning something he already knew. But it didn't seem important.

The next day, the two of them had ground school in the morning and flight training during the afternoon. Minter took Stecker up first, and spent two hours having him practice the skills necessary to get an aircraft off the ground, to make turns, and then to get it back on the ground again. He spent the last half hour with Stecker shooting touch-and-go landings, with Stecker following him through on the controls.

He did essentially the same thing when he gave Pickering his two hours, except that he devoted the last hour to touch-and-goes, and the last fifteen minutes of that to having Pickering actually make the landings and takeoffs.

But when the two hours were up, and he had permitted Pickering to taxi the Yellow Peril from the runway to the parking ramp himself, instead of ordering him to shut it down, he climbed out of the forward cockpit, knelt on the wing root beside the rear cockpit, and looked intently into Pickering's face.

"I can't think of any reason why you shouldn't take it up yourself, Pickering, can you?"

Pickering smiled. "No, sir," he said.

"Then do so, Lieutenant," Minter ordered, and got off the wing root.

Pickering had some trouble, Minter saw, taxiing the Yellow Peril back to the runway. And for a moment he really thought Pickering was about to collide with another Yellow Peril on the center line of the runway.

Just enough trouble to give Minter pause to consider that maybe he had done the wrong thing, that just maybe Pickering really didn't have any experience, and that he should not be sending him up to solo with the absolute minimum of five hours' instruction.

But then the tower flashed the green lamp at Pickering's Yellow Peril, giving him permission to take off. The Yellow Peril began to move down the runway. The tail wheel came off the ground smoothly and when it should have, and a moment later, very smoothly, the Yellow Peril was airborne.

And Pickering followed the orders he had been given for his first solo flight: Take off, enter the landing pattern, and land. That's all.

Except when he was in the line of Yellow Perils waiting for their turn to land, he swung the Yellow Peril from side to side. Just once. It was a gesture of joy and exuberance. Minter decided that he would not mention it once Pickering was back on the ground, as he was now ninety-five percent sure he soon would safely be.

The landing was as smooth as Minter expected it to be. But what surprised him was the look on Pickering's face when he taxied to the parking ramp and shut the Yellow Peril down. It was the same look—mingled awe, relief, pride, and even a little disbelief—that Minter had learned to expect from other young men who had really just made their first solo flight.

And when he'd climbed down from the Yellow Peril he looked at Minter and said, "Jesus Christ, that's something, isn't it?"

"That really was your first time, wasn't it?" Minter blurted.

"Yes, sir," Pickering said. The question obviously confused him.

"Don't let it go to your head, Pickering," Minter said. "The University of California did a study that proved conclusively that any high-level moron can be taught to fly."

(Two)
Gayfer's Department Store
Pensacola, Florida
20 February 1942

Second Lieutenant Malcolm S. Pickering, USMCR, could see Martha Sayre Culhane two aisles away. She was standing before triple full-length mirrors as she held a black dress to her body and examined her reflection thoughtfully.

Martha wore a light brown sweater and a brown tweed skirt. A single coil of pearls around her neck had shifted so that it curled around her left breast. And she was wearing loafers and bobby socks.

She was, Pick thought, the most exquisitely feminine creature he had ever seen. Just looking at her made his throat tight and dry, and his heart change its beat.

She was across a two-aisle no-man's land of ladies' lingerie—glass counters stacked high with underpants and brassieres and girdles and slips. Headless-torso dummies had been placed here and there on the counters, dressed in more or less translucent brassieres and pants.

The intimate feminine apparel made Pick uncomfortable. And so did being where he was, and why. Without being aware that he was doing it, he closed his eyes and shook his head.

Martha nodded, as if making a decision, and then stepped away from the triple mirror and out of Pick's sight.

He moved an aisle away and saw her enter a dressing room and close its curtain. "May I help you, Lieutenant?" a female voice said, behind him, startling him.

"No," he said. "No, thank you. Just browsing."

He looked at the counters immediately around him. He had moved to the expectant-mother section. The dummies here displayed nursing brassieres.

She must think I'm crazy! Obviously, I am.

The hem of the curtain over Martha's dressing room was eighteen inches off the floor. He saw Martha's tweed skirt drop to the floor. Then she stepped out of it and scooped it up. And then, over the top of the curtain, he could see her hands and arms as she pulled the sweater off over her head.

He could imagine her now, in his mind's eye, standing behind the curtain wearing nothing but her string of pearls and her brassiere and her underpants.

He closed his eyes and shook his head again, and when he opened them he could see her hands as she stepped into the black dress and pulled it up.

And then a moment later, she came out and went back to the triple mirrors and looked at herself again. She had not zipped

up the black dress, and he could see the strap of her brassiere
stretched taut over her back.

And then he walked toward her, taking long, purposeful
strides that shortened and grew hesitant as he came close.

"Surprise, surprise," he said, as jovially as he could
manage. "Fancy running into you here!"

"I don't know why you're surprised, Pick," Martha said,
looking directly at him. "You followed me from the air
station."

He felt his face color.

"I soloed today," he blurted. "A couple of hours ago."

"Good for you," she said.

"Christ!" he said, furious and humiliated.

"I didn't mean that the way it sounded," Martha said.
"Congratulations, Pick. Really. I know what it means, and I'm
happy for you."

"I want to celebrate," Pick said.

"You should," Martha said. "It's a bona fide cause for
celebration."

"I mean, with you," Pick blurted.

"I was afraid of that," she said.

"I thought maybe dinner, and then . . ."

She shook her head, and held up her left hand with her
wedding and engagement rings on it.

"It sometimes may not look like it, Pick, but I'm in
mourning."

"You go out with Captain Mustache," Pick blurted.

She laughed a delightful peal of laughter.

"Is that what you call him?" Martha said. "Marvelous! You
better pray he doesn't hear you. Jimmy is very proud of his
mustache."

"You go out with him," Pick persisted.

"That's different," Martha said. "He's a friend."

"And I can't be your friend?"

"You know what I mean," Martha said. "Jimmy was *our*
friend. He was best man at the wedding."

"I'll settle for being your friend," Pick said.

"You don't take no for an answer, do you?" Martha said.

"Usually, I take anything less than 'oh, how wonderful' for
no," Pick said.

"Well, Mr. Pickering," Martha said, "I'm truly sorry to

disappoint you, but not only will I not go out with you, but I would consider it a personal favor if you would stop following me around and staring at me like a lovesick calf.''

"Jesus!"

"I'm a *widow*, for God's sake," Martha went on furiously. "I'm just not interested, understand? I don't know what you're thinking—"

She stopped in mid-sentence, for Second Lieutenant Pickering had turned and fled down the aisle.

Martha told herself that there was really no reason for her to be ashamed of herself for jumping on him that way, or to be sorry that she had so obviously and so deeply hurt his feelings.

She *was* a widow, for God's sake.

Greg, my wonderful Greg, was killed only two months and twelve days ago. Only a real bitch and a slut would start thinking about another man only two months and twelve days after her husband, whom she had loved as much as life itself, had been killed. And if that handsome, arrogant sonofabitch was any kind of a gentleman he would understand that.

Martha Sayre Culhane vowed that she would never again think of the terrible hurt look in Pick's eyes when she told him off. It would not bother her, she swore, for she would simply not think about it.

Let him look at some other girl, some other woman, with those eyes. That would get him laid, and that, certainly, was all he was really after anyway. He had probably stood in front of a mirror and practiced that look.

Goddamn him, anyway! What did he think she was?

She went back in the dressing room and took the black dress off. She did not buy it.

She went from Gayfer's Department Store to the bar at the San Carlos. She waited for Jimmy Carstairs to come in. By the time he came in, she was feeling pretty good.

When she woke up the next morning, she remembered two things about the night before. She'd had a scrap with Jimmy Carstairs, who had refused to let her drive herself home. And that once—or was it twice?— she had tried to call Pick on the house phone. He had had no right to walk away from her like that before she had finished telling him off, and she had been determined to finish what she had started.

There had been no answer in the penthouse, even though Martha remembered letting the telephone ring and ring and ring.

(Three)
San Diego Navy Base, California
21 February 1942

Although it was surrounded by a double line of barbed-wire-topped hurricane fencing, the brig at Diego was not from a distance very forbidding. It looked like any other well-cared-for Naval facility.

But inside, Lieutenant Commander Michael J. Grotski, USNR, thought as he waited to be admitted to the office of the commanding officer, it was undeniably a prison. Cleaner, maybe, but still a prison. Until November 1941, Lieutenant Commander Grotski had been engaged in the practice of criminal law in his native Chicago, Illinois. He had spent a good deal of time visiting clients in prison.

"You can go in, Commander," the natty, crew-cutted young Marine corporal in a tailored, stiffly starched khaki uniform said as he rose from his desk and opened a polished wooden door. Above the door was a red sign on which was a representation of the Marine insignia and the legend "C. F. KAMNIK, CAPT. USMC BRIG COMMANDER."

The "C," Commander Grotski knew, stood for "Casimir." He had come to know Captain Kamnik pretty well. They were not only two good Chicago Polack boys in uniform, but they had both once served as altar boys to the Reverend Monsignor Taddeus Wiznewski at Saint Teresa's. Monsignor Wiznewski had installed a proper respect for what they were doing in his altar boys by punching them in the mouth when Mass was over whenever their behavior fell below his expectations.

They had not been altar boys at the same time. Captain Kamnik was six years older than Lieutenant Commander Grotski. And he had enlisted in the Marine Corps when Grotski was still in the sixth grade at St. Teresa's parochial school. But it had been a pleasant experience for the both of them to recall their common experience, and to find somebody else from the old neighborhood who was a fellow commissioned officer and gentleman.

"Good morning, Commander," Captain Kamnik said as he

rose up behind his desk and grinned at Grotski. "How can the Marine Corps serve the Navy?"

"Oh, I just happened to be in the neighborhood and I thought I would drop in and ruin your day."

"Let me guess," Kamnik said, first closing the office door and then going to a file cabinet. From this he took out a bottle of Seagram's Seven Crown. Then he continued, "You are about to rush to the defence of some innocent boy out there, who has been unjustly accused."

"Close, but not quite," Grotski said, taking a pull from the offered bottle and handing it back. Kamnik took a pull himself, and then put the bottle back in the filing cabinet. Technically, it was drinking on duty, one of many court-martial offenses described in some detail in the *Rules for the Governance of the Navy Service*. But it was also a pleasant custom redolent of home for two Polack former altar boys from the same neighborhood.

Kamnik looked at Grotski with his eyes raised in question.

"You have a fine young Marine out there named McCoy, Thomas Michael," Grotski said.

It was evident from the look on Kamnik's face that he had searched his memory and come up with nothing.

"McCoy?" he asked, as he went to his desk and ran his finger down one typewritten roster, and then another. "Here it is," he said. *"Ex*-Marine. He's on his way to do five-to-ten at Portsmouth." Portsmouth was the U.S. Naval Prison.

"Not anymore, he's not," Grotski. "You have his file?"

"Somewhere, I'm sure. Why?"

"You're going to need it," Grotski said, simply.

Captain Kamnik walked to the door and pulled it open.

"Scott, fetch me the jacket on a prisoner named McCoy. He's one of those general prisoners who came in from Pearl. On his way to Portsmouth."

"Aye, aye, sir," the corporal said.

Kamnik turned to Grotski.

"You going to tell me what this is all about?"

"After you read the file," Grotski said. "Or at least glance at it. I'll throw you a bone, though: I have the feeling the commanding general of the joint training force in Diego is more than a little pissed at me."

"Really? You don't mind if I'm happy about that?"

"I'm flattered," Grotski said.

Corporal Scott entered the office a minute later, carrying a seven-inch-thick package wrapped in water-resistant paper and sealed with tape. On it was crudely lettered, "McCoy, Thomas Michael."

The package contained a complete copy of the general court-martial convened in the case of PFC Thomas M. McCoy, USMC, 1st Defense Battalion, Marine Barracks, Pearl Harbor, Hawaii, to try him on charges that on the twenty-fourth day of December 1941, he had committed the offense of assault upon the person of a commissioned officer of the U.S. Navy in the execution of his office by striking him with his fists upon the face and on other parts of his body.

The record showed that PFC McCoy was also charged with having committed an assault upon a petty officer of the United States Navy in the execution of his office by striking him with his fists upon the face and on other parts of his body, and by kicking him in the general area of his genital region with his feet.

The record showed that PFC McCoy was additionally accused of having been absent without leave from his assigned place of duty at the time of the alleged offenses described in specifications 1 and 2.

The record showed that in secret session, two-thirds of the members present and voting, a general court-martial convened under the authority of the general officer commanding Marine Barracks, Pearl Harbor, T.H., had found PFC McCoy guilty of each of the charges and specifications; and finally that, in secret session, two-thirds of the members present and voting, the court-martial had pronounced sentence.

As to specification and charge number 1, PFC McCoy was to be reduced to the lowest enlisted grade, suffer loss of all pay and allowances, and be confined at hard labor for a period of five to ten years at Portsmouth or such other Naval prison as the Secretary of the Navy may designate, and at the completion of his term of imprisonment, be dishonorably discharged from the Naval service.

As to specification and charge number 2, PFC McCoy was to be reduced to the lowest enlisted grade, suffer loss of all pay and allowances, and be confined at hard labor for a period of three to five years at Portsmouth or such other Naval prison as the Secretary of the Navy may designate, and at the completion of his term of imprisonment, be dishonorably discharged from the Naval Service.

As to specification and charge number 3, PFC McCoy was to be reduced to the lowest enlisted grade, suffer loss of all pay and allowance, and be confined at hard labor for a period of six months in the U.S. Navy brig at Pearl Harbor, or such other place of confinement as the Commanding General, Marine Barracks, Pearl Harbor, T.H., may designate.

"Another of your innocent lambs, I see, Commander," Captain Kamnik said.

"Lovely fellow, obviously," Grotski said.

"So what about him?"

Grotski handed a single sheet of paper to Kamnik.

OP-29-BC3
L21-[5]-5
SERIAL 0002

FROM: THE COMMANDER IN CHIEF, PACIFIC FLEET
TO: GENERAL OFFICER COMMANDING,
             MARINE BARRACKS, PEARL HARBOR

REFERENCE: RECORD OF TRIAL, MCCOY, PFC THOMAS MICHAEL, USMC

1. THE REVIEW REQUIRED BY LAW OF THE TRIAL, CONVICTION, AND SENTENCING OF PFC MCCOY HAS BEEN COMPLETED BY THE UNDERSIGNED.

2. THE REVIEW REVEALED THAT THE COMPOSITION OF THE GENERAL COURT-MARTIAL WAS NOT IN KEEPING WITH APPLICABLE REGULATIONS AND LAW. (SEE ATTACHMENT 1 HERETO.)

3. IT IS THEREFORE ORDERED THAT THE FINDINGS AND SENTENCE IN THE AFOREMENTIONED CASE BE, AND THEY HEREBY ARE, SET ASIDE.

E. J. KING
ADMIRAL, USN

"You mean we're going to have to try this character again?" Captain Kamnik asked. "What about the 'composition' of the court-martial?"

"The law requires that 'all parties to the trial,'" Grotski said, "be present for all sessions of the court. They weren't. The trial lasted three days. Three times, one officer or another was called away. The court reporter, apparently a very thorough individual, put it in the record every time somebody left, and when they came back."

"I can't imagine why they would be called away," Kamnik said, sarcastically. "It's not as if there's a war on, or anything important like that."

"CINCPAC really doesn't review these cases himself," Grotski said. "He gives them to a lawyer on the judge advocate's staff to review, and he generally goes by his recommendations. Whoever reviewed this saw that members of the board kept wandering in and out."

"You're not telling me we have to go through the whole goddamned trial again?" Kamnik said.

"No," Grotski said. "You remember I said the general is pissed at me?"

"What about?"

"Well, by the time the case was reviewed, McCoy was already on his way to Portsmouth . . . here, in other words. So this was sent here for action. And the general called me in and said that somebody had fucked up in Hawaii, and that we were going to have to try Brother McCoy all over again, and would I please see that it was done very quickly and efficiently, and that I was to personally make sure that no member of the board left the room for any purpose while the trial was on.

"So I said, 'Aye, aye, sir,' and read the file. Then I went back to see the general and told him that in my professional judgment, we could not retry Brother McCoy. For two reasons: The first was double jeopardy. He'd already been tried. The government had its shot at him. They should not have gone on with the trial with any member of the court missing, but they did. That was not McCoy's fault. He was there. And I told the general that it was not the responsibility of his defense counsel to object; that he was almost obliged to take advantage of mistakes the prosecution made. And then I told him that even if they sort of swept that under the rug and tried him again here, McCoy was entitled to face his accusers. The Navy would have to bring here from Pearl (or from wherever they are now) the officer he punched out, and the shore patrolman, plus all of

McCoy's buddies who had previously testified that McCoy was just sitting there innocently in the whorehouse when the shore patrol lieutenant came in and viciously attacked him for no reason that they could see."

"You mean this sonofabitch is going to get away with punching out an officer? A shore patrol officer?" Captain Kamnik asked incredulously.

"Think of it this way, Casimir," Commander Grotski said dryly, " 'it is better that one thousand guilty men go free than one innocent man be convicted.' "

"But the sonofabitch is guilty as hell! Innocent, my ass!"

"He was entitled to a fair trial, and he didn't get one," Grotski said. "I must say the general took this better than you are."

"I thought you said he was pissed," Kamnik said.

"At me. As the bearer of bad news. He doesn't seem to be annoyed with Brother McCoy nearly as much. As a matter of fact, he even had a thought about where PFC McCoy can make a contribution to the Marine Corps and the war effort in the future."

"What does that mean?"

"I'm here to 'counsel' McCoy," Grotski said. "You're welcome to watch, but only if you can keep your mouth shut."

"I wouldn't miss this for the world," Kamnik said. "You want him brought here?"

"That would be very nice, Captain Kamnik," Grotski said. "I appreciate your spirit of cooperation."

"Scott!" Captain Kamnik called. The natty corporal stuck his head in the door. "Do you know where to find the sergeant of the guard?"

"He's out here, sir. He's waiting to see you."

"Ask him to come in, please."

The sergeant of the guard was the meanest-looking sonofabitch Commander Grotski had seen in some time, a bald, stocky staff sergeant of thirty or so, with an acne-pocked face. Grotski searched for the word, and came up with "porcine." The sergeant of the guard was porcine, piglike, a mean boar pig.

The sergeant of the guard came to attention before Kamnik's desk.

"What's on your mind, Sergeant?" Kamnik asked.

"I didn't know that the captain was busy, sir."

"Don't mind me, Sergeant," Grotski said amiably.

The sergeant still hesitated.

"Go on, Sergeant," Captain Kamnik said.

"The captain said he wanted to hear," the sergeant of the guard reluctantly began, "of an 'incident.'"

"Yes, I did."

"We had a little trouble with one of the transits, sir," the sergeant of the guard said.

"Oh?"

"He gave one of the guards some lip, sir," the sergeant of the guard said. "And then he assaulted two guards. The point of it is, sir, before we could restrain him, he busted PFC Tober's nose."

"The situation is now under control?"

"Oh, yes, sir," the sergeant of the guard said. "But I thought you'd want to hear right away about PFC Tober. I sent him over to the dispensary."

"And the transient?"

"We have him restrained, sir. I was going to ask the captain's permission to keep him in the box until we can ship him out of here."

"The 'box,' Sergeant?" Commander Grotski asked, innocently.

"That's what we call our 'solitary detention facility,'" Captain Kamnik explained.

"Oh, I see," Grotski said. "And just out of idle curiosity, what's the name of the prisoner who broke the guard's nose?"

The sergeant of the guard looked at Captain Kamnik for permission to reply. Kamnik nodded.

"McCoy, sir," the sergeant of the guard said. "He's a mean sonofabitch, a general prisoner on his way to Portsmouth. He's gonna do five-to-ten. Assault on an officer and some other stuff."

"Curiosity overwhelms me," Commander Grotski said. "I would like to see this villain."

The sergeant of the guard looked distantly uncomfortable. He looked to Captain Kamnik for help and got none.

"Do you suppose you could bring him here, Sergeant?" Commander Grotski asked.

"Commander," the sergeant of the guard said, "you don't really want to see to this character, do you?"

"Oh, but I do. Go get him, Sergeant."

The sergeant of the guard again looked in vain for Captain Kamnik's help.

When he had gone, Commander Grotski asked, "Are you a betting man, Casimir?"

"Sometimes," Kamnik said.

"How about three will get you five that this McCoy will fall down the stairs on his way here?"

"It happens, Commander," Kamnik said. "I do my best to stop it, but sometimes it happens."

Five minutes later General Prisoner Thomas Michael McCoy was led into the brig commander's office. He was dressed in dungarees. A ten-inch-high letter "P" had been stenciled to the thighs of his trousers and onto the rear of his jacket. He was in handcuffs, and the handcuffs were chained to a thick leather belt around his waist. His ankles were encircled with heavy iron rings, and the rings were chained together, restricting his movement to a shuffle.

His hands were swollen, and red with iodine. There was more iodine on his face, on his mouth, and above his eyes. His face was swollen, and in a few hours both of his eyes would be dark.

They must have been really pissed at him, which was not surprising, since he broke a guard's nose, Commander Grotski thought. *Otherwise the marks of his beating would not be so visible.*

"What happened to your face?" Commander Grotski asked.

General Prisoner McCoy thought about his reply for a moment before he gave it.

"I fell down in the shower," he said.

"I fell down in the shower, *sir,*" Grotski corrected him.

"I fell down in the shower, sir," McCoy dutifully parroted.

"That will be all, Sergeant," Commander Grotski said. "When we need you, we'll call for you."

The sergeant is worried that the moment he's out of the room, Grotski thought, *McCoy will tell us that three, four, maybe five guards got him in the box and had at him with billy clubs, or saps, or whatever they thought would cause the most pain. That's against the* Regulations for the Governance of the Naval Service.

"You really fell down in the shower, McCoy?" Grotski

asked, when the sergeant of the guard had gone, closing the door after him.

"Yes, sir," McCoy said, after thinking it over.

"Tough guy, are you?" Grotski asked.

McCoy didn't answer.

"I asked you a question, McCoy," Grotski said.

"I guess I'm as tough as most," McCoy said, and remembered finally to add, "sir."

"You don't know what tough is, you dumb Mick sonofabitch," Grotski said. "And you're the dumbest sonofabitch I've seen in a long time. You don't even know what you're facing, do you? It hasn't penetrated that thick Mick head of yours, has it? You're really so dumb you think you can take on Portsmouth, don't you?"

McCoy didn't reply.

"That sergeant isn't even very good at what he did," Grotski said. "He's nowhere near good enough to get himself assigned to Portsmouth. At Portsmouth, he would be a rookie. When they beat you at Portsmouth, they got it down to a fine art. No marks. It just hurts. And how long are you going to be in Portsmouth, McCoy?"

"They gave me five-to-ten, sir," McCoy said.

"Let me tell you how it works. The first time you look cockeyed at somebody at Portsmouth, you dumb Mick, they'll give you a working over that'll make the one you just had feel like your mother kissed you. And then they'll add six months on your sentence for 'silent insolence.' And every time you look cockeyed at a guard there, you'll get another working over, and another six months, until one of two things happens. You won't look cockeyed at anyone, or you will fall down the stairs and break your neck. Then they'll bury you in the prison cemetery. You don't really understand that, do you?"

"I'm going to keep my nose clean, sir," McCoy said.

"Bullshit! You're not smart enough to keep your nose clean," Grotski said, nastily.

He let that sink in.

"You wouldn't even know what to do, would you, you stupid sonofabitch, if I told you I can get you out of Portsmouth?"

McCoy looked at him uncomprehendingly.

Finally, he said, "Sir?"

"If I was in your shoes, you miserable asshole, and

somebody told me he could get me out of Portsmouth, I would get on my knees and ask him what I had to do, and pray to the Blessed Virgin that he would believe me when I said I would do it."

McCoy looked at him, his eyes widening.

And then he dropped to his knees. He tried to raise his hands together before him in an attitude of prayer, but his handcuffed wrists were chained to the leather belt around his waist, and he could move them only slightly above his waist.

"You tell me what I have to do, sir, and I'll do it. I swear on my mother's grave!"

"And now you pray, you miserable bastard," Grotski ordered. "And out loud!"

McCoy looked at him, frightened and confused.

"What do I pray?"

"Say your Hail Marys, you pimple on the ass of the Marine Corps," Grotski ordered icily.

"Hail Mary, full of grace," McCoy began, "the Lord is with thee. Blessed art thou amongst women and blessed is the fruit of thy womb, Jesus. Holy Mary, Mother of God, pray for us sinners now and at the hour of our death. Amen."

Grotski looked at Captain Kamnik, then nodded his head in an order for him to leave the room.

He closed the door to the office after them.

"He's pretty good at that, Casimir," he said. "Do you think maybe he was an altar boy, too?"

"Jesus!" Kamnik said, and then spotted the sergeant of the guard. "Wait outside please, Sergeant," he ordered.

When he looked at Grotski, Grotski was grinning broadly.

"Now what?"

"It's what is known as psychological warfare," he said. "I'll let him keep it up a while until I'm sure he is in the right state of mind, and then I'll offer him a chance to redeem himself."

"How?" Kamnik ordered.

"You ever hear of a Lieutenant Colonel Carlson?" he asked. Kamnik shook his head. "No."

"Well, he's apparently on the general's shitlist, too. Some kind of a nut. He's being given some kind of commando outfit. The general said when I got McCoy out of here, he thought it would be nice if McCoy volunteered for it. I had the feeling he wouldn't be all that unhappy if McCoy got himself blown away as one of Carlson's commandos."

"And you think he'll volunteer?"

"I'm not going to let him off his knees until he does," Commander Grotski said.

XIV

(One)
The San Diego Yacht Club
1400 Hours, 28 February 1942

The Yellow Cab dropped Second Lieutenant Kenneth J. McCoy, USMCR, wearing dungarees, at the end of Pier Four at the yacht club. The driver was not accustomed to carrying dungaree-clad Marines—for that matter Marines period—to the yacht club. And he watched curiously as McCoy walked down the pier and finally crossed the gangplank onto the *Last Time*. Then he shrugged his shoulders and drove off.

McCoy slid open the varnished teak door to the lounge and stepped inside.

Ernie Sage and Dorothy Burnes were there, listening to the radio. Dorothy was sitting uncomfortably in one of the armchairs, draped in a tentlike cotton dress. Ernie Sage, wearing very brief shorts and a T-shirt, jumped up from one of the couches when she saw him.

"What are you doing home so early?" she asked as she crossed the room to him. She grabbed his ears, pulled his face to hers, and kissed him wetly and noisily on the mouth. "Not that I'm not glad to see you, as you can see."

Dorothy laughed.

"They gave me the afternoon off," McCoy said.

"You should have called me, I would have come for you," Ernie said. She put her arm around him and pressed against him, confirming his suspicion that there was nothing but Ernie under the T-shirt.

"It was quicker catching the bus," he said.

"And how did you get here?"

"In a cab."

"And what did that cost?"

"Buck and a half, with the tip."

"Mr. Moneybags," Ernie said.

Ernie's attitude toward money—she was a real cheapskate—was another of the things about her that continually surprised him. With the exception, maybe, of Pick Pickering, she was the richest person he had ever known, but she was really tight about some things, like his taking a taxicab. It really bothered her.

He reached down and pinched her tail under the shorts, confirming that there was nothing but her under there, either.

She yelped in mock protest and jumped away from him.

"You want something to eat? A beer? A drink? Anything?"

"I thought you would never ask," McCoy said. "About anything."

"You better watch him." Dorothy laughed. "You would be amazed the kind of trouble that sort of thing can get you into."

"How goes it, Dorothy?" McCoy asked.

"How do you think?" Dorothy replied, patting her stomach. "I'm beginning to think it has to be triplets."

"Well?" Ernie asked.

"Well, what?"

"You want something to eat? Or to drink?"

"That wasn't the original offer," McCoy said.

"It must be something the Corps puts in their food," Dorothy laughed.

"Well?" Ernie pursued.

"What I need now is a shower," McCoy said, and started across the lounge to the passageway to the cabins.

"Why did they give you the afternoon off?" Ernie said. "I thought you were supposed to get transferred today?"

"I was," he said. "And tomorrow they're sending me to Northern California." He saw the look on her face, and quickly added, "Just for a couple of days."

Then he entered the passageway to avoid further explanation.

Ernie was in their cabin when he came naked out of the bathroom. She had a plate in one hand and a bottle of Schlitz in the other.

"Sardines on saltines," she said. "And Schlitz. And I could be talked into anything, too, if that was a bona fide offer."

And then she looked at him, and her face colored, and she laughed, deep in her throat.

"And I see it was," she said.

"You do that to me," he said. "I think it's something you put in the sardines."

"I wish I knew what it was," she said as she put the tray and the beer down on the bedside table. "We could give the formula to my father on a royalty basis and get rich."

She pushed the shorts down off her hips and then pulled the T-shirt over her head.

"Oh, baby," McCoy said huskily as she walked to him and put her arms around him.

"Are you going to tell me what you're going to do in Northern California?" Ernie asked, her face against his chest.

"I've got to call," he said. "You can listen."

"Before, or after?"

"After," he said.

"You don't know how lucky you are you gave the right answer," Ernie said as she pulled him backward onto the bed.

"Colonel Rickabee." The voice came over the telephone flat and metallic.

"Sir, I'm sorry, I asked for Captain Sessions," McCoy said.

"What's the matter, McCoy?" Rickabee replied. "You don't like me?"

Ernie, who was lying half on top of McCoy, giggled, and then she moved higher up so that she could hear better.

When there was no reply from McCoy, Colonel Rickabee said, "What is it exactly that you feel you can tell Sessions and can't tell me?"

"Nothing, sir," McCoy said.

"Good!" Rickabee said, gently sarcastic.

"I went over to the Second Raider Battalion today, sir."

"How did it go?"

"It went smoothly, sir. I was further assigned to Baker Company, as a platoon leader, but that's not what they're going to have me doing."

"What *happened*, McCoy? Take it from the beginning. Tell me about the red flags, and the a cappella choir singing the *Internationale*."

"Nothing like that, sir," McCoy said, chuckling.

"Did you see Colonel Carlson?"

"Yes, sir."

"And Captain Roosevelt?"

"Yes, sir."

"Was either of them howling at the moon?"

Ernie giggled so loudly that Rickabee heard her.

"Is there someone with you?" he asked, now deadly serious. "I presume you are using a secure line?"

"The line is secure, sir," McCoy said.

"Okay, once again. Take it from the beginning."

"The adjutant was waiting for me when I showed up to take the reveille formation, sir. He said he had my orders transferring me to the Raiders, and there was no sense complaining about them, because the battalion commander had already gone to the Second Joint Training Force personnel officer trying to keep me."

"Another of many ways Colonel Carlson is endearing himself to the rest of the Corps," Rickabee said dryly, "is by kidnapping their best people. Go on."

"So they sent me over to the Second Raider Battalion in a truck," McCoy said. "And I reported to the adjutant. And he sent me in to report to Colonel Carlson."

"Roosevelt?"

"I didn't see him until later, sir."

"Go on."

"Colonel, it was just like my reporting in to the Third Battalion," McCoy said. "Colonel Carlson shook my hand and welcomed me aboard. Told me I was joining the best outfit in the Corps, and that it was a great opportunity for me, a great challenge . . . the usual bullshit."

"I hope Carlson didn't sense your cynicism," Rickabee said. "You are supposed to be bright-eyed and eager, McCoy."

"Colonel, he makes sense," McCoy said. "I wasn't making fun of him. What I was trying to say was that it was like reporting in anywhere else."

"As opposed to what?"

"I read that letter, sir, the one Roosevelt wrote, where he wanted to have 'leaders' and 'fighters' and the rest of that Red Army stuff."

"And there was none of that?" Rickabee asked.

"Not what I expected, sir."

"Explain."

"First, he talked about what the Raiders were supposed to do. I mean, the raid business, shaking the Japs up by hitting them where they didn't expect to get hit. The *Commando* business. And then he said that the mission was so important that the Corps had given him top priority for personnel and equipment, and that meant the personnel—"

"Let me interrupt," Rickabee said. "Do you think he believes the Corps thinks the Raider mission is so important that he has carte blanche?"

"Sir?"

"That he can have anything, do anything, he wants?"

"He sure sounded like he did. But on the other hand, you could hardly expect him to say anything else."

Rickabee snorted. "Go on."

McCoy mimed wanting a cigarette. Ernie leaned across him to the bedside table and picked up his Lucky Strike package and Zippo. In the process, she rubbed her breast across his face. McCoy wondered if it had been an accident, and realized, pleased with the realization, that it had not been.

"Then he said because he had such high-class enlisted men, it would be possible to treat them differently."

"How differently?" Rickabee asked softly.

"I want to say 'better,'" McCoy said. "But that's not quite it. He said they can be given greater responsibility. . . . Colonel, what I think he was saying is that he thinks you can get more out of the men if they're making the decisions. Or some of the decisions. Or if they *think* they're making the decisions."

"You sound as if you're a convert," Rickabee said, dryly.

"When Colonel Carlson says it, it doesn't sound so nutty as when I try to tell you about it," McCoy said.

"Anything specific?" Rickabee asked.

"He said that he's been both an enlisted man and an officer, and that what really pissed him off as an enlisted man was when the officers had special privileges and rubbed them in the enlisted men's faces, and that he wasn't going to let that happen in the Raiders."

"Interesting," Rickabee said.

"I think I know what he means, Colonel," McCoy said. "He doesn't want to burn down the officers' club. All he's saying is that if you're in the field, and the men are sleeping on the ground, the officers should not have bunks and sheets."

"Neither do I," Rickabee said. "That doesn't sound like the revolution."

"I'm beginning to think, Colonel, that if Roosevelt hadn't written that nutty 'fighters' and 'leaders' letter—''

"But he did," Rickabee interrupted. "And if he hadn't, there probably would be no Raider battalions."

"Yes, sir."

"Did Colonel Carlson say anything else out of the ordinary? Anything unusual?"

"No, sir."

"How long were you with him?"

"About fifteen minutes, sir. Then he sent me down to the company."

"Baker Company, you said?"

"Yes, sir. Captain Coyte, Ralph H."

"What about him?"

"Looked like a real Marine to me. Seemed to know what he was doing. And like a nice guy."

"And he gave you a platoon?"

"Yes, sir, but I never got there. He was still feeling me out. I hadn't been there ten minutes, when Captain Roosevelt showed up."

"What did he want?"

"He told Captain Coyte that he was going to borrow me. He told him I used to be in a heavy-weapons company in the Fourth Marines and knew about weapons, so he was going to send me up to some Army ordnance depot near San Francisco to make sure the Army didn't give us all junk when we drew weapons."

"Okay," Colonel Rickabee said. "That makes sense."

"And then he gave me the rest of the day off."

"What did you think of Roosevelt?"

"I liked him, too," McCoy said. "He acts like a Marine."

"And he wasn't walking around with a copy of the Communist Manifesto in his pocket?"

"No, sir." McCoy chuckled.

"Well, it looks like you're in, and nobody's suspicious," Rickabee said. "So all you have to do is keep your mouth shut and your eyes open."

"Yes, sir."

"I want to make the point, McCoy, that we want to hear about anything unusual, *anything* unusual."

"Yes, sir," McCoy replied. "The weapons are a little unusual, sir."

"What do you mean by that?"

"Well, what I'm going to draw—*try* to draw—from the Army, are shotguns and carbines."

The U.S. Carbine, Caliber .30, M1 was an autoloading shoulder arm with a fifteen-round magazine. It fired a pistol-sized cartridge, and was intended to replace the .45 Colt automatic pistol. The later M2 version was fully automatic, and there was later a thirty-round magazine.

"That's just the sort of thing I mean," Rickabee said. "By shotguns, I presume you mean twelve-gauge trench guns?"

"Yes, sir. From the First World War. And carbines. I've never even seen a carbine."

"Well, then, if you're the weapons expert, it will be a case of the blind leading the blind, won't it?" Rickabee said.

"I guess so," McCoy said.

"Anything else?"

"Roosevelt told me that they're going to give everyone a knife and a pistol," McCoy said.

"I heard about that," Rickabee said. "Anything else?"

"I ran into Gunnery Sergeant Zimmerman."

"You knew he was being sent out there, didn't you?"

"Yes, sir. Captain Sessions told me."

"Sessions felt," Colonel Rickabee said, "and I agreed, that it might be handy for you to have somebody out there you could trust. Another set of eyes."

"Zimmerman thinks that the Raiders are a great idea," McCoy said.

"You didn't tell him what you're doing out there, did you?"

"No, sir, of course not."

"Then leave it that way, McCoy. Zimmerman can be an extra set of eyes and ears in the ranks for you."

"I understand, sir," McCoy said. "He wouldn't understand that. I'm not so sure I do."

"And that's all?"

"Yes, sir."

"I relay herewith the best wishes of Captain Ed Banning," Rickabee said.

"Thank you, sir," McCoy said. "He's with you in Washington?"

"Actually, he's in the Naval hospital in Brooklyn," Rickabee said.

"What's wrong with him?" McCoy asked quickly.

"He was blind for a while," Rickabee said. "You didn't know that?"

"No, sir," McCoy said, shocked.

"Well, it was apparently psychosomatic," Rickabee said. "Which means no evident physical damage. He can see now, but the medics want to check him out carefully."

"Yes, sir."

"Okay, that seems to be it. Check in with me when you come back from San Francisco. Let me know how you made out with the Army. And anything else that comes to mind."

"Aye, aye, sir."

"So long, McCoy," Colonel Rickabee said. "Keep up the good work."

The line went dead.

McCoy put the handset back in its cradle, and then looked at Ernie.

"Any questions?" he asked.

"Sergeant Zimmerman's here?" Ernie asked.

"Uh-huh."

"Why don't you have him to dinner?" Ernie said.

"It doesn't work that way," McCoy said. "Officers don't socialize with enlisted men."

"You're a snob," she said. "Who would ever know?"

"What would Marty Burnes think?" McCoy said, teasingly.

"Fuck him, it's our boat," Ernie said.

McCoy chuckled. *"Fuck him?"* he parroted. "When I met you, you didn't use words like that."

"When I met you, I was a virgin," Ernie said. "Cussing like a Marine is not the only bad habit I learned from you."

She lowered her head to his chest and nipped his nipple, and then she jumped out of bed and went into the bathroom.

McCoy picked up the telephone again and called Camp Elliott and spoke with the sergeant major of the Second Raider

Battalion. He told him that if it were possible, he would like to have Gunnery Sergeant Zimmerman go with him to Northern California.

"We were in the Fourth Marines together, Sergeant Major, and he knows about weapons," McCoy said.

"And, with respect, sir," the sergeant major said, chuckling, "you old China Marines stick together, don't you?"

"Let me tell you, sometime, Sergeant Major, how it was in the Old Corps."

"Do that," the sergeant major, who was twice McCoy's age, said, laughing. "I'll have Zimmerman at the motor pool when you get there, Lieutenant."

(Two)
U.S. Navy Hospital
Brooklyn Navy Yard
2 March 1942

The headshrinker was wearing a white medical smock with an embroidered medical insignia on the breast, but there was no name tag with his rank on it. And since the Navy did not wear rank insignia on the collar points of their white shirts, Banning could not tell what rank he was. He could have been anything, to go by his age, from a junior grade lieutenant to a lieutenant commander.

"Come in, Captain Banning," the headshrinker said, when he saw Banning in the outer office.

Banning was in pajamas and a blue bathrobe, his bare feet in cloth hospital slippers.

"Good morning, sir," Banning said. "I was told to report to you."

"I'm Dr. Toland," the headshrinker said. "I've been looking forward to this."

"Why?" Banning challenged. It sounded like a bullshit remark.

The headshrinker looked at him intently for a moment, and then smiled.

"Actually, because I thought you would be more interesting than my general run of patients. These go from bed-wetting sailors trying to get out of the service to full commanders experiencing what we call the 'midlife crisis.' You're my first battle-scarred veteran."

Banning had to chuckle. "And you're the one who decides whether or not I'm crazy, right?"

"If I were in your shoes, Captain, that would annoy me too," Dr. Toland said. "So let me get that out of the way. I find you to be remarkably stable, psychologically speaking, considering what you've gone through."

"I just walked in here," Banning said. "Can you decide that quickly?"

"Sit down, Banning," Dr. Toland said. "I'll get us some coffee, and we can go through the motions."

Banning expected a corpsman, or a clerk, to bring coffee, but instead Toland walked out of the office and returned with two china mugs.

"You take cream and sugar?" he asked.

"No, black's fine," Banning said, taking the cup. "Thank you."

"The way it works," Toland said, "unless somebody walks in here wild-eyed and talking to God, is that I consider the reason an examination was requested; the aberrations, if any, that the patient has manifested; and the stress to which he has been subjected. Taking those one at a time, I'm a little surprised that you're surprised that they wanted you examined."

"I don't quite follow that," Banning said.

"According to General Forrest," Dr. Toland said, "the duties they have in mind for you are such that they just can't take the chance that you will either get sick, physically as opposed to mentally; or that you will suddenly decide you're Napoleon."

Banning looked at him sharply. He had not expected to hear General Forrest's name. He wondered if Toland was telling him the truth or whether this was some kind of a headshrinker's game. After a moment he concluded that Toland was telling the truth and that he had been discussed by this headshrinker and the Deputy Chief of Staff for Intelligence, USMC. Then he wondered why that had happened. Why was he important enough for Forrest to spend time talking about him to a headshrinker?

"That seems to surprise you," Toland said, and Banning knew that *was* a headshrinker's question.

"I'm just a captain," Banning said.

"Not for long," Toland said. "One of the questions on

General Forrest's mind was whether or not it was safe to make you a major."

Banning was surprised at that, too, but when he looked at Dr. Toland for an explanation, Toland was going through a stack of papers on his desk. He found what he was looking for, took a pen from a holder, and signed his name on each of four copies. Then he handed one to Banning.

"The significant part is on the back side," Toland said.

It was a Report of Physical Examination. In the "Comments" block on the reverse side there was a single typewritten line and a signature block:

"Captain Edward J. Banning, USMC, is physically qualified without exception to perform the duties of the office (Major, USMC) to which he has been selected for promotion.

"Jack B. Toland, Captain, Medical Corps, USNR"

Banning looked at Toland with mixed surprise and relief. Toland didn't look old enough to be a captain. (A Naval captain is equivalent to a colonel, USMC.) And he was surprised to learn—in this way—that he was being promoted. But mostly, he was enormously relieved to read the words *physically qualified without exception*.

Toland smiled at him.

"We watched you while we were running you through the examinations," Toland said. "What I was afraid we might find was a tumor. That's sometimes the case when there is an unexplained loss of sight."

"What was it, then?"

"I think it falls into the general medical category we refer to as, *'we don't know what the hell it is,'*" Toland said. "If I had to make a guess, I'd say it was probably either a brain concussion or that the nerves to the eyes were somehow bruised, so to speak, by concussion. I understand you were shelled twice, and pretty badly."

"Yes, sir," Banning said.

"Well, whatever it was, *Major* Banning, I think you can stop worrying about it."

"I'm astonished at my relief," Banning blurted. "I suddenly feel—hell, I don't know—like a wet towel."

"That's to be expected," Toland said. "What's unusual is that someone like you would admit it."

Banning looked at him, but didn't reply.

"You could do me a service, Banning, if you would," Toland said.

"Sir?"

"Other men are going to be blinded," Toland said. "Some of them are already coming back. It would help me if you could tell me what it's like."

"Frightening," Banning said. "Very frightening."

Toland made a gesture, asking him to go on.

"And then I got mad," Banning said. "Furious. Why me? Why hadn't I been killed?"

Toland nodded, and then when Banning said nothing else, he asked, "Suicide? Any thoughts of suicide?"

Banning met Toland's eyes for a long moment before he replied. "Yes," he said.

"Why didn't you?" Toland asked.

"I had a cocked pistol in my belt when I took the bandages off," Banning asked.

"And do you think you would have—could have—gone through with it?"

"Yes," Banning said, simply.

"Because you didn't want to face life without sight?"

"Because I was useless," Banning said. "I'm a Marine officer."

"And didn't want to be a burden to your family?"

"The only family I have, aside from the Corps, is a wife. And I left her on the wharf in Shanghai. God knows where she is now."

"I knew you were married," Dr. Toland said. "I didn't know the circumstances. That makes it a little awkward."

"Sir?"

"My next line was going to be 'Well, now that we're through with you, you're entitled to a thirty-day convalescent leave. A second honeymoon at government expense.'"

"Christ!" Banning said.

"What's worse is that it's not 'do you want a convalescent leave?', but 'you *will* take a thirty-day convalescent leave,'" Toland said. "That's out of my hands. No family anywhere? Cousin, uncle . . . ?"

"None that I want to see," Banning said. "I'd really rather go back to duty."

Toland shook his head, meaning "that's out of the question."

"The BOQ rooms here are supposed to be the cheapest hotel rooms in New York City," Toland said. "Dollar and a half a day. Be a tourist for a month."

Banning looked at him doubtfully.

"You'd be able to get a lot of the paperwork out of the way," Toland pursued. "And get yourself some new uniforms."

"Sir?"

"Our benevolent government, Major Banning," Dr. Toland said dryly, "is not only going to finally pay you, once they get your service records up to date, but is going to compensate you for the loss of whatever you were forced to leave behind in the Far East. Household goods, car, everything. And I understand the only uniform you have is the one you were wearing when you came in here. You'll have to make up a list of what you lost, and swear to it."

"I hadn't thought about that," Banning admitted.

"You'll have a good deal of money coming to you," Toland said. "And a newly promoted major should have some decent uniforms. Hell, you'll be able to afford going to Brooks Brothers for them."

"Brooks Brothers?" Banning parroted, and then laughed.

"Is that funny?"

Banning cocked his head and chuckled.

"The day the Japanese came ashore in the Philippines," he said, "I was on a bluff overlooking the beach. There's a couple of companies of Marines, Fourth Marines, on the beach, with nothing but machine guns. The artillery we were supposed to have, and the bombers, just didn't show up. There's half a dozen Japanese destroyers and as many troop ships offshore. And just before the invasion started, a mustang second lieutenant, a kid named McCoy, joined me. He worked for me as a corporal in China, and he was in the Philippines as a courier. So he came running, like the cavalry, with a BAR and loaded down with magazines." (The Browning Automatic Rifle is a fully automatic, caliber-.30-06 weapon, utilizing 20-round magazines.) "The Japanese started their landing barges for the beach, and the destroyers started to fire ranging rounds. And then McCoy, absolute horror in his voice, says 'Oh, my God!' and I looked at him to see what else could possibly be wrong. And he says, 'My pants! My pants! They're going to be ruined, and you wouldn't believe what I paid for them. I bought them in *Brooks Brothers!*' "

Toland laughed, and then asked, "What happened to him?"

"They dropped a five-inch round on us a couple of minutes later, and the next thing I knew I was in the basement of a church. McCoy had carried me there."

"Well, when he gets back, the government will replace his pants, too," Toland said.

"He's back," Banning said. "He was a courier, and he got out." He chuckled. "And he probably got off the plane with the form for the loss of his trousers already filled out. McCoy is a very bright young man."

"If he's a friend of yours," Toland said, "you could use part of your leave to go see him."

"That's not possible," Banning said, shortly.

Toland's eyebrows rose but he didn't respond.

"If you're going to be here—and this is a request, Major—I really would like to talk to you some more about your feelings when you thought you were blind."

"Sure," Banning said. "If you think it would be helpful."

"It would," Toland said. "I'd be grateful."

Banning nodded.

"There's one final thing, Banning," Toland said. "A little delicate. One of the reasons they give convalescent leave is because of the therapeutic value of sexual intercourse."

Banning's eyebrows rose.

"Seriously," Toland said. "And while I am not *prescribing* a therapeutic visit to a whorehouse . . ."

"I take the captain's point," Banning said.

"Good," Toland said.

XV

Camp Elliott, California
3 March 1942

At the regular morning officer's call, Colonel Carlson reported the arrival of the 240 carbines from the Army Ordnance Depot, and then turned toward McCoy and called his name.

McCoy rose to his feet.

"Sir?"

"For those of you who haven't had a chance to meet him," Carlson said, "this is Lieutenant Ken McCoy. He's fresh from Quantico, but don't prejudge him by that. Before he went through Quantico, he was a noncom with the Fourth Marines in Shanghai."

McCoy was uncomfortable; and then he was made even more so by First Lieutenant Martin J. Burnes, who turned around to beam his approval of the attention McCoy was being paid by Colonel Carlson. But Carlson was not through.

"I sent McCoy, rather than someone from S-Four, to get the carbines from the Army," Carlson said, "because, of all the people around here, I thought he and Gunnery Sergeant

Zimmerman, another old China Marine, would do the best job of bringing back what I sent them to get—despite the roadblocks I was sure the Army would put in their path. I didn't think they'd take either 'no' or 'come back in two weeks' for an answer. If it got down to it, I was sure that they were coming back with the carbines if they had to requisition them at midnight when the Army was asleep."

Carlson waited for the expected chuckles, and then went on: "There's a moral in that, and for those who might miss it, I'll spell it out: *The right men for the job, no matter what the Table of Organization and Equipment says they should be doing.* What everybody has to keep in mind is the mission. The rule is to do what has to be done in the most efficient way. Without regard to rank, gentlemen. An officer loses no prestige getting his hands dirty doing what has to be done, so long as what he's doing helps the Raider mission."

McCoy sat down.

"I'm not through with you, McCoy," Colonel Carlson said. McCoy stood up again.

"McCoy, if you had to make sure everybody in the battalion got a quick but thorough familiarization course in the carbine—say, firing a hundred rounds—how would you go about it?"

The question momentarily floored McCoy, not because he didn't have a good idea how it should be done, but because lieutenant colonels do not habitually ask second lieutenants for suggestions.

But he explained what he thought should be done.

Carlson considered McCoy's suggestions for a moment, and then asked: "What about an armorer?"

"Gunny Zimmerman, sir, until he can train somebody to take over," McCoy said.

"Okay, Lieutenant, do it." He then addressed the other officers. "McCoy was in the heavy weapons with the Fourth Marines in China. Until somebody better equipped comes along, he's our new-and-special-weapons training officer; and until armorers can be trained, Sergeant Zimmerman will handle that."

McCoy sat down again, now convinced that Carlson was through with him. He was pleased with what had happened. He agreed that Carlson was making it official that the Raiders were to assign the best-qualified man to the job no matter what his billet was, and it was sort of flattering to have his recommendations about how to set up a familiarization program accepted without change.

"What do I have to do, McCoy? To keep you on your feet? Put a grenade on your chair?" Carlson said, amused rather than angry.

"Sorry, sir," McCoy said, jumping to his feet in embarrassment.

"We have another problem that McCoy is going to help us solve. Man's third-oldest weapon, the first two being the rock and the stick, is the knife. From what I've noticed, most of our people think that the primary function of a knife is to open beer cans. But actually, in the hands of somebody who knows what he's doing, a knife is a very efficient tool to kill people. For one thing, it doesn't make any noise when it's used. There are a lot of self-appointed experts in knife fighting around. The problem with them is that by and large they are theoreticians rather than practitioners. Very few of them have ever used a knife to take a life."

McCoy sensed what was coming, and winced.

"In addition to that, people being trained in the lethal use of a knife seem to sense that their instructors don't *really* know much more about using a knife on another individual than they do; and consequently, they don't pay a lot of attention to what the instructor's saying."

There were more agreeable chuckles, and Carlson waited for them to subside before he went on.

"When McCoy was in Shanghai, they called him *'Killer,'*" Carlson said. "And with just cause. One night he was ambushed by four Italian Marines who wanted to rearrange his facial features and turn him into a soprano. They picked on the wrong guy. He had a knife, and before that little discussion was over, two of the Italian Marines were dead, and one other was seriously wounded."

There was silence in the room now, and all faces were turned to McCoy. Marty Burnes's face mirrored his amazement.

"McCoy was trained in knife fighting by a real expert," Carlson went on. "Captain Bruce Fairbairn of the Shanghai Municipal Police. Fairbairn designed a fighting knife—called, for some reason, the Fairbairn. McCoy carries his up his left sleeve strapped hilt down to his wrist so he can get at it in a hurry. Maybe, if you ask him very nicely, he'll show it to you.

But in any event, we're going to teach our people how to use a knife for something besides opening beer cans, and I announce herewith the appointment of Lieutenant 'Killer' McCoy as instructor in knife fighting . . . in addition to his other duties, of course."

Lieutenant Marty Burnes applauded, and after a moment's hesitation, the others joined in.

When it had died down, Carlson said, "*Now* you can sit down, Killer."

When the officer's call was over, McCoy ran after Colonel Carlson, who was walking with Captain Roosevelt toward battalion headquarters.

"Sir, may I see you a moment?"

"Sure, Killer," Carlson said. "But first, why don't you show Captain Roosevelt your fighting knife?"

"Sir, I'm not carrying a knife," McCoy said.

"If I had the reputation for being a world-class knife fighter, Killer," Carlson said, "I don't think anyone would ever catch me without my knife."

"Sir," McCoy blurted, "I'm not a knife fighter."

"*Ab esse ad posse valet elatio,* McCoy," Carlson said.

"Sir?"

"That means, in a very rough rendering, that the facts stand for themselves," Carlson said.

"Well, the facts are that I'm not a knife fighter," McCoy said, firmly.

Carlson switched to Cantonese.

"I know that, and you know that," he said. "But it *is* true that you did have to kill those Italians with a knife, and that they called you '*Killer*' in Shanghai. That story will be all over the battalion by noon. And when you start to teach knife fighting, you will have a very attentive audience."

"Sir," McCoy replied in Cantonese, "I don't know how to teach knife fighting. I only saw Captain Fairbairn once, at a regimental review. He doesn't know I exist, and he certainly never taught me anything."

"He did write a very good book on the subject," Carlson said. "I happen to have a copy of it. I'll get it to you in plenty of time for you to read it and adapt it to your purposes before your first class."

McCoy didn't reply.

"Were you listening in officer's call, Killer? When I talked about getting the best man for the job?"

"Yes, sir," McCoy said.

"You're it," Carlson said. "You're a clever young man, McCoy. Much more clever than people at first believe. You know what I want you to do, and I expect you to give it your best shot."

"Aye, aye, sir," McCoy said, in English.

"May I ask what that was all about?" Roosevelt asked.

"Killer was telling me that he doesn't have his knife today," Carlson said, "but that he will carry it with him in the future, and the next time he sees you, he'd be happy to show it to you."

"Fine." Roosevelt beamed.

"Anything else on your mind, Killer?" Colonel Carlson asked.

"No, sir," McCoy said, and then blurted, "Sir, I would really appreciate it if you didn't call me 'Killer.'"

Carlson smiled sympathetically. "I'm afraid that falls under the category of public relations, McCoy. We could hardly call our world-class knife fighting expert anything else, could we? Not and get the same reaction from the Raiders."

McCoy didn't reply.

"If there's nothing else, Killer," Carlson said, "you may return to your duties."

McCoy saluted.

"Aye, aye, sir."

"I'd really like to see your knife, Killer," Captain Roosevelt said.

(Two)
Camp Elliott, California
7 March 1942

Second Lieutenant Kenneth J. McCoy, Gunnery Sergeant Ernst Zimmerman, and a detail of twelve Marines from Able Company had come to the range in two Chevrolet half-ton pickups and a GMC 6×6^1 at dawn.

---

[1] A two-and-one-half-ton-capacity, canvas-bodied truck, called "6×6" (pronounced "six-by-six") because all of its six wheels could be driven. Six-by-six was something of a misnomer, because the double axles at the rear usually held eight wheels.

The 6×6 dragged a water trailer, and all the trucks were heavily laden and full. There were stacks of fifty-five-gallon garbage cans; stacks of buckets; bundles of rags; stacks of oblong wooden crates with rope handles; stacks of olive drab oblong ammunition cans; five-gallon water cans; five-gallon gasoline cans; and an assortment of other equipment, including eight gasoline-powered water heaters.

The detail from Able Company had come under a sergeant and a corporal; and Gunnery Sergeant Zimmerman—with a confidence that surprised McCoy, who remembered Zimmerman as a mild-mannered motor sergeant in the 4th Marines—quickly and efficiently put them to work.

All but one of the garbage cans were filled with water from the trailer and then placed twenty yards apart in a line.

Zimmerman watched as the sergeant set up one of the water heaters in one of the garbage cans and then fired it off. Satisfied that he could do the same thing with the other heaters (these were normally used to boil water in garbage cans set up at field kitchens to sterilize mess kits), he turned to what else had to be done.

He ordered the cans of ammunition removed from the Chevrolet pickup that had brought McCoy to the range and stacked inside the range house. On each olive drab can was lettered, in yellow:

CALIBER .30 US CARBINE
110 GRAIN BALL AMMUNITION
480 ROUNDS PACKED
4 BANDOLIERS OF 12 10-ROUND STRIPPER CLIPS

He next ordered that one of the garbage cans, four of the five-gallon cans of gasoline, and a bundle of rags be loaded in the back of the pickup.

Then he went to one of the heavy oblong wooden crates with rope handles removed from the 6×6. These crates were also stenciled in yellow:

10 US CARBINES CAL .30 M1
PACKED FOR OVERSEAS SHIPMENT IN COSMOLINE
DO NOT DESTROY CONTAINER INTEGRITY WITHOUT SPECIFIC
AUTHORIZATION

There was a good deal of container integrity. The cases were wrapped with stout wire. When Zimmerman had cut the wire loose, he saw the lid to the case was held down by eight thumbscrews. When these were off, he looked around and borrowed a ferocious-looking hunting knife from the nearest Raider, who looked about eighteen years old and as ferocious as a Boy Scout.

When he pried the lid of the case loose, there was a piece of heavy, tarred paper over the contents. Zimmerman cut it free. Inside the case were ten heavy paper-and-metal envelopes. Zimmerman took two of them out and handed them to the Raider from whom he had borrowed the hunting knife.

"Put these in the back of the lieutenant's pickup," he ordered.

Zimmerman then sought out the detail sergeant.

"Twenty-four cases," he said. "Ten carbines per case. Two hundred forty carbines, less two the lieutenant has. I want to see two hundred and thirty-eight carbines out of their cases when I get back here. And I want to see twelve people busy boiling the Cosmoline off twelve carbines."

"Where you going, Gunny?" the buck sergeant asked.

"To inspect the range with the lieutenant," Zimmerman said, gesturing down range.

He then walked to the pickup, got behind the wheel, and drove the truck past the one-hundred, two-hundred, and three-hundred-yard ranges to a dip in the ground fifty yards from the five-hundred-yard target line. When the pickup went into the dip, it was invisible to the people on the firing line.

McCoy and Zimmerman got out of the cab of the truck.

"How are we going to do this?" Zimmerman asked.

"Carefully," McCoy said.

He climbed into the bed of the truck, picked up the garbage can, and lowered it to the ground. Zimmerman took one of the five-gallon cans of gasoline, opened it, and poured it into the garbage can. And then, as McCoy picked up one of the metal-foil envelopes from the bed of the truck and carefully tore the top off, Zimmerman poured the gas from the other three cans into the garbage can.

Inside the envelope was a very small rifle, not more than three feet long, with its stock curved into a pistol grip behind the trigger. It was covered with a dark brown sticky substance. McCoy delicately lowered the small rifle into the gasoline in the garbage can, and then repeated the process with the second metal foil envelope.

Then the two of them began, carefully, to slosh the weapons around in the gasoline.

The removal of Cosmoline from weapons by the use of gasoline or other volatile substance was strictly forbidden by USMC regulations. It was also the most effective way to get the Cosmoline off—far more effective than boiling water.

The sharp outlines of the small rifle began to appear as the Cosmoline began to dissolve.

"Don't breath the fumes," McCoy cautioned.

Zimmerman passed the barrel of the carbine he was holding to McCoy.

"I got a can," he said.

He went to the truck and took from it an empty No. 10 can. He took a beer-can opener from his pocket and punched small drain holes around the bottom rim. Then he set the can down, unfolded a piece of scrap canvas on the bed of the truck, and then took one of the small rifles from McCoy.

He disassembled the small rifle into the stock and action, handed the stock and the forestock (a smaller piece of wood, which sat atop the barrel) to McCoy, sloshed the now-exposed action in the gasoline again, and then took it to the piece of canvas, where he took it down into small pieces and put them into the No. 10 can.

McCoy, meanwhile, using a rag and a toothbrush, stripped the stock and forestock of Cosmoline. When he was satisfied, he took the wooden pieces to the truck and laid them down. Zimmerman sloshed the parts in the No. 10 can around, then wiped them with a rag and scrubbed them with a toothbrush.

They worked quickly, but without haste. Soon, both of the rifles were on the scrap of canvas, free of Cosmoline. Except for the trigger group, they were stripped down to their smallest part.

"You think we have to take these down?" McCoy asked, looking doubtfully at the complex arrangement of small parts and springs.

Zimmerman picked up the second trigger group assembly and studied it carefully. "No," he said, issuing a professional judgment, "I don't think so."

"I don't suppose you've got a book?" McCoy asked. "So we can figure out how to put it back together?"

Zimmerman produced a small, paperbound manual, the U.S. Army Technical Manual for the U.S. Carbine, Caliber .30, M1, from the breast pocket of his dungarees, and displayed it triumphantly.

"You may turn into a passable gunny yet," McCoy said.

"Fuck you, McCoy," Zimmerman said, as he thumbed through the book looking for the disassembly instructions. When he found it, he opened the small book wide, breaking its spine so that it would lay flat.

Then, after carefully oiling each part and consulting the drawings in the book, they put the small rifles back together.

They worked the actions and dry-fired the weapons to make sure they were operable.

"What do we do about the gas?" Zimmerman asked.

"Dump it out, leave the can here until later," McCoy ordered. He took Zimmerman's carbine from him and climbed back into the pickup. Zimmerman tipped the garbage can on its side, watched for a moment as the sandy soil soaked up the gasoline, and then got behind the wheel.

They were gone no more than fifteen minutes. Steam was now rising from the water-filled garbage cans, and the men they had left were sloshing carbines around in it. It would be a long and dirty job using boiling water, McCoy thought, but there was no other way for these guys to do it. Doing it with gasoline was something only old Marines could handle safely; these kids, and that included their sergeant, would just blow themselves up using gas.

It did not occur to him that both the sergeant and the corporal, and at least two of the Raiders, were as old as, or older than, he was. He and Zimmerman had done a hitch with the 4th Marines. They were Marines, China Marines, and the others were kids.

As McCoy walked down the line of steaming garbage cans, Zimmerman went to the 6 × 6, pulled out a large flat cardboard carton, and took from it two large two-hundred-yard bull's-eye targets. Then he looked around and saw a tall, good-looking kid who didn't seem to have much to do.

He snapped his fingers, and when he had the kid's attention, beckoned to him with his finger.

"You might as well learn how to do this," Zimmerman said, and demonstrated the technique of making glue from flour and water in a No. 10 can.

When the glue had been mixed, Zimmerman led the kid to the one-hundred-yard line. There, target frames, constructed of two-by-fours with cotton "target cloth" stretched over them, were placed on the ground. He showed the kid how to brush the flour-and-water paste onto the target cloth, and then how to rub the targets smooth against it. Then they hoisted the target frames erect, put their legs into terra cotta pipes in the ground, and walked back to the firing line.

Zimmerman saw that a red (firing in progress) pennant had been hoisted on the flagpole, and that McCoy, with the sergeant, the corporal, and several kids watching him, had found the carbine magazines and other missing parts, and was trying to finish the assembly process.

"Gunny," Lieutenant McCoy said sternly, "do you know how to put the sling on this piece?"

"Yes, sir," Gunnery Sergeant Zimmerman said, confidently, even though he had absolutely no idea how to do it.

The carbine sling was a piece of canvas. Unlike the Springfield and Garand rifles, which had sling swivels top and bottom, however, the carbine sling fitted into a sling swivel mounted on the front side of the weapon with a "lift-the-dot" fastener. McCoy had figured out that much for himself.

He was having a problem fastening the rear end of the sling. Zimmerman took the carbine from McCoy. The right side of the stock of the carbine had, near the butt, a three-inch-long slot cut into it. In the center of the slot, there was a hole cut all the way through the stock. The left side of the stock had been inlet, the cut obviously designed to accommodate the sling.

There was a metal tube intended to fit into the slot of the right side of the stock. And the sling was intended to go through the stock from the left side, loop around the metal tube, and then pass through the stock again, holding the sling in place.

The problem Lieutenant McCoy was having, Gunnery Sergeant Zimmerman saw, was that when he looped the sling around the tube, it wouldn't fit in the hole. And it obviously had to, for otherwise the metal tube would fall off.

Zimmerman took the metal tube in his hands.

"This, sir," he announced, "is the sling keeper."

At that moment, he noticed that one end of the tube was knurled. He unscrewed it. There was a piece of wire, flattened at one end, under the cap.

"Which, as you can see," Zimmerman said, "also contains the oiler."

He screwed the cap back in place, and wondered what the hell he was going to do now. And then inspiration struck. He knew how the goddamned thing worked.

"To insert the sling, sir," he pontificated, "*first* you insert the sling keeper/oiler—I'm not exactly sure of the nomenclature, sir—into the stock, and *then* you feed the sling around it."

It was only a theory, but it was all he had to go on; so he tried it, and it worked. The metal tube was securely inside the slot in the stock, and the sling was in place.

"In that manner, sir," Gunnery Sergeant Zimmerman said.

"Very good, Gunny," Lieutenant McCoy said.

"It's really very simple, sir," Gunnery Sergeant Zimmerman said.

"Sergeant," McCoy said, "the gunny and I are going to test-fire these weapons. Pass the word to your men, and make sure they keep well back of the firing line."

"Aye, aye, sir," the sergeant said. "Sir, are we going to get to fire them?"

"You'll be the first to fire when the company shows up," McCoy said.

Zimmerman opened an ammunition can and took from it an olive drab cotton bandolier. It had six pockets, each of which held two ten-round stripper clips separated by a strip of paperboard. He freed one of the small, shiny cartridges and looked at the base. It was stamped FC 42.

He showed it to McCoy.

"Brand-new, sir," he said, obviously impressed.

"That's the first brand-new ammo I've ever seen," McCoy said.

Zimmerman examined a stripper clip and a carbine magazine carefully, and he saw where one end of the stripper clip was obviously designed to fit over the lips of the magazine. He put it in place and shoved down with his thumb. The cartridges slipped into the magazine.

He looked at McCoy and saw that McCoy had been watching him. McCoy loaded a stripper clip into each of two magazines.

Then they walked to the firing line. McCoy sat down, and Zimmerman followed his example. He made as much of a sling as he could from the canvas strap, then shifted himself around until he was in what he considered to be a satisfactory shooting position.

Then he looked over his shoulder and around the range to make sure none of the kids had wandered into a dangerous position. Just to be sure, he counted heads. They were all in sight. He raised his voice.

"Ready on the right, ready on the left. Ready on the firing line. The flag is up, the flag is waving, the flag is down, commence firing!"

He lined up the sights on the bull's-eye and let off a round as well as he could. The trigger was stiff, heavy as hell, he thought. Probably because it was brand new. There was very little recoil; and the muzzle blast, while sharp, was less than he expected.

They fired slowly and carefully. Zimmerman was finished before McCoy took the carbine from his shoulder.

"Both clips?" Zimmerman asked.

"Might as well," McCoy said, and exchanged clips and resumed firing.

When they had finished, and McCoy had issued the formal commands to clear all weapons and leave the firing line, they handed the carbines to the sergeant and walked to the targets at the one-hundred-yard line.

There were twenty holes in each target. Zimmerman's were scattered around the bull's-eye, and McCoy's were at the lower left of the target. What counted, however, was not the location of the holes, but the size of the group. Sight adjustment would move the group.

"Piece of shit," Zimmerman said, disgustedly, reaching up and laying his extended hand with the thumb on one hole and the little finger on another. "That's eight fucking inches, for Christ sake, at a hundred yards."

"Some of them were fliers," McCoy said. "And some were from a fouled barrel, and the triggers are stiff because they're new."

"Bullshit, McCoy," Zimmerman said. "It's a piece of shit, and you know it."

"Get some rounds through them," McCoy insisted. "Let the sears wear in a little and you can cut those groups in half."

"Down to five inches?" Zimmerman said, sarcastically.

"Ernie, this thing is not supposed to be a rifle. It's to replace the pistol," McCoy said. "I don't know about you, but I can't put ten rounds from a forty-five into five inches at a hundred yards rapid fire.''

Zimmerman looked at him.

"I'm not sure I could do it with a Thompson, either," McCoy insisted. "This thing fires fifteen rounds, and with the recoil, you're right back on the target as fast as you can pull the trigger. It's not a piece of shit, Ernie."

"Well, maybe to *replace* the pistol," Zimmerman grudgingly agreed.

"That's what it's for," McCoy said.

"Here they come," Zimmerman said, jerking his head toward the firing line.

A column of men, four abreast and fifty deep, was double-timing up the range road. They were in dungarees and wearing field gear, except for rifles and helmets. It was Company B, 2nd Ranger Battalion, which McCoy expected. But he had not expected it to be led by the company commander, or to be accompanied by its officers. He thought the Baker Company gunny would probably bring them out.

"Issue and familiarization firing of the US Carbine, Caliber .30, M1, 16 Hours," as the training schedule called it, was really the gunny's business; but the Old Man was at the head of the column, and all the other officers except the executive officer were in the column behind him.

Zimmerman reached up, worked his fingers under the target, and jerked it free of the target cloth.

"What did you do that for?"

"I don't want anybody to see me all over a hundred-yard target that way," Zimmerman said, as he balled the target up in his hands.

McCoy laughed, and then started trotting to the firing line so he would be there when the column double-timed up.

Captain Coyte turned the company over to the gunny, and walked toward McCoy.

McCoy saluted.

"Good morning, sir," he said. "I didn't expect to see the captain out here."

"I've never seen a carbine," Captain Coyte said. "Just include me in, Killer. It's your show."

"Aye, aye, sir," McCoy said.

"I thought I heard firing," Captain Coyte said.

"Yes, sir, Gunny Zimmerman and I test-fired two of them."

"Is that a couple of them on the table?" Coyte asked, nodding toward one of the four rough wooden tables behind the firing line. Without waiting for an answer, he walked toward the table, gesturing to the other officers to join him.

When he got to the table, he picked up one of the carbines, looked into the open action to confirm that it was not loaded, and then released the operating rod, threw it to his shoulder, drew a bead on the one target remaining, and dry snapped it. He tried, and failed, to get the bolt to remain open, and then looked at McCoy for help.

"There's a little pin on the rear operating-rod lever, Captain," McCoy explained. "Hold it back, push the pin in."

Captain Coyte succeeded in keeping the action open.

"I suppose this is the wrong word to use on a weapon," he said. "But it's kind of cute, isn't it?"

"If you think of it as a replacement for the pistol, sir," McCoy said, "it's not bad."

"Accuracy?"

"We managed to get ten shots into about eight inches at one hundred yards," McCoy said.

Captain Coyte's eyebrows went up. "There are a couple of reasons that might have happened," he said.

"I think, from a clear bore, with maybe a hundred or two hundred rounds to smooth it up, we can tighten those groups, sir."

"If you could cut them in half, that would still give you four inches," Captain Coyte said thoughtfully. "I now understand, I think, your reference to thinking of it as a replacement for the pistol."

"Captain, why don't you let me put up some targets and let you and the other officers fire?" McCoy asked. "The way I had planned to run this was to have the men clean their pieces—"

Coyte looked around. "McCoy, it's your range, and your class," he said. "If that could be done without fouling up your schedule . . ."

"Yes, sir."

"Well, then," Captain Coyte said, "in the interest of efficiency, not because I dare think that rank has its privileges, let's do it, Killer."

There was a smile in his eyes, and McCoy knew that he was mocking Colonel Carlson's "no special privileges" philosophy. He was surprised that a captain would mock the battalion commander, but especially that he would do so for the amusement of the junior second lieutenant in his company.

It took no more than fifteen minutes for McCoy to paste the holes in his target and then to give Captain Coyte enough quick instruction to understand what he was doing, and for Coyte to fire twenty rounds at the target.

By the time they were finished, Baker Company's gunny had broken the company down into four groups, and one group was gathered around each of the tables. At the first table, Zimmerman was demonstrating to a group of NCOs the disassembly technique on one of the two carbines they had cleaned with gasoline. The idea was that the NCOs would then go to the other tables and try disassembling the partially cleaned weapons themselves.

The system McCoy had dreamed up out of his head, and then modified after suggestions from Zimmerman, seemed to be working. The bottleneck was going to be getting the carbines free of Cosmoline, but nothing could be done about that. The safety precautions were in place. There would be inspections by platoon sergeants of weapons before they were shown to the gunnys, and finally Zimmerman would inspect them himself.

He saw that Zimmerman had also just about selected the armorer for the carbines. One of the kids. He had seen him mixing paste and pasting targets.

McCoy glanced at the tables and the faces. They were mostly kids, he thought, some of them as young as seventeen. And some he suspected were seventeen using somebody else's birth certificate.

And then he did a quick double take. There was a familiar face at the next-to-the-last table. At first it seemed incredible, but then there was no question about it at all. One of the Raiders struggling to get a good look at a sergeant taking a carbine to pieces was Tommy. Thomas Michael McCoy. PFC Thomas Michael McCoy, USMC, was Second Lieutenant Kenneth J. McCoy's little brother.

Younger brother, McCoy thought. *The sonofabitch is even bigger than I remembered. And meaner looking.*

"You look stunned, McCoy," Captain Coyte said. "Was my marksmanship that bad?" McCoy was startled, and it showed on his face when he looked up at Coyte.

"McCoy?"

"Sir, I just spotted my kid brother. The PFC with the broken nose, by Table Three?"

"I saw the similarity in name when he reported in," he said. "He reported in from Pearl. They must have lost his records, for he has a brand-new service record."

"They give you a new service record when they throw out a court-martial sentence, too," McCoy said.

"But we don't know that, do we, McCoy?" Coyte said. "So far as I'm concerned, so far as the Raiders are concerned, he has a clear record."

Their eyes met for a moment, and then Coyte went on, "If this is going to be a problem, McCoy, I can try to have him transferred."

"No problem, sir," McCoy said. "I can handle the sonofabitch."

"I'm sure you can, Killer," Captain Coyte said.

XVI

(One)
Annex #2, Staff NCO Club
Camp Elliott, California
10 March 1942

Gunnery Sergeant Ernst Zimmerman, USMC, sat alone on a wooden folding chair at one of the small, four-man tables of the club. He was freshly showered and shaved, and in freshly washed dungarees. His feet were on a folding chair.

Annex #2 of the staff NCO club was a Quonset building. It was intended to provide a place for the staff noncommissioned officers—the three senior pay grades—to go for a beer when they came off duty tired, hot, and dirty. The wearing of the green uniform was prescribed for the main staff NCO club.

Annex #2 was simple, in fact crude. The bar, for instance, ran a third of the length of the building and was made of plywood. After it was built, someone had gone over the surface with a blow torch, which brought out the grain of the wood. Then it had been varnished. There were fifteen stools at the bar, and a dozen of the small tables. There was a juke box and four slot machines. Two took nickels, one took dimes, and one quarters.

252

Zimmerman never played the slot machines. He would play acey-deucey for money, or poker, and he had been known to bet on his own skill with the Springfield rifle, but he thought that playing the slots was stupid, fixed as they were to return to the staff NCO club twenty-five percent of the coins fed to them.

And he had never been in the main staff NCO club. He thought it was stupid to get all dressed up in greens, just to sit around with a bunch of other noncoms and tell sea stories. Green uniforms had to be cleaned and pressed, and that cost money. You could get hamburgers and hot dogs and bacon, lettuce, and tomato sandwiches and french fries at the main club, but Zimmerman thought it was stupid to buy your food when the Corps was providing three squares a day.

If you really wanted a good meal, Zimmerman reasoned, take liberty off the base and go to some civilian restaurant and get a steak.

There was a row of whiskey bottles behind the bar, but Zimmerman rarely had a drink. He had nothing against the hard stuff, just against buying it by the drink at thirty cents a shot. For the price of ten drinks, you could get a bottle, and there were a lot more than ten shots in a bottle.

Annex #2 offered a two-quart pitcher of draft beer for forty cents. They also offered little bags of Planter's peanuts for a nickel. Zimmerman liked peanuts, but he didn't like to pay a nickel for half a handful, so he bought them in cans in the PX for twenty-nine cents, two or three cans at a time, when he bought his weekly carton of Camel cigarettes. He kept them in his room. When he was going to Annex #2 for a pitcher of beer, he dumped half a canful of peanuts on a piece of paper, folded it up, and carried it with him. He figured that way he could eat twice as many peanuts with his beer for the same money.

All things considered, Zimmerman was satisfied with his present assignment. He sort of missed being around a motor pool, but you couldn't work in a motor pool if you were a gunnery sergeant, and it was nice being a gunny. He had never expected to become a gunny. Probably a staff sergeant, or maybe even a technical sergeant. But not a gunny. It was either the building of the Corps for the war, or else there had been a fuck-up at Headquarters, USMC, and some clerk was told to make him a staff sergeant and he hadn't been paying attention and had made a gunny instead. But he wasn't going to ask, or complain, about it. If there was a fuck-up, it would be straightened out.

He had liked being a gunny in the 1st Separate Battalion at Quantico. He had liked it better before they had transferred the company from Quantico to the 2nd Separate Battalion out here, and he had been a little worried when they had renamed the outfit the 2nd Raider Battalion.

It was supposed to be all volunteer. That wasn't so. Nobody had asked him when they'd transferred him from the motor pool at Parris Island whether he wanted to volunteer, and nobody had said anything about volunteering for anything since he'd been out here, either.

They were running the asses off the volunteers, a lot of time at night; but since he had been working for McCoy, he had been relieved from all other duties. That didn't mean it wasn't hard work, but the work McCoy had him doing made more sense than what everybody else was doing, especially the running around in the dark and the "close personal combat" training.

He didn't say anything about it, of course, but there was a lot of bullshit in the Raider training. They all thought they were going to be John Wayne, once they got to the Pacific, cutting Japanese throats. They seemed to have the idea that the Japs were obligingly going to stand still and raise their chins so they could get their throats cut.

Zimmerman knew that aside from McCoy, and maybe Colonel Carlson, he was one of the few people who had even seen a Japanese soldier up close. And the ones he had seen looked like pretty good soldiers to him. Some of the Japs he had seen were as big and heavy as he was. Most of the Raiders, especially the kids (which meant most of the Raiders; Zimmerman had heard that eighty-two percent of the enlisted men were under twenty years old), had the idea that Japs were buck-teethed midgets who wore thick glasses.

Colonel Carlson was trying to make them understand that wasn't so, that the Japs were tough, smart, and well trained. But the kids thought he was just saying that to key them up. They wouldn't change their minds until some Jap started to stick one of those long Jap bayonets in them.

There were some things the Raiders were doing that made sense to Zimmerman. Everybody was getting, or was supposed to get, a .45 in addition to whatever weapon he would be issued. In the Old Corps, that didn't happen. Only people in crew-served weapons, plus some senior noncoms, and officers, got .45s. Most people couldn't hit the broad side of a barn with a pistol, but still it made sense to give people one in case something went wrong with their basic weapon.

Except, Zimmerman thought, that the Raiders were going apeshit over Thompsons and carbines, trying to get them issued instead of what they should have, these new eight-shot self-loading .30–06 Garands.

In all his time in the Corps, Zimmerman had known only two people who could handle a Thompson properly. Major Chesty Puller, who was a short, stocky, muscular sonofabitch (in Zimmerman's mind, Puller, not Gunnery Sergeant Lou Diamond, was the Perfect Marine) and could handle the recoil with brute strength; and McCoy. McCoy, compared to Puller, was a little fucker, but he had learned how to control the recoil of a Thompson by controlling the trigger. He got off two-round bursts that went where he pointed them, and he could get off so many two- and three-round bursts that he could empty the magazine, even a fifty-round magazine, just about as fast as Major Puller, who just pulled the trigger and held it back and used muscles to keep ten-, fifteen-, even twenty-round bursts where he wanted them to go.

Aside from McCoy and Puller and, he now remembered, a gunnery sergeant with the Peking Horse Marines, everybody else he had ever seen trying to deliver accurate rapid fire from a Thompson had wound up shooting at the horizon. Or the moon.

But it was classy, *salty,* to have a Thompson, and everybody was breaking their ass to get one. In the Old Corps, you took what the book said, period. But Colonel Carlson, McCoy had told him, had been given permission to arm the Raiders just about any way he wanted to. If a Raider, officer or enlisted, could come up with almost any half-assed reason why he should have a Thompson, more often than not, they let him have one.

Zimmerman had personally stripped down and inspected ninety-six of the fuckers—half of them brand new, and half of them worn-out junk—that they'd got from the Army and that McCoy had sent him after.

But most of the officers loved the Thompsons. Though if

they couldn't talk themselves into one of those, they wanted carbines. Maybe there was something to what McCoy had said, that the carbine was intended to replace the pistol. But he was about the only one that ever said that. Everybody else wanted it because they thought it would be a lot easier to haul around than a Springfield or a Garand.

And then there were the knives. Every sonofabitch and his brother in the Raiders was running around with a knife, like they were all Daniel Boones and they were going to go out and scalp the Japs, for Christ sake.

McCoy was the only Marine Zimmerman ever knew who had ever used a knife on anybody. There had been some guys in Shanghai who'd gotten into it with the Italian Marines during the riots with Springfield bayonets, but that was different. Bayonets weren't sharp, and they had been used almost like clubs, or maybe small, dull swords. And so far as Zimmerman remembered hearing, none of those Italian Marines had died.

Two of the four Italian Marines who had jumped McCoy in Shanghai had died. McCoy had opened them up with his Fairbairn, which was a knife invented by a Limey captain on the Shanghai Municipal Police. It was a sort of dagger, razor sharp on both edges, and built so that the point wouldn't snap off if it hit a bone. McCoy's wasn't a *real* Fairbairn, but a smaller copy of one run up by some Chinese out of an old car spring. It was about two-thirds as long as the real one. The real Fairbairn was too big to hide inside your sleeve above your wrist and below your elbow; McCoy's Baby Fairbairn was.

McCoy was now carrying his Fairbairn. When Zimmerman had asked him why, McCoy had first said, *"Because Carlson told me to."* And then he jumped all over his ass, saying he had a big mouth and that he should have kept it shut about what happened in Shanghai. Zimmerman had told him, truthfully, that he hadn't said a goddamned word about that, but he wasn't sure McCoy believed him.

Well, everybody in the goddamned Raiders knew about it now, and was calling him "Killer," the officers to his face, and the others behind his back. Until they stopped it, a lot of the kids were even trying to go around with their knives strapped to their wrists. That didn't work, but they thought it was salty as hell.

All this salty knife and submachine-gun bullshit was fine in training, Zimmerman thought; but if the Raiders ever got to do what everybody thought they were going to do—sneak ashore in little rubber boats from destroyers-converted-to-transports onto some Jap-held island and start, like John Wayne and Alan Ladd in some bullshit movie, to cut throats and shoot up the place—they were going to find out it was a hell of a lot different from what they thought.

Only once in his life had Gunnery Sergeant Ernst Zimmerman found himself in a situation where armed men were really trying to kill him. Forty or fifty Chinese "bandits," who were working for the Japs, had ambushed him and a Marine officer named Sessions when they had become separated from the rest of a motor supply convoy.

He hadn't shit his pants or tried to hide or run or anything like that. He'd just stood there with a .45 in a hip holster and just absolutely forgot he had a weapon, until McCoy had come charging up like the goddamned cavalry taking Chinese down with a Thompson. Even *then* he hadn't done anything. McCoy had had to scream at him, *"Shoot, for Christ's sake!"* before he took the .45 out and started to use it to save his own ass.

Zimmerman didn't think that would happen again—after he had "woken up," he had done what had to be done—but he wondered how these Raiders who were swaggering around Camp Elliott with their knives and carbines and Thompsons were going to react when they found themselves facing some Jap who was as big as they were, and who wasn't wearing thick glasses and didn't have buck teeth and was about to shoot them or run them through with a bayonet.

Baker Company's gunnery sergeant, Danny Esposito, appeared at the table with a pitcher of beer in one hand and a mug in the other. He was a large, heavy, leather-skinned man of thirty (either a Spaniard or an Italian, Zimmerman wasn't sure which), and he was wearing greens.

"You saving this table?" he asked.

"Sit down," Zimmerman said.

"You ready?" Gunnery Sergeant Esposito asked, holding his pitcher of beer over Zimmerman's mug.

"Why not?"

Esposito topped off Zimmerman's mug, and then sat down. Zimmerman pushed the piece of waxed paper with the peanuts over to him. Esposito scooped some up, tossed them in his mouth, and nodded his thanks.

"Scuttlebutt says that if somebody's got a worn-out Thompson and wants one of the new ones," Gunnery Sergeant Esposito said, "you're the man to see."

"You want a Thompson?" Zimmerman asked evenly.

"One of my lieutenants," Esposito said. "I put a hundred rounds through a Garand, and I sort of like it. It ain't no Springfield, of course, but I'm getting two-, two-and-a-half-inch groups."

"The Garand is a pretty good weapon," Zimmerman said. "People don't like it 'cause it's new, that's all."

"What about the Thompson? Can you help me out?"

"I'll see what I can do," Zimmerman said. "That why you come looking for me?"

"What makes you think I come looking for you?"

"You're all dressed up," Zimmerman said.

Esposito shrugged and drained his beer mug and refilled it before he replied.

"I was hoping maybe I'd run into you, Zimmerman," he confessed.

"You did," Zimmerman said.

"Out of school?" Esposito asked.

Zimmerman nodded.

"You're pretty tight with Lieutenant McCoy," Esposito said.

"We was in the Fourth Marines together," Zimmerman said. "He's all right."

"Scuttlebutt says he had you to dinner," Esposito said. "On some yacht, where he's shacked up."

"That's what the scuttlebutt says?" Zimmerman replied.

"What do you know about his brother?"

"Not much," Zimmerman asked.

"I got an old pal at the Diego brig," Esposito said.

"What'd he do?" Zimmerman said.

"I said 'at,' not 'in,'" Esposito said, before he realized that Zimmerman was pulling his leg. "*Shit*, Zimmerman!"

"What about your pal at the brig?"

"He says McCoy—*PFC* McCoy was in there," Esposito said. "You know anything about that?"

Zimmerman shook his head. "No."

"He was supposed to be on his way to Portsmouth to do five-to-ten for belting an officer."

"That's what you heard, huh?" Zimmerman said.

"I also found out when he reported in here, he had just had full issue of new uniforms, and he's got a brand-new service record."

"What does that mean?"

"It means I got the straight poop from my friend at the brig," Esposito said. "If they vacate a general court-martial sentence and turn somebody loose, they give him a new service record. And since general prisoners don't have uniforms, except for dungarees with a 'P' painted on them, they give them a new issue."

"If I was you, Esposito," Zimmerman said, "I wouldn't be running off at the mouth about this."

"Because of Lieutenant McCoy, you mean?"

"Because if the Corps gave him a new service record, it means the Corps wants him to have a clean slate. Don't go turning over some rock."

"How would your friend Lieutenant McCoy react if I kicked the shit out of his little brother?"

"Why would you want to do that?" Zimmerman asked.

"For one thing, he's a wisenheimer," Esposito said. "For another, he thinks he's a real tough guy. He beat the shit out of two of my kids. No reason, either, that I can get out of anybody, except that he wanted to show people how tough he is. And he's running off at the mouth, too. About his brother, I mean. What's with the shack job on the yacht? Is that true? And while I'm asking questions, what's the real poop about Lieutenant McCoy?"

Zimmerman lit a Camel with his Zippo, and then took a deep pull at his beer mug.

"What do you mean, real poop?"

"He really kill a bunch of Italian Marines with that little knife of his?"

"*Two* Italians," Zimmerman said. "He killed *two* Italians. Stories get begger and better every time they get told."

"You was there?"

"I was there," Zimmerman said.

"Mean little fucker, isn't he?" Gunnery Sergeant Esposito said, approvingly. "I heard fifteen, twenty Italians. I knew that was bullshit."

"It was twenty *Chinamen*," Zimmerman said. "Not Italians, *Chinamen*."

"No shit?"

"Okay, we're out of school, right?" Zimmerman said. He waited for Esposito to nod his agreement and then went on. "McCoy and I were buddies in the Fourth. We had a pretty good rice bowl going. We ran truck supply convoys from Shanghai to Peking. We got pretty close. One time the convoy got ambushed. Chinese bandits, supposed to be. Actually the Japs were behind it. McCoy killed a bunch of them—twenty, anyway, maybe more—with a Thompson."

"No shit?" Esposito said, much impressed.

"You don't want to get him mad at you, Esposito," Zimmerman said. "You was asking about the boat—"

"*Yacht,* is what the brother says," Esposito said. "And the rich broad who lets him drive her LaSalle convertible."

"One thing at a time . . . Christ, what do you guys do, spend all your time gossiping about your officers like a bunch of fucking women?"

Esposito gave Zimmerman a dirty look, but didn't say anything.

"First of all," Zimmerman went on, "the LaSalle is McCoy's. He come home from China with a bunch of money—"

"Where'd he get it?"

"He's a goddamned good poker player," Zimmerman said. "And on top of that, he was lucky, real lucky, a couple of times."

Esposito nodded his acceptance of that.

"So he bought the LaSalle; that's his," Zimmerman said. "And so we both wound up here. And like I said, we were buddies. But he's now an officer, so he can't come in here, and I can't go to the officers' club. So he has a girl friend. A *real nice* girl, Esposito, you understand? I personally don't like it when you say 'shack job.' And she lives on a boat, not a yacht, a boat. And McCoy tells her about me and his kid brother, and she says bring us to dinner. So we go. And that's it. We had dinner and drank some beer, and then McCoy drove us back out here."

"I figured it was probably something like that," Esposito said. "His brother's got a real big mouth."

"I saw that myself," Zimmerman agreed.

"And he's a mean sonofabitch, too," Esposito said. "I told you; he really beat the shit out of a couple of my kids."

"I don't want to put my nose in where it ain't welcome,"

Zimmerman said. "But, maybe, if you would like, I could talk to the brother."

"I don't know," Esposito said, doubtfully. "You think he'd listen to you? He sure as shit don't listen to me when I try to talk to him."

"You start beating up on him, you're liable to lose your stripes," Zimmerman said.

"Well, shit, Zimmerman, if you think you could do any good," Esposito said.

"It couldn't hurt none to try," Zimmerman said.

"What the hell," Esposito said. "Why not? And what about the Thompson?"

"You take the old one to the armory, tomorrow," Zimmerman said. "And tell the armorer I said to swap it for you."

"You want to split another pitcher of beer?"

"Nah, hell, I got to get up in the wee hours. But thanks anyway."

Ten minutes later, Gunnery Sergeant Ernst Zimmerman was outside the enlisted beer hall, known as the Slop Chute.

There was a cedar pole ten feet from the entrance. Seventy-five or so knives were stuck into it. Zimmerman had heard about the cedar pole, but it was the first time he had seen it. There was a regulation that the Raiders could not enter the Slop Chute with their knives. So rather than going to his barrack or tent to leave his knife there, some ferocious Raider had stuck it in the cedar pole and reclaimed it when he left the Slop Chute. The idea had quickly caught on.

"Dodge fucking City," Zimmerman muttered under his breath, disgustedly.

He pushed the door open and walked inside, grimacing at the smell of sour beer, a dense cloud of cigarette smoke, and the acrid fumes of beer-laden urine.

"Hey, Mac, no knives," a voice behind him said. Zimmerman turned and saw there was a corporal on duty at the entrance. Zimmerman didn't reply. Finally, the corporal recognized him. "Sorry, Gunny," the corporal added. "Didn't recognize you at first."

Zimmerman looked around the crowded room until he spotted PFC Thomas McCoy, who was sitting with half a dozen others at a crude table drinking beer out of a canteen cup.

He walked across the room to him.

"Hey, whaddasay, Gunny!" one of the others greeted him, cheerfully. "You want a beer?"

"I want to see McCoy for a minute, thanks anyway," Zimmerman said.

"What the hell for?" PFC McCoy replied. He was a little drunk, Zimmerman saw.

Zimmerman, on the edge of snapping, "Because I said so, asshole! On your feet!", stopped himself in time and smiled. "Colonel Carlson's got a little problem he wants you to solve for him."

The others laughed, and a faint smile appeared on McCoy's face. He got to his feet.

"This going to take long?" he asked.

"I don't think so," Zimmerman said.

He motioned for McCoy to go ahead of him, and then followed him across the room and out of the building. McCoy went to the cedar post, jerked one of the knives from it, and slipped it into the sheath on his belt.

"Where we going?" he asked.

"Right over this way," Zimmerman said, "it's not far."

Behind the Slop Chute building was a mixed collection of other buildings, some frame with tar-paper roofs, some Quonsets, and some tents. Here and there a dim bulb provided a little light.

Zimmerman went to the door of one of the small frame buildings, took off his dungaree jacket and his hat, and hung them on the doorknob.

"What's this, Gunny?" McCoy asked, suspiciously.

"You know what it means, you fucking brig bunny," Zimmerman said. "It means that right now you can call me 'Zimmerman,' 'cause right now, I ain't a gunny. I just hung my chevrons on the doorknob."

"What the hell is wrong with you?" McCoy asked.

"Nothing's wrong with me," Zimmerman said. "What's wrong is wrong with you, asshole."

"I don't know what the fuck you're talking about, Gunny, but if you think I'm going to get in it with you and wind up back in the brig, you have another think coming."

"You're not going back to the brig," Zimmerman said, moving close to him. "Having his brother in the brig would embarrass Lieutenant McCoy, and you've embarrassed him enough already, brig bunny."

"I wish I believed that," McCoy said. "I would like nothing better than to shove your teeth down your throat."

"Have a shot," Zimmerman said. "Look around, there's nobody here. And your brother's an officer. He wouldn't let them put you in the brig on a bum rap."

"Fuck you," McCoy said.

"I thought that you were supposed to be a tough guy," Zimmerman said. "I guess that's only when you're picking on kids, right?"

McCoy balled his fists, but kept them at his side.

"Come on, tough guy," Zimmerman said. "What's the matter, no balls?"

McCoy threw a punch, a right, with all his weight behind it.

Zimmerman deflected the punch with his left arm and kicked McCoy in the crotch.

McCoy made an animal sound, half scream and half moan, and fell to the ground with his hands at his crotch and his knees pulled up.

"You *cocksucker*," he said indignantly, a moment later. "You *kicked* me."

Zimmerman kicked him again, in the stomach.

"That's for calling your brother's lady friend a 'shack job,'" Zimmerman said, conversationally. He kicked him again. "And that's for calling me a 'cocksucker.' You got to learn to watch your mouth, brig bunny."

McCoy was writhing around on the ground, gasping for breath, moaning as he held his scrotum.

Zimmerman, his arms folded on his chest, watched silently. After several minutes, McCoy managed to sit up.

"Are you getting the message, tough guy? Or do you want some more?"

"You don't fight fair," McCoy said, righteously indignant. "You kicked me, for Christ's sake!"

"Get up then, Joe Louis," Zimmerman said. "Try it with your fists."

McCoy took several deep breaths, and then got nimbly to his feet, balled his fists, and took up a crouched fighting posture.

"I must have missed," Zimmerman said, almost wonderingly. "Usually when I kick people, they stay down."

"You cocksucker!" McCoy said, and charged him. He threw a punch. Zimmerman caught the arm, spun around, and threw McCoy over his back. McCoy landed flat on his back. The air was knocked out of him.

Zimmerman walked to him and kicked him in the side. "I *told* you," he said. "*Don't* call me a cocksucker."

With a massive effort, McCoy got his wind back and struggled to his knees. And then he heaved himself upright.

Zimmerman slapped him twice with the back of his left hand across the face, and then with the heel of his right hand across the throat. The first blow was hard enough to make McCoy reel, and the second sent him flying backward, his hands to his throat, gasping for breath. And then he fell heavily onto his backside.

Zimmerman stepped up to him and kicked him in the side again. McCoy bent double and threw up.

"I hit you with my open hand," Zimmerman said, conversationally. "If I had hit you with the side of it,"—he demonstrated with his left hand—"you would have a broken nose, and you wouldn't be able to talk for a week. If I had hit you hard enough, I would have crushed your Adam's apple and you would choke. The only reason I didn't do that is because your brother is a friend of mine, and he might feel bad about it."

"Jesus Christ!" McCoy said, barely audibly.

"The next time, McCoy, that I hear that you said one fucking word out of line, or that you took a poke at anybody, I'm going to be back and give you a real working over. Tough guy, my ass!"

He walked over to McCoy and raised his foot to kick him again.

McCoy scurried away as best as he could.

Zimmerman lowered his foot and laughed.

"*Shit!*" he said, contemptuously. And then he walked to the small building, put his dungaree jacket back on, and walked off.

PFC Thomas McCoy waited until he was really sure that he was gone, and then he got to his feet. His balls hurt, and his sides, and inside, and it hurt him to breathe.

He took a handkerchief from his pocket and wiped at the vomitus on his jacket and trousers and boots. Then, gagging, he staggered off toward his barrack.

(Two)
The Foster Peachtree Hotel
Atlanta, Georgia
14 March 1942

Second Lieutenant Richard J. Stecker, USMC, stood with a glass of Dickel's 100-proof twelve-year-old Kentucky sour mash bourbon whiskey in his hand, looking out the window of his bedroom in the General J. E. B. Stuart suite. It was raining—it looked as if it couldn't make up its mind to snow or rain—and the wind had blown the rain against the windowpane. Stecker idly traced a raindrop as it slid down.

He was more than a little pissed with his buddy, Second Lieutenant Malcolm S. Pickering, USMCR, for a number of reasons, all attributable to Pick's infatuation with the female Stecker thought of alternately as "the Admiral's Daughter" and "the Widow."

Stecker was either sorry for the poor sonofabitch—who really had a bad case of puppy love for Martha Sayre Culhane, or unrequited love, or the hots, or whatever the hell it was—or pissed off with him about it.

At the moment, the latter condition prevailed.

From yesterday at noon until fifteen minutes ago, there had come a ray of hope:

At noon yesterday, using a concrete beam foundation of one of the hangars at Saufley Field for a table, they had been having their lunch (a barbecue sandwich and a pint container of milk) when Pick, out of the blue, spoke up. "How would you like to get laid?"

"Are you seeking to increase your general fund of knowledge, Pickering, or do you have some specific course of action in mind?"

"I was thinking we might drive to Atlanta," Pick said, "and take in the historical sights. They have a panorama of the Battle of Atlanta, which should be fascinating to a professional warrior such as yourself. There are also a number of statues of heroes on horseback, which I'm sure you would find inspirational."

"I thought you said something about getting laid?"

"That, too," Pick said.

"You realize, of course, that if we go to Atlanta, you won't be able to hang around the lobby of the San Carlos panting for a glimpse of the fair Martha?"

"Fuck fair Martha," Pick said, just a little bitterly, and then quickly recovered. "Which might be a good idea, come to think of it."

"I heard it takes two," Dick said.

"Do you want to go to Atlanta, or not?"

It was necessary to get permission to travel more than a hundred miles from the Pensacola Navy Air Station. And before they could run down Captain Mustache and obtain his approval, it was after six. As a result they got to the Foster Peachtree Hotel after midnight. The bar wasn't closed, but there were no females dewy-eyed with the thought of consorting with two handsome and dashing young Marine officers.

That didn't seem to bother Pick. He was interested in drinking, and the two of them closed the bar long after everyone else had left. Stecker wondered why the bartender hadn't thrown them out, until he remembered that Pick's grandfather owned the hotel.

And Pick of course waxed drunkenly philosophic about his inability to get together with the Admiral's Daughter. Dick Stecker had heard it all before, and he was bored with it.

"I'll make a deal with you, Pick," he said. "You won't mention Whatshername's name all weekend, and I will not pour lighter fluid on your pubic region and set it on fire while you sleep."

In the morning, Pick slept soundly, snoring loudly, until long after ten.

Then, determinedly bright and cheerful, he went into Stecker's room, ordered an enormous breakfast from room service, and then explained that they really shouldn't eat too much, for they were meeting his Aunt Ramona for lunch at quarter to one.

"Your *Aunt Ramona?*" Dick asked, disgustedly.

"My Aunt Ramona loves me," Pick said. "And I always try to see her when I am in Atlanta. Only the cynical would suggest I do this because dear Aunt Ramona usually is accompanied by two or more delightful young belles, straight from *Gone with the Wind.*"

"No shit?"

"You will have to watch your foul mouth, Stecker," Pick said. "There is nothing that will chase away a well-reared

South'ren lady quicker than a foul-mouthed Marine. And if you talk dirty, my Aunt Ramona will rap you over the head with her cane.''

Aunt Ramona was not what Dick Stecker had been led to expect. She turned out to be a good-looking redhead, wearing a silver fox hat to match her knee-length silver fox coat. She was in her thirties, Stecker judged, as he watched her give her cheek to Pick to kiss.

"Aunt Ramona," Pick said, on his very good manners, "may I present my good friend, Lieutenant Richard Stecker? Dick, this is Mrs. Heath."

"I'm very pleased to meet you, Lieutenant," she said, extending a diamond-heavy hand with a gesture that would have done credit to the Queen of England.

"My pleasure, ma'am," Stecker said.

"If I had known you were coming, before ten o'clock this morning, Pick," Aunt Ramona said, "I would have set something up."

"I realize this has inconvenienced you," Pick said politely.

"You have always been an imp," Aunt Ramona said. "But I am glad to see you."

And then the girls appeared.

One was a blonde, and the other was a redhead, and they were gorgeous.

The first thing Dick Stecker thought was that they were not going to get laid. Not the same day they met these gorgeous creatures. Probably not until after they had walked down an aisle with them to be joined together in holy matrimony. Then he thought, *That doesn't matter. Just being with them is enough. You just don't often get to meet girls like this.*

They had thick Southern accents, which Dick Stecker found absolutely enchanting, and names to match. The blonde's name was Catherine-Anne, and the redhead's Melanie. Melanie had light blue eyes and a most enchanting way of licking at her lips with the tip of her delicate red tongue. And she, even more than Catherine-Anne, seemed to be fascinated to meet a West Point graduate who had gone into the Marines and was learning to be a Naval aviator.

They had lunch in the high-ceilinged main dining room—an elegant, delicious lunch, which Dick Stecker thought was very appropriate for the circumstances. There had even been champagne.

"This is a celebration," Aunt Ramona said. "And—as wicked as this might make me sound—I'd just *love* to have some champagne."

When the champagne was delivered and poured, and they all touched their glasses, Melanie had met Dick Stecker's eyes over the rim of her glass.

And three times, by accident of course, her knee had brushed against his under the table. The last two times she had pulled it away, of course, but she had also looked into his eyes.

Everything had at first gone swimmingly. They had had a second bottle of champagne. There was a string quartet, and they had danced. Both of them danced with Aunt Ramona first, of course, and then with the girls. When he had finally gotten his arms around Melanie, her perfume made him a little dizzy, and she seemed oblivious to her breasts pressing against his abdomen.

Pick seemed interested in Catherine-Anne, and she in him; and that all by itself seemed to be a blessing. All that had to be done now was to ask to take them to dinner. And get rid of Aunt Ramona, of course.

And then Aunt Ramona looked at her diamond-encrusted watch and cried in her ladylike way, "I had absolutely no *idea* it was so late! Girls, we have to go this *minute!*"

Pick jumped to his feet, and Dick had been sure that what he was going to do was make his move. He was a smooth sonofabitch, and there was no question that he would say precisely the right thing, and in precisely the right way, and that the result would be that they would get to take Catherine-Anne and Melanie to dinner. Maybe starting with early cocktails.

But he didn't. He kissed his goddamned aunt on the cheek and told her it had been nice to see her. And then he smiled at the girls and told them it had been a pleasure to make their acquaintance and that he hoped sometime to see them again.

And that was it. Melanie gave Dick one of those looks, and her hand; but then she was gone, following the other two out of the dining room.

"Jesus Christ, you blew that!" Dick snapped.

"Blew what?"

"They're *gone!* Goddamnit! Didn't you *notice?*"

"As opposed to what?" Pick had asked, innocently.

"I thought we were here to get laid," Dick whispered furiously and a little too loudly. Heads turned.

"You really didn't think . . . Aunt Ramona's friends?"

"I thought maybe dinner."

"They just met you, Dick," Pick explained. "Things just aren't done that way in Atlanta."

"Why not?"

"Well, if we get back here, maybe the next time I could get Aunt Ramona to give me their phone numbers, and maybe we could get them to meet us somewhere for a drink."

"What about now, for Christ's sake? What's wrong with now?"

"Can I say something to you without offending your feelings?" Pick said.

"I don't know," Dick said. "Right now, you're on pretty thin ice."

"You don't know much about girls like that," Pick said, seriously. "That's not a criticism; it's a simple statement of fact."

"So what? I can learn."

"You sort of liked the redhead, didn't you?" Pick asked.

"Melanie, her name is Melanie," Dick said. "Yeah, I did."

"Well, like I said, the next time we're here, if we come back, *maybe* I can get Aunt Ramona to put a good word in for you."

"But not now, huh?" Dick said, resignedly.

"Did you really think that something would happen?"

"Ah, hell, I guess not."

"I really feel bad about this," Pick said, as he signed his name to the bill and got up. "I really feel that I gave you the wrong impression about girls like that."

"Forget it," Dick said.

He followed Pickering out of the dining room and to the bank of elevators.

"Where are we going now?"

"Nature calls," Pick said.

"Yeah, me too," Dick said.

When they were in the suite, Pick touched Dick's arm.

"Hey, buddy," he said, "I've got an important phone call to make. Would you mind staying in your room until I yell?"

"You mean we drove seven hours just so we can't get laid and you can call your fucking widow?" Dick exploded.

Pick looked as if he had been about to say something but had changed his mind. Dick Stecker was instantly ashamed of himself.

"I'm a horse's ass," he said. "Good luck when you call her."

"Take the bar with you, why don't you?" Pick said.

"What?"

Pick pointed. There was something in the suite now that hadn't been in it when they had gone downstairs to meet Aunt Ramona, a cart mounted on huge brass wheels and holding an assortment of bottles, an ice bucket, and even two bottles of champagne.

"I'm liable to be some time," Pick said.

"In that case, I will take it," Dick said.

"Gimme one of the champagne bottles," Pick said, and took one from the cooler.

Then he turned his back on Stecker and started to open the champagne.

Stecker pushed the cart into his bedroom. He didn't want any champagne. For one thing, there didn't seem to be any point in drinking something romantic if you were alone in a hotel room. And for another, it tasted to him like carbonated vinegar.

He examined the bottles, selected the bourbon, made himself a drink, and then went to look out the window.

Always look for the bright side, he told himself. *At least you're here, in the fanciest hotel room you have ever seen. And you at least met her, and maybe you can come back. And the day isn't over. There is always hope.*

Dick had been looking out the window for perhaps five minutes when there was a knock at his door.

"I'm here by the window," he said, "contemplating jumping."

"Oh, don't do that," a soft Southern female voice said. "There's all sorts of interesting ways to spend a rainy afternoon."

Dick Stecker did not, literally, believe what he saw when he turned from the window to face the door.

Melanie was there. She had a smile on her face, and a champagne glass in her hand, and she was stark naked.

"Holy Christ!" Dick said.

Melanie walked slowly across the room to him. Her boobs,

he thought, were absolutely gorgeous. And she was a real redhead.

"Can you handle that all right, Lieutenant?" Pickering called. "Or should I make you up a flight plan?"

Dick's eyes snapped to the open door. Pickering was standing there, one hand holding a bottle of champagne, the other wrapped around Catherine-Anne's waist. Catherine-Anne was wearing nothing but a smile and a garter-belt. She was not a real blonde.

Melanie walked up to Dick and started to unbuckle his Sam Browne belt. When Dick looked at the door again, it was closing. He heard Pickering laugh. And then he turned his attention to Melanie.

On the way back to Pensacola the next day, Pick furnished Dick with an explanation. Ramona Heath was a madam, not his aunt. He had known her for years—since he been a sixteen-year-old bellhop. She had a stable of girls with which she traveled all over the country. Her girls were expensive, because they were the best. Most of her middle-aged clients were perfectly willing to close their eyes to the fact that the fees were paid by the people trying to sell their product and to allow themselves to think their charm and good looks were responsible for their being in bed with beautiful young women.

"I'm surprised," Jack said.

"Surprised? We went to get laid; we got laid."

"I mean, in good hotels," Stecker said. "Does that make me seem naive?"

"My grandfather once said," Pick said, "not to me, of course, but I heard about it, that the only thing he had against a paying guest coupling with an elephant in his room was that it was sometimes hard to clean the carpet."

"What did that little joke of yours cost you?" Stecker asked.

"Nothing. I tried to pay her—we danced, remember?—but she said no. She said I should think of it as her contribution to the war effort."

"Jesus Christ, Pickering, you're amazing."

"Yeah, I am," Pickering said, and there was something rueful in his tone of voice that made Dick Stecker look at him.

"Now what's wrong?"

"Well, I went to get laid. And I got laid. Getting it to stand up took all the skill at the command of the hooker, which I must say was most imaginative and thorough. And when it was over, I felt like a piece of dog shit. *How could I be unfaithful to good old Whatshername?"*

"Oh Jesus, Pick, I'm sorry," Stecker said.

"What the fuck am I going to do, Dick?" Pick asked plaintively.

Stecker said the only thing he could think of. "Hang in there, buddy," he said. "Just hang in there."

XVII

(One)
The New York Public Library
1215 Hours, 25 March 1942

Carolyn Spencer Howell was thirty-two years old. She was tall, chic, and much better dressed than most of the other librarians in the Central Reading Room of the New York Public Library on Forty-second Street, and she wore her black hair parted in the middle, and long enough to reach her shoulder blades. She had begun—not without feeling a little foolish and wondering what her real motives were—what she thought of as her special "research project" four days before.

Although one saw more and more men in uniform on the streets these days, one did not encounter many in the library, except in the lobby waiting out the rain. But there was one who was spending considerable time in the Central Reading Room, and Carolyn Spencer Howell found him very interesting. She had no way of knowing, of course, how long he had been coming into the Central Reading Room before she noticed him; but since she had noticed him ten days earlier, he had come in every day.

He was a Marine, and an officer. She knew that much about

the military services. Marines wore a fouled anchor superimposed on a representation of the world as their branch-of-service insignia. Officers wore pins representing their rank on the epaulets of their tunics and overcoats, and in the case of this man, on his collar points. Carolyn had to go to the Britannica to find out that a golden oak leaf was the insignia of a major.

From the time she had first noticed him, the Marine major had followed the same schedule. He arrived a few minutes after nine in the morning and went to the periodicals, where he read that day's *New York Times,* and then the most recent copies available of the *Baltimore Sun* and the San Diego *Union Leader.* He could have just been killing time, which of itself would be interesting, but he seemed to be looking for something particular in the newspapers.

When he came into the library every day, the Marine major had with him an obviously new leather briefcase, in which he carried two large green fabric-bound looseleaf notebooks, a supply of pencils, two fountain pens, cigarettes, and a Zippo lighter and a can of lighter fluid. She had once watched while he refilled his lighter. It was unusual to carry a supply of lighter fluid around with you, but it seemed to make sense if you thought about it.

He would make notes in one of the two notebooks, writing in pencil in one of them and in ink in the other. When he had finished reading the newspapers, he would come to the counter—sometimes to Carolyn Spencer Howell, and sometimes to one of the other girls—and fill out the little chits necessary to call up material from the stacks.

The first words he ever said to Carolyn Spencer Howell were "Would it be possible to get the *New York Times* from November fifteenth, nineteen forty-one, through, say, December thirty-first?"

"Of course," she said, "but it would make quite an armful. How about four days at a time? Starting with November fifteenth, nineteen forty-one?"

"That would be fine," the major said. "Thank you very much."

He had a nice, deep, masculine voice, she thought, and spoke with a regional accent that told her only that he was not a New Yorker. And there was something a little unhealthy about him, she thought. He didn't look quite as robust and outdoorsy as she expected a Marine major to look.

On the plus side, he had nice, warm, experienced eyes.

The second time he spoke to her, the major asked if by any chance the library had copies of the *Shanghai Post*.

"Well, yes, of course," she said. "Up to when the war started, of course."

"Could I have them from November first, nineteen forty-one . . . up to the last?"

"Certainly."

While he was reading the *Shanghai Post*, Carolyn noticed something strange. The major was just sort of staring off into space. There was a strange, profoundly sad look on his face. And in his eyes.

Some of the other requests he made of Carolyn Spencer Howell were of a military or politico-military nature. For instance, she got for him the text of the Geneva Conventions on Warfare, and several volumes on stateless persons. He was especially interested in Nansen passports.[1]

Most of his requests concerned the Japanese, which was understandable, but what in the world was a major of Marines doing spending all day, every day, in the public library? Didn't the military services have more information on the enemy than a public library could provide?

An even more disturbing thought came to Carolyn Spencer Howell. Was he *really* a Marine officer? Or some character who had simply elected to put on a service uniform? This was New York City, and anything was possible in New York, even in the main reading room of the public library. This unpleasant thought was fertilized when Carolyn realized that the major's uniforms were brand new. There was even a little tag that he had apparently missed stitched below one of the pockets on one of his blouses.

Yet he wore decorations, or at least the little colored ribbons that represented decorations, on the breast of his uniform. And for some reason she came to believe that these were the real thing—which made *him* the real thing. Finding out what they

---

[1] In 1920, the League of Nations authorized an identity/travel document to be issued to displaced persons, in particular Russians who did not wish to return to what had become the Soviet Union. It came to be called the "Nansen passport" after Fridtjof Nansen, League of Nations High Commissioner for Refugee Affairs.

represented became important to Carolyn. She thought of it as her "research project."

He had four ribbons. And when he came to the counter, she looked at them carefully and later made notes describing their colors. She checked her notes for accuracy when she had reason to walk through the reading room.

One had a narrow white stripe at each end, then two broader red stripes, and a medium-sized blue stripe in the middle. Next to it was one that was all purple, except for narrow white stripes at each end. And there was a little gold pin on this one, an oak leaf maybe. Another one was all yellow, with two narrow red-white-and-blue bands through it. And there was another yellow one, this one with two white-red-white bands *and* a blue-white-red band. This one had a star on it.

Carolyn was, after all, a librarian; she was trained to do research. Thus it wasn't hard to find out what the ribbons represented. The one that sat on top of the other three was the Bronze Star Medal, awarded for valor in action. The purple one was the Purple Heart, awarded for wounds received in action. The little pin (officially, according to *United States Navy Medals and Decorations, Navy Department, Washington D.C., January 1942, 21 pp., unbound,* an *oak leaf cluster*) signified the second award. Or, in other words, it said he had been wounded twice. The mostly yellow one with the star on it was awarded for service in the Asiatic-Pacific Theater of Operations; the star meant participation in a campaign. The other mostly yellow one was the American Defense Medal, whatever that meant.

That meant that the somewhat pale and hollow-eyed major was a bona fide hero. Either that or that he was a psychotic subway motorman who was enduring his forced retirement by vicariously experiencing the war—dressing up in a Marine officer's uniform and spending his days reading about the war in the public library.

Today, the Marine officer, with an armload of books, came directly to Carolyn Spencer Howell's position behind the counter.

"I wonder if you could just keep these handy?" he asked, "while I go have my lunch."

"Certainly," Carolyn said, and then she blurted, "I see you've seen service in the Pacific."

For the first time he looked at her, really looked at her as an individual, rather than as part of the furnishings.

"I was in the Pacific," he said, and then, "I'm surprised you know the ribbons. Few civilians do."

"I know them," Carolyn heard herself plunge on. "And you've been wounded twice. According to the ribbons."

"Correct," he said. "You have just won the cement bicycle. Would you care to try for an all-expense-paid trip to Coney Island?"

And then his smile vanished. He looked at her intently, then shook his head and started to laugh.

"What were you about to do?" he asked. "Call the military police?"

She felt like a fool, but she was swept along with the insanity.

"I was just a little curious how you could have served in the Pacific and be back already," she said.

"Would you believe a submarine?" he asked, chuckling. He reached in his pocket and took his identity card from his wallet and handed it to her.

It had a photograph of him on it, and his name: BANNING, EDWARD J. MAJOR USMC.

"Now will you guard my books for me while I have lunch?" he asked.

"I'm sorry," Carolyn Spencer Howell said, flushing. Then she lowered her head and spoke very softly.

There was no reply, and when she looked up, he was gone. Carolyn Spencer Howell shook her head.

"Oh, damn!" she said so loudly that heads turned.

Fifteen minutes later, she walked into a luncheonette on East Forty-first Street and headed for an empty stool. A buxom Italian woman with her hair piled high on her head beat her to it, and Carolyn turned in frustration and found herself looking directly at Major Edward J. Banning, USMC, who was seated at a small table against the wall.

"You wouldn't be following me, would you?" he asked. Carolyn flushed, and started to flee.

Banning stood up quickly and caught her arm.

"Now, I'm sorry," he said. "Please sit down. I'm about finished anyway."

She sat down.

"I have made an utter fool of myself," she said. "But I wasn't really following you. I often come here for lunch."

"I know," Banning said. "I've seen you. I hoped maybe you'd come here for lunch today."

She looked at him.

"I've been thinking," he said. "Under the circumstances, I would have thought I was suspicious, too."

"Would you settle for 'curious'?" Carolyn asked.

"You were suspicious," he said. "Why should that embarrass you?"

A waitress appeared, saving her from having to frame a reply. She ordered a sandwich and coffee, and the waitress turned to Banning.

"If the lady doesn't mind me sharing her table, I'll have some more coffee," he said.

"Please," Carolyn said quickly.

She looked at him. Their eyes met.

"You remember me asking for stuff on Nansen passports?" Banning asked. She nodded. "The reason I wanted to find out as much as I can is that my wife, whom I left behind in Shanghai, is traveling on a Nansen."

"I see," she said.

"I wanted that out in front," Banning said.

"Yes," Carolyn Spencer Howell said. And then she said, "I was married for fifteen years. My husband turned me in on a younger model. It cost him a good deal of money. I had to find a way to pass the time, so I went back to work in the library."

He nodded.

We both know, she thought. *And he knew before I did. I wonder why that doesn't embarrass me? And what happens now?*

They walked back to the library together. Just before she was to go off shift, he walked to the counter and asked her how she would respond to an invitation to have a drink before he got on the subway to go back to Brooklyn. She said she would meet him for a drink in the Biltmore Hotel. She would meet him under the clock . . . he couldn't miss the clock.

And so after work they had a drink, and then another. When the waiter appeared again, she said that she didn't want another just now. Then he asked her if she was free for dinner, and she told him she was, but she would have to stop by her apartment for a moment.

In the elevator, she looked at him.

"I can't remember one thing we talked about in the Biltmore," she said.

"We were just making noise," he said.

"I don't routinely do this sort of thing," Carolyn Spencer Howell said softly, as they moved closer together.

"I know," he said.

Afterward, she went to the Chinese restaurant on Third Avenue, and returned with two large bags full of small, white cardboard containers that Ed Banning said looked like they held goldfish.

Then she took off her clothes again, and they ate their dinner where she had left him, naked, in the bed.

(Two)
Bachelor Officers' Quarters
U.S. Navy Hospital
Brooklyn, New York
0930 Hours, 26 March 1942

The spartan impersonality of the bachelor officers' quarters struck Major Edward J. Banning the moment he pushed open the plate-glass door and walked into the lobby. It was in some ways like a small hotel.

There was a reception desk, usually manned by a petty officer third. But he wasn't there. And the lobby and the two corridors that ran off it were deserted.

The lobby held a chrome-and-plastic two-seater couch; a chrome-and-plastic coffee table in front of the couch; and two chrome-and-plastic chairs on the other side of the coffee table. There was a simple glass ashtray on the coffee table, and nothing else.

The floor was polished linoleum, bearing the geometric scars of a fresh waxing. There were no rugs. Two photographs were hanging on the walls, one of the Battleship *Arizona*, the other of a for-once-not-grinning-brightly Franklin Delano Roosevelt. There was a cork bulletin board, onto which had been thumbtacked an array of mimeographed notices for the inhabitants.

A concrete stairway led to the upper floors. Its railings were steel pipe, and its stair-tread edges were reinforced with steel.

Banning went to the desk and checked for messages by leaning over the counter for a look at the row of mailboxes where a message would be kept. There was no message, no letter. This was not surprising, for he expected none.

Banning went up the concrete stairs to the second floor. It was identical to the first, except there was no receptionist's desk. That space was occupied by a couch-and-chairs-and-table ensemble identical to the one in the lobby, which left the center of the second floor foyer empty. There was an identical photograph of President Roosevelt hanging on the wall, next to a photograph of two now-long-obsolete Navy biplane fighters in the clouds.

Halfway down the right corridor, his back to Banning, the petty officer who usually could be found at the reception desk was slowly swinging a large electric floor polisher across the linoleum. Banning walked down the left corridor to his room.

The reason he noticed the spartan simplicity of the BOQ, he realized, was that forty-five minutes earlier, he had walked down a carpeted corridor illuminated by crystal chandeliers to an elevator paneled in what for some strange reason he had recognized as fumed oak, and then across carpets laid on a marble floor past genuine antiques to a gleaming brass-and-glass revolving door spun by a doorman in what looked to be the uniform of an admiral in the Imperial Russian Navy.

"Good morning, Mrs. Howell," the doorman had politely greeted Carolyn. "It's a little nippy. Shall I call a cab?"

"No, thank you," Carolyn had said. "I'll walk."

The doorman's face had been expressionless. Or at least his eyebrows had not risen when he recognized Mrs. Carolyn Howell coming out of the building with a Marine. Nevertheless, Carolyn's face had colored, and Banning had seen that she was embarrassed.

She had quickly recovered, however, and almost defiantly took his arm before they walked down the street.

The sex had been precisely what the doctor had ordered. From the moment he had kissed her in the elevator on the way up, there had been no false modesty, no pushing him away, no questions about what kind of a woman did he think she was. She wanted him—or at least a man—just about as bad as he had wanted her—or at least a woman.

She had told him later, and he had believed her, that it had been the first time for her since the trouble with her husband.

"It *is* like riding a bicycle, isn't it?" she had asked, with a delightfully naughty—and pleased—smile as she forked a shrimp from one of the little cardboard Chinese take-out containers. "You don't forget how. Except that I feel, with you, like you've just won the Tour de France."

And it had been, aside from the sex, a very interesting (or perverse?) experience to lie naked in Carolyn's bed and tell her about Milla, while she, with genuine sympathy in her eyes, was kneeling naked beside him. To think that Milla would like Carolyn, and Carolyn would like Milla. And to wonder if he was really a sonofabitch for feeling that somehow Milla, if she knew about Carolyn, would not be all that hurt, or pissed off. That she might even be happy for him.

He reached his room, found the key, and pushed the gray metal door open.

The BOQ room was furnished with a bed; a straight-backed chair; a chest of drawers; a chrome-and-plastic armchair; a small wooden desk; and a framed photograph of a broadly smiling Franklin Delano Roosevelt.

Lieutenant Colonel F. L. Rickabee, USMC, in uniform, was sitting in the straight-backed chair, his feet on the bed, reading the *New York Times*. He had removed his uniform blouse, revealing that he used suspenders to hold up his trousers. There were other straps around his torso, which only after a moment Banning recognized as the kind that belonged to a shoulder holster.

"Ah, Banning," Rickabee said, "there you are. All things come to him who waits."

"Good morning, sir."

"I feel constrained to tell you that I caught the four A.M. milk train from Sodom on the Potomac in the naive belief that by so doing I could catch you before you went out."

"If you had called, sir . . ." Banning said.

Rickabee swung his feet off the bed, refolded the newspaper carefully, and tossed it on the bed. When he faced Banning, Banning saw the butt of what he thought was probably a Smith & Wesson Chief's Special in the shoulder holster.

"No problem," Rickabee said. "It gave me the chance to talk with Captain Toland about you, which was also on my agenda. And it also gave me my very first chance to play secret agent."

"Sir?"

"I asked the white hat on duty downstairs to let me into your room. He told me it was absolutely against regulations." He bent over the bed, took what looked like a wallet from his blouse, and tossed it to Banning. "So I got to show him that. He was awed."

Banning caught it and opened it. Inside was a gold badge and a sealed-in-plastic identification card. The card, which carried the seal of the Navy Department, held a photograph of Rickabee, and identified him as a special agent of the Secretary of the Navy, all questions about whom were to be referred to the Director of Naval Intelligence.

Banning looked at Rickabee.

"I think I could have ordered him to set the building afire," Rickabee said. "It had an amazing effect on him. You could almost hear the trumpets." He held his hand out for Banning to return the identification.

Banning chuckled and tossed the small folder back to him.

"Very impressive, sir," he said.

"In the wrong hands, a card like that could be a dangerous thing," Rickabee said.

"Yes, sir, I can see that," Banning said.

A leather folder came flying across the room. Banning just managed to catch it.

"That's yours," Rickabee said. "You're a field-grade officer now, so I suppose it won't be necessary to tell you to be careful with it."

Close to astonishment, Banning opened the folder. It held the same badge and card, except that his photograph peered at him from it.

"You also get a pistol," Rickabee said, pointing to a large, apparently full, leather briefcase. "Since I didn't think you'd have to repel boarders between here and San Diego, I took the liberty of getting you a little Smith & Wesson like mine."

A dozen questions popped into Banning's mind.

"Sir—" he began.

"Let me talk first, Ed," Lieutenant Colonel Rickabee interrupted him. "It will probably save time."

"Yes, sir," Banning said.

"General Forrest sent me here," Rickabee said. "My first priority was to settle to my own satisfaction the question of your mental stability. Dr. Toland's diagnosis—that there is nothing wrong with you that a good piece of ass wouldn't cure—confirmed my own. Toland told me that the way you handled yourself when you thought you were blind was as tough a test of your stability as he could think of."

Banning waited for Rickabee to go on.

"So you are now officially certified as an officer who, because of the extraordinary faith placed in his ability and trustworthiness by both the Assistant Chief of Staff for Intelligence of the Marine Corps, and the Commandant, can be entrusted with the highest-level secrets of the Corps, and with some extraordinary authority," Rickabee said.

"Jesus Christ," Banning said. "What the hell does that mean?"

"Just what I said," Rickabee said. "Secret one is that General Forrest at this time yesterday morning was cleaning out his desk and wondering how he was going to tell his wife that he was being retired from the Corps in disgrace—a disgrace that was no less shameful because the reasons were secret."

"Forrest? Christ, he's a good man. What the hell—"

"At two yesterday afternoon, the Commandant summoned General Forrest to his office and told him that he had reconsidered; that the needs of the Corps right now—there being no one available with his qualifications and experience to replace him—were such that he would not be retired."

"Colonel," Banning said, "I don't have any idea—"

"Major General Paul H. Lesterby was retired from the Corps as of oh-oh-oh-one hours this morning," Rickabee went on. "Colonel Thomas C. Wesley—"

"Used to be with Fleet Marine Force Atlantic?" Banning interrupted.

Rickabee nodded. "And more recently, he was Plans and Projects in the Commandant's office. Wesley is now on a train for California, where he will function as special assistant to the commanding officer of the supply depot there until the Commandant makes up his mind whether he will be retired, or court-martialed. The Commandant was honest enough to tell Wesley that he would prefer to court-martial him, and the only thing that was stopping him was the good of the Corps."

"What the *hell* did he do?"

"You know Evans Carlson, I understand?"

"Yes, sir."

"From this point, Ed, as you will see, we are getting into an even more sensitive area," Rickabee said, and went into his briefcase. First he took out a small revolver in a shoulder holster and laid it on the bed. Then he handed Banning a thick stack of papers. "These documents were given to the Commandant the day before yesterday. I can't let them out of my hands. You'll have to read them now. When I get back to Washington, the whole file will be burned, and I am to personally report to the Commandant that it has been burned.''

The first document in the stack was stamped SECRET. It was entitled, ''Report of the Activities of Evans Carlson, late Major, USMC, during the period April 1939–April 1941.''

Halfway down the stack was Captain James Roosevelt's letter to the Major General Commandant of the Marine Corps. At the bottom of the stack, also stamped SECRET, were transcripts of telephone conversations between Lieutenant Colonel Rickabee or Captain Edward Sessions and Second Lieutenant K. J. McCoy.

''I wondered what McCoy was doing at Elliott,'' Banning said when he had finished reading everything and was tapping the stack on his chest of drawers to get it in order.

''Any other questions?'' Rickabee asked.

''You want an honest response to that?'' Banning asked.

''Please,'' Rickabee said.

''This is a despicable thing to do to Carlson,'' Banning said.

''Yes, it was,'' Rickabee said. ''And that was one of the more printable terms used by the Commandant to describe it.''

''Was?''

''Was,'' Rickabee confirmed. ''Just as soon as the Commandant saw it, it was over. Except for cleaning up the mess, of course.''

''How did it happen?'' Banning asked. ''How did it get started in the first place?''

''The goddamned Palace Guard got carried away with its own importance,'' Rickabee said. ''Wesley took it upon himself to save the Corps from Carlson. He enlisted General Lesterby in that noble cause, and then the two of them went to Forrest with their little idea. When Forrest balked, they led him to believe they were acting for the Commandant.''

''Jesus Christ!''

''And that goddamned Wesley suckered me, too,'' Rickabee said. ''There was no question in my mind that he was working for the Commandant. Otherwise—''

''It's hard to believe,'' Banning said. But when he heard what he had said, he offered a quick clarification. ''I mean, a colonel and a major general. Jesus Christ!''

''I think the real reason the Commandant's mad at Forrest is that Forrest was apparently willing to believe the Commandant was capable of something like that. Fortunately, I'm only a lieutenant colonel, and lieutenant colonels are supposed to be stupid. The Commandant treated me with condescending contempt, and spelled out very slowly and carefully what he wants me to do about cleaning up the mess."

"That involves me? You said something about Diego," Banning asked.

"The Commandant told me—this was during the eighteen-hour period General Forrest thought he was being retired in disgrace, and there was nobody to deal with but me—that the worst thing you can do to a commander is let him know his superiors question his ability. If necessary, the Commandant is prepared to go to California and apologize to Carlson and assure him of his personal confidence in him. But he hopes that Carlson doesn't know we sent an officer out there to spy on him, and that an apology won't be necessary."

"Apologies being beneath the dignity of the Commandant?" Banning asked, sarcastically. "You don't suppose he could be worried that President Roosevent will find out about this half-cocked spying operation?"

Rickabee hesitated a moment before he replied. "I'm sure he is," he said finally. "And the damage to the Corps if that happens is something I don't even like to think about. If the President found out, the Commandant would have to go. And that would be bad for the Corps, for all the reasons that come quickly to mind."

Banning grunted.

"But having granted that, Ed, no, I don't think apologizing would bother the Commandant at all. But *making* the apology would be an admission that there was doubt in Carlson's loyalty and ability—doubt high enough within the Corps to have the Commandant personally involved. What the Commandant wants to know is whether Carlson knows, or strongly suspects, what's been going on. That's where you come in."

"How?"

"The forward element of the First Raider Battalion will leave Quantico one April for Diego, and sail for Hawaii as soon as shipping can be found for them. The Second Battalion, Evans Carlson's, is supposed to complete their training at Camp Elliott on Fifteen April. There will be an inspection of the Second Raider Battalion by officers from Headquarters,

USMC. You will be part of that delegation, charged, as an experienced regimental S-Two, with having a look at Carlson's intelligence section. Not, if I have to say it, as somebody assigned to us. You'll prepare the usual report, which will make its normal passage through channels. You will also be prepared, immediately on your return, to tell the Commandant personally whether or not you think Carlson suspects anything."

"Lovely job," Banning said, dryly.

"Check with McCoy, of course. And there's somebody else out there you probably should talk to. You remember Master Gunnery Sergeant Stecker?"

"Did a hitch with the Fourth? Has the Medal of Honor?"

"He's a captain, now, in Diego. At Second Joint Training Force headquarters. He works for Colonel Lou Harris, and Harris has had him greasing Carlson's ways. If approached discreetly, you might ask him if Carlson has smelled a rat."

"I don't know if he would talk to me. He's a starchy sonofabitch."

"He's a good Marine," Rickabee said. "Use your judgment, Ed."

"I get the picture, sir," Banning said. "When do I go?"

"Your leave is over two April," Rickabee said. "I've got orders for you. You are assigned to the office of the Inspector General, Headquarters, USMC, on that date, and to the inspection team for the Second Raiders. They will have left Washington one April. You've got a rail priority, and Sergeant Gregg—you remember him?"

Banning shook his head. "No."

"Gregg got you a compartment on the Twentieth-Century Limited to Chicago, and then on whatever they call that train with the observation cars—"

"I know what you mean," Banning said. "I can't think of the name."

"Well, anyway, after you cruise through the Rockies in luxury to Los Angeles, you take a train called the Lark to San Diego. The inspection team will return to Washington by air. You'll travel with them."

"Aye, aye, sir." Banning said.

"By the time you get to Washington, have your mind made up," Rickabee said. "The Commandant has a tough call to make, and he'll have to make it pretty much on what you decide."

Banning grunted, and nodded his head thoughtfully.

"I knew the good life was too good to last," he said.

XVIII

(One)
Company B, 2nd Raider Battalion
Camp Elliott, California
26 March 1942

The men of Baker Company were spread out on both sides of the dirt road—hardly more than a path—in the hills above Camp Elliott when the jeep drove up. The platoon leader and Gunnery Sergeant Esposito were standing up. And a few of the men were sitting up, but most of them were flat on their backs, still breathing heavily. Gunny Esposito had elected to have them pass the last five minutes before the break at double-time. After forty-five minutes of marching at quick time with full field gear, including a basic load of ammo, five minutes of double-time feels like five hours.

The jeep was driven by the company clerk. Unlike the stereotype of most company clerks, Baker Company's company clerk looked like the fullback he had been on the Marion (Ohio) High School "Tigers" before he had enlisted in the Corps three days after Pearl Harbor. You had to have a "C" average to remain eligible for varsity football, and since Rocky Rockham wasn't too comfortable with geometry or English, the coach had suggested that if he wanted to play football, he better take something he could do well in, something that would bring his grade average up, like typing.

At Parris Island the personnel clerk had asked Rocky Rockham if he had any skills, like typing. And Rocky told him that he could type pretty good, forty-five words a minute. Naturally the personnel clerk hadn't believed him, and made him take a test. Rocky Rockham didn't look like somebody who could type, but he passed the test, and he left Parris Island for the Joint Training Force at Diego as a clerk/typist.

Rocky quickly realized that telling the personnel clerk that he could type had been a mistake. He had joined the Corps to kill Japanese, to pay the buckteethed bastards back for Pearl Harbor and Wake Island, not to sit at a fucking typewriter in a fucking office, filling out fucking requisition forms.

At the reveille formation one day, there had been a call for volunteers to serve in something called the 2nd Separate Battalion. The first sergeant told them the 2nd Separate Battalion was going overseas as soon as they finished their training. So Rocky volunteered. That was what he wanted, getting overseas, and out from behind the typewriter.

"Well, lad," the first sergeant of Baker Company said, smiling at him the day he reported aboard, "I'm damned glad to see you. You can really type forty-five words a minute?"

A minute after that, not smiling, the first sergeant of Baker Company pointed out to PFC Rockham that he was in the Marine Corps, and the Marine Corps didn't give a flying fuck what *he* wanted to do. He would do what the Corps told him to do, and if he was smart, he would do it wearing a fucking smile. He was now Baker Company's company clerk, and that was fucking *it*.

When Rocky wrote home that he had been made a corporal, he didn't add that he was the company clerk of Baker Company, 2nd Raider Battalion, USMC; just that he was in the Raiders and hoped to soon be killing Japs.

Rocky stopped the jeep, and walked over to the lieutenant who was taking the march for the Old Man. He saluted and delivered his message.

"Go get him, Gunny," the lieutenant ordered.

Gunny Esposito turned around.

"McCoy!" he bellowed. "Up here! On the double!"

PFC Thomas M. McCoy, still breathing heavily, still red-faced, pushed himself off the ground and trotted to where Gunny Esposito stood with the lieutenant and Rocky Rockham.

"Throw your gear in the vee-hicle," Gunny Esposito said, "and go with Corporal Rockham."

"Where'm I going, Gunny?"

"In the vee-hicle with Corporal Rockham," Gunny Esposito explained.

When they were bouncing back down the hill, McCoy asked Rockham where he was going.

"Able Company," Rockham said. "You been transferred."

"What the fuck for?"

"Who the fuck knows?" Rockham asked rhetorically. "First sergeant give me your service record, told me to collect you and your gear and take you over to Able Company."

PFC McCoy naturally concluded that Zimmerman, that fat, mean cocksucker, was responsible. He had seen Zimmerman three, four times since the night Zimmerman had taken him from the Slop Chute and worked him over. And it was always the same thing. Zimmerman would motion for him to come over to wherever he was standing.

"I hear you been keeping your mouth shut and your nose clean," Zimmerman had said. "Maybe you aren't as dumb as you look, brig bunny."

When Rockham dropped him off at the Able Company orderly room, with his sea bag, his records, and all his gear, McCoy put the bag and his field gear by the side of the door, and then he complied with the order painted on the door to "KNOCK, REMOVE HEADGEAR, WAIT FOR PERMISSION TO ENTER."

"Come!" a voice called.

McCoy stepped inside.

"You're McCoy," the company clerk announced. The company clerk was a little fucker with glasses.

"I was told to report here," McCoy said.

The first sergeant looked up from his desk. He was a mean-looking sonofabitch, a tall, skinny Texan.

"You got your gear, I hope?" the first sergeant asked. When McCoy nodded, he motioned to McCoy to hand him his service record.

He opened the envelope, took out all the records it

contained, and picked out the service record itself, leaving the clothing forms and the shot records and all the other documents on the table. Then he stood up and walked through a door under a sign reading "MERWYN C. PLUMLEY, 1ST LT, USMC, COMMANDING," carrying the service record with him.

He was inside maybe two minutes before he opened the door and stuck his head out.

"McCoy, report to the commanding officer."

McCoy walked to the open door and followed the protocol. He rapped twice on the doorjamb with his knuckles, waited until he was told to come in, and then he marched in. He stopped eighteen inches from Lieutenant Plumley's desk, coming to attention; and then, looking six inches over the officer's head, he barked, "Sir, PFC McCoy reporting to the company commander as ordered, sir."

"Stand at ease, McCoy," Lieutenant Plumley said. McCoy spread his feet and put his hands in the small of his back. Now he could look at Lieutenant Plumley. When he did, he saw that Plumley was examining him very carefully.

"Gunnery Sergeant Zimmerman has been talking to me and to First Sergeant Lowery about you, McCoy," Lieutenant Plumley said.

Well, that fucking figures!

"When the lieutenant talks to you, McCoy, you say 'Yes, sir,'" First Sergeant Lowery snapped.

"Sorry, sir," PFC McCoy said.

"Tell me, McCoy," Lieutenant Plumley said, "why you did so badly with the BAR in Baker Company?"

What the fuck is that all about?

"Sir, I qualified with the BAR," McCoy said.

"Marksman," Lieutenant Plumley said. "Only Marksman."

Record firing scores qualified a marine as Marksman, Sharpshooter, or Expert. Marksman was the lowest qualifying score, and extra pay was given those qualifying as Expert.

"Sir," McCoy blurted, "the BAR I had was a piece of shit, one of them worn-out ones we got from the Army."

"And you think you could do better if you had a better weapon?"

"Yes, sir," McCoy said.

"So does Gunnery Sergeant Zimmerman," Lieutenant Plumley said.

"He's sure big enough," First Sergeant Lowery said. There was a faint hint of approval in his voice. McCoy looked at him in surprise.

"Gunnery Sergeant Zimmerman, as you know, McCoy," Lieutenant Plumley said, "has been temporarily assigned other duties. But when we deploy, he will come back to the company. He is naturally interested in what he will find here when he comes back."

"Yes, sir," McCoy said.

"We're short a couple of squad leaders," Lieutenant Plumley said. "And when the first sergeant and I discussed this with Gunnery Sergeant Zimmerman, he recommended that you be transferred from Baker Company and be given one of those billets."

"Sir?" McCoy was now completely baffled. He was sure he hadn't heard right.

"Gunny Zimmerman has recommended that you be given one of the squad-leader billets. It carries with it a promotion to corporal," Lieutenant Plumley said. "That's why I was curious when I saw that you'd only made Marksman when you fired for record."

"Yes, sir," McCoy said.

"If the first sergeant could arrange for you to requalify, with a weapon in first-class condition, do you think you could do better than Marksman?"

"Yes, sir."

"Well, then, we'll do it this way. We will assign you temporarily as a BAR fire-team leader," Lieutenant Plumley said. "Sergeant Lowery will arrange for you to requalify. If you make Sharpshooter—I would hope Expert—I'll give you your corporal's stripes. Fair enough?"

"Yes, sir."

"Do you have anything else, First Sergeant?"

"No, sir."

"Then that will be all for now, Sergeant," Lieutenant Plumley said. "I would like a word with McCoy alone."

"Aye, aye, sir," First Sergeant Lowery said, and walked out of the office, closing the door behind him.

Plumley looked at McCoy.

"There's something about me I think I should tell you, McCoy," he said. "I don't listen to scuttlebutt. I don't like scuttlebutt."

"Yes, sir."

"If someone comes to me with a clean service record, so far as I am concerned, he has a clean record. So far as I am concerned, you have reported aboard with a clean record. Do you take my point?"

"Yes, sir," McCoy said.

Lieutenant Plumley smiled and reached across the desk with his hand extended.

"Welcome aboard, McCoy," he said. "You come recommended by Gunny Zimmerman, and therefore I expect good things of you."

"Thank you, sir."

"You're dismissed, McCoy," Lieutenant Plumley said.

McCoy came to attention, did an about-face, and marched out of the office.

First Sergeant Lowery was waiting for him in the outer office.

"Come on, I'll show you where you'll bunk," he said. Outside the orderly room, he picked up McCoy's field gear and carried it for him.

Halfway to the barrack, he laid a hand on McCoy's arm.

"I understand you're pretty good with your fists, McCoy."

"I guess I'm all right," McCoy said.

"You use your fists in Able Company, McCoy, and I'll work you over myself. And compared to me, what Zimmerman did to you will be like being brushed with a feather duster."

McCoy looked at him.

"You understand me?" First Sergeant Lowery asked.

"Yeah, I understand you."

First Sergeant Lowery smiled, and patted McCoy, a very friendly pat, on the shoulder.

"Good," First Sergeant Lowery said. "Good."

(Three)
The New York Public Library
1415 Hours, 26 March 1942

Carolyn Spencer Howell had expected Major Edward Banning to join her for lunch. But when he hadn't been there, and after she had finally given up on him and gone to eat, she knew she had to come to terms with the reality of what had happened.

The conclusion she drew was that she had made a grand and glorious ass of herself. That, for reasons probably involving the moon, but certainly including the fact that she was a healthy female with normal needs, as well as the fact that Ed Banning was a good-looking healthy male, she had played the bitch in heat. And she'd done everything a bitch in heat does but back up to the male, rub her behind against him, and look over her shoulder to see what was keeping him from doing what she wanted done.

She had even performed the human version of that. Before they kissed in the elevator, she had with conscious and lascivious aforethought pressed her breasts against him.

All this morning Carolyn relived with surprise and embarrassment her shamelessly lewd behavior with him in her apartment. The reason she thought of nothing else all morning was that until the reality dawned on her, she had wondered how she would behave when he returned from Brooklyn.

The last thing he said to her when she left him at the subway entrance was that he would go change his uniform and come back. He even kissed her. Rather distantly, she thought even at the time, but a kiss was a kiss. Once she reached the library there had been time to consider what she had done: She had allowed one of the patrons to buy her a drink, following which she had taken him directly to bed.

Her worrying started when she began to imagine how she was going to be able to look him in the eye when he came back from Brooklyn. But after he hadn't returned by eleven (when she thought she would take him into the staff lounge, which you could do for a "friend," and give him a cup of coffee and maybe a Danish), she began to worry, to give her imagination free rein.

By noon, one theory of the several that had occurred to her seemed to stand the test of critical examination. The point of this one was that he was *not* entirely a sonofabitch. He had at least been decent enough to tell her he was married. And she was now convinced that he was indeed a Marine officer.

Yet he had been very vague about what exactly he did as a Marine officer, and where he did it. And in fact, now that she had time to think about it, it no longer seemed entirely credible that he was in New York on leave simply because his family was gone and he had no place else to go, and New York seemed as good a place as any to take a holiday.

If he was so bored with his leave, why was he on leave?

And viewed with the cold and dispassionate attitude that she believed she had reached by one o'clock—when it was apparent that he was not going to come—his melodramatic story of the White Russian wife left on the pier in Shanghai clearly served two purposes. First, it told her he was married, so don't get any ideas. And second, it clearly infected the heart of the librarian with terminal nymphomania and inspired her to perform sexual feats right out of the Kama Sutra. He had probably enormously embellished the original tale as soon as he had realized how much of it she was so gullibly willing to swallow.

Over lunch (preceding which she had a Manhattan to steady her nerves and keep her from throwing the ashtray across the room), she remembered what her father told her when she told him she was going to divorce Charley: "Everybody, sooner or later, stubs their toe. When that happens, the thing to do is swallow hard and go on to what happens next."

And so, by the time she walked back in the library, Carolyn was at peace with herself. She accepted the situation for what it was, and she was already beginning to see small shafts of sunlight breaking through the black cloud. All she had done was make a fool of herself, and thank God, no one knew about it. Except, of course, Henry the Doorman; and he was just the doorman. In her state of temporary insanity, she could have introduced Banning to her colleagues in the library. With her state of rut in high gear, it would have been clear to any of her colleagues that she had more of an interest in Major Ed Banning than as a fellow lover of books.

And being absolutely brutally honest about it, she hadn't come out of the encounter entirely empty-handed. Obviously, she had wanted to be taken to bed, and Ed had certainly done that with great skill and finesse. She would not need such servicing again any time soon.

Now she would simply put Major Ed Banning out of her mind.

And then, *there* he was, in the Central Reading Room. He was sitting at a table close to the counter. He quickly rose up, with a worried look on his face, when he saw her approach him.

"Hello," he said.

"Hello," Carolyn said.

"I thought you would be interested to know that you don't work here," he said.

"I beg your pardon?"

"I called up and asked to speak to you—"

"You did?"

He's obviously lying. After some thought, he has decided to come back for another drink at the well.

"And a woman said there was no one here by that name," Ed Banning said.

"Oh, really?"

"So I called back, thinking I would get somebody else, and I got the same woman, and she said, in righteous indignation, 'I told you there is no Mrs. Powell on the staff.'"

My God, he doesn't even know my name!

"It's *Howell*," Carolyn said. "With an 'H.'"

"Well, that explains that, doesn't it?" Ed Banning said. And then he looked at her and blurted, "I was afraid that maybe you had told her to say that, that you just wished I would go away."

"No," Carolyn said, very simply.

"I got my orders," Ed said. "That's why I was delayed. That's what I was trying to tell you on the telephone."

"Where are you going?" she asked.

"The West Coast," he said.

"When are you going?"

"Two April," Ed said. "That's a week from today."

"Oh," she said.

"Are you free for dinner?" Ed asked.

"Dinner?"

"I don't want to intrude in your life, Carolyn," Ed Banning said. "But I had hoped that we could spend some time together."

"Oh," she said.

"Dinner?" he asked again, and when there was no immediate reply, "Maybe tomorrow night?"

My God, he's afraid I'll say no.

"What are your plans for this afternoon?" Carolyn asked.

"I have to go to Brooks Brothers," Banning replied.

"Brooks Brothers?" She wasn't sure she had heard correctly.

"When I replaced my uniforms, I didn't buy as much for the tropics as I should have," he said.

"Meaning you're headed for the tropics . . . the Pacific?"

"Meaning that I realized this morning that I don't have enough uniforms," he said.

Is that the truth? Or does he know he's on his way to the Pacific and doesn't want to tell me?

"That's all you have planned?" Carolyn asked.

"That's it."

"For this afternoon, or for the rest of the week?"

"For the week," Ed Banning said.

"I thought maybe you'd be going home or something," she said.

"I thought I told you," he said. "Like a lot of Marines, the Corps's home."

Carolyn looked into his eyes.

"Wait for me in the lobby," she said. "It'll take me about five minutes to tell my boss I'm going, and to get my coat."

When she went outside, he was at the bottom of the stairs, standing by one of the concrete lions that seem to be studying the traffic on Fifth Avenue passing the library. It was snowing, and there was snow on the shoulders of his overcoat and on his hat.

She went quickly down the stairs and put her hand under his arm, and then she absolutely shocked herself by blurting, "Hi, sailor, looking for a good time?"

He touched her gloved hand for a moment and smiled at her.

"Have any trouble getting the afternoon off?" he asked.

"I told my boss I was just struck with some kind of flu," Carolyn said, "that'll keep me from work for a week."

"Can you get away with it?" he asked.

"Sure," she said. "Now, aside from Brooks Brothers, what would you like to do?"

His eyebrows rose. She nudged him with her shoulder.

"Aside from that, I mean," she said.

He shrugged.

"Is there some reason you have to stay in the city?" Carolyn asked, as they started to walk across Fifth Avenue to Forty-first Street.

"No," he said. "The only thing I have to do is get on the Twentieth-Century Limited on two April at seven fifty-five in the evening. Why do you ask?"

"How do you feel about snow?" she asked.

"I hate it," he cheerfully admitted.

"How about snow outside?" Carolyn pursued. "On fields. Unmarked, except maybe by deer tracks?"

"Better," he said.

"With a fireplace inside? Glowing embers?"

"A loaf of bread, a glowing ember, and thou?"

"Beside you in the wilderness," Carolyn said. "I have a place in Bucks County. Overlooking the Delaware. An old fieldstone canal house."

"And you want to go there?"

"I want to go there with you," she said.

"Christ, and I was afraid you were trying to get rid of me," Banning said.

Carolyn squeezed his arm. She didn't trust her voice to speak.

(Four)
Battalion Arms Room
2nd Raider Battalion
Camp Elliott, California
1300 Hours, 9 April 1942

There are few things that frighten the United States Marine Corps. One of them is the acronymn "IG," for "Inspector General," which usually means not only the officer bearing that title but his entire staff. This ranges from senior noncommissioned officers upward, and what they do is visit a unit and compile long lists of the unit's shortcomings in all areas of military endeavor.

When a visit from the IG is scheduled, the unit to be inspected instantly begins a frenzied preparation for the inspection, so that the IG will find as little wrong as possible. The IG *will* find something wrong, or else the IG (including the staff) would not be doing the job properly. No IG report has ever said that the unit inspected was perfect in every detail of its organization, personnel, and equipment. The best a unit can hope for is that the shortcomings the IG will detect will be of a minor, easily correctable nature.

The fear, and the resultant near-hysteria, is compounded when the phrase "from Washington" is appended to "IG." Colonels who could with complete calm order a regimental attack across heavily mined terrain into the mouths of cannon, and master gunnery sergeants who would smilingly lead the attack with a fixed bayonet, break into cold sweats and suffer stomach distress when informed their outfit is about to be inspected by "the IG from Washington." There is a reason for this concern. An IG evaluation of "Unsatisfactory" is tantamount to the announcement before God and the Corps that they have been weighed in the balance and found not to be Good Marines.

The 2nd Raider Battalion was not immune to IG hysteria. There were several "preinspections" before the "IG from Washington's" inspection, during which the staff examined the equipment and personnel of the Raiders and searched for things the IG would likely find fault with. And there were twice as many pre-preinspections, in which platoon leaders and gunnery sergeants sought to detect faults that would likely be uncovered by the battalion brass during their preinspections.

Depending on the individual, experience with IG inspections tends to lessen the degree of hysteria. Inasmuch as Second Lieutenant Kenneth J. McCoy had gone through four annual IG inspections while an enlisted man with the 4th Marines, he had not been nearly as concerned with the preinspections—or even with the "IG from Washington" inspection itself—as had been First Lieutenant Martin Burnes (whose permanent presence, and that of his wife, aboard the *Last Time* was now an accepted fact of life).

McCoy was so experienced with IG inspections, in fact, that he knew the rules of the game, and took several precautionary steps in his own area of responsibility (weaponry) to keep the IG inspectors happy. He was aware that IG inspectors would keep inspecting things until they found something wrong. So he gave them something to find.

After details of Raiders who'd been sent up from the companies to the armory had cleaned the crew-served and special (shotguns, et cetera) weapons to Gunnery Sergeant Zimmerman's highly critical satisfaction, and after they had all been laid out for the IG's inspection, Second Lieutenant McCoy and Gunnery Sergeant Zimmerman had gone through them and fucked things up a little here and there. While Zimmerman partially unfastened a sling on a Thompson, for example, McCoy would rub a finger coated with grease over the bolt of a Browning Automatic Rifle, or on the barrel of one of the Winchester Model 1897 12-gauge trench guns.

When it came, the inspection went as McCoy thought it would. The inspecting officer was a captain who took a quick look around and then turned over the actual inspection to a chief warrant officer, a tall, leathery-faced man named Ripley who looked as if he had been in the Marine Corps since the Corps had gone ashore at Tripoli. Gunnery Sergeant Zimmerman had subtly, if quickly, let Chief Warrant Officer Ripley know that Second Lieutenant McCoy had been in the heavy-weapons section of the 4th Marines in Shanghai. This had disabused Mr. Ripley of the notion that, for some inexplicable reason, the Raiders had turned their armory over to a baby-faced candy-ass second john fresh from Quantico—which is what he had thought when he first set eyes on Lieutenant McCoy.

Chief Warrant Officer Ripley then, for a couple of minutes, searched for discrepancies of the type to be expected in any repository of arms, such as dirt and fire hazards and inadequate records. Then he looked for such things as malfunctioning weapons not properly tagged, so they could be repaired. And then he detail-stripped several weapons selected at random, searching for specks of dirt or rust. Finding none, he then compiled his list of minor discrepancies: *"excess lubricant on three (3) Browning Automatic Rifle bolts; improperly fastened slings on two (2) Thompson submachine guns; and grease on barrels of two (2) shotguns, trench M1897."*

By then it was evident to him that the baby-faced second john knew how to play the game. What the hell, he was an old China Marine, too.

Then he grew serious.

"Out of school, Lieutenant, where'd you and the gunny hide the junk weapons?" Ripley asked. His voice sounded like gravel.

"No junk weapons," McCoy said. "That's them."

"The Army liked you, right, Lieutenant?" Ripley asked, dryly sarcastic. "And gave you all good stuff and none of their junk?"

"After the third, or fourth, or fifth time we gave them their junk back," McCoy replied, "they got tired. Or maybe they ran out of junk. But these weapons are all ours, and there is no junk."

Ripley believed him. His rule of thumb about judging officers, especially junior lieutenants, was to believe what their gunnys thought of them. And this gunny obviously thought highly of this second lieutenant.

The inspection of the armament and armory had taken the

full afternoon allotted to it on the plan of inspection, but three and a half of the four hours were spent by McCoy and Zimmerman showing the warrant officer the exotic, nonstandard weapons Colonel Carlson had obtained using his special authority to arm the Raiders as he saw fit, and then listening to the warrant officer's sea stories about what it had been like in the 4th Marines in the old days, when he'd been there in '33–35.

Chief Warrant Officer Ripley had never before had the chance to closely examine three of the special weapons Carlson had acquired for the Raiders. One of them was the Reising caliber .45 ACP submachine gun. Invented by Eugene G. Reising, the closed-breech, 550-round-per-minute weapon had gone into production in December 1941. McCoy had learned the Army had received several hundred of them, and had told Colonel Carlson, and Carlson had promptly signed a requisition for two hundred of them.

"If we don't like them, we can always give them back, can't we, McCoy?"

Ripley had never even heard of the Reising before he found it in McCoy's special-weapons arms room. But he had heard a lot about the other two, though he'd never actually seen them: These were the brainchild of a Marine, Captain Melvin Johnson, USMCR, who (as a civilian) had submitted the first models to the Army Ordnance Corps in 1938.

The Johnson rifle was a self-loading .30-06 rifle with a unique rotary ten-shot magazine and an unusual eight-radial-lug-bolt locking system. Barrels could be replaced in a matter of seconds.

The Johnson light machine gun was a fully automatic version of the rifle, with a magazine feeding from the side; a heavier stock with a pistol grip; and a bipod attached to the barrel near the muzzle.

Warrant Officer Ripley was fascinated with them. And after a solemn examination, he pronounced the Reising to be *"a piece of shit"*; the Johnson rifle to be *"twice as good as that fucking Garand"*; and the Johnson machine gun *"probably just as good as the Browning automatic rifle."* Lieutenant McCoy agreed with Ripley about the Reising; and he too thought that the Johnson rifle was probably going to be a good combat weapon (because its partially empty magazine could be reloaded easily; the en bloc eight-round clip of the Garand could not be reloaded in the rifle); and he thought the BAR was a far better weapon than the Johnson. But he kept his opinions to himself, deciding that he was in no position to argue with a chief Warrant officer, whose judgment was certainly colored by the fact that the Johnsons were invented by a Marine.

Second Lieutenant McCoy and Gunnery Sergeant Zimmerman were relieved, but not really surprised, when Warrant Officer Ripley showed them the clipboard on which was the pencil copy of his report. (A neatly typewritten report in many copies would be prepared later.) He had found their armory "Excellent" overall (one step down from the theoretical, never—in McCoy's experience—awarded "Superior"); and aside from "minor, readily correctable discrepancies noted hereon" there was no facet of their operation that would require a reinspection to insure that it had been corrected.

Gunnery Sergeant Zimmerman then produced a jug he just happened to come across where someone had hidden it behind a ceiling rafter, and they had a little nip.

"The brass'll keep at it for a while," Ripley said. "Between us China Marines, most of 'em got a real hard-on for Carlson. What the fuck is that all about?"

"I think it's because he got out of the Corps and then came back in," McCoy said. "And then got promoted."

"Carlson got out of the Corps?" Ripley said, obviously surprised. "I didn't know that. How come?"

McCoy shrugged his shoulders.

"I was with him in Nicaragua when he got the Navy Cross," Ripley said with a touch of pride in his voice. "The last I heard, he had the Marine detachment at Warm Springs. What'd he do, piss off the President?"

"I don't think so," McCoy said. "Otherwise the President's son wouldn't be the exec."

"No shit?" Chief Warrant Officer Ripley said. "That tall drink of water is really the President's son? I thought they were pulling my chain."

"That's him," McCoy said.

"I'll be goddamned," Ripley said.

"Is the brass going to fuck with your report? So they can stick it in Carlson?" McCoy asked.

"I call things like I see them," Ripley said indignantly. "You guys are more shipshape than most. And nobody fucks with my reports. Shit!"

"Well, this isn't the first time I heard that they're trying to stick it to Carlson," McCoy said. "And there are some real sonsofbitches around."

"When they handed me this shitty assignment—I'd rather be with the First Division; hell, I'd rather be *here*—the Commandant himself told me if anybody tried to lay any crap on me, I was to come to him personal."

XIX

XIX

(One)
Aboard the Yacht Last Time
San Diego Yacht Club
1900 Hours, 9 April 1942

Major Edward J. Banning, Captain Jack NMI Stecker, and Lieutenants McCoy and Burnes were sitting on teak-and-canvas deck chairs with their feet on the polished mahogany rail at the deck. Music and the smell of something frying came up from the portholes of the galley.

"You look deep in thought, Jack," Banning said.

"You really want to know what I'm thinking?" Stecker replied. "That there are two kinds of Marines. There is the one kind, the ordinary kind, the *Campbell's Baked Beans with Ham Fat* kind; and then there's the *steak* kind. That one"—he pointed at McCoy—"is the steak kind. I don't know how they do it, but they always wind up living better than other people."

He smiled at McCoy. "No criticism, McCoy. I'm jealous. Christ, this is real nice."

Banning chuckled. "I know what you mean, Jack," he said. "When all the other PFCs in the Fourth were playing acey-deucey for dimes with each other in the barracks, McCoy was

304

playing poker for big money in the Cathay Mansions Hotel with an ex–Czarist Russian general, and he was living in a whorehouse the General owned."

"Jesus!" McCoy said. "Be quiet, Ernie'll hear you."

Stecker and Banning laughed.

"I didn't know you knew about that," McCoy said to Banning.

"I know a good deal about you that you don't know I know," Banning said, a little smugly.

"The first time I saw him, he was a corporal; but he was driving that big LaSalle," Stecker said, pointing down the wharf. "I was a *technical sergeant* before I drove anything fancier than a used Model A Ford."

"This seems to have developed a leak, Ken," Banning said, examining his bottle of Schlitz. "It's all gone."

"I'll get you another, sir," First Lieutenant Martin J. Burnes, USMCR, said quickly, taking the bottle from Banning's hand and scurrying down the ladder to the aft cockpit.

"There's another proof of your theory, Jack," Banning said. "When *I* was a second lieutenant, *I* did the running and fetching for first lieutenants."

Stecker chuckled.

"He's all right, Major," McCoy said. "Eager as hell. *Gung ho!*"

Marty Burnes returned almost immediately with four bottles of Schlitz.

"Here you are, sir," he said, respectfully, handing one of the bottles to Banning, and then passing the others around.

"Burnes," Jack Stecker said, "McCoy just accused you of being '*gung ho!*' I keep hearing that phrase around here. What's that all about?"

"You never heard it in China?" Banning asked, and then before Stecker could reply, he went on. "Oh, that's right. You had your family with you. No sleeping dictionary. You weren't *really* a China Marine then, were you, Jack? *No speakee Chinaman.*"

McCoy snorted.

"It's a Chinese phrase, sir," Burnes said, almost eagerly. "It means 'all pull together.'"

"What's that got to do with the Raiders?" Stecker pursued.

"Cooperate, sir, for the common good. Do something that has to be done, even if it's not your responsibility."

"Give me a for-example," Banning asked, politely.

"Oh, for example, sir," Burnes said, "suppose an officer is walking around the area, and he sees that a garbage can is knocked over. Instead of finding somebody, an enlisted man, to set it up, he would do it himself. Because it should be set straight, sir, for the common good of the unit."

Banning looked at McCoy and saw that his eyes were smiling.

Burnes sensed that the example he had given was not a very good one. "You can explain it better than I can, Ken," Burnes said. "You tell the major."

"First of all," McCoy said, in Cantonese, "it doesn't mean 'all pull together.' It means something like 'strive for harmony.' And while it strikes me, and probably strikes you, as the night soil of a very large and well-fed male ox, you can see from this child that the children have adopted it as holy writ. What's wrong with it?"

Burnes's eyes widened, first at the flow of Chinese, and then as Major Banning choked on his beer. He went to Banning and vigorously pounded his back until Banning waved him off.

"You all right, sir?" Burnes asked, genuinely concerned.

"I'm fine," Banning said. "It went down the wrong pipe."

"Well, Burnes," Stecker said. "We know who had those dictionaries, don't we? Nobody likes a wiseass second lieutenant, McCoy."

Ernie Sage came onto the forward deck skillfully balancing a tray in her hands. The tray held two plates of hors d'ouevres, one with bacon-wrapped chicken livers, the other with boiled shrimp and a bowl of cocktail sauce. She was wearing a T-shirt and shorts. The front of her T-shirt was emblazoned with a large, red Marine Corps insignia.

"Steak," Stecker said. "See my point?"

Ernie smiled nervously, wondering if that meant disapproval of the T-shirt.

Banning laughed.

"I'm not so sure all these hors d'ouevres are a good idea," Ernie said. "The steaks are enormous. Ken ran into some China Marine he knew working in the commissary."

Stecker laughed out loud in delight, and Banning shook his head.

Ernie smiled with relief; they did not disapprove of her shorts and T-shirt. But now that she thought about it, she did. It was a dumb idea, something she had done in hurt and anger. Her mother had called the day before, and they had gotten into it. The conversation had started out politely enough, but that hadn't lasted long. And her mother had played her ace: *"I just hope you know how you're hurting your father's feelings, how it hurts him to have his friends seeing his daughter acting like . . . like nothing more than a camp follower."*

"Nice to talk to you, Mother," Ernie said. "Call again sometime next year," and then she'd hung up.

But it had hurt, and she'd cried a little, and then she'd stopped that nonsense. But then she had been downtown, and she'd seen a half dozen real camp followers, the girls who— either professionally or otherwise—plied their trade in San Diego bars patronized by Marines. They had been wearing Marine Corps T-shirts, and Ernie had wondered if she was really like them, and then she'd decided it didn't matter whether she was or not, her mother thought she was.

And she'd gone into a store and bought the T-shirt.

"I'm glad that the steaks are enormous, because so is my appetite," Banning said.

"Good," she said, smiling.

"Ernie, take these two with you, will you please?" Banning said. "I've got to have a quiet word with Jack Stecker."

When McCoy and Burnes had followed Ernie off the deck, Banning nodded after them.

"Very nice," he said.

"The hors d'ouevres, or McCoy's lady friend?" Stecker asked.

"Both," Banning said. "but especially her. She's all right, Jack."

"Yes, she is," Stecker said.

"I understand you've been greasing Evans Carlson's ways," Banning said.

"Oh, so that's what this all about," Stecker said.

Banning didn't reply directly.

"See a lot of him, do you?"

"Every other day," Stecker said.

"I've got a couple of questions I'd like to ask," Banning said.

"Let me save you some time, Major," Stecker said. "No, I don't think he's either crazy or a Communist."

"Why did you say that, Jack?" Banning asked.

"Isn't that what you wanted me to say? That he is? So they can relieve him and put these Raider battalions out of business?"

"No," Banning said. "As a matter of fact, it's not. I have it on the highest authority—relayed from General Holcomb himself—that Carlson is none of the unpleasant things he's being accused of."

Stecker met his eyes. "I'm really relieved to hear you say that," he said.

"There's some scuttlebutt that an officer has been sent out here to spy on Carlson," Banning said. "You pick up any of that?"

"Yeah, I've heard that," Stecker said.

"Do you think Carlson has?"

"Oh, I'm sure he has," Stecker said. "But I don't think he knows it's McCoy."

"McCoy?" Banning said.

"Come on, Ed, we've known each other too long to be cute," Stecker said.

"Please respond to the question," Banning said, formally. "What gave you the idea McCoy is in any way involved in this?"

"All right," Stecker said after a moment. "Because I happen to know that McCoy went from the Platoon Leader's Course at Quantico to work for Rickabee in Washington, and I took the trouble to find out that's not on his service record; his record says he was a platoon leader at Quantico until he came out here."

"You mention any of those theories of yours to Carlson?"

"No," Stecker said. "Frankly, I was tempted."

"Why didn't you?"

"Because I have been around the Corps long enough to know the shit's going to hit the fan sooner or later, and I didn't want to get splattered," Stecker said. "And also because I like McCoy, and I knew this wasn't his idea."

"The shit has already hit the fan," Banning said. "General Paul H. Lesterby was retired; Colonel Thomas C. Wesley's been assigned to the supply depot at Murdoch, while the Commandant makes up his mind whether or not to court-martial him."

Stecker's face grew thoughtful. His eyebrows rose, he pursed his lips, and he cocked his head to one side. "The scuttlebutt I got on that," he said, "was that Lesterby had a mild heart attack and that Wesley finally was recognized for the horse's ass he's always been."

"Do you think Carlson believes that?"

"I suppose he does," Stecker said. "Why that line of questions?"

"Although he will do so if necessary," Banning said, "which is to say if he thinks—which means I tell him—that Carlson knows about the officer Lesterby sent out here, the Commandant would really rather not come out and formally apologize to Carlson."

"Carlson? He better worry about having to apologize to the President," Stecker said.

"If he thought it would be the best thing for the Corps, I think the Commandant would resign in the morning," Banning said. "*I* don't think that would be good for the Corps."

"Neither do I," Stecker said. "How the *hell* did you get involved in this? You used to be a good, simple, honest Marine."

"Well, Jack, I didn't volunteer for it," Banning said, a little coldly.

"I'm sorry, I shouldn't have said that," Stecker said. "I can't imagine why the hell I did. I'm sorry."

"Forget it," Banning said.

"To answer your question, Ed," Stecker said, "if Carlson is worried about having a spy in his outfit, he doesn't seem concerned. I think he would have said something to me if he did. Or, probably, now that I think about it, suspected that it was me. I don't think he thinks it's one of his officers, and I'm almost positive he doesn't suspect McCoy of anything."

Banning nodded.

"But if you want, I can ask him," Stecker said. "Discreetly, of course. I'm going to see him tomorrow at eleven hundred."

"No, this is it," Banning said. "I'm flying back to Washington at oh-nine-hundred. To report to the Commandant as soon as I get there."

"I really wish I could be more helpful," Stecker said.

"You've been very helpful," Banning said.

"So what happens to McCoy?" Stecker said.

"It would raise questions if he were suddenly relieved from the Raiders," Banning said.

"So who really pays for this idiocy is a nice young kid—a

fine young officer," Stecker said bitterly. "Lesterby gets to draw his pension, and Wesley, too, and McCoy gets his ass blown away playing commando on some unimportant little island in the South Pacific."

"I thought you were all for Carlson and his Raiders," Banning said, surprised.

"I think the whole idea of Raiders is stupid from start to finish," Stecker said. "You didn't ask me that."

The smell of charring beef began to float up to the flying bridge.

Stecker sniffed. "Are we about finished?" he asked. "Oddly enough, after this conversation of ours, I still have an appetite."

Banning set his beer bottle down and stood up. "Thank you, Jack," he said.

When they went into the main cabin, they saw that the women had changed. Ernie Sage was now wearing a pale yellow cotton dress, which she wore with a single strand of pearls that Banning knew were real, and had cost what a Marine second lieutenant made in three months.

The table had been very elegantly set in the main lounge of the *Last Time*. There was gold-rimmed bone china, crystal glasses, and heavy sterling. There were two bottles of wine on the table, and a reserve supply, plus a bottle of brandy, on a sideboard.

Banning reflected that Ernie Sage seemed to have grasped what was expected of the wife of a junior officer when entertaining in their quarters a field-grade officer. Except she wasn't married to Killer McCoy, and this yacht was not exactly what came to mind when you thought of the quarters of a second lieutenant living off the post.

McCoy seemed to have read his mind.

In Chinese, he asked, softly, "It's a long way from that one-room apartment of mine over the whorehouse in Shanghai, isn't it?"

Banning laughed. McCoy started to pour the wine. He did it naturally, Banning thought. He was perfectly at ease with it, and even with this elaborate arrangement of crystal, china, and silver. He wondered if McCoy himself knew how much he had changed since Shanghai.

"You know, I knew that Ken spoke Chinese—" Marty Burnes gushed.

"Two kinds, plus Japanese, and God only knows what else," Banning interrupted.

"But I didn't really *believe* it until I heard the two of you talking," Burnes concluded.

"The day I met him," Ernie said, "he took me to a Chinese restaurant in Chinatown in New York City. And spoke Chinese to them. I was awed."

"Knowing all those languages," Jack Stecker said innocently, "I wonder if the greatest contribution he can make to the Marine Corps is in the armory of the Second Raider Battalion."

Banning looked toward Stecker and found Stecker's eyes on his. He did not reply, but he had already made up his mind that one of the first things he was going to do when he got back to Washington was try to justify getting McCoy out of the Raiders. Stecker was of course right. Second Lieutenants who spoke Japanese and two kinds of Chinese were in very short supply and should not be expended while they were trying to paddle up to some obscure Japanese-held island in a rubber boat.

He looked away from Stecker and found Ernie Sage's eyes on him. She had nice eyes, he thought. Perceptive eyes. But what he saw in them now was sad disappointment that he had not responded to Stecker. And that meant, Banning decided, that Ernie Sage knew what McCoy was doing here.

The dumb, lovesick sonofabitch told her! He knew that was expressly forbidden. He isn't even married to her, for Christ's sake!

And then he was forced to face the shameful fact that Major Edward J. Banning, that professional intelligence officer of the U.S. Marine Corps, that absolute paragon of military virtue, had only a week before shown his credentials to a civilian female for no better reason than that he wanted to look good in her eyes.

Banning decided that if McCoy had told Ernie at least some of what he was really doing with the 2nd Raider Battalion at Camp, Elliott, he had done so with a reason, and only after thinking it over. The cold truth to face was that McCoy had almost certainly had a better reason for telling Ernie than he had for showing Carolyn his credentials.

Banning spent the night aboard the *Last Time;* and in the morning, McCoy drove him to the airfield, where a Navy

Douglas R4D was waiting to fly the "IG from Washington" team back to Washington.

As he gave McCoy his hand, there was time to tell him what he had decided.

"You've done a good job here, Ken, in a rotten situation," Banning said. "I'm going to try to talk Rickabee into getting you out of here. I'm not sure he will, but I'm going to try."

(Two)
Headquarters, 2nd Raider Battalion
Camp Elliott, California
23 April 1942

Though it appeared loose and informal—everyone sat on the ground in the shade—and Colonel Carlson pointedly did not use the official term, there was a 2nd Raider Battalion officers' call in everything but name. Colonel Carlson probably did not like the official term, McCoy thought, because there was an implied exclusion of enlisted men from an official officers' call. But with the exception of a very few enlisted men (the sergeant major; the S-3 [Plans & Training] and S-4 [Supply] sergeants; two of the first sergeants; and three gunnery sergeants, including Zimmerman), everybody at the meeting was an officer, and most of the battalion officers had been summoned and were present.

A week or so before, Captain Roosevelt gave a lecture on the Rules of Land Warfare, a subject that McCoy was more than casually familiar with. Because of the situation in China at the time, there had been frequent lectures on the Rules of Land Warfare in the 4th Marines. And as he listened to Roosevelt, McCoy reflected that he had been lectured on the Rules of Land Warfare so often that he knew most of them by heart. But McCoy did learn one thing during Roosevelt's lecture: Roosevelt used two terms McCoy had never heard before. Since he did not have an appetite to stand up and confess his ignorance, McCoy wrote the terms down, intending to look them up in a dictionary.

As it happened, the dictionary did not turn out to be necessary. When he asked Ernie about it, she questioned him about what he wanted to look up, and then she explained the meaning of *de facto* and *de jure*.

And now he realized that those terms fit this case: Carlson's meeting, with everybody sitting on the ground in the shade of the battalion headquarters building, was a *de facto* officers' call, even if Carlson was reluctant to make it a *de jure* officers' call.

The first item on the agenda was significant. Carlson told his officers and senior noncoms that, as of that day, the 2nd Raider Battalion had officially completed its stateside training, and that Admiral Nimitz (Commander in Chief, Pacific Fleet) had so officially informed Admiral King, and had requested transportation for the battalion to Hawaii, where they would be trained in rubber-boat techniques and in making landings from submarines.

Additionally, Carlson continued, the advance element of the "competition" (which everyone knew meant the 1st Raider Battalion) had sailed from San Diego aboard the USS *Zeilin* 11 April, more than likely for Samoa, although that was just a guess, and in any event should not be talked about.

Then he told them that a report from Major Sam Griffith[1] had "somehow come into hand."

"Griffith thinks our organization of the 2nd Raider Battalion is the way the entire Corps should go," Carlson said, with just a hint of smugness in his dry voice. "That is to say, six line companies and a headquarters company, as opposed to the competition's four line companies, a heavy-weapons company, and a headquarters company. And he has made that a formal recommendation to the Commandant."

There was a round of applause, and Carlson grinned at his men.

"And he agrees, more or less, with our organization[2] of the companies as well," Carlson went on. "He agrees more than he disagrees."

There was another round of applause.

And then, on the subject of mortars, Carlson told them that the decision by the brass had not been made, but that he hoped it would "go our way."

---

[1] As a captain, Griffith had been sent with Captain Wally Greene to observe and undergo British Commando training. He was regarded within the Marine Corps as an expert on commando, or Raider, operations.

[2] Each company consisted of two rifle platoons, plus a company headquarters. Each platoon, under a lieutenant, consisted of three squads. Each squad consisted of a squad leader, and a three-man fire-team, armed with a BAR, an M1 Garand, and a Thompson submachine gun.

There were two mortars available, a 60-mm and an 81-mm. The 81-mm was the more lethal weapon. It was capable of throwing a nearly seven-pound projectile 3,000 yards (1.7 miles). It was standard issue in the heavy-weapons company of a Marine infantry battalion. On the other hand, the 60-mm's range, with a three-pound projectile, was just about a mile.

For a number of reasons (with which McCoy, who fancied himself a decent man with either weapon, agreed completely), Carlson was opposed to the Raiders carrying the 81-mm mortar into combat. For one thing, the kind of combat the Raiders anticipated would be close range, and the 60-mm would be better for that purpose. More importantly, considering that the Raiders planned to enter combat by paddling ashore in rubber boats, a ready-for-action 81-mm mortar weighed 136 pounds. It would of course be broken down for movement, but the individual components—the tube itself, and especially the base plate— were heavy as hell, and were going to be damned hard to get into and out of a rubber boat. As would the ammunition, at seven pounds per round.

It was not, furthermore, a question of choosing *either* the 60-mm *or* the 81-mm. The TO&E provided for *both* 81-mm *and* 60-mm mortars in each company; and that meant that if they did things by the book and took the 81-mm too, they would have to wrestle two kinds of mortars and two kinds of ammunition into and out of the rubber boats.

But Carlson told him that he thought he had come up with a convincing argument against the Raiders following standard Marine Corps practice requiring an 81-mm mortar platoon in each company: Such a platoon would exceed the carrying capacity of the APDs.[3] If the 81-mm mortar platoon went along on the APDs, it would be necessary to split the companies between several ships. That obviously was a bad idea.

"But there are those," Carlson said, "close to the Deity in Marine Corps heaven who devoutly believe the Corps cannot do without the eighty-one-millimeters. So I have proposed that

---

[3]Grandly known as High Speed Transports, the APDs, which were supposed to transport Raiders on missions, were in fact modified World War I–era "four-stacker" destroyers. Two of their four boilers and their exhaust stacks had been removed, and the space reclaimed converted to primitive troop berthing. They were "high speed" only when compared to freighters and other slow-moving vessels.

we drag them along with us—without personnel—in case we
need them. In which case, they would be fired by the sixty-
millimeter crews.''

McCoy thought Carlson was absolutely right about the
mortars, and he hoped that the brass would let him have his
way. But he wondered if they actually would. He had not
forgotten Chief Warrant Officer Ripley's disturbing remark
about the "brass really having a hard-on for Carlson." He
knew they hadn't changed that attitude because the Commandant had blown his stack about spying on Carlson. A lot of the
brass, and even people like Captain Jack Stecker, thought the
whole idea of Raiders was a lousy one. Which meant that a lot
of people were still going to be fighting Carlson at every step.
If Carlson said the moon was made of Camembert, they would
insist it was cheddar.

"That will be all, gentlemen," Colonel Carlson said, a few
minutes and a few minor items later. "Thank you. If there are
no questions . . ."

There were questions. There was always some dumb
sonofabitch who didn't understand something. But finally the
questions had been asked and answered, and Carlson waved
his hand in a gesture of dismissal. In a regular unit, the exec
would have called attention and then dismissed them after the
commanding officer had walked away. Doing it Carlson's way,
McCoy thought, made more sense.

Colonel Carlson called out to him as McCoy started to get to
his feet.

"McCoy, stick around please. I'd like a word with you."

"Aye, aye, sir," McCoy said.

Carlson went into the building, after motioning for McCoy
to follow. When he went inside, the sergeant major waved him
into Carlson's office. Captain Roosevelt was there.

"Stand at ease, McCoy," Carlson said, and searched
through papers on his desk. Finally he found what he was
looking for and handed it to McCoy. It was a TWX.

ROUTINE
HEADQUARTERS USMC WASH DC 1545 21APR1942
COMMANDING OFFICER
2ND RAIDER BN
CAMP ELLIOTT CALIF
  THERE EXISTS THROUGHOUT THE MARINE CORPS A CRITICAL
SHORTAGE OF OFFICER PERSONNEL FLUENT IN FOREIGN

LANGUAGES. RECORDS INDICATE THAT 2ND LT KENNETH R MCCOY PRESENTLY ASSIGNED COMPANY B 2ND RAIDER BN IS FLUENT IN CHINESE JAPANESE AND OTHER FOREIGN LANGUAGES. UNLESS HIS PRESENT DUTIES ARE CRITICAL TO THE 2ND RAIDER BATTALION IT IS INTENDED TO REASSIGN HIM TO DUTIES COMMENSURATE WITH HIS LANGUAGE SKILLS.

YOU WILL REPLY BY THE MOST EXPEDITIOUS MEANS WHETHER OR NOT SUBJECT OFFICER IS CRITICAL TO THE MISSION OF YOUR COMMAND.

BY DIRECTION

STANLEY F. WATT COLONEL USMC OFFICE OF THE ASSISTANT CHIEF OF STAFF FOR PERSONNEL

"You don't seem especially surprised, McCoy," Colonel Carlson said in Cantonese.

"No, sir," McCoy answered, in the same language. "Major Banning told me there was a shortage of people who could speak Chinese and Japanese."

Carlson smiled, and nodded at Roosevelt. "The Big Nose doesn't know what we're talking about, does he?"

Chinese often referred to Caucasians as "Big Noses."

"No, sir," McCoy said, now in English.

"Then in English," Carlson said.

"Thank you, gentlemen," Captain Roosevelt said.

"Well, McCoy, are you critical to the Raiders?" Carlson asked.

"I don't know, sir," McCoy said.

"Well, let me put it this way, then, Lieutenant," Carlson said. "In your opinion, can you make a greater contribution to the Corps doing what you're doing with the Raiders, or doing whatever Major Banning has in mind for you to do? And I don't think there is any more question in your mind than there is in mine that Ed Banning is behind that TWX."

"Straight answer, sir?"

"I certainly hope so," Carlson said.

"I think I can do more here, sir," McCoy said.

"Huh," Carlson snorted. "Go buy yourself a bigger hat, Lieutenant McCoy. I am about to designate you as Critical to the Second Raiders."

"Thank you, sir."

"Not even the Big Nose is critical," Carlson said, in Cantonese, and smiled benignly at Captain Roosevelt, who smiled back. "Only you and me, McCoy."

McCoy grinned back.

Still in Cantonese, Carlson went on: "I don't think you need to know the name of the island, yet, McCoy, so I won't give it to you. But for our first mission, we are going to conduct a raid on a *certain* island. That's subject to change, of course, but I have a hunch it won't. The reason I'm telling you this much is that it is currently projected that we will be transported in submarines, rather than the converted destroyers. That will limit the force to no more than two hundred people. I want you—alone, don't confer with anyone else—to start thinking how we'll have to structure that force, and equip it."

"Aye, aye, sir," McCoy said, in English. "Does that mean I will go with the assault force, sir?"

"Uh-huh," Carlson said. "I thought you'd want to go."

"Oh, yes, sir," McCoy said.

And then he thought, *Oh, shit! What the hell have I done?*

XX

(One)
The San Carlos Hotel
Pensacola, Florida
8 August 1942

Second Lieutenant Richard J. Stecker, USMC, was in direct violation of the uniform regulations of the U.S. Navy Air Station, Pensacola, which, in addition to specifying in finite detail what a properly dressed officer would wear when leaving the post, took pains to specifically proscribe the wearing of flight gear except immediately before, while participating in, and immediately after aerial flight.

He was wearing a gray cotton coverall, equipped with a number of zippered pockets. This was known to the Naval Service as "Suit, flight, aviator's, cotton, tropical," and to Stecker, who had copied Pick Pickering's description, as "Birdman's rompers." Sewn to the breast of the rompers was a leather patch, stamped in gold with Naval aviator's wings and the words "STECKER, R.J. 2ND LT USMC." Pick said they did that so that professional Marines could look down and see who the Marine Corps said they were.

The flight suit was dark with sweat. Enormous patches of it

spreading from the back and the armpits and the seat nearly overwhelmed the dry areas. The patches were ringed with white, remnants of the salt taken aboard in the form of salt pills and then sweated out.

Stecker was aware that he was learning bad habits from Pick Pickering. Or, phrased more kindly, that Pickering had given him insight into the functioning of the Naval establishment that had not previously occurred to him. Previously, he had obeyed regulations, no matter how petty, because they were regulations and Marine officers obeyed regulations. He had in fact cautioned Lieutenant Pickering (a friendly word of advice from a professional Naval establishment person to a temporary officer and gentleman): "You're gonna get your ass in a crack if they catch you driving home in your flight suit," he'd told him.

Lieutenant Pickering had not only been unrepentant, but had patiently pointed out to Lieutenant Stecker the flaws in his logic.

"First of all, I don't intend to get caught. I drive through the woods, not past the Marine guard at the gate. Secondly, I think the MPs have better things to do than establish roadblocks to catch people wearing flight suits. And I come into the hotel through the basement, not the lobby. I think the chances of my getting caught run from slim to none. But, for the sake of argument, what if I'm caught? So what?"

"You'll find yourself replying by endorsement,"[1] Stecker argued.

"And I will reply by endorsement that since officers who live in quarters on the post can go from the flight line to their quarters in their rompers, I thought I could go directly to my quarters so attired. And that if I have sinned, I am prepared to weep, beat my breast, pull out my hair, and in other ways manifest my shame and regret."

"You can get kicked out of here."

"Oh, bullshit! We're nearly through this fucking course. They might throw us out for showing up on the flight line drunk, or something else serious like that. But so much time and money has been invested in us, and they need pilots so

---

[1] When an officer was caught doing something he should not be doing, such as being out of uniform, he would receive a letter from his commanding officer specifying the offense and directing him to "reply by endorsement hereto" his reasons for committing the offense.

bad, they're not going to throw anybody out for wearing rompers off base."

And he was right, of course.

Lieutenant Stecker had spent three hours that afternoon between six and ten thousand feet over Foley, Alabama. He had been at the controls of a Grumman F4F-3 wildcat, engaged in mock aerial combat with an instructor pilot.

The Wildcat had been rigged with a motion picture camera. The camera was actuated when he activated the trigger that would normally have fired the six .50-caliber Browning machine guns with which the Wildcat was armed.

The film was now being souped, and they would look at it in the morning. Dick Stecker knew that in at least four of the engagements, the film from the gun camera would show that he had successfully eluded his IP and then gotten on his IP's tail and "shot him down."

It had been almost—not quite, but almost—pleasant tooling around at six, seven thousand feet with the twelve hundred horsepower of the Wright XR-1830-76 moving the Wildcat at better than three hundred knots. And, although he had consciously fought getting cocky about it, it had been satisfying to realize that he had acquired a certain proficiency in the Wildcat. The odds were that in about two months, certainly within three, he would be flying a Wildcat against the Japanese.

When the training flight was over, however, it was not at all pleasant. He opened the canopy before he had completed his landing roll at Chevalier Field. By the time he had taxied to the parking ramp, the skin of the aircraft was too hot to touch, and he was sweat-soaked. The temperature had been over one hundred degrees for three days, and the humidity never dropped out of the high nineties.

He actually felt a little faint as he walked to the hangar, carrying a parachute that now seemed to weigh at least one hundred pounds. His IP came into the hangar red-faced and sweat-soaked, and went directly to the water cooler, where he first drenched his face in the stream, and then filled a paper cup and poured it over his head.

The post-flight critique was made as brief as possible. Then the IP had walked to his car in his rompers and drove off. That left Stecker with a choice: He could be a good little second lieutenant who obeyed all the rules. Or he could do what he ended up doing. What he did was get in his car and drive through the woods to the Foley Highway and then to the hotel.

He parked the car behind the hotel and entered through the basement. He planned to use the service elevator, but it wouldn't answer his ring, so he had to summon a passenger elevator.

With my luck, he thought, *the elevator will stop in the lobby, answering the button-push of the base commander, who will be accompanied by the senior Marine Corps officer assigned to Pensacola.*

But the elevator rose without stopping to the top floor, and there was no one in the small foyer when the door opened. Stecker crossed quickly to the penthouse door, put his key in, and opened it. A wave of cold air swept over him. The basement of the building was not air-conditioned, and the allegedly air-conditioned elevators seldom were.

Stecker emitted a deep, guttural groan of relief.

Then he worked the full-length zipper on the rompers to its lower limit and spread the sweaty material wide. When the cold air struck his lower chest, he groaned appreciatively again.

Then he walked into the penthouse and found it was occupied.

The occupant was a female. The female was clothed in brief shorts and a T-shirt decorated with a red Marine Corps insignia. And she was smiling at him. Not a friendly smile, Stecker quickly relized, but a "see the funny man, ha ha" smile.

"What am I expected to say in reply to your groans?" Ernie Sage asked. "You Tarzan, me Jane?"

"Not that I really give a damn," Dick Stecker said, "but how did you get in here?"

"I told them I was Pick's sister," Ernie said. "Where is he?"

"I'm Dick Stecker," Dick said.

"How about this to start a conversation, Dick Stecker?" Ernie said. " 'Your fly's open.' "

"Oh, Jesus," he groaned and dived for it.

"To quickly change the subject, you were telling me where Pick is," she said.

"He took off about an hour after we did," Stecker said. "He should be here in about an hour."

"Took off for where?"

"Local," Stecker said. "Training flight. Mock dogfights."

She turned and went to the bar, returned with a bottle of beer, and handed it to him.

"You look like you could use this," she said. When she saw the surprise on his face, she added, "Yes, I did make myself right at home, didn't I?"

"You didn't say who you were?"

"Just another Marine camp-follower," she said. "Mine has gone overseas, so I figured I'd better latch on to another."

"Ah, come on," Stecker said.

"I'm Ernie Sage," she said. "I'm the closest thing Pick has to a sister."

"Oh, sure. The one he's always talking to on the phone. In California."

"Used to," she said. "My second lieutenant's gone. Now I'm back in New York."

"I'm Dick Stecker," Stecker repeated.

"I know," she said. "I know your father. I like him; Pick likes you. Our acquaintance is off to a flying start."

"What brings you here?" Stecker asked.

"I have been holding Pick's hand about the Sainted Widow for months. Now it's his turn to hold mine for a while."

"Is there anything I can do?"

"Can you miraculously transport me to Camp Catlin?"

"I never even heard of it," Stecker said.

"That's surprising," Ernie said. "According to Pick, you're a walking encyclopedia of military lore."

"Where is it?"

"It's in—on?—Hawaii. And if you can't miraculously transport me there, why don't you take a shower? I can smell you all the way over here."

"Do you always talk like that?" Stecker asked, shocked but not offended.

"Only to friends," Ernie said. "And any son of Captain Jack NMI Stecker, any friend of Pick's, et cetera et cetera . . ."

"I'm flattered," Stecker said.

"And well you should be," Ernie said. "Go bathe; and when you come out, you can give me a somewhat more accurate picture of the Sainted Widow than the one I got from Pick."

"How do you know the one you got from Pick isn't accurate?"

"No one, not even me, is that perfect," Ernie said. She pointed toward one of the bedrooms. "Go shower."

Stecker took a shower, and put on a khaki uniform. When he came out, Ernie Sage was leaning on the glass door leading to the patio.

"How much further along are you than Pick?" she asked, smiling at him.

"I beg your pardon?"

"You're wearing wings," Ernie said. "I thought you got those only when you're finished training."

"When you finish the school," he said. "We got rated the first of the month."

"Then you're finished?"

"Yes, we are. Now we're getting trained in F4F-3s."

"I thought—Pick told me—they were going to send you to Opa-something for that?"

"Opa-locka," Stecker said. "Farther down in Florida. They usually do. But they have some F4F-3s, and qualified IPs here . . . and Pick and I make up a class of two, so we stayed here."

"Congratulations," Ernie said.

"Excuse me?"

"On being a Naval aviator," she said.

"Oh," Stecker said. "Thank you."

"Now tell me about the Sainted Widow," Ernie said.

"I'm not sure I should," Stecker said.

"Think of me as a kindly old aunt," Ernie said.

"That would be hard," Stecker said. "You don't look anything like a kindly old aunt."

"I think I should tell you that my boyfriend is a Raider," Ernie said. "Their idea of a good time is chewing glass. I have no way of knowing what he would do if he thought someone was paying me an unsolicited compliment."

"That would be 'Killer' McCoy," Stecker said. "Pick's told me all about him."

"Did he tell you that Killer McCoy and I were sharing living accommodations, without benefit of marriage, at what I have now learned to call Diego?" Ernie asked.

"Yeah," Stecker said. "As a matter of fact, he did."

"Well, now that he's told you my shameful secret, you tell me his. What's this Sainted Widow done to him?"

"I don't think she's done anything to him," Stecker said. "That's what you could call the root of the problem."

By the time Pick walked in the door (in a crisp tropical worsted uniform, without a drop of sweat on him, which sorely tempted Stecker to spill the beer he handed him into his lap), Stecker had covered the dead-in-the-water romance between Pick and Martha Sayre Culhane in some detail.

He had explained to Ernie that he believed, or at least hoped, that the romance was beginning to pass. Since the Navy had kept them busy flying, Pick simply didn't have time to moon over his unrequited love. And when they did have a Sunday off, Pick drank—but not too much, for he knew he would have to fly the next day.

Stecker went on to tell her that he thought it was a shame they hadn't gone to Opa-locka for fighter training. That would have gotten Pick out of Pensacola. And once he was out of Pensacola, he believed that Martha Sayre Culhane would, however slowly, begin to fade. In his opinion, absence did not make the heart grow fonder.

And then, after Pick arrived, his role and Ernie's were reversed. Ernie, with a couple of drinks in her, revealed how much she missed Ken McCoy and how worried she was about him. Pick and Stecker tried to comfort her, after their peculiar fashion: Pick told her, for instance, that it was her romance she should be worried about, not Ken McCoy's life. He told her that she was responsible for teaching McCoy bad habits. Which meant that at this very moment, he was probably on some sunny, wave-swept Hawaiian beach with some dame wearing a grass skirt.

In time, Pick and Ernie got more than a little smashed. And Stecker found himself making the decisions and driving. They went to Carpenter's Restaurant, where he made them eat deviled crabs and huge mounds of french-fried potatoes, to counter the alcohol.

That didn't seem to work with Pick, who slipped into a sort of maudlin stupor, but it seemed to sober up Ernie. Consequently, she was acutely aware of the look on Dick Stecker's face when Martha Sayre Culhane walked into Carpenter's with Captain Mustache and two other couples. And she followed his eyes and turned to him with a question on her face.

Dick Stecker nodded as he put his finger quickly before his lips, and he then glanced at Pick, begging her not to let him know.

She nodded her understanding of the situation.

But there was nothing Dick Stecker could do when Ernie Sage saw Martha Sayre Culhane go into the ladies' room. Ernie suddenly jumped to her feet and went in after her.

When Martha Sayre Culhane came out of the stall, a young woman wearing a T-shirt with a large red Marine Corps emblem on was it sitting on the makeup counter. The young woman examined her shamelessly, and said "Hi!"

"Hello," Martha said, a little uncomfortably. She took her comb from her purse and ran it through her hair. Then she took out her lipstick and started to touch up her lips.

"Funny," Ernie said. "You really are nearly as beautiful as Pick thinks you are."

"I beg your pardon?"

"You don't look like a selfish bitch, either," Ernie went on. "More like what Dick Stecker says, 'the Sainted Widow.' I guess you work on that, huh?"

"Who the hell are you?"

"Just one more Marine Corps camp-follower," Ernie said.

"I don't know what this is all about, but I don't like it," Martha said.

"We have something in common, believe it or not," Ernie said.

"I can't imagine what that would be," Martha said.

"I got one of those telegrams," Ernie said. "From good ol Frank Knox. He regretted that my man was 'missing in action and presumed dead.'"

Martha looked at Ernie.

"I'm sorry," she said.

"As things turned out, he wasn't dead," Ernie said. "I told you that to explain what we had in common. I know what it's like."

Martha started to say something, but stopped.

"At the moment, I'm crossing my fingers again," Ernie said. "No, I'm not. I'm *praying*. Mine's back in the Pacific. He's an officer in the Second Raider Battalion."

"What is it you want from me?" Martha said.

"I want to talk to you about Pick," Ernie said. "He's in love with you."

"I don't really think that's true," Martha said.

"It's true," Ernie said. "Take it from me. I've known Pick since we used to play doctor. I know about him and women. He's *in love* with you."

"Well, I don't happen to be in love with him, not that it's any of your business," Martha snapped.

"So what?" Ernie said. "Lie about it. You're going to have to stop playing the sainted widow sooner or later. Give it up now. Give that poor, frightened, wonderful sonofabitch a couple of weeks, a couple of months, however long he's got before they ship him off to the Pacific. It won't cost you anything. You might even like it. I've never heard any complaints. And if you don't, Martha, and he gets killed, too, you'll regret it the rest of your life."

"You're crazy," Martha said. "My husband—"

"Is dead," Ernie said. "And he's not coming back. I told you, I know what that feels like. Pick is alive. *He's in love with you*. Stop being so goddamned selfish!"

Ernie pushed herself off the counter and walked out of the room.

When the Sainted Widow came out of the ladies' room two minutes later, she looked as if she had been crying. She gazed around the room, found Pick, and stared at him for almost a minute before turning and rushing out of the restaurant.

And a moment after that, Captain Mustache crossed the room, obviously in pursuit of the Sainted Widow. They did not return to the restaurant.

Stecker would have really liked to ask what had gone on in the ladies' room. He couldn't ask, of course, with Pick sitting right there.

(Two)
Pearl Harbor, Territory of Hawaii
8 August 1942

In compliance with Operations Order (Classified SECRET) No. 71-42, from Commander in Chief, United States Pacific Fleet, Task Group 7.15 (Commander John M. Haines, USN) got underway at 0900 hours, Hawaiian time.

Task Group 7.15 consisted of the submarines USS *Argonaut* (Lt. Commander William H. Brockman, Jr., USN) and USS *Nautilus* (Lt. Commander J. H. Pierce, USN); and Companies A and B, 2nd Raider Battalion, USMC (Lt. Colonel Evans F. Carlson, USMCR).

The mission of Task Group 7.15 was to land a force of Marines on Makin Island, where they were to engage and destroy the enemy; to destroy any enemy matériel stocks they found; to destroy any buildings, radio facilities, and anything else of military or naval value; and then to withdraw.

There was never any consideration given to holding Makin Island once it had been taken. It would have been impossible to supply, much less reinforce. And there was nothing the Americans wanted with the island anyway.

It was a *raid,* the purpose of which was to force the Japanese to reinforce *all* of their islands, in order to attempt to prevent subsequent Raider raids. To do so, it was reasoned, would force the Japanese to assign troops and matériel to protect all their islands, and that the troops and matériel so assigned would therefore not be available for use elsewhere.

There would also be some positive public relations aspects of a successful raid; the American ego was still smarting from Pearl Harbor and the fall of the Philippine Islands. In that sense, it would be the Navy's answer to the Air Corps's bombing of the Japanese homelands by a flight of B-25 aircraft commanded by Lieutenant Colonel Jimmy Doolittle.

There were some cynics. They claimed it made absolutely no sense to spend so much time and effort putting several hundred Marines ashore on an island of little importance—and which we did not intend to keep, anyway. Such a raid would indeed force the Japanese to station men on all of their islands, but doing so would pose fewer problems for the Japs than it would, in the future, for the United States. After the Makin Raid, they believed, we would have to fight our way ashore on every island we wished to take and keep. And *that* would cost lives.

There were even those who said that the whole Raider concept was a Chinese fire drill, because the President's son was involved and because the Commandant didn't have the balls to tell the President the whole idea was a drain on manpower and resources that could be better used elsewhere.

The dissent was heard, duly noted, and ignored.

The *Argonaut*[2] was a one-of-a-kind submarine. She was designed in 1919 to be something of a copy of the German U-Cruiser class, and she was intended for use for both long-distance cruising and underwater mine laying. She was launched at Portsmouth on November 10, 1927, and commissioned on April 2, 1928. Powered by two German-made MAN

---

[2]She was to be sunk by Japanese destroyers between Lae and New Guinea on 10 January 1943.

diesel engines developing 3,175 horsepower, she was capable of making fifteen knots on the surface. And her electric motors would move her at eight knots submerged. She was armed with two six-inch cannon, three .30-caliber machine guns, and four 21-inch torpedo tubes. Immediately after Pearl Harbor, she had gone through a refit at Mare Island Navy Yard, converting her to a transport submarine.

The *Nautilus* was one of two submarines of the Narwhal class. Generally similar to the *Argonaut,* she did not have a mine-laying capability. When she was launched at Mare Island in March 1930, she had MAN diesels, but these were replaced by Fairbanks Morse engines just before World War II. She had two aft-firing torpedo tubes plus four forward firing and was armed, like the *Argonaut,* with two 6-inch Naval cannon.

Both vessels were considerably larger than "fleet" submarines of the period, and for this reason had been chosen to transport the elements of the 2nd Raider Battalion charged with making an attack upon the Japanese-held Makin atoll, which lay 2,029 nautical miles to the southwest, roughly halfway between Hawaii and Australia.

The *Argonaut* and the *Nautilus* were led through the antisubmarine cables and other defenses of Pearl Harbor, and for some distance at sea by a patrol craft (PC 46), which stood by while (at 1500 hours) the submarines dived to test hull integrity and to determine trim. At 2015 hours, the *Argonaut* left the formation, under orders to visually reconnoiter the Makin atoll before the arrival of the *Nautilus.*

At 2100 hours the patrol craft was released as escort and the *Nautilus* got underway to rendezvous with the *Argonaut* off Makin Atoll.

(Three)
Makin Island
0530 Hours, 17 August 1942

Not surprising Second Lieutenant Kenneth J. McCoy one little bit, the landing was all fucked up.

The faithful Gunnery Sergeant Zimmerman, leading a couple of squads, was at his side as they lay in the sand fifteen yards off the beach. The trouble with the situation was that Zimmerman was with Able Company, and Lieutenant McCoy was performing his duties as a platoon leader with Baker Company. He didn't know where Zimmerman was supposed to be, except that it wasn't here.

A large Raider came running up and dropped on his belly beside McCoy. "How's it going?" he asked cheerfully.

Under the circumstances, McCoy decided, since they were where they were, and since the large Raider was his little brother, he would not deliver a lecture on the proper manner for a corporal to address a commissioned officer and gentleman. Then he noticed the awesome weapon, a Boys antitank rifle,[3] with which Tom was armed.

"Where'd you get that, Tommy?" McCoy asked.

"I gave it to him," Zimmerman said, softly. "We got orders to bring the sonofabitch and he's the only one big enough to carry it, much less shoot it."

McCoy chuckled.

"I'm going to blow some Jap general a new asshole," Tommy said confidently. "A *big* new asshole."

McCoy looked up at the sky. It was lighter than it had been; dawn was obviously breaking, but it was still dark. Too dark, he decided, to order Zimmerman to go look for his officers and find out where he was supposed to be. That would just add Zimmerman and his bunch to those already milling around in the dark.

"Stay here," McCoy said, and crawled back to the beach. Then he stood up, because he couldn't see lying down.

The force had been loaded into eighteen rubber boats. And they had planned to land at several points along the seaside shore of Butaritari Island. But at the last minute (when, in McCoy's private opinion, Colonel Carlson had seen how fucked up the offloading from the subs into the boats had gone), Carlson had the word passed that everybody was to land at Beach "Z," which was across the island from Government House.

What everybody called "Makin *Island*" was correctly "Makin *Atoll*," a collection of tiny islands forming a small hollow triangle around a deep-water lagoon. The base of the triangle, shaped like a long, low-sided "U," was Butaritari Island, the largest of the islands. Off its northern point was

---

[3] A British weapon, essentially an oversize bolt-action rifle. Loaded, on its monopod, it weighed almost forty pounds. Fed with a top-mounted clip, the .55-caliber weapon fired a tungsten-cored bullet larger than the U.S. .50-caliber machine-gun round. It had proved ineffective against German tanks, but it was believed it would be effective against lighter armored Japanese vehicles.

Little Makin Island. When they had finished here, the Raiders were scheduled to attack and to destroy what personnel and matériel might be found there.

What civilization there was on Butaritari Island was all on the lagoon side—wharves running out from warehouses and buildings to the deep water of the lagoon. To the north of the built-up area were Government Wharf and Government House, now the Japanese headquarters. That was where the vast bulk of the Japanese forces were supposed to be.

McCoy counted rubber boats. He counted fifteen; that meant three were missing.

On the beach somewhere out of sight? Or swamped?

A trio of Raiders came running down the beach in a crouch, their weapons (Thompsons and Garands) at the ready.

"Whoa!" McCoy ordered.

Somewhat sheepishly they stopped, stood erect, and looked at him. Privately hoping it would set an example, McCoy had elected to arm himself with a Garand rather than with any of the array of gung ho automatic weapons in the arms room. He thought that the planned operation called for rifles . . . and not submachine guns that most people couldn't shoot well anyway, or carbines, whose effectiveness as a substitute for a rifle he questioned.

Their faces were streaked with black grease, and they were wearing what looked like, and in fact were, khaki uniforms that had been dyed black. There was no more India ink in the drafting offices at Camp Catlin, but the Raiders had the black uniforms Carlson couldn't find in quartermaster warehouses anywhere.

"We've been looking for you, Lieutenant," the corporal said, somewhat defensively.

"Where are you?" McCoy asked, clearly meaning the rest of the platoon.

The corporal gestured down the beach behind him. "About a hundred yards, sir."

"You run into anybody from Able Company?" McCoy asked.

"Yes, sir, there's a bunch of them down there, sir," the corporal said.

"You two stay here," McCoy ordered the two Raiders. Then he pointed at the corporal. "You go get the others," he said, and pointed inland. "I'm about fifteen yards in there."

"Aye, aye, sir," the corporal said, and started down the beach.

Colonel Carlson appeared, coming up the beach.

McCoy saluted.

"Oh, it's you, McCoy," Carlson said. "Getting your people sorted out?"

"Yes, sir," McCoy said. "I've got at least a platoon of Able Company with me. I'm about to send them down the beach."

"Good," Carlson said. "But despite the confusion, so far so good."

"Yes, sir," McCoy said.

The unmistakable crack of a .30-06 cartridge broke the stillness, clearly audible above the hiss of the surf.

"Oh, *shit!*" McCoy said, bitterly.

There was no following sound of gunfire. Just the one shot.

"What was that?" one of the Raiders asked, when neither Colonel Carlson nor McCoy spoke.

"That was some dumb sonofabitch walking around with his finger on the trigger," McCoy said furiously. "He might as well have blown a fucking bugle."

"I think this might be a good time for you to join your men, McCoy," Colonel Carlson said, conversationally, and then walked back down the beach.

XXI

(One)
Butaritari Island, Makin Atoll
0700 Hours, 17 August 1942

At a quarter to six, a runner from Lieutenant Plumley's Able Company had reported to Colonel Carlson that his point (that is, the leading elements of Plumley's troops) was at Government Wharf and that he had captured Government House without resistance. Carlson sent the runner back with orders for Plumley to move down the island in the direction of the other installations, that is to say, southeast, or to the left.

Carlson had expected the bulk of Japanese forces to be in the vicinity of Government House, and had made his plans accordingly. Now it seemed clear to him that the Japanese were in fact centered around On Chong's Wharf, about two miles away. If he had known that, he could have ordered Plumley to move quickly down the island, so that he could get as far as possible before he encountered resistance.

But once the presence of the Raiders on Butaritari became known to the Japanese—and the goddamned fool who had fired his Garand had taken care of that—the situation would change rapidly. If *he* were the Japanese commander, Carlson reasoned,

332

he would move up Butaritari's one road as fast as he could, until he ran into the enemy.

Carlson's prediction was quickly confirmed. Another runner appeared, saluted, and, still heaving from the exertion of his run, announced, "We got Japs, Colonel."

Carlson extended his map.

"Show me where, son," he said, calmly.

When the runner pointed to the Native Hospital, Carlson nodded. His professional judgment was that the Japanese commander had established his line at the best possible place; the island was only about eleven hundred feet wide at that point.

He turned to his radio operator and told him to try to raise either of the submarines. So far Carlson's radio communication with the submarines had been just about a complete failure, but his time, he was lucky.

"I got the *Argonaut*, sir," the radio operator reported.

Carlson snatched the microphone and requested Naval gunfire on both the island (to shell Japanese reinforcement routes) and the lagoon, where two small ships were at anchor.

"We do not, repeat not," the *Argonaut* replied, "have contact with our spotter."

"Then fire without him," Carlson snapped, and tossed the microphone to the radio operator.

There came almost immediately the boom of the cannon firing, and then the whistle of the projectile in the air. Then there was the sound of a shell landing on the island, and almost simultaneously an enormous plume of water in the lagoon.

"Get them again, if you can," Carlson ordered the radio operator. "Tell them to keep it up."

Without thinking about it, without realizing he was doing it, Carlson counted the rounds fired by the cannon on the submarines, just as a competitive pistol shooter teaches you to habitually count shots. When the booming stopped, he was up to sixty-five, and both of the ships in the lagoon were in flames.

And then the *Nautilus* called him, and before the voice faded, Carlson heard that the Japanese-language linguist aboard the *Nautilus* had heard the Japanese send a message in the clear reporting the Raider attack and asking for reinforcements. Carlson asked if there had been a reply, but the radio was out again.

That made Carlson think of McCoy, and to wonder if it would not have been smarter to leave him aboard the *Nautilus* or not even bring him along at all. Japanese-speaking Americans were in short supply.

A moment later, McCoy showed up in person.

"I thought you would want to know what we're facing, sir," he said, and pointed out on Carlson's map the locations of four Japanese water-cooled machine guns, two grenade launchers, and a flame thrower.

"They got riflemen, a bunch of them, filling in the blanks in the line," McCoy said, pointing, "and snipers in the tops of most of the coconut trees along here."

"You didn't want to send a runner?"

"I didn't have one handy that I trusted with a map, sir," McCoy said.

"Well, then, Lieutenant, you can just keep running. Go find the Baker Company commander and tell him I said to get moving, down the island."

"Aye, aye, sir," McCoy said, and ran off.

In the next four hours, a procession of runners reported that Baker Company was making slow but steady progress down the island.

At 1130, two Japanese Navy Type 95 reconnaissance planes appeared over the island, flew back and forth for fifteen minutes, dropped two bombs, and then flew away. Carlson knew that meant the *Argonaut* and the *Nautilus*, essentially defenseless against aircraft, had dived, and there was no longer any reason even to try to raise them on the radio.

The *Nautilus* surfaced again at 1255, but immediately dived again after their radar detected a flight of twelve aircraft approaching the island. The submarines would remain submerged until 1830 hours.

At 1330, the Japanese aircraft arrived over Butaritari Island. It was quite an armada: two four-engined Kawanishi flying boats (bombers); four Zero fighters; four Type 94 reconnaissance bombers; and two Type 95 seaplanes. They promptly began to bomb and strafe the Raiders, and they kept it up for an hour and a half, but without doing much real damage.

Then, apparently convinced they had wiped out whatever antiaircraft capability the Raiders might have had, one of the four-engined Kawanishis and one of the Type 95s landed in the lagoon. They were promptly engaged by .30-caliber Raider machine-gun fire. The Type 95 caught fire. And the Kawanishi hurriedly taxied out of .30-caliber range and began to discharge its passengers—thirty-five Japanese soldiers intended to reinforce the Butaritari garrison—apparently oblivious to the fact that a slow but steady fire from a Boys .55-caliber antitank rifle was being delivered.

When the Kawanishi made its takeoff, it almost immediately entered into a series of violent circling maneuvers. The last of these sent it, with an enormous splash, into the lagoon.

The Japanese aircraft that remained over Butaritari then left, but more Zeros returned at 1630 and bombed and strafed the island for another thirty minutes. From the way they were flying and choosing to drop their bombs, it was evident to Carlson that there was little if any communication between the Japanese defenders of Butaritari and the aircraft that came to their assistance: The Zeros were attacking a portion of the island he had ordered the Raiders out of (to better counter Japanese sniper fire). And the Japanese had promptly moved into this position. The Zeros were consequently attacking Japanese positions and troops.

By 1700, Carlson understood that he had an important decision to make. He had two options. His mission was to destroy enemy forces and vital installations, and to capture prisoners and documents. So far, the Raiders had killed a number of Japanese, but there were no prisoners, no documents, and no serious damage to installations.

Choice One was to continue his advance.

But the operations plan called for the Raiders to evacuate Butaritari at some time between 1930 and 2100. And it also called for attacking Little Makin Island the next morning.

Choice Two was to hold his present position and make a very orderly withdrawal by stages to the beaches, the boats, and ultimately the submarines. If he did that, he would be in a position to attack Little Makin on schedule. After some thought, he decided that made the most sense.

By 1900, Carlson had established (under his own command; he felt it his duty to be the last Marine off the beach) a covering force for the disengagement, and the bulk of the Raiders were on the beach, loading the rubber boats for the return to the submarines, which had surfaced at 1845, and were now prepared to cover the withdrawal with Naval gunfire in addition to taking the Raiders aboard.

But now he was facing another enemy, the sea. The surf, which had posed no serious problems as they landed, now wouldn't let them off the island. This came as a surprise; for the waves were not especially large. And until he actually got in them, he didn't see what the problem was. They were moving very fast, and succeeding waves piled in very quickly. The trouble was that the waves were crowded too close together for the boats to operate.

Raiders walked their boats into the surf, and they generally managed to get past the first four waves without trouble. But then the agony started. Only a few of the outboard engines could be made to start, and those that they did get running were quickly drowned as waves crashed over the bows of the rubber boats and soaked coils and points.

After that, the Raiders tried paddling.

But paddling rhythmically and furiously for all they were worth, the Raiders could not make it past the rollers coming into the beach; they would make it over one roller only to be hit and thrown back by the next before they could gain momentum.

Boats filled to the gunwales. The Raiders bailed furiously. Then they loosened the outboard motors and dropped them over the side. And then they got out and pulled the boats by their own efforts, by swimming.

Surf turned boats over, which sent the Raiders' weapons, ammunition, and equipment to the bottom. But even empty, it was impossible to get the boats past the wave line.

After an hour, Carlson ordered back to the beach everybody that had not made it through the close-packed waves. When he got there, he found that less than half of the boats had made it through the surf. Thus more than half of the Raiders were still on the beach, and they were exhausted. Most of them had lost their weapons and equipment and rations. And there were a few wounded men, including four stretcher cases. These men were in pain, and obviously in no condition to keep trying to get off the beach.

So Carlson ordered all the boats pulled well up on the shore. He collected what weapons there were, set up a perimeter defense, and did what he could for the wounded. Then he formed teams to keep trying (it was possible that the surf was a freak condition, which would pass) to get through the surf, one boat at a time.

Carlson conducted a nose count. There were 120 Raiders still on the beach. And then, as if to suggest that God was displeased, it began to rain.

As soon as daylight made it possible, the Raiders tried Carlson's idea of forcing their boats through the surf one at a time. When one boat made it, another tried, and when it made it, then another tried. The wounded, Carlson knew, could not be extracted this way, and he would not leave them. He therefore ordered Captain Roosevelt into one of the boats so he could assume command of the Marines on the submarines. When he was sure Roosevelt had made it, he ran another nose count. Now there were seventy men on the beach.

At 0740, five Raiders aboard the *Nautilus* volunteered to take a boat with a working motor as close to shore as it could manage. Then one of the Raiders swam ashore from it with a message from Commander Haines that the subs would lay off the island as long as necessary to get the Raiders off the beach.

Then Japanese Zeros appeared. And the subs made emergency dives. The Japanese strafed the beach, and then turned their attention to the rubber boat with its volunteer crew. Nothing more was ever seen of it—or of them.

When Roosevelt, whose rubber boat had been the fourth and last to make its way through the rollers, started counting noses aboard the *Nautilus*, he came across Lieutenant Peatross and the remaining eight of the men who had been with him in his rubber boat during the initial landing.

He was convinced that Peatross and his men had been swamped. But they hadn't. The current had taken them a mile farther down the beach than any of the others, where they had made it safely ashore. When they heard the firing, they had literally marched toward the sound of gunfire. And then he and his men had spent the day harassing the Japanese rear. They had burned down his buildings, blown up a radio station, and burned a truck.

And in compliance with orders, still not having made their way through Japanese lines to the others, they had at 1930 gotten back in their rubber boat and made it through the surf to the waiting submarine.

During the afternoon of August 18, Carlson moved what was left of his forces to Government House on the lagoon side of the island. There they found a sloop. And for a short while (until it was determined that the sloop was unseaworthy), there was a spurt of hope that they could use it to get off the island.

Meanwhile, a radio was made to work long enough to establish a brief tie with the *Nautilus*. Evacuation would be attempted from the lagoon side of the island at nightfall.

Carlson sent men to manhandle the boats from the seaside beaches across the narrow island to the lagoon. Then he led a patrol toward the Japanese positions. He stripped the deserted office of the Japanese commander of what he had left behind (including his lieutenant general's flag, which the Raiders forwarded to Marine Commandant Holcomb). And then they burned and blew up one thousand barrels of Japanese aviation gasoline.

The fire was still burning at 2308 hours, when Colonel Carlson, believing himself to be the last man off the beach, went aboard the *Nautilus*.

There was no question of attacking Little Makin Island. For one thing, they would be expected. And the men not only had no weapons, they were exhausted.

The Raid on Makin Island was over. The *Nautilus* and the *Argonaut* got underway for Pearl Harbor.

(Two)
Pearl Harbor Navy Base, Territory of Hawaii
26 August 1942

It is a tradition within the submarine service for the crew to stand to on deck as the boat eases up to its wharf on return from a patrol. In keeping with this tradition, men were standing on the deck of the *Nautilus*. In fact, the deck was crowded; for in addition to the crew, the Marine Raiders who'd been "passengers" on the boat were on the deck, too.

The Raiders would have failed an inspection at Parris Island (or anywhere else in the Marine Corps). And they would have brought tears to the eyes of the gunnery sergeant of a Marine detachment aboard a battleship, a cruiser, or an aircraft carrier.

They were not at attention, for one thing. For another, no two of them seemed to be wearing the same uniform. Some were in dungarees, some in dyed-black khaki, some wore a mixture of both uniforms, and some wore parts of uniforms scrounged from the *Nautilus*'s crew. Some wore steel helmets, some fore-and-aft caps, and some were hatless.

There was a Navy band on the wharf, and it played

"Anchors Aweigh" and the "Marines' Hymn," and the Raiders watched with their arms folded on their chests, wearing what were either smiles of pleasure or amused tolerance.

The Pearl Harbor brass came aboard after that. And on their heels corpsmen started to offload the stretcher cases and ambulatory wounded. A line of ambulances, their doors already open, waited on the wharf behind the gray staff cars of the brass and the buses that would carry the Raiders.

Lieutenant W. B. McCracken, Medical Corps, USNR, was wearing, proudly, dyed-black trousers and an unbuttoned Marine Corps dungaree jacket—as if to leave no question that he had been the doc of Baker Company, survivor of the Makin Raid, as opposed to your typical natty, run-of-the-mill chancre mechanic. McCracken walked up to Second Lieutenant Kenneth J. McCoy, USMC, grabbed his dungaree jacket, and looped a casualty tag string through a button hole.

"Go get in an ambulance, Killer," he said.

"I don't need it," McCoy said.

It was neither bravado nor modesty. He had not, in his mind, been wounded. A wound was an incapacitating hole in the body, usually accompanied by great pain. He had been *zinged* twice, *lightly* zinged. The first time had been right after they'd started moving down the island. A Japanese sniper in a coconut tree had almost got him, or almost missed. A slug had whipped through his trousers, six inches above his knee, grazed his leg, and kept going. It had scared hell out of him, but it hadn't even knocked him down.

Almost immediately, he had seen another muzzle flash and fired four shots from his Garand into the coconut tree. The Jap's rifle had then come tumbling down, and a moment later the sniper followed it—at least to the length of the rope he'd used to tie himself up there.

After that McCoy had pulled his pants leg up, then opened his first aid packet and put a compress on the hole, which was a groove about as wide as his pinky finger and about as long as a bandage. And then he'd really forgotten about it. Or rather, the wound hadn't been painful until that night, when he'd waded into the surf and the salt water had gotten to it and made it sting like hell.

And he had been *zinged* again the next morning, when he'd led a squad down the island to see what the Japs were up to. He had been looking around what had been a concrete-block wall when a Japanese machine gun had opened up on them. A slug had hit the blocks about two feet from him, and a chunk of concrete had clipped him on the forehead. It had left a jagged tear about three inches long, and it had given him a hell of a headache, but it hadn't even bled very much. And it was not a real *wound*.

The doc on the *Nautilus* had put a couple of fresh bandages, hardly more than Band-Aids, on him; and until now, that had been the end of it. He had spent the return trip trying to come up with a casualty list: who had been killed; who was missing from the fucked-up landing and the even more fucked-up withdrawal from the beach; and who, if anybody, was still unaccounted for. He hadn't thought of much else after it had become apparent to him that they had left as many as eight people on the beach.

"Hot showers," Doc McCracken said, pushing him toward the gangplank, "sheets, mattresses, good chow, and firm-breasted sweet-smelling nurses. Trust me, Killer."

Doc McCracken was smiling at him.

"What the hell," McCoy said. "Why not?"

It took about two hours before he had gone through the drill and was in a room in the Naval hospital with something to eat. A couple of doctors had painfully removed the scabs and dug around in there as if they hoped to find gold. Then they'd given him a complete physical. And of course the paper pushers were there, filling in their forms.

McCoy was just finishing his second shower—simply because it was there, all that limitless fresh hot water—and putting on a robe over his pajamas, and getting ready to lie on his bed and read *Life* magazine, when Colonel Carlson pushed open the door and walked into the room. He was still in mussed and soiled dungarees. McCoy supposed he'd come to the hospital to check on the wounded. The *real* wounded.

"Go on with what you were doing," Carlson said, as McCoy started to straighten up to attention. "Go on, get on the bed. It's permitted. Then tell me how you feel."

"I don't think I really belong here, Colonel," McCoy said, climbing onto the bed.

"Clean sheets and a hot meal," Carlson said, smiling.

"That's what the doc said, sir," McCoy said.

"I'm about to go out to Camp Catlin," Colonel Carlson said. "I thought I'd drop by and say 'so long.'"

"Sir?"

Carlson dipped into the cavernous pocket of his dungaree jacket and came out with a sheet of teletype paper, which he handed to McCoy.

PRIORITY
HEADQUARTERS USMC WASH DC 8AUG42
COMMANDING OFFICER
2ND RAIDER BN
FLEET MARINE FORCE PACIFIC
　　YOU WILL ON RECEIPT ISSUE APPROPRIATE ORDERS DETACH-
ING SECOND LIEUTENANT KENNETH J. MCCOY USMCR FROM
COMPANY B 2ND RAIDER BN AND TRANSFERRING HIM TO
HEADQUARTERS USMC.
　　TRAVEL FROM HAWAII TO WASHINGTON BY AIR IS DIRECTED
PRIORITY AA2.
BY DIRECTION
STANLEY F. WATT COLONEL USMC OFFICE OF THE ASSISTANT
CHIEF OF STAFF FOR PERSONNEL

McCoy looked at Carlson.

"Well, you'll be in here for forty-eight hours," Carlson said. "That'll give us time to get your gear from Catlin to you."

"I guess they really need linguists, sir," McCoy said.

"Certainly, they do. Linguists are valuable people, McCoy. There's far too few of them—you did notice that TWX was dated 8 August—for the Corps to risk losing one of them storming some unimportant beach."

Their eyes met.

"When you get to Washington, McCoy, say hello to Colonel Rickabee for me."

McCoy saw that Carlson was smiling.

"You've known all along, then, sir?"

"Not everyone in the Corps thinks I'm a crazy Communist, McCoy," Carlson said. "I've still got a few friends left who try to let me know what's going on."

"Oh, shit!" McCoy said.

"Nothing for you to be embarrassed about, McCoy,"

Carlson said. "You're a Marine officer. A *good* Marine officer. And good Marine officers do what they're told to do, to the best of their ability."

He stepped to the bed and put out his hand.

"Take care of yourself, son," he said. "I was glad you were along on this operation."

And then he turned and walked out of the room.

(Three)
Navy Air Station
Pensacola, Florida
29 August 1942

Second Lieutenant Malcolm S. Pickering's first response to the knock at the penthouse door was to simply ignore it. Either it would go away or Dick Stecker would get up and answer it.

It was Saturday morning, and they had drunk their Friday supper.

They were finished at Pensacola. Orders would be cut on Monday, 31 August, certifying that Second Lieutenants Pickering and Stecker were rated as fully qualified in F4F-3 aircraft, and placing them on a ten-day-delay-en-route leave to where-ever the hell the Marine Corps was sending them.

It was occasion to celebrate, and they had celebrated until the wee hours.

The knocking became more persistent, and Pickering finally gave in. Wrapping a sheet around his middle, calling out "Keep your pants on!" he walked to the door and jerked it open.

It was Captain James L. Carstairs, USMC, *Captain Mustache,* in his usual impeccable uniform.

"Good morning, sir," Pickering said.

"May I come in?" Captain Carstairs asked. "You alone?"

"I'm alone," Pickering said. "But . . . Captain Carstairs, Stecker has a guest."

"The one with her hair piled two feet over her head?" Captain Carstairs said. "And the enormous bazooms?"

"Uh . . ."

"We saw you last night," Captain Carstairs said. "I rather doubt that in your condition you saw us, but we saw you."

"I saw you, sir," Pickering said. "I didn't know you had seen us."

"You should have come over and said hello," Captain Carstairs said. "I had the feeling Mrs. Culhane rather wished you would."

Pickering looked at him in surprise, and blurted what popped into his mind.

"Is that why you're here? To tell me that?"

"Unfortunately, no," Captain Carstairs said, and handed Pickering a yellow Western Union envelope.

"What's this?"

"Keep in mind the other possibility," Carstairs said. "The word is they left a lot of people on the beach."

Pickering ripped the envelope open.

GOVERNMENT
WASHINGTON DC
5PM AUGUST 28 1942
SECOND LIEUTENANT M. S. PICKERING, USMCR
NAVY AIR STATION PENSACOLA FLORIDA
 THE SECRETARY OF THE NAVY REGRETS TO INFORM YOU THAT YOUR FRIEND SECOND LIEUTENANT KENNETH J. MCCOY USMCR 2ND RAIDER BATTALION WAS WOUNDED IN ACTION AGAINST THE JAPANESE ON MAKIN ISLAND 17 AUGUST 1942. HE HAS BEEN REMOVED TO A NAVAL HOSPITAL AND IS EXPECTED TO FULLY RECOVER. FURTHER DETAILS WILL BE FURNISHED AS AVAILABLE.
FRANK KNOX JR SECRETARY OF THE NAVY

"There's another word in the lexicon," Captain Carstairs said, "one they did not use. The adjective 'seriously,' as in 'seriously wounded.' And they included the phrase 'fully recover.'"

"Yeah," Pickering said, and then looked at Carstairs. "Thank you."

"My curiosity is aroused," Carstairs said. "Doesn't he have a family?"

"Not one he gives much of a damn about," Pickering said. "He's got a brother, but he's in the Raiders, too."

"He came through it, that's what counts," Carstairs said. "That's all that counts."

"Oh, Christ!" Pickering said, having just then thought of it. "Ernie!"

"Who's Ernie?"

"His girl friend," Pick said. "I'll have to tell her."

"Why?" Carstairs said, practically. "If he's not seriously hurt, he'll write her and tell her. Why worry her?"

"Because she would want to know," Pick flared. "Jesus Christ!"

"Keep your cool, Pickering," Carstairs said. "Think it over. What would be gained?"

"Yeah," Pick said. "This is not the first telegram from the Secretary of the Navy—" He stopped. "I am about to have a drink. Would you like one?"

"I thought you would never ask," Captain Carstairs said.

Pick made drinks, and then told Captain Mustache about the first telegram from the Secretary of the Navy about Ken McCoy when he had been in the Philippines, the one that said he was "missing in action and presumed dead." They made enough noise to raise Dick Stecker and his guest from their bed.

They had another couple of drinks, and then ordered room service breakfast, and in the end Pick decided he would not call Ernie, not now. It made more sense to wait and see what happened. There was no sense getting Ernie all upset when there was nothing at all that she could do.

Captain Mustache stayed with them. He even got a little smashed, and it had all the beginnings of a good party. Now that they were about to be certified as fully qualified brother Naval aviators, it was fitting and proper for him to associate with two lowly second lieutenants as social equals.

Sometime during the evening, Captain Mustache told him that he had just about given up on Martha Sayre Culhane. It had become clear to him that she was just not interested.

Pickering recalled that the next morning (now Sunday) when some other sonofabitch was knocking at the door.

As Pick staggered to open it, he remembered telling Captain Mustache that he knew just how he felt. And then Captain Mustache had said something else: He thought it wasn't absolutely hopeless for Pick, and that it was a shame Pick was about to ship out.

Pick jerked the door open. It was Captain Mustache again.

"Why didn't you just crap out on the couch?" Pick asked, somewhat snappishly.

"I took the brunette in the glasses home, remember?" Captain Mustache said, and then added, demonstrating,

"You've got another one," and handed him a yellow Western Union envelope.

"Oh, shit, now what?" Pick asked.

The second telegram, to his relief and confusion, appeared to be identical to the first. He was afraid that it would be one expressing the condolences of the Secretary of the Navy.

"What the hell is this?" he asked. "A duplicate? In case I didn't get the first one?"

"I don't know," Carstairs answered. And then they saw that the two telegrams were not identical. The second said McCoy had been wounded on August 18; the first had said August 17.

"I guess he got shot twice," Carstairs said, "and the paperwork just got caught up."

"I'm going to have to call Ernie," Pick said, firmly. "She has a right to know."

"Can I have a hair of the dog?" Captain Mustache asked. "Make me one, will you? I think I'm going to need it."

It took Ernie so long to answer her phone that he was afraid she wasn't at her apartment, but finally, she came on the line.

"What is it?" she snapped.

"This is Pick, Ernie," he said.

"What do you want at this time of the morning?" she snapped.

"I've got a little bad news," Pick said, gently.

"About what?" she asked, now with concern in her voice.

"About Ken," Pick said. "Ernie, did you read in the paper or hear on the radio about the Marine Raiders and Makin Island?"

"Yes," she said. "What the *hell* are you talking about?"

"I'm talking about Ken," Pick said.

"Just a minute," Ernie said, and went off the line. And stayed off.

"Hello?" Pick said, finally.

"Hello, yourself," Ken McCoy's voice came over the wire. "You have a lousy sense of timing, asshole. Did I ever tell you that?"

"When did you get back?"

"I got into Washington about ten last night," McCoy said. "And I caught the four A.M. train into New York. I've been here about an hour and a half. Get the picture?"

"Sorry to have bothered you, sir," Pick said, and hung up.

Captain Mustache handed him a drink. Pick looked at it and set it down.

"Our twice-wounded hero is in New York," he said. "I don't know how the hell he worked that, but I'm not really surprised."

"Well, there's our excuse to celebrate again," Carstairs said.

"No," Pick said.

"No?" Carstairs asked.

"Actually, I think I'll go to church," Pick said.

"Well, sure," Carstairs said, uncomfortably, forcing a smile.

(Four)
Navy Air Station Chapel
Pensacola, Florida
30 August 1942

Chaplain (Lieutenant Commander) J. Bartwell Kaine, USNR, who until three months before had been rector of the Incarnation Episcopal Church of Baltimore, Maryland, was pleased to see the two Marine second lieutenants at his morning prayer service.

It had been his experience since coming to Pensacola that few, too few, of the officer aviation students attended worship services of any kind, and that those who did went to the nondenominational Protestant services at 1100. He was interested in keeping, so to speak, Episcopalian personnel within the fold, and there was no question in his practiced eye that the two handsome young Marines in the rear pew were Episcopal. They knew the service well enough to recite the prayers and doxology from memory, and they knew when and how to kneel.

Chaplain Kaine made a special effort, when the service was over, to speak to them, to let them know they were more than welcome, and to invite them to participate in the activities of what he referred to as "the air station Episcopal community."

They informed him that while they appreciated the offer of hospitality, they had finished their training and were about to leave Pensacola.

Then Second Lieutenants Pick Pickering and Dick Stecker walked to Pickering's car and got in. As Pickering pushed the starter button and got the Cadillac running, Stecker spoke:

"Even though I'm aware of the scriptural admonition to

'judge not, lest ye be judged,' why is it that I have the feeling that you dragged me over here more in the interests of your sinful lusts of the flesh than to offer thanks for your buddy coming through all right?"

"Fuck you, Dick," Pickering said, cheerfully.

"What made you think she'd be there? And if she had been, what makes you think she would have rushed into your arms?"

"I saw the picture of her father in the base newspaper. He's a vestryman. It was worth a shot."

"You're desperate, aren't you?" Stecker replied, half mockingly, half sympathetically.

"You're goddamn right I am. We're leaving here Tuesday."

"You're nuts, Pick," Stecker said, not unkindly.

"I'm in love, all right? People in love are allowed to be a little crazy."

"What you need is a piece of ass," Stecker said. "It has amazing curative powers for crazy people. Let's go back to the hotel and commit every sin—except worshipping graven images."

"Let's go sailing," Pickering said.

"Let's do what?"

"Sailing. Boats, sails. You *have* been on a boat?"

"How are we going to do that?"

"Trust me, my son," Pickering said solemnly. "Put thy faith in me, and I will work miracles."

Five minutes after they passed the Marine guard on the Pensacola Navy Air Station, Pickering turned off Navy Boulevard. Five hundred yards beyond he passed between two sandstone pillars.

"You *did* notice the sign?" Stecker asked, dryly.

"The one that said 'Pensacola Yacht Club'?"

"The one that said 'Members Only.'"

"Oh, ye of little faith," Pickering said.

"You really think she's going to be in here?"

"There was another story about her father," Pickering said, "in the Pensacola newspaper. In addition to being an admiral, he's the vice commodore here."

"Jesus, you are desperate."

"It also said they serve a buffet brunch, starting at ten," Pickering said. "Admirals have to eat, just like human beings. Maybe he brought his daughter with him."

"And what if he did? Presuming we don't get thrown out on

our asses, what are you going to do, just walk up and say, 'Hi, there'?"

"Why not?" Pickering said, smiling at Stecker as he parked the car and pulled the emergency brake on.

A portly, suntanned man in a blue blazer with an embroidered patch on the pocket walked up to them as they entered the lobby of the yacht club.

"Good morning, gentlemen," he said. "Meeting someone?"

"Gee," Stecker said, under his breath, "we lasted a whole ten seconds before we got caught."

"No, we thought we'd try the buffet," Pickering said.

The man in the blazer looked uncomfortable, making Stecker think that he disliked throwing servicemen out of his yacht club, even if that was precisely what he was about to do.

"Gentlemen," he said, "I'm afraid this is a private club—"

"But you are affiliated with the American Yachting Association?" Pickering asked, as he took out his wallet.

"Yes, of course," the man said.

Pickering searched through the wallet and came up with a battered card and handed it over.

"Welcome to the Pensacola Yacht Club, Mr. Pickering," the man said, smiling, and handing him the card back. "I won't have to ask, will I, what brings you into our waters?"

"Our Uncle Samuel," Pickering said.

"Well, let me show you to the dining room," the man said. "If you don't think it's too early, the first drink is traditionally on the club."

"How nice," Pickering said.

The corridor from the lobby to the dining room was lined with trophy cases and framed photographs.

"Well, there's a familiar face," Pickering said, pleased, pointing to a photograph of a large sailboat with its crew. They were standing along the port side, hanging on to the rigging, and they were obviously delighted with themselves.

A thin strip of typewritten legend on the photograph said, "FAT CHANCE, 1st Place, Wilson Cup, San Francisco-Hawaii 1939."

"That was the 'thirty-nine Wilson Cup," the man from the yacht club said. "Jack Glenn, one of our members, was on her."

"Fat Jack," Pickering said. "But please note that splendid sailor about to fall off the bowsprit."

Stecker looked. It was Pickering, as obviously drunk as he was delighted with himself, holding on firmly to the bowsprit rigging.

"That's you," Stecker accused.

"Indeed," Pickering said.

From the look on the man from the yacht club, Stecker decided, the Pensacola Yacht Club was theirs.

"God is in his heaven," Pickering said solemnly. "Prayer pays. All is right with the world."

"What the hell?" Stecker asked, and then looked where Pickering was looking.

A rear admiral, a woman obviously his wife, and Martha Sayre Culhane were coming down the corridor.

"Well, hello, there," Mrs. Sayre said, offering her hand to Pickering. "It's nice to see you again, Lieutenant. You're a sailor, too?"

"Quite a sailor, Mrs. Sayre," the man from the yacht club said. He pointed to the photograph. "He was on the *Fat Chance* with Jack Glenn."

"Good morning, Martha," Pickering said.

"Hello, Pick," Martha said.

She did not seem nearly as glad to see Pickering as Pick was to see her.

"Since no one seems to be about to introduce us, gentlemen," Admiral Sayre said, "I'll introduce myself. I'm Admiral Sayre."

"How do you do, sir?" Pickering said politely.

"Jim, this is Lieutenant Pickering," Mrs. Sayre said. "I'm afraid I don't know this—"

"Stecker, ma'am," Stecker said. "Dick Stecker."

"We're here for the brunch," Mrs. Sayre said. "Why don't you join us?"

"We wouldn't want to intrude," Stecker said.

"That's very kind, thank you very much, we'd love to," Pickering said.

"I'd like to thank you for doing this, Dick," Mrs. Jeanne Sayre said to Stecker.

"Ma'am?" Stecker asked.

They were in the cabin of the *Martha III*, a twenty-eight-foot cruising sailer, now two miles offshore, and heeled twenty degrees from the vertical in nasty choppy seas. Jeanne Sayre had boiled water for tea on a small stove. Stecker had welcomed the opportunity to get out of the spray by helping her. When he had come below, Martha was with her father in the cockpit, and Pick was way up front, just behind what Stecker had earlier learned (looking at the photo in the yacht club) was the "bowsprit."

"I'm sure you and Pick had other plans for this afternoon," Jeanne Sayre said.

"This is fine," he said. "I'm glad to be here."

"Even though you're going to have to have your uniform cleaned, if it's not ruined, not to mention buying shoes, which have already been ruined?" she asked, smiling tolerantly.

"I've never had a chance to do something like this before," Stecker said.

"My husband too rarely gets the chance to do anything like this," Jeanne Sayre said. "He really works too hard, and he's reluctant—he's really a nice guy—to ask his aides to 'volunteer.' I saw his eyes light up when he heard Pick was a real sailor. I didn't have the heart to kick him under the table when he asked if anybody would like a little sail."

"Pick's having a fine time," Stecker said, smiling.

He'd be having a much better time, of course, if it wasn't for you, the admiral, and me; and it was just him and your well-stacked daughter sailing off into the sunset on this goddamned little boat.

The boat at the moment started to change direction. Stecker's eyes reflected his concern.

"We're turning," she said. "I guess my husband decided we're far enough offshore."

The *Martha III* came to a vertical position, and then started heeling in the other direction.

"Man overboard!" a male voice, obviously the admiral's, cried.

For a moment, Stecker thought it was some sort of joke in bad taste, but then he saw the look on Mrs. Sayre's face, and knew it was no joke. Obviously, Pick, playing Viking up front, had lost his footing and gone into the water. There was a quick sense of amusement—serves the bastard right—quickly replaced by a feeling of concern. The water out there was choppy. People drowned when they fell off boats, particularly into choppy water.

He followed Jeanne Sayre as she went quickly to the cockpit. He looked forward. Pick hadn't gone overboard. He was halfway between the bow and the cockpit. And he had taken his blouse off.

Pick ripped a circular life preserver free and threw it over the side; and then, in almost a continuous motion, he made a quick running dive over the side. He still had his socks on, Stecker saw, but he had removed his shoes.

Stecker looked over the stern. Surprisingly far behind the boat, he saw Martha Sayre Culhane's head bobbing in the water, held up by an orange life preserver.

Mrs. Sayre had taken her husband's position at the wheel, and while she watched both her husband (who was lowering the mainsail) and her daughter behind her in the water, she was trying to start the gasoline auxiliary engine.

The moment it burst into life, Admiral Sayre lowered the sail all the way.

"Bring her around!" he ordered, and then pushed past Stecker to get a boat hook from the cabin.

Stecker felt both useless and absurd.

He searched the water and found first Martha and then Pickering. Pickering was swimming with sure, powerful strokes to Martha, towing the life ring behind him on its line.

It seemed to take a very long time for the *Martha III* to turn, but once she was through the turn, she seemed to pick up speed. When Stecker saw Martha again, Pick was beside her in the water.

It took three minutes before the *Martha III* reached them. Mrs. Sayre expertly stopped the boat beside them, and then Stecker and Admiral Sayre hauled them in, first Martha, and then Pickering. They were blue-lipped and shivering.

"Take them below, and get them out of their clothes," Admiral Sayre said. "There's still some blankets aboard?"

"Yes," his wife said.

The admiral looked around the surface of the water, located a channel marker, and pointed it out to Stecker.

"Make for that," he ordered. "I'll relieve you in a minute."

"Aye, aye, sir," Stecker said, obediently. And for the first time in his life he took the conn of a vessel underway.

When he went to the cabin, Admiral Sayre—seeing that his

wife had already stripped their daughter of her dress and was working on her slip—faced Pickering aft before he ordered him out of his wet clothing. Pick stripped to his underwear, and then Admiral Sayre wrapped a blanket around his shoulders.

"I'll hang your pants and shirt from the rigging. You'll look like hell, but it will at least be dry," the admiral said.

"Thank you, sir," Pick said.

"Why the hell did you go over the side?" the admiral demanded.

"I thought maybe she was hurt," Pick said.

"Well, I'm grateful," the admiral said. He looked down the cabin. "You all right, honey?" he asked.

"A little wet," Martha said.

"I'll do what I can to dry your clothes," her father said. "Jeanne, you go topside and take the helm."

"Aye, aye, Admiral, sir," his wife replied, dryly sarcastic.

Now wrapped, Martha and Pick looked at each other across the cabin.

And then Pick crossed the cabin to her.

"You want to tell me what that was all about?" Martha asked.

"If I had a bicycle, I would have ridden it no hands," Pick said.

She walked past him to the ladder to the cockpit, and turned and walked in the other direction.

"It was a dumb thing to do," Martha said. "You weren't even wearing a life jacket. You could have drowned, you damn fool."

"So could you have," Pick said slowly. "And if you were going to drown, I wanted to drown with you."

"Jesus," she said. And she looked at him. "You're crazy."

"Just in love," he said.

"My God, you are crazy," she said.

"Maybe," Pick said. "But that's the way it is. And this was my last chance. We're leaving Tuesday."

"Jim Carstairs told me," Martha said, and then: "Oh, Pick, what are you doing to me?" she asked, very softly.

"Nothing," he said. "What I would like to do is put my arms around you and never let you go."

Her hand came out from under her blanket and touched his face. His hand came out and touched hers, and then his arms went around her, as he buried his face in her neck.

This served to dislodge the blankets covering the upper portions of their bodies. Martha had removed her brassiere, and was wearing only her underpants. As if with a mind of its own, Pick's hand found her breast and closed over it.

"My God!" she whispered, taking her mouth from his a long, long moment later. "My parents!"

They retrieved their blankets.

When Admiral Sayre came into the cabin no more than a minute later, they were on opposite sides of the cabin, Martha sitting down, Pick leaning agains a locker.

But maybe it wasn't necessary. They had color in their faces again. Martha's face, in fact, was so red that she could have been blushing.

"You two all right?"

"Yes," Martha said.

"Couldn't be better, sir," Pick Pickering said.

Postscript

Kwajalein Island
16 October 1942

The following is factual. It is taken from *"Record of Proceedings of a Military Commission convened on April 16, 1946, at United States Fleet, Commander Marianas, Guam, Marianas Islands," under the authority of Rear Admiral C. A. Pownall, USN, the Commander, Marianas Area, to deal with the cases of Vice Admiral Koso Abe, Captain Yoshio Obara, and Lieutenant Commander Hisakichi Naiki, all of the Imperial Japanese Navy:*

Early in October, a Lieutenant Commander Okada, who was a staff officer of the Central Japanese Headquarters, visited Kwajalein in connection with an inspection of Japanese defense fortifications. While he was there, Vice Admiral Abe, Kwajalein commander, solicited Commander Okada's assistance in securing transportation to Japan of nine prisoners of war, Marine enlisted men who had been captured following the Makin Island operation and brought to Kwajalein. The Imperial Japanese Navy had been unable, or unwilling, so far to divert a vessel to transport the prisoners.

Commander Okada replied to Vice Admiral Abe that *"from*

now on, it would not be necessary to transport prisoners to Japan; from now on, they would be disposed of on the island [Kwajalein]'' or words to that effect.

On October 11, 1942, Vice Admiral Abe delegated the responsibility of disposing of the prisoners to the Commanding Officer, 61st Naval Guard Unit, Imperial Japanese Navy, Captain Yoshio Obara, IJN, a career naval officer and a 1915 graduate of the Imperial Japanese Naval Academy. The Marine prisoners of war were then being held by the 61st Naval Guard unit.

Vice Admiral Abe's orders to Captain Obara specified that the executioners, as a matter of courtesy to the prisoners of war, hold the grade of warrant officer or above.

There was a pool of approximately forty warrant officers (in addition to officers of senior grade), none of whom was initially willing to volunteer for the duty. When prevailed upon by Captain Obara and Lieutenant Commander Naiki, however, three warrant officers stepped forward, as did an enlisted man, who would serve as "pistoleer."

Lieutenant Commander Naiki proposed to dispose of the Marine prisoners on October 16, which was the Yasakuni Shrine Festival, a Japanese holiday honoring departed heroes. This proposal received the concurrence of Captain Obara and Vice Admiral Abe.

A site was selected and prepared on the southwestern part of the island.

Captain Obara ordered that the evening meal of October 15, 1942 for the prisoners include beer and sweet cakes.

On October 16, the Marine prisoners were blindfolded and had their hands tied behind them. They were moved from their place of confinement to a holding area near the disposal site and held there until Vice Admiral Abe and Captain Obara arrived, in full dress uniform, by car from activities in connection with the Yasakuni Shrine Festival.

The Marine prisoners were then led one at a time to the edge of a pit dug for the purpose, and placed in a kneeling position. Then they were beheaded by one or another of the three warrant officers—using swords, according to Japanese Naval tradition. The services of the pistoleer, who would have fired a bullet into their heads should there not be a complete severance of head from torso, were not required.

A prayer for the souls of the departed was offered, under the direction of Vice Admiral Abe, who then left.

A woven fiber mat was placed over the bodies, and the pit filled in. Additional prayers were offered, and then the disposal party was marched off.

On 19 June 1947, Lieutenant Colonel George W. Newton, USMC, Provost Marshal of Guam, reported to the Commandant of the Marine Corps that, in accordance with the sentence handed down by the Military Commission, Vice Admiral Abe, Captain Obara, and Lieutenant Commander Naiki, late of the Imperial Japanese Navy, had that day been, by First Lieutenant Charles C. Rexroad, USA, hanged by the neck until they were dead.

ABOUT THE AUTHOR

W.E.B. Griffin, who was once a soldier, belongs to the Armor Association; Paris Post #1, The American Legion; and is a life member of the National Rifle Association and Gaston-Lee Post #5660, Veterans of Foreign Wars.

A captivating novel of valor and adventure
from the bestselling author
of the Corps series.

W.E.B. GRIFFIN

HONOR BOUND

It is fall 1942. Three U.S. military experts are about to undertake a mission unlike any they have ever experienced. An ace Marine aviator fresh from Guadalcanal, an Army second lieutenant demolition expert, and an Army staff sergeant counterintelligence specialist are teamed up and sent to Buenos Aires, where their mission is to sabotage by any means necessary the resupply of German ships and submarines. If they are to succeed, they have to be very cunning . . . and very lucky.

Available in hardcover in bookstores everywhere

G. P. Putnam's Sons
A member of The Putnam Berkley Group, Inc.